HAROLD ROBBINS

The compelling novel of a woman's sensational journey from Broadway actress to best-selling author . . . a journey that takes her into the half-world of topless bars and love-for-sale clubs, and the twilight world of drugs and alcohol, as she moves restlessly from man to man and woman to woman.

Books by Harold Robbins

The Adventurers
The Betsy
The Carpetbaggers
The Dream Merchants
Dreams Die First
The Inheritors
The Lonely Lady
Memories of Another Day
Never Love a Stranger
The Pirate
79 Park Avenue
A Stone for Danny Fisher
Where Love Has Gone

Published by POCKET BOOKS

HAROLD ROBBINS

THE LONELY LADY

PUBLISHED BY POCKET BOOKS NEW YORK

POCKET BOOKS, a Simon & Schuster division of
GULF & WESTERN CORPORATION
1230 Avenue of the Americas, New York, N.Y. 10020

Published by arrangement with Simon and Schuster
Library of Congress Catalog Card Number: 76-1895

ISBN: 0-671-41713-4

First Pocket Books printing March, 1977

30 29 28 27 26

Printed in the U.S.A.

This book is dedicated to the memory of
Jacqueline Susann and Cornelius Ryan,
Both of whom had not only the gift of life within them
But the courage to live it to the very end.
I miss you, my friends.

You get real cooled out if you're an "achievement"-oriented woman. No matter how high a price you pay, you're alone when you get anywhere—in a way that no man ever has to be.

—Phyllis Chesler, *Women and Madness*

Book One

SMALL TOWN

Chapter 1

SHE SAT at the top of the stairs and cried.

As she came out of the anesthesia, she saw the little girl weeping, her face covered by her hands and long golden-brown hair. She had seen the image of herself thousands of times in that fractional moment between waking and sleeping—ever since the death of her father.

Her vision cleared and the doctor's face looked down at her, smiling. "Everything's okay, JeriLee," he said.

She glanced around the room. There were several women on rolling beds near her.

The doctor answered the question before she asked it. "You're in the recovery room," he said.

"What was it?" she asked. "A boy or a girl?"

"Does it matter now?"

"It does to me."

"It was too soon to tell," he lied.

A hint of tears came into the corners of her eyes. "It seems like an awful lot of trouble to have gone through and not know what it might have been."

"It's better this way," he said reassuringly. "Now try and get some rest."

"When can I get out of here?" she asked.

"This afternoon, as soon as I get the results of the tests."

"What tests?"

"Routine," he said. "We think you may have an Rh problem. If so, we have a shot we can give you so that there will be no complications with your next pregnancy."

She stared at him. "Would there have been with this one?"

"There was a possibility."

"Then maybe it was a good thing that I had the abortion."

"Probably. But after this try to be more careful."

"There won't be another abortion," she said firmly. "The next one I keep. I don't give a damn what anyone says. And if the father doesn't like it he can go fuck himself."

"You have plans?" he asked in a shocked tone.

"No. But you won't give me the pill because of the clotting factor and I keep rejecting the I.U.D. I feel kind of stupid walking around with a diaphragm and a tube of Delfen in my handbag all the time."

"You don't have to go to bed with every man you meet, JeriLee," the doctor said. "It doesn't prove anything."

"I don't go to bed with every man I meet," she retorted. "Only those I want to."

The doctor shook his head. "I don't understand you, JeriLee. You're too bright to let yourself in for something like this."

She smiled suddenly. "That's one of the hazards of being a woman. A man can ball all he likes and nothing happens to him. But a woman can get knocked up. She's the one who has to be careful. I thought the pill was going to even things up and it's just my luck I can't take it."

The doctor gestured to a nurse. "I've got one pill you can take," he said, scribbling on his prescription pad. "It will help you sleep for a while."

"Will I be able to work tomorrow?" she asked.

"I'd rather you waited a few days," he said. "It won't hurt if you rest a bit longer. You may be bleeding rather heavily. The nurse will take you back to your room now. I'll see you later when I discharge you."

The nurse took the prescription from him and began to roll the bed away. "Wait a minute," JeriLee said. The nurse stopped. "Jim."

The doctor turned back. "Yes?"

"Thank you," she said.

He nodded and the nurse pushed her through the

swinging doors and down the corridor to the elevator. She pressed the call button and looked at JeriLee with a professional smile. "Now, that wasn't too bad, was it, honey?"

JeriLee stared up at her. "It was fucking hell," she said, her eyes beginning to fill with tears. "I've just killed my baby."

"Why are you crying, JeriLee?" her aunt asked as she came out of her mother's room and found her sitting on the steps.

The child turned up her tearstained face. "Daddy's dead, isn't he?"

Her aunt did not answer.

"He won't be coming back like Mommy said?"

The woman bent down and picked her up, holding her close. "No," she said softly. "He won't be coming back."

The tears stopped. "Mommy lied to me," JeriLee said accusingly.

Her aunt's voice was soft. "Your mother wanted to spare you, child. She didn't want to hurt you."

"But that's not what she told me to do. She said I must always tell the truth no matter what."

"Come, let me wash your face with cold water," her aunt said. "It will make you feel better."

Obediently JeriLee followed her aunt into the bathroom. "Will Mommy tell Bobby?" she asked as her face was being sponged.

"Your brother's only four years old. I don't think he's old enough to understand."

"Shall I tell him?"

Her aunt met her questioning gaze. "What do you think you should do, JeriLee?"

JeriLee saw the warm sympathy in her aunt's eyes. "I don't think I will," she said thoughtfully. "Maybe he is too young."

Her aunt smiled and kissed her cheek. "That's very wise, JeriLee. That's a very grown-up decision for an eight-year-old to make."

JeriLee was pleased by the warmth of the approval.

But in later years she was strangely regretful. It was her first adult decision and it had been a compromise.

Later that night when she was still lying awake, she heard her mother come up the steps and go into her room. She waited for the familiar sound of her father's footsteps to follow after he had turned out the lights downstairs. When they did not come, she knew she would never hear them again. Then she turned her face into the pillow and began to cry for him.

She had been just a little over three years old on that day when her mother dressed her carefully in a white bouffant cotton dress and brushed the golden-brown ringlet of curls around her face. "Be very careful about your dress. I want you to look very pretty today," her mother had said. "We're meeting Daddy at the train. He's coming home."

"Is the war over, Mommy?"

"No. But Daddy is out of the service now. He's been discharged."

"Why, Mommy? Is he hurt?"

"A little bit. Nothing serious," her mother answered. "He hurt his leg and walks with a slight limp. But you mustn't say anything about it. Pretend you don't notice."

"Okay," JeriLee said. She turned and looked at herself in the mirror. "Do you think Daddy will recognize me now that I'm all grown up?"

"I'm sure he will," her mother said laughingly.

In a town the size of Port Clare the return of the first discharged veteran would not go unnoticed. The mayor, the town council and the high school band had all been mustered out for the occasion. Across the front of the small railroad station hung a large white banner imprinted with red and blue lettering:

WELCOME HOME, BOBBY.

It was typical of Robert Gerraghty that he decided not to get off on the station side of the tracks but jumped off on the other side because it was nearer home.

Frantically the crowd searched the platform for the missing hero. "You sure he's supposed to be on this train?" the mayor asked JeriLee's mother with mounting frustration.

Her mother was near tears. The train was beginning to roll out of the station. "That's what he said in his letter."

At that moment a shout came from the far end of the platform. "There he is!"

Robert Gerraghty was almost a block away, walking briskly in the other direction. When he heard the shout he put down his bag, took off his army cap and scratched his head.

The high school band broke into "Hail the Conquering Hero," and the mayor, forgetting his dignity, scrambled across the tracks.

In the confusion, the crowd followed and the mayor, giving up all their elaborate plans, made his speech in the middle of the dusty street. "We are gathered here to honor the return of one of Port Clare's own, a genuine hero, wounded in the service of his country, Private First Class Robert F. Gerraghty . . ." The noise of the band was so great that he was forced to stop.

Her father held JeriLee in one arm, his other arm around her mother. JeriLee kept tugging at his sleeve. He turned to her, smiling. 'What is it, JeriLee?"

"Were you shot in the leg?" she whispered.

He laughed. "No, darling."

"But Mommy says you were hurt. That you walk with a limp."

"That's true." He nodded. "But I wasn't wounded in action." He saw the puzzled look on her face. "I guess your daddy was stupid enough to let a truck run over him."

"Then you're not a hero," she said with disappointment.

He put his face close to hers and, smiling, held a silencing finger to his lips. "I won't tell if you won't."

She began to laugh. "I won't tell anybody," she promised. Then she thought for a moment. "Can I tell Mommy?"

He grinned and kissed her cheek. "I think Mommy already knows." He looked into her face. "Did anyone ever tell you that you look exactly like Shirley Temple?"

She smiled, forcing the dimples into her cheeks. "Everybody says that, Daddy," she said proudly. "And Mommy says that I sing and dance better than she does."

"Will you sing and dance for me when we get home?"

She threw her arms around his neck. "Yes, Daddy."

"Hold that!" a photographer called out. "We want that one for the paper."

JeriLee held her brightest Shirley Temple smile, but somehow the mayor got his face in front of her and when the picture finally appeared on the front page of the Port Clare *Weekly Bulletin* all you could see of JeriLee was her arms around her father's neck.

JeriLee was dozing when the nurse came in with her lunch. For a moment she was startled. Yesterday had been so vivid in her thoughts that today seemed an intrusion. Her father had been a very special man, laughing at the world around him, the town of Port Clare and all its hypocrisies. "Nothing makes sense anymore, JeriLee," he had said to her. "Someday they'll discover the war has really changed the world. Freedom is more than a word for nations, it's really a very personal thing."

Then, she had not known what he meant. All she knew was that her mother was angry with him a great deal of the time and often took it out on her. Her brother, born less than a year after her father returned, escaped the brunt of it. But she was growing up and much too much like her father, her mother often said.

The nurse gave her a menu. "The doctor said you can have anything you like as long as you eat lightly."

"I'm not hungry," she said.

"You have to eat something," the nurse insisted. "Doctor's orders."

She glanced briefly at the menu. "Hot roast beef sandwich. No gravy. Jell-O and coffee."

The nurse nodded. "Good. Now roll over and let us give you this shot."

JeriLee looked at the needle. "What's that for?"

"Didn't the doctor tell you? It's for the Rh factor. In case you get pregnant again you won't have any trouble with the child."

JeriLee turned on her side. The nurse was quick and efficient. She scarcely felt the needle. "I don't intend to get pregnant again," she said.

The nurse laughed, turning away. "That's what they all say, honey. But they all come back."

JeriLee watched her leave the room. Supercilious bitch. White uniforms make them think they know everything. She leaned back against the pillows. She felt tired but not as weak as she had expected. What was it she had heard them say about abortions? Today it was no worse than treating a cold. Maybe they were right.

She looked out the window. The Los Angeles morning smog had lifted and the day was bright and sunny. She wished she had thought of having a telephone in the room. But they had told her she would be there only a few hours. Instead the Rh thing was going to hold her up almost all day.

She wondered how the meeting was going. Her agent should be with the producer right now. She wanted very badly to do the screenplay of her book herself. The first writer they had hired had botched it up completely. Finally they had come to her.

Her agent was high. He was sure the producer was over a barrel and he wanted to sock it to him. He was thinking of asking a hundred thousand dollars. She thought he was crazy. That was more than they had paid for the book, and she would have been willing to write it for nothing.

"Leave it to me," the old man had said soothingly. "This is my business. I know how to handle it. Besides we can always come down."

"Okay," she had finally agreed reluctantly. "But don't blow it."

"I won't," he'd promised, then looking at her, asked, "Where will you be tomorrow afternoon in case I should have to get in touch with you?"

"Probably home."
"And if not?"
"Cedars."
He'd looked at her in surprise. "What are you going there for?"
"A D. and C."
"You?" he asked with shock in his voice.
"Why not?" she retorted. "After all, I am a woman. Women sometimes get pregnant. Even in this day and age."
He became very solicitous. "Do you have everything you need? I can drive you—"
"You're sweet, Mike," she interrupted. "But it's all arranged. There's nothing to worry about."
"Will you call me then? When it's over?"
"As soon as I get home."
He got out of his chair and walked her to the door. "You take care now."
"I will," she promised.
Freedom was a very personal thing, her father had said. She wondered what he would have thought if he'd known what she had done today.
Probably he would have only wanted to be sure she was doing what she wanted to do, that she was making her own choice. For him that had been what freedom was about.
But the world had not completely caught up with his way of thinking. Her mother was unchanged. She would have been appalled if she'd known. And so would many others. Even among some of her so-called liberated friends abortion was in many ways still a dirty word.
She looked down at the luncheon tray in front of her. The roast beef had a pale anemic hospital look about it. Tentatively she began to cut the rubbery meat, then put down her knife and fork in disgust. She really wasn't hungry anyway.
She looked out the window at the bright California day. It was not a bit like Port Clare in January. Remembering one snowy day with the freezing cold wind coming off the Sound as she walked down the road to catch the bus to school, she actually shivered. The snow

had fallen the night before and felt crisp and clean under her galoshes as she made her way down the sidewalk. The plows had been out all night and the snow was banked neatly on the sides of the road. She climbed over a bank and came down on the road where the snow was turning brown and dirty from the passing cars. In the distance the bus came into view.

It seemed like such a long time ago. Almost another age. And in a way it was.

Chapter 2

"YOU ALMOST always die," the man said.

She turned from the bus window and looked at him. For the three months she had been taking this bus to Port Clare Central High the man had been in the seat next to her. This was the first time he had ever spoken.

"Yes," she said, her eyes unexpectedly filling with tears.

He stared past her out the window. "The snow. Why is it always the damn snow?" he asked, speaking to no one.

"I'm going to die," he went on matter-of-factly.

"My father died," she said.

For the first time he focused on her. A shade of embarrassment crept into his voice. "I'm sorry," he apologized. "I didn't realize I was talking aloud."

"It's all right."

"I didn't mean to make you cry."

"I'm not crying," she said defiantly.

"Of course," he said quickly.

She felt a strange pain in her stomach. She realized with a sense of shame that she hadn't thought about her father for a long time. In a way it had been almost too easy for her stepfather to push him from her mind.

The man's face seemed thin and pinched. "Do you go to Central?"

"Yes."

"What term?"

"Sophomore."

"You look older," he said. "I would have thought you were a senior."

A faint flush came over his pale skin. "I hope I— I mean—I don't want to offend. I just don't know too much about young girls."

"That's okay," she said. "People are always taking me for older."

He smiled, recognizing that he had pleased her. "Forgive me anyway," he said. "I'm Walter Thornton."

Her eyes widened. "You're that—?"

He didn't allow her to finish. "I'm that Walter Thornton," he said quickly.

"But"—she hesitated—"you ride the bus every morning."

He laughed. "You know a better way to get to the station?"

"But you have two plays and a movie on Broadway at the same time."

"I also don't drive." He looked at her. "How do you know so much about me?" he asked curiously.

"Everybody knows about you," she said.

"Not high school kids. They know about actors, not writers."

"I'm going to be a writer," she said.

"Why not an actress?" He was curious. "You're beautiful enough."

She blushed. "Why? Is it wrong for me to want to be a writer?"

"No," he said. "It's just unusual. Most girls want to go to Hollywood and become a movie star."

"Maybe I'll do that too," she said thoughtfully.

The bus began to slow down. They were at the railroad station. He got to his feet and smiled at her. "I'll see you tomorrow. We'll talk some more."

"Okay," she said. Through the window she watched

the tall thin figure in the flapping raincoat disappear in to the waiting 8:07 New York express.

Her boy friend, Bernie Murphy, was waiting for her in front of the school. "Do you know who I met on the bus today?" she asked excitedly. "Walter Thornton! Imagine that? I've been sitting next to him every day for three months and I didn't even know who he was."

"Who's Walter Thornton?" Bernie asked.

"Who's Mickey Mantle?" she retorted with disgust.

When JeriLee was ten years old two things happened that were to change her life. The first was that her mother remarried. The second was that she wrote a story which she then produced as a play on the final day of school.

She called it "A Gory Fairy Tale." And it was. For by the time the curtain fell everyone on stage had died.

As writer, producer and director, she cast herself in the only dual role, that of the cook who had been put to death by the king and then risen from the grave as a witch who came back for revenge.

JeriLee loved the feeling of power. During that brief period she was the most important girl in the fifth grade.

For the first time she could feel the impact she had on other people and instinctively she recognized that the words she had written were the source of the heady sense of power.

Later, clutching her award for creative writing, her face still smudged with the black soot makeup of the witch, she went to her mother and announced her decision.

"I'm going to be a writer, Mommy."

Her mother, who was sitting with Mr. Randall of the Farmer's Bank, smiled vaguely. She had scarcely watched the performance. She was too busy thinking about John Randall's proposal the previous night. "That's nice, dear," she said. "But I thought you wanted to be an actress."

"I did," JeriLee answered. "But I changed my mind."

"I thought you looked beautiful on the stage," her mother said. "Didn't you, John?"

"She was the most beautiful girl there," John Randall agreed heartily.

JeriLee stared at them. They had to be blind. The whole point of the makeup was to make her look like an ugly witch. "My makeup was horrible," she said.

Her mother smiled reassuringly. "Don't you worry, dear," she said. "We thought you looked beautiful."

Later they went to dinner at the Port Clare Inn, a candlelit restaurant which overlooked the Sound.

"We have something very important to tell you, dear," her mother began over dessert.

JeriLee scarcely looked at her. She was too busy watching the drunken couple who were openly fondling each other at the corner table.

"JeriLee!" her mother said sharply.

JeriLee looked at her mother.

"I said we had something very important to tell you."

She became the dutiful child. "Yes, Mother."

Her mother spoke awkwardly. "Ever since your father died . . . well, you know how difficult it has been for me to take care of you and your brother while going to work in the bank every day."

JeriLee was silent. She was beginning to understand. But she didn't know whether she liked what was coming.

Her mother glanced at Mr. Randall for support. He nodded reassuringly. Under the table her hand sought his. "We thought it would be nice if the two of you had a father again," she said, then added quickly, "Bobby is almost six years old now and a boy should have a father to do things with. You know, ballgames, fishing, things like that."

JeriLee looked first at her mother, then at Mr. Randall. "You mean you want to marry him?" There was a note of disbelief in her voice. Mr. Randall and her father were nothing alike. Her father had always been laughing and full of fun, while Mr. Randall almost never smiled.

Her mother fell silent.

For the first time Mr. Randall spoke. Soothingly, as if he were talking to a client of the bank who had been questioning an error on his monthly statement. "I'd make a very good father to the two of you. You're a very lovely girl and I like your brother very much."

"Don't you like me too?" she asked with a child's unerring logic.

"Of course I do," he answered quickly. "I thought I made that quite clear."

"You didn't say it."

"JeriLee!" Her mother's voice was sharp again. "You have no right to speak like that to Mr. Randall."

"It's all right, Veronica," he said soothingly. "I like you very much, JeriLee, and I would be proud if you would have me as your father."

JeriLee looked into his eyes and for the first time saw the hidden warmth and kindness. She responded immediately but didn't know what to say.

"I know I can never take the place of your real father but I love your mother and will be very good to all of you," he said earnestly.

JeriLee smiled suddenly. "Can I be the flower girl at the wedding?"

John Randall laughed in relief. "You can be anything you want," he said, covering her mother's hand with his. "Except the bride."

A year after they were married, John Randall formally adopted the two children and her name became JeriLee Randall. A curious sadness came over her the first time she wrote her new name. Now there would be almost nothing left to remind her of her father. Bobby, who had never really known him, had already forgotten. And she wondered if, in time, she would too.

Chapter 3

John Randall looked over the top of his New York *Times* as his daughter came to the breakfast table. She came quickly around the table and kissed him on the cheek. He caught a quick scent of perfume as she went to her chair.

Her voice was bright with suppressed excitement. "Good morning, Daddy."

He smiled, looking at her. He was genuinely fond of her. None of the individual features that made up her face were beautiful. Her nose was perhaps a trifle too long, her mouth a bit too wide, her dark blue eyes over high cheekbones too large for the size of her face, but somehow together they had an incredible effect. Once you looked at her you could never forget her. She was beautiful.

He could see that this morning she had taken extra care with her appearance. Her hair looked even silkier than usual and her skin was shining clean. He was glad that she didn't use makeup as so many of the girls did nowadays. "Something must be happening," he said.

She looked at him over the bottle of milk she was pouring on her cornflakes. "What, Daddy?"

"I said something's going on."

"Nothing special."

"Come on now," he said gently. "Has a new boy come into the class?"

She laughed, shaking her head. "Nothing like that."

"Still Bernie?"

She blushed but didn't answer.

"There has to be something."

"Daddy," she said reproachfully, "why does it always have to be a boy?"

"Because you're a girl."

"It's nothing like that," she said. "But I did meet someone yesterday. On the bus."

"On the bus?" he echoed, puzzled.

She nodded. "He sat down yesterday right next to me. Imagine that, Daddy? For three months he's been sitting next to me and I never knew who he was."

"He?" Now he was really puzzled. "Who?"

"Walter Thornton," she said. "I always thought he was only here for the summer. I never knew he lived here all the time."

"Walter Thornton?" he asked, a note of disapproval in his voice.

"Yes. America's greatest writer."

The disapproval in his voice became more apparent. "But he's a communist."

"Who said so?" she challenged.

"Senator McCarthy, more than two years ago. He took the fifth before the committee. And everybody knows what that means. When the news came out, the bank seriously considered asking him to take his business somewhere else."

"Why didn't you?"

"I don't know," he answered. "We felt sorry for him, I guess. After all, we are the only bank in town and it would be inconvenient to make him go out of town."

JeriLee had heard enough talk about the banking business to absorb an idea of how it was run. "Did he maintain heavy balances?" she asked shrewdly.

He flushed. She had put her finger on it. When all was said and done, the man probably had greater cash balances than any other client of the bank. The weekly income was fantastic. "Yes," he admitted.

Having made her point, she was silent.

He stared at her. She was not like other girls or even other women he had known. Certainly her mother did not have the same ability to cut through to the bone the way she did. In many ways she seemed to think like a man. Still there was nothing about her that was not female.

"What's he like?" he asked curiously.

"What's who like?" Veronica asked, bringing the eggs and bacon from the kitchen.

"Walter Thornton. JeriLee met him on the bus yesterday."

"Oh, him? I read in the papers he's going through a divorce." She went to the dining-room door and called up the stairs, "Bobby! You come right down and have your breakfast. Otherwise you'll be late for school."

Bobby's voice echoed faintly through the door. "It's not my fault, Mom. JeriLee was hogging the bathroom all morning."

Veronica came back into the room and sat down at the table. "I don't know what I'm going to do with him. Every day he comes up with another excuse."

John looked across the table at his daughter and smiled. She was blushing. "Don't get upset," he said to his wife. "Things like that happen sometimes. I can always drop him off on my way to the bank."

Veronica turned to her daughter. "What is he like?" she asked. "Mr. Smith at the market says that whenever Mrs. Thornton came in she smelled of liquor. At times he even suspected she might be drunk. They all felt sorry for him."

JeriLee shrugged her shoulders. "He seems very nice. Quiet. You wouldn't think he is who he is."

"Did you tell him you wanted to be a writer?" her mother asked.

JeriLee nodded.

"What did he say?"

"He thought it was nice. He was very polite."

"Maybe he will look at some of your things. He could give you advice."

"Oh, Mother!" JeriLee exclaimed. "A man like that wouldn't bother reading the work of a schoolkid."

"I don't know, you never—"

"I don't think she should trouble him," John interrupted. "JeriLee's right. The man is a professional. It would be very unfair to ask him. He's probably got more important things to worry about."

"But—" Veronica began.

Again he interrupted. "Besides he's not exactly the kind of person JeriLee should be associated with. He's very different than us. He has different standards. Everyone knows that communists have very loose morals."

"He's a communist?" Veronica asked.

John nodded. "Mr. Carson says that the bank has to be very careful in our dealings with him. We don't want anyone to get the wrong ideas about us."

Mr. Carson was president of the bank, the leading Republican and the most important man in Port Clare. For the past twenty years he had personally selected the mayor of the town, although he himself was too modest to want the office for himself.

Veronica was impressed. "Well, if Mr. Carson thinks so—"

"I think that's unfair!" JeriLee burst out. "There are many people who think that Senator McCarthy was worse than the communists."

"Senator McCarthy is a real American. He was the only one standing between us and the communists. The way Truman was acting, we were lucky if we didn't give the whole country away." John's voice was positive.

"Your father is right, dear," Veronica said. "The less you have to do with him the better."

Suddenly JeriLee found herself near tears. "I'm not doing anything with him, Mother. He just sits in the seat next to me on the bus."

"That's all right, JeriLee." Her mother's voice was soothing. "Just be careful you don't let people see you talking too much to him."

Bobby came tearing into the room, pulled his chair to the table and began helping himself to eggs and bacon.

"What's the matter?" Veronica asked sharply. "Have you forgotten your manners? Not even a 'good morning'?"

"Good morning," Bobby grumbled, his mouth full.

He looked at JeriLee. "It's all her fault anyway. If she didn't spend so much time in the bathroom I wouldn't be late."

"Take it easy," John said. "I'll drop you off at school."

Bobby smiled triumphantly at JeriLee. "Gee, Dad, thanks."

For a brief moment JeriLee had a twinge of hatred for her brother and the male kinship he had with their father. Maybe that was the way it was supposed to be. After all, she was a girl. But that did not make it right. It wasn't reason enough to make her feel isolated from their world.

She rose from the table. "I'll be going now."

"All right, dear," her mother said, beginning to gather the dishes.

She went around the table and dutifully kissed her mother and father. Then she picked up her schoolbooks, went out into the street and began walking toward the bus stop.

Mr. Thornton wasn't on the bus that morning, nor the following morning or the morning after that. A few days later she read that he had gone to Hollywood for the filming of his latest picture, and that he was then going on to London, where one of his plays was being produced. It wasn't until the following summer that, the day after she turned sixteen, she saw him again. By that time she was no longer a girl. She was a woman.

Physically she had matured long before. Her breasts had begun developing soon after she was eleven. By the time she was twelve she started having her periods. At fifteen there were still traces of baby fat in her face but during that winter it disappeared, leaving her cheeks with long interesting planes. She noticed the thickening of the hair under her arms and around her pubis. Like all the girls, she began shaving under her arms and using a deodorant. But she also became aware of other changes that had taken place within her.

It began in the spring, when as a member of the girls' cheerleading squad she came on the field where the baseball team was practicing. Like the other girls, she wore the loose sweatshirt with an orange and black PC emblazoned across the white shirt and the very short skirt that barely came to the top of her thighs.

They took up their position in front of the stands which ran from behind home plate down toward first and third base. Miss Carruthers, the phys ed teacher, lined them up, their backs to the players on the field. Since JeriLee had been on the squad the year before, Miss Carruthers had her standing next to her as she led them through the various cheers.

After about fifteen minutes Mr. Loring, the baseball coach, came over to her. "Miss Carruthers, may I talk to you for a moment please?"

"Of course, Mr. Loring." She stood waiting for him to continue.

He cleared his throat. "Privately."

She nodded and followed him to the front of the visitors' dugout. After looking around carefully to see that they were out of earshot he turned to her. "Miss Carruthers," he growled, "what are you trying to do to my team?"

She was bewildered. "I . . . I don't understand."

"Can't you see?" he snapped. "In the fifteen minutes you've been out there, my boys have missed two easy pop flies, the outfielder stepped into a pothole and the pitcher caught a line drive with his stomach."

She still didn't understand. "Mr. Loring, what has that got to do with me?"

He almost exploded. "You got to get those girls out of there or I won't have any team left by the time the season starts."

"Mr. Loring!" she exclaimed indignantly. "My girls are in no way interfering with your players. They are merely doing their jobs."

"Their jobs are to cheer the team on," Loring snarled. "Not tease them out of their minds. Look at that one." He pointed. "Everything's sticking out on her."

"You mean JeriLee?"

"That's the one!" he said angrily. "Those aren't buttons on the front of her shirt!"

Miss Carruthers was silent for a moment as she watched JeriLee. There was no doubt about her female animal quality. Her nipples were hard and clearly defined, even under the loose sweatshirt. "I see what you mean," she said thoughtfully.

"You'll have to do something about her," he said. "Make her wear a brassiere or something."

"All my girls wear brassieres," she retorted.

"Then get her one that fits!" he snapped.

Just then there was a loud crash from the far end of the field. An outfielder ran headlong into the fence and fell to the ground. Immediately the other players began to gather around him. The coach hurried down the field. By the time he got there, the boy was sitting up groggily.

"God damn it, Bernie!" the coach shouted angrily. "What are you trying to do? Kill yourself?"

"No, sir. I was just trying to catch the ball but I lost it in the sun."

Loring turned and looked up at the sky. "Sun? What sun?" he shouted. "The sky is covered with clouds."

Then he looked down the field and saw JeriLee. Even at this distance he could see the motion of her breasts. Suddenly he couldn't take any more. "Miss Carruthers!" he yelled. "Get those girls off my field!"

Bernie was waiting for JeriLee after practice. He fell into step with her as they walked toward the bus stop.

"Did you hurt yourself, Bernie?" she asked.

He shook his head.

"You really hit that fence. You ought to look where you're going. What was on your mind?"

"I was watching you," he admitted.

"That's silly. You're supposed to keep your eye on the ball."

"I know. That's what the coach said."

"Then why were you watching me?" she asked.

"You don't know?"

"No," she said with annoyance. "I don't know."

"You grew since last year."

"Of course I did, stupid. So did you."

"I don't mean like that," he said, raising his hand over his head. "I mean like that." He held his two hands out in front of his chest.

"You mean—?"

He nodded. "Just like Marilyn Monroe. That's what all the fellows say."

She flushed and involuntarily glanced down at herself. "They're stupid," she said but at the same time she felt her nipples harden and a warm feeling come over her.

Chapter 4

THE BEACH CLUB at the Point opened for the season in mid-May. The summer people began coming from New York, first for weekends, and later, when school closed, they moved out full time. By then the club would be crawling with children during the week, and on weekends their fathers would be stretched out burning from the sun, exhausted by an overdose of tennis or golf. And every Saturday night there would be a big buffet dinner and dance for the members.

A job at the club was a plum for the local kids. It was Bernie who first gave JeriLee the idea that she should apply.

"I'm going to work at the club this summer," he announced.

"Doing what?"

"Lifeguard."

"But you're not a good swimmer. Even I can swim rings around you."

He smiled at her. "They know that."

"And they still hired you?"

He nodded. "They figure I'm big. The kids'll listen to me."

She nodded. At seventeen he was already well over six feet tall, with broad shoulders and a muscular body.

"Besides they've already got two crackerjack swimmers guarding the beach. That's where they really need them. I'll be working the pool. That's easy."

"That's where all the city girls hang out," she said, feeling a strange twinge of jealousy. "You'll really have it made."

He blushed. "Cut it out, JeriLee. You know I don't look at other girls."

"Even when they come on with those two-piece suits —you know, the French ones they call bikinis?"

"They still won't be you," he said awkwardly. After a pause, he asked, "Why don't you get a job out there?"

"Doing what?"

"I heard Mr. Corcoran telling somebody they were looking for waitresses. It's not a bad job. Just a few hours at lunch and dinner. In between, your time is your own. We could see a lot of each other then."

"I don't know," she said indecisively. "I don't think my father would like it. You know how he feels about the summer people."

"Why don't you ask him?"

"What makes you think I can get the job?"

"Mr. Corcoran said many of the girls he interviewed weren't pretty enough. He said it's very important for the club to have good-looking people around." He looked at her. "You'd have no trouble."

She smiled. "You really think so?"

He nodded.

"Maybe I will ask my father then."

Her father agreed that it was a good idea. He had noticed her development and the sudden interest the boys had taken in her and had been concerned that when school was out there wouldn't be enough to keep her occupied. Once he had given his approval and arranged the interview with Mr. Corcoran, her employment was assured, since the bank held the first mortgage on the club.

Until school closed she worked weekends only. Middays she served lunch by the pool. On Saturday night she was at the clubhouse dining room.

Lunch was not a problem, because the menu was simple—hamburgers and hot dogs mostly and a few other sandwiches with side orders of cole slaw, potato salad and french fries. Once lunch was over, about three-thirty, she was on her own until six o'clock, when she reported to the main dining room to help set up the tables.

The three other girls with whom she worked in the main dining room had already put in two seasons at the club and knew the ropes. As a result, JeriLee found herself stuck with all the dirtiest jobs. Dinner was also made more difficult by the fact that the maitre d' and the chef were Italian brothers who created an air of panic by screaming at each other in Italian and at everyone else in broken English.

After school closed and the summer families were in residence, there was a dance every Saturday night. Small orchestras were brought from the city, and when the dining room closed JeriLee and the other girls would drift over to the bar where the dance floor had been set up and sit on the terrace listening to the music and watching the members dance. Bernie was one of the two boys who bused the small cocktail tables set up around the dance floor, and she would wait for him to take her home, usually around one o'clock in the morning.

His father had gone in with him on the purchase of a 1949 Plymouth Belvedere convertible, and the payments took up almost all of Bernie's salary. During that summer, between his responsibilities for the car and his job, Bernie seemed to acquire a maturity along with the dark summer tan and the sunbleached hair. He was no longer a boy.

The girl members at the club also had their effect on him. As lifeguard at the pool, he was one of the few boys who were always around and so it was inevitable that they would try to exercise their charms on Bernie.

JeriLee saw it when in the afternoons she would change into a swimsuit and go out to the pool to cool off. The girls were always sending him for Cokes or cigarettes or towels or asking him to help them with their strokes or dives. She felt a twinge of jealousy as she saw Bernie glow under the attention. But she never said anything that would indicate she had noticed.

Instead she would slip into the pool and begin to swim back and forth in strong steady laps until her arms were like lead. Then she would climb out of the pool at the far end, away from his lifeguard's chair, stretch out on a towel on the concrete edge of the pool and read a book. When it was time for her to return to work, she would gather up her towel and leave the pool without a backward look.

After a while Bernie began to notice and one night on the way home he asked, "How come you don't talk to me when you come down to the pool in the afternoon?"

"Keep your eyes on the road," she said, not answering his question.

"You mad at me about something?"

"No," she said shortly. "You know the rules. Mr. Corcoran doesn't like the help to mix when the members are around."

"Come on, nobody pays attention to that and you know it."

"Besides, you're always too busy." Her voice took on a New York tone. "Bernie, is my stroke too short? Bernie, I would love a Coke. Bernie, would you get me a light?"

"You sound like you're jealous."

"I am not!"

"It's part of my job," he said defensively.

"Of course," she said with a note of sarcasm.

Silently Bernie followed the road that led out to the Point. He pulled into the parking area overlooking the Sound and stopped the motor. There were only a few other cars parked, their motors off and the lights out. It was still early. When the clubs and bars closed after two o'clock, the area would be full. A faint sound of music came from one of the car radios.

He turned and reached for her. She brushed his hand away. "I'm tired, Bernie. I want to go home."

"You are jealous."

"I just don't like them making a fool of you, that's all."

"They're not making a fool of me," he said quickly. "I'm supposed to be nice to the members."

"Sure."

"Besides there's not one of them that can hold a candle to you, JeriLee. They're all so phony and artificial."

"Do you mean that?"

He nodded.

"Even Marian Daley?" Seventeen and blond, Marian Daley had always been indulged by her doting parents. She wore the briefest bikinis at the club and was said to be even wilder than the New York girls.

"She's the phoniest of them all," he said. "The boys know she's the biggest teaser around."

Without knowing it, he had said exactly the right thing. She softened. "I was beginning to wonder," she said. "She never lets you alone."

"She never lets any guy alone," he said, clinching his case. He reached for her again.

She slid next to him, lifting her face for his kiss. His mouth was warm and soft. After a moment she let her head fall on his shoulder. "It's so quiet here," she said softly.

"Yes," he said, raising her face to his and kissing her again. This time his lips were harder and more demanding.

She felt his excitement and her own response. Her heart began to pound. She opened her mouth slightly and his tongue found its way inside. A warmth ran through her, leaving her peculiarly weak. She pressed herself harder against him.

His hands slipped from her shoulders, cupping her breasts. He felt her nipples hardening. "Oh, Jesus!"

he moaned softly, fumbling with the buttons of her blouse.

Her hand caught his, stopping him. "No, Bernie," she said softly. "Don't spoil it."

"You're making me crazy, JeriLee," he whispered. "I just want to touch them. Nothing else."

"It's not good. You know it leads to other things."

"Oh, Christ!" he swore, suddenly angry. He pulled his hands away. "You're a worse tease than Marian Daley. At least she lets a guy feel her tits."

"Then you did go with her," she accused.

"I did not!" he retorted, lighting a cigarette.

"I thought you weren't supposed to smoke."

"I'm not in training," he snapped.

"Then how do you know about her if you didn't go with her?"

"I know some of the guys who did. And I could have too."

"Then why didn't you? If that's what you want?"

"I don't want her. I want you. You're my girl. I don't want any other."

She saw that his face was hurt and troubled. "Bernie, we're much too young to feel like that," she said gently.

But even then she knew that there were currents running inside her that were bringing her closer and closer to the brink of her own sexual awareness.

Chapter 5

"YOU'RE NEW AROUND HERE, aren't you?"

She was lying face down at the side of the pool and when she opened her eyes the first thing she saw was his white city feet. She rolled to one side and, squinting against the sun, looked up.

The boy was tall, not as tall or broad as Bernie but wiry with curly black hair. He smiled. "I'll buy you a Coke."

She sat up. "No, thank you," she said politely.

"Come on," he said. "We're all friends here."

She shook her head. "I work here. It's against the rules."

"Stupid rules." He grinned and held out his hand. "I'm Walt."

"I'm JeriLee," she said. She took his hand and found herself being pulled to her feet.

"I'll buy you the Coke anyway," he said. "I'd like to see them try and stop me."

"No. Please. I don't want to make waves."

She picked up her towel. "Besides I have to set the tables for dinner." She started to walk away.

"Maybe I'll see you at the dance later."

"We're not allowed to do that either."

"Then we can go to a juke joint."

"It will be too late. I'll have to go home then."

"Something tells me that you don't want to go out with me."

Without answering, she hurried away, a strange feeling knotting the pit of her stomach and creating a trembling in her legs.

She saw him again with a group of boys and girls in the dining room that evening. He was seated next to Marian Daley and seemed engrossed in her conversation. When he glanced up and saw her walking by, he nodded and smiled. She went through the swinging doors into the kitchen feeling once more than strange sensation of weakness. She was glad that he wasn't at one of her tables.

"Coming to the dance?" Lisa, one of the waitresses, asked as they were putting away the last of the dishes.

JeriLee finishing drying her hands. "I don't think so. I think I'll just go home."

"They say the singer with the new orchestra is just like Sinatra."

"I'm too tired. If you see Bernie tell him that I've

gone straight home. I can still make the eleven-thirty bus."

"Okay, see you tomorrow."

"Right," JeriLee replied. "Have fun."

She heard the faint sound of the music as she walked past the clubhouse. In her mind she pictured the dance floor.

He was dancing with Marian Daley, who was pressing herself tightly against him. Her full breasts swelled over the top of her dress and she was smiling wet-lipped into his face. He was looking down at her and dancing even closer than before. Then he was whispering something in her ear. She laughed and nodded and a moment later they were leaving the floor on the way outside to his car.

It all seemed so real that for a second she expected to meet them in the parking lot. She began to hurry as if to avoid seeing them, then she stopped abruptly.

JeriLee, she said to herself, what's the matter with you? You must be going crazy!

"Going to the bus, JeriLee?" said a voice from behind her.

She turned. It was Martin Finnegan, one of the beach boys who bused in the dining room on Saturday nights. They all thought he was rather strange because he kept mostly to himself. "Yes, Martin."

"Mind if I walk with you?"

"Okay."

Silently he fell into step with her. They had walked almost a block before he spoke. "Did you and Bernie have a fight?"

"No. What makes you think that?"

"I never saw you take the bus before."

"I was just too tired to stay for the dance tonight. You never stay for the dances, do you?" she asked.

"No."

"Don't you like to dance?"

"Sure."

"Then, why don't you stay?"

"I have to be up early to go to work."

"You don't start on the beach until ten-thirty."

"I work at Lassky's Sunday mornings and have to be at the station at five to pick up the New York papers." He looked at her. "During the week you get the *Herald Tribune* every morning, but on Sundays you get the *Times* as well."

"How do you know that?"

"I make up the papers for the home routes. I know exactly what papers everyone reads."

"That's interesting."

"It sure is. It's amazing how much you can learn about people just from knowing what papers they read. For example, your father's boss, Mr. Carson. His favorite paper in the *Daily Mirror*."

"The *Daily Mirror*? I wonder why."

He smiled. "I know why. It's the only paper that has complete race results from all the tracks in the country. I often wonder what people would think if they knew that the president of the only bank in town played the horses?"

"Do you really think he does?"

"Lassky calls it the closet horse player's *Green Sheet*. That's strictly a horse-racing paper."

They were almost at the bus stop. "Are you going steady with Bernie?" he asked.

"Bernie is a good friend."

"He says you're his girl."

"I like Bernie but he has no right to say that."

"Would you go out with another guy if he asked you?"

"I might."

"Would you go out with me?"

She didn't answer.

"I haven't got the money that Bernie's got an' I haven't got a car but I could spring for a movie and a Coke one night if you want." There was a hesitant tone in his voice.

"Maybe we'll do that one night," she said gently. "But if we do, we go dutch."

"You don't have to do that. I could afford that much, really I can."

"I know but that's the way I do it with Bernie,"

"You do?"
"Yes."
"All right then," he said, smiling suddenly. "Gee, that makes me feel good. I wanted to ask you out so many times but I was always afraid to."
She laughed. "It wasn't too difficult, was it?"
"No," he said. "One night next week?"
"Sure."
The bus squeaked to a stop in front of them and the door opened. He insisted on paying her fare, and since it was only a dime she let him.
"Gee, JeriLee," he said, "you really are very nice."
"You're not so bad yourself, Mr. Finnegan." She noticed that he had been carrying a book. "What's that you're reading?"
"The Young Manhood of Studs Lonigan, by James T. Farrell."
"I never heard of it. Is it any good?"
"I think so. In some ways it reminds me of my own family. It's about an Irish family on the South Side of Chicago."
"Will you lend it to me when you're finished?"
"I got it from the library. I'll renew it and give it to you next week."
She looked out the window. They were nearly at her stop. "I get off here."
He got up with her. "I'll walk you to your house."
"You don't have to do that. I'll be all right."
"It's almost midnight," he said firmly. "I'll walk you home."
"But you'll have to wait a half hour for another bus."
"That's okay."
At her door she turned to him. "Thank you very much, Martin."
He shook her hand. "Thank you, JeriLee. Don't forget you said we could go to a movie."
"I won't forget."
"And I won't forget to give you the book," he said. "Good night."
"Good night, Martin." She watched him go down the porch steps, then turned and went into the house.

Her parents were in the living room watching television. They looked up as she came in. "I didn't hear Bernie's car," her mother said.

"I took the bus. I didn't hang around for the dance."

"Are you all right, dear?" Veronica asked.

"I'm okay, Mom. Just a little tired, that's all."

"Did you come home alone?" John asked. "I don't know whether I like that this late at night. Next time maybe you ought to call and I can come and get you."

"I wasn't alone. Martin Finnegan saw me to the door." She sensed a change in her father's expression. "He really was very nice. Very polite."

"He may be, but his family has a bad reputation. His father hasn't worked in years and he and his wife spend all their time in bars. I don't know how they manage to get along."

"Martin isn't like that. Do you know he works at Lassky's every morning as well as at the Beach Club?"

"That's very nice, but all the same I would be careful about seeing too much of him. I don't want people to think I approve of a family like that."

"I don't see what business it is who we see or don't."

"When you're a banker, everything you do is your neighbor's business. How else do you think you can get them to place their faith in you?"

She thought of Mr. Carson and what Martin had told her. For a moment she was tempted to mention it to her father but then she kept silent. "I'm tired," she said. "I'm going to take a hot both and go to bed."

She kissed her parents good night and went up the stairs to her room. She started the water in the tub and began to undress. She thought first of Martin and then of Walt. Again the peculiar warmth flowed through her and her legs felt strangely weak.

She stared at her naked body in the mirror over the dresser. The whiteness of her breasts contrasted with the tan of the rest of her body. Her nipples hurt and seemed to be trying to burst from her breasts. Wonderingly, she touched them. An excitement radiated through her body, culminating in a flush of heat in her pubis. She put a hand on the dresser for support.

She lowered herself into the warm tub and leaned back. There was an aching in her groin and a prickly sensation in her breasts that she had never felt before. The warm water flowed around her soothingly. Slowly she began to lather herself with soap. Her hand moved down her body, increasing her painful pleasure. Almost as if in a dream, she touched her pubis, the soap turning to lather on her fur. She leaned back, closing her eyes as the warm excitement mounted in her. The movements of her hand became almost automatic.

As Walt's face appeared before her all the muscles in her groin expanded, then contracted in an exquisite, agonizing flash of white fire. She almost screamed aloud in the throes of her first orgasm. Then it passed, leaving her limp, contented, yet strangely empty.

Is this what love is really like? she wondered to herself. And even into the night, while she lay sleepless in her bed, she kept on wondering.

Chapter 6

SUDDENLY IT WAS everywhere around her—in the magazines, newspapers and books she read, in the movies she saw, in the ads and commercials on television, in the conversation of her friends. And it all pointed to a growing awareness of her own inner sexuality.

It seemed as if Walt had triggered a reaction that was pulling her down a road she was not sure she wanted to travel. Unsure of these new feelings, she fought the impulse to explore without really knowing what it was she wanted to discover.

Her dreams were filled with sexual fantasies involving everyone she knew, even her parents and her brother. And in the morning she would awake tired from the struggle with sleep.

She began to masturbate regularly. At first only in her bath, then in bed. But in a little while even that was not enough. The day between waking and sleeping was much too long. By this time she had become so expert in self-manipulation that she could take herself off almost in a matter of minutes. At work she would disappear into the rest room several times a day and carefully lock the door. Frantically she would hike up her dress and pull down her panties. Then she would lean back on the toilet seat and give herself up to the sweet sensations her fingers gave her. A few minutes later she would be back at work as if nothing had taken place.

During this time of inner turmoil her surface appearance seemed almost unchanged. Perhaps she was more rigid in her relations with boys than she had been before, because she did not trust herself. She began to avoid contact with boys, even Bernie, whenever possible. Now she no longer waited for him to take her home but left early so that she could retire to the safety of her own bed.

One day Bernie finally confronted her. "What's the matter, JeriLee? Did I do something wrong?"

She flushed. "I don't know what you're talking about. There's nothing the matter."

"It's more than two weeks since we've been alone. You never let me take you home anymore."

"I'm just too tired to wait around for you to get through, that's all."

"You sure?"

"I'm sure."

"Will you wait for me tonight then?"

She hesitated a moment, then nodded. "Okay." With a choking feeling that brought her close to tears, she went into the dining room to begin setting the tables for dinner.

He turned the car into the parking area at the Point. "Don't stop, Bernie," she said tensely. "I'm really very tired."

"I just want to talk to you, that's all," he said, switching off the motor. The music from the car radio drifted into the night air. He took out a cigarette and lit it.

"You're still smoking."

"Yeah." He looked across the seat at her. She was sitting up against the door as far away from him as she could get. "Don't you like me anymore, JeriLee?"

"I like you just as much as I always did."

"Is there someone else?" he asked. "I know you went to the movies with Martin a couple of weeks back."

She shook her head.

"I don't understand it," he said in a puzzled voice.

"Take me home, Bernie."

"JeriLee, I love you."

That broke the dam. Suddenly she was crying, her hands covering her face, her body shaking with sobs.

He reached across the seat and drew her to him. "JeriLee," he asked softly, "what's the matter?"

"I don't know," she said, her voice muffled against his shoulder. "I think I'm going crazy. I think such crazy thoughts."

"What thoughts?"

"I can't talk about them. It's too horrible." She regained her self-control. "I'm sorry."

"There's nothing to be sorry about. I only wish I could help."

"Nobody can help. It's something I have to do myself."

He placed a hand under her chin and, turning her face up to him, kissed her gently. At first her lips were soft and quivering, then suddenly her tongue forced its way into his mouth.

For a moment he felt surprise, then he responded to her excitement. Roughly he pulled her closer, crushing her breasts against him.

Tentatively he let one hand cup her breast. He heard her breath quicken but she did not push him away as she always had. Emboldened by her lack of resistance, he slipped his hand into her dress and under her brassiere. He felt the warm flesh of her breast and the nipple hardening against his fingers. As she moaned and began to shiver, he felt himself straining painfully against his tight trousers. "JeriLee!" he groaned, pushing her back across the seat almost covering her with his body.

He fumbled with her dress and one breast sprang free. He put his face down and took the thrusting nipple into his mouth. Grinding against her, his hardness pressed into her mound even through the cloth of his pants.

The sensation was too exquisite. His orgasm took him by complete surprise. He shuddered spastically, his ejaculation flowing uncontrollably into his trousers. "Oh, Jesus!" he said. And stopped.

For a moment she continued moving, her eyes closed tightly. Then she too stopped and opened her eyes.

He stared into them. There was something in her expression he had never seen before. It was as if she had discovered and confirmed something she had always known. He sat up and looked down at her. He had soaked through his trousers and onto her dress. "I'm sorry," he said.

"That's all right," she said quietly.

"I lost my head. I stained your dress."

She sat up slowly. "Don't worry," she said. Suddenly she appeared very calm.

"It won't happen again, I promise."

"I know," she said. "Now will you take me home?"

"You're not angry with me, are you?"

"No, Bernie, I'm not angry with you," she said softly. Then she smiled and kissed his cheek quickly. "Thank you."

"For what?"

"For helping me to understand."

He drove her home without knowing what she meant.

Oddly enough it was easier after that. Having confirmed her own worst suspicions about herself, she began to accept her own sexuality. Unfortunately she had no one to talk to. Her mother would be the last person in whom she would confide.

Veronica was part of that prewar generation in which the rules were strict and simple. Good girls didn't, bad girls were punished or made pregnant. In her own bed she was always reserved and proper. Even with her first husband, JeriLee's father, who had the capacity to arouse her to a point almost beyond her control, she managed to stop just before she came to orgasm. And she never felt the lack. A good woman had many other things to occupy her mind. Sex was incidental; the important things were to keep a good home and bring up a proper family. And she was fortunate that her second husband was as conservative as she was.

To his great disappointment, John Randall had not gone to war. He had volunteered but had always been turned down. And so while others left for the service he remained in his job at the bank and, as one of the few younger men, almost automatically gained promotions. Veronica Gerraghty had first come to work at the bank during the war while her husband was away. And even then he had been very impressed with her.

She was not like most of the young married girls who told you how much they missed their husbands while hinting at dates and promising other things. She was quiet and pleasant and smiled often, but it was a friendly smile, not an invitation. After her husband came home he did not see her except when she would come to the bank to make a deposit or a withdrawal. On those occasions she would always stop at his desk and ask how he was. And she was always nice.

Then tragedy had struck. Her husband had been killed in a car accident on the highway just out of town late one night. There were rumors about the accident. Bob had always been wild. And that night he had been drinking and was seen with a woman who was known to have a bad reputation. But none of these facts ever appeared in the newspaper account of the death of Port Clare's first war hero.

John Randall remembered checking into the file following his death. For a man as erratic as he had been, Bob Gerraghty's affairs were in remarkably good order. At the time, he thought that Mrs. Gerraghty was probably responsible. There was about eleven thousand dollars in the joint savings account, and seven hundred in checking. The records indicated that he owned more than two thousand dollars in war savings bonds at maturity value. The mortgage the bank held on their home for twenty-five thousand dollars was completely paid off by the insurance clause, as was another small personal loan of one thousand dollars that he had made just the month before. There was G.I. insurance for ten thousand dollars which had been converted to a civilian policy. He had heard there were several other small policies the amount of which he did not know. In addition the widow would be eligible for service and social security pensions for herself and the children. All of which meant that she fared far better than most people thought.

John Randall had sent Veronica a note of condolence and received a polite reply thanking him. A few weeks after the funeral she came to the bank and he helped her rearrange the accounts under her own name. After that he had not seen her for almost two months, when she came to ask if there was a job for her. While there was no great pressure on her financially, she said she would feel better if she knew she was helping to provide for herself. He thought that she displayed a great deal of good sense. If only more women were like her, they would have fewer problems. Fortunately, a job had just opened up and she began work the following week as the teller at the savings account window.

She had been there for a little more than three months when he asked her out.

She hesitated. "I don't know. It may be a little too soon. People might not like it."

He nodded in appreciation. He knew what she was thinking. Mr. Carson, the bank president, was a strict Presbyterian and had his own ideas of how his employees should act. He was continually railing about the erosive influence of modern thinking on the moralities of the country. "I'll wait a little longer," Randall promised.

"Thank you," she said.

Another three months went by before they had their first date—a movie and dinner. She was home by eleven o'clock and he said good night to her at the front door. He nodded to himself as he went down the walk to his car. It was a lovely little house—neat, well kept and in a good neighborhood. She would make a very good wife for some man, even a future bank president.

They went to Niagara Falls on their honeymoon. On the first night John stood at the window in his new pajamas and silk robe, the gift bottle of champagne the hotel gave each newlywed couple icing in the bucket near him. The literature had promised a view of the falls but had neglected to mention that only a tiny corner was visible between the two hotels facing them. As he squinted into the cloudy sky he heard Veronica come into the room behind him.

She was wearing a silk chiffon nightgown with lace inset over her breasts under a transparent peignoir. There was an almost frightened look on her face.

"Would you like some champagne?" he asked.

She nodded.

Awkwardly he opened the bottle. The cork popped and ricocheted from the ceiling. He laughed. "That's the way a good champagne can be told from a bad one. If the cork pops."

She laughed.

He filled the two glasses and handed one to her. "A toast," he said. "To us."

They sipped the wine. "It is good," she said.

"Come here and look out the window," he invited.

She looked into his eyes for a moment, then shook her head. "I think I'll go to bed. I'm a little bit tired from the long drive."

He watched her place her peignoir on a chair, get into bed and close her eyes. "Is there too much light for you, dear?" he asked.

She nodded without opening her eyes.

He pressed the wall switch and went around to the other side of the bed. He could hear her soft breathing. Tentatively he put out a hand and touched her shoulder.

She did not move.

He turned her face toward him. In the faint light he saw that her eyes were open. "You'll have to help me," he said embarrassedly. "I've never . . . you know . . ." His voice failed.

"You mean—?" she began.

"Yes," he answered. "I could have, I suppose, but I knew I could never bring myself to do it with anyone but my wife."

"I think that's beautiful," she said. Her fear was suddenly gone. At least he would not be like Bob, always comparing her with other women and always insisting that it would never be good until she got something out of it. She had made the right choice. John Randall would be a good husband. "John," she whispered.

"Yes?"

She reached out her arms to him. "The first thing you do is come here and kiss me."

Slowly she led him through the mysteries of her body until the trembling eagerness in him was almost more than he could stand, then she closed her hand around his bursting shaft and guided him into her.

With an involuntary groan, he came almost immediately in a long shuddering orgasm. She slipped her hand between his legs as Bob had taught her and cupped his testicles, applying a slight pressure to make sure they were completely emptied. He moaned again at her touch. Then he was silent, breathing heavily. She moved out from under him.

He touched her face in wonder. "I never felt anything like that before."

She didn't answer.

"Was it good for you?"

"Very good."

"I heard that if a man came too quickly the woman didn't get anything out of it."

She smiled. "That's not true. Maybe certain kinds of women. But not normal ones. This is everything I ever wanted."

"You're not just saying that?" he asked anxiously.

"I mean it. I never had anything as good, even with Bob. I'm very satisfied."

"I'm glad," he whispered.

She bent forward and kissed him. "I love you."

"I love you." A note of wonder came into his voice. "You know . . . I think . . . I'm getting excited again."

"Try not to think about it. More than once a night can cause serious strain. You might hurt yourself."

"Touch me," he said "I'm hard again."

She let him put her hand on him. He seemed carved from rock. She was surprised. Even Bob had never recovered so rapidly.

"I think this once it won't do any harm," he said. "Put me inside you."

Almost reluctantly she guided him into her again. This time he lasted slightly longer but still exploded in a few minutes. He groaned in a strange combination of pleasure and pain as his almost empty testicles strained to express the semen.

He rolled onto his side, looking at her. He was still breathing heavily. "You know you may be right," he said.

"I am right," she said. She kissed his check. "Now try to get some sleep," she said gently. "It will be all right tomorrow."

And from that moment on that was the way it was.

Chapter 7

WHEN HE SAW HER, Bernie came down from his lifeguard's perch at the deep end of the pool. He walked over to where she had spread out her towel. "You're not angry about last night, JeriLee?" he asked.

She smiled at him. "Should I be?"

"I didn't mean to—"

"It's okay," she said quickly. "Nothing really happened. Besides I liked it too."

"JeriLee!"

"Is there anything wrong in that? Didn't you like it?"

He didn't answer.

"Why shouldn't I?" she asked. "Boys aren't the only ones who have feelings."

"But, JeriLee," he protested, "girls are supposed to be different."

She laughed. "If they are, there are an awful lot of girls doing something they don't like."

"I don't understand you, JeriLee. One day you're one way, the next another."

"At least I conform as far as that is concerned," she said. "Girls are said to be changeable." She laughed. "You ruined my dress. I told my mother I spilled something on it in the kitchen."

"It's not funny. I felt guilty as hell about it all night."

"Don't be. Next time just be more careful."

"There won't be a next time, JeriLee. I won't lose my head again."

She looked at him quizzically.

"I mean it. I respect you too much."

"You mean you won't do it even if I want you to?"

"You don't want it, JeriLee," he said with conviction.

"If that's what you think, why did I let you do it?"

"Because you lost your head too."

"No, Bernie, that's not the reason. I let you do it because I wanted you to do it. Suddenly I discovered why I was feeling so strangely, why I was always nervous and upset. It's because I was trying to run away from the feelings inside me."

"You don't know what you're saying, JeriLee."

"I'm being honest, Bernie. I'm not pretending to myself that I didn't want it or like it. Maybe now I'll find a way to cope with it."

"JeriLee, nice girls don't feel like that." He was upset. "Maybe you ought to talk to somebody."

"Who? My mother?" JeriLee asked sarcastically. "I can't talk to her. She would never understand."

"Then what are you going to do?"

"The same thing you're doing. Maybe in time we'll know what it's all about."

He walked back to his stand without answering. All that afternoon he watched her. Nothing was right anymore. He was sorry he had started the whole thing with her.

"Did you finish the book?" Martin asked when she returned it to him.

"Yes."

"What did you think?"

"There were parts of it I didn't understand. Most of the time I felt sorry for all of them. They seemed so lost and unhappy no matter what they did."

"What is it you didn't understand?"

"You said that it reminded you of your own family. You're nothing like Studs Lonigan."

"I could be if I allowed myself to drink the way he did," Martin said. "And my parents are as hypocritical as his. They're always preaching at me but they don't live the way they say I should."

"Did you ever make it with a girl the way he did?"

Martin blushed. "No."

"Do you do anything else?"

"I . . . I don't know what you mean," he stammered.

"I think you do."

He turned fiery red. "Golly, JeriLee, people don't ask questions like that."

"You're blushing," she said. "Do you like it?"

He didn't answer.

"How often do you do it?"

"That's not fair, JeriLee. How would you like it if I asked you a question like that?"

"Maybe you're right," she said after a moment. "I went over to the library myself and took out two more books by James Farrell. You know, I like him. At least he's honest."

"He's a good writer," Martin said. "I tried to get my father to read him but he wouldn't. He said he'd heard all about him from Father Donlan in church, and that he had been excommunicated because of the dirty words in his book."

JeriLee nodded. "I know. When I took out the books, the librarian looked at me kind of funny. She said she thought I might be too young for James Farrell."

He laughed. "Sometimes I wonder what they think we are. Children?"

JeriLee stood on the terrace listening to the music through the open doors of the lounge. The black orchestra had been playing at the club for the last several weeks. At first some members had objected. They said that the only reason Mr. Corcoran had hired them was because they were cheaper than the white orchestras. But from the first night they played, all except the die-hards admitted they were the best orchestra the Beach Club had ever had.

JeriLee and Lisa were sitting on the railing when the music stopped and the orchestra came out on the terrace. They moved off to one side, talking among themselves. After a few moments the boy singer walked over to the railing and stood looking out over the water.

"That last number was very beautiful," JeriLee said to him. "You sounded just like Nat King Cole."

"Thank you."

She had the vague feeling that he did not like her compliment. "I bet everybody says that. You must get sick of hearing it."

He turned to look at her. His eyes were appraising. "That's what folks want to hear," he said in a soft accent.

She felt the faint antagonism. "I'm sorry," she said. "I meant it as a compliment."

He seemed to relax. "We have to give the people whut they want."

"There's nothing wrong in that."

"I guess not," he admitted.

"I'm JeriLee Randall," she said. "I work here."

"I'm John Smith. I work here too." Then he laughed.

She laughed with him. "John Smith. Is that really your name?"

His eyes brightened. "No. But my pappy always warned me. Never tell white folk your real name."

"What is your name?"

"Fred Lafayette."

"Fred, I'm pleased to meet you," she said, holding out her hand.

He shook her hand, then looked into her face. "Jeri-Lee, I'm pleased to meet you."

"And I really do like your singing," she said.

"Thank you." He was smiling now. The orchestra was filing back into the room. "I got to go now. See you later."

"He even looks like Nat King Cole," Lisa whispered as he went inside.

"Yes," JeriLee replied thoughtfully. She felt the warm excitement and her hand still tingled from his touch. She wondered if it would be like that with every boy she met or whether there had to be some special attraction. She turned to her friend. "Lisa, will you answer an honest question?"

"Sure," Lisa answered.

"Are you a virgin?"

"JeriLee! What kind of a question is that?"

"Are you?"

"Of course," she said indignantly.

"Then you wouldn't know."

"What?"

"What it's like?"

"No," Lisa said shortly.

"Don't you ever wonder?"

"Sometimes."

"Did you ever ask anybody about it?"

"No," Lisa answered. "Who is there to ask?"

"I know what you mean."

"I guess it's something every girl has to find out for herself," Lisa said.

JeriLee thought her friend had, in her own way, just about summed it up.

Chapter 8

THE SUN BEAT DOWN, spreading its warmth through her body. She dozed, her face resting on her arms, her eyes closed against the light. She knew the voice the moment he spoke even though she had heard it only once and that almost a month ago.

"Hi, JeriLee. I'm back and I still want to buy you a Coke."

She looked at the feet first. They had now been bronzed by the sun. "Where have you been?" she asked.

"In California, visiting my mother," he said. "They're divorced." He paused. "Are you still worried about the rules?"

She shook her head. As the season went on, the rules about fraternization between employees and members had been relaxed. She learned from Lisa that it was the same every year. She rose to her feet. He was taller than she remembered.

He took her arm casually as they walked toward the cabana bar. It seemed that an electric current ran through his hand, creating a tingling where he touched her. She felt a slight weakness in her legs and a knotting in her stomach. She wondered why it was stronger with him than with anyone else.

He gestured at one of the small tables under an umbrella. "Sit here," he said. "It's cooler than at the bar. I'll bring the drinks."

"I'll have a cherry Coke," she said.

He returned in a moment with the Coke for her and a can of beer for himself. He sat down opposite her and smiled. "Cheers," he said and took a large swallow from the can.

She sipped at the Coke through the straw. He was older than she had thought. He had to be over eighteen to get a beer.

"Is it good?" he asked.

She nodded.

"Has it been good so far this summer?"

"Okay."

"The weather, I mean."

"I know."

An awkward silence descended upon them. After a few minutes he spoke. "You're the first person I looked for when I came in."

Her gaze was direct. "Why?"

He smiled. "Maybe it's because you're so pretty."

"There are prettier girls." She was neither coquettish nor dissembling. It was merely a statement of fact.

"That's a matter of opinion," he said, smiling. "You see, I didn't forget your name. I bet you forgot mine."

"Walt."

"What's the rest of it?"

"You never told me the rest of it."

"Walter Thornton Jr. What's the rest of your name?"

"Randall," she answered. She looked at him. "Is your father the—?"

"Yes. Do you know him?"

"Not really. He just sat next to me on the bus every morning on his way to the station."

He laughed. "That's my father all right. He won't drive."

"Is he here now?" she asked. "I heard he had gone to Europe."

"He came in yesterday. I flew in from Los Angeles to meet him."

"I didn't know he was a member," she said. "I never saw him in the club."

"He never comes to the club. I don't think he's ever been here. He bought the membership for my mother. She used to complain she had nothing to do while he was away."

"Oh," she said, disappointed. "I thought I might be

able to talk with him. I want to be a writer and I think he's really good."

"I can get Dad to talk with you."

"Thank you," she said.

He smiled. "Now maybe I can get you to talk to me."

"I am talking to you."

"Not really. Mostly you're just answering questions."

"I don't know what to talk about."

"That's honest." He laughed. "What are you interested in?"

"I told you. I want to be a writer."

"Besides that. Do you like sports? Dancing?"

"Yes."

"That's not much of an answer."

"I'm afraid I'm not very interesting. I'm not like the girls you know."

"How do you know that?"

"They know how to have a good time. I don't. Port Clare isn't a very interesting place to grow up in. Nothing much ever happens here."

"Are you coming to the dance tonight?" he asked.

She nodded.

"Maybe I'll see you there?"

"Okay." She got to her feet "Thanks for the Coke. I've got to go now."

"See you later." He watched her walk toward the clubhouse. She was right about one thing. She was not like the other girls he knew. In one way or another they were all cock teasers and, oddly enough, he had the feeling that was a game she would never play.

The muscles of her stomach relaxed as she walked back to the clubhouse. It was strange the effect he had on her. The sudden intense awareness of self, and the rising sexual heat. All the time she had been with him she was aware of the constant wetness between her legs.

She went into the locker room, stripped off her swimsuit and got under a cold shower. But it didn't seem to help. While soaping herself she touched her pubis and almost sank to her knees with the quick intensity of her orgasm.

After a moment she regained her self-control and

leaned her head against the cold tile wall of the shower stall. There was something wrong with her. Very wrong. She was sure that none of the girls she knew were going through what she was.

"Looks like you goin' to lose youah little friend, Fred." Jack, the drummer, said, gesturing with his stick at the dance floor.

JeriLee and Walt were moving by in a slow fox trot. He was holding her close, too close, Fred thought. There was an expression on her face he had never seen before, an intensity he could almost sense. Abruptly he segued into a fast Lindy. The orchestra stumbled for a moment, then caught up with him.

Jack grinned. "Ain't goin' to he'p. You jes been playin' it too cool, man."

"She's not like that," Fred whispered fiercely. "She's just a straight kid."

"I ain' arguin'. She straight all right. But she also ready. That sweet li'l white pussy is ripe an' beggin' to be picked."

"What makes you such an expert?" Fred asked angrily.

"Becuz I only got two things on my mind, man. Drums an' pussy. If'n I ain't thinkin' about one, I'm thinkin' 'bout t'other." He laughed. "You better believe it."

Fred looked back at the dance floor but JeriLee and Walt were gone.

The moment she came into his arms on the dance floor he had felt her breasts pressing against him through his thin shirt. She wasn't wearing a brassiere. He was sure of it. Instantly he felt himself growing hard and tried to move his hips slightly away from her so that she would not know. But she moved along with him, sighed slightly and rested her head on his shoulder.

"Hey," he said.

She raised her face.

"Do you always dance like this?"

"I don't know. I just follow," she said.

"Do you know what you're doing to me?" he asked. "I'm getting very excited."

Her eyes were level. "I didn't know I was doing that. I thought you were doing it to me."

"You mean you're excited too?"

"I think if you let go of me I'd fall. My legs feel so weak."

He stared at her. He had been wrong. All the time he had thought she was just an innocent little girl. Abruptly the orchestra broke into a fast number. He stopped and looked down at her. "JeriLee, let's get out of here."

"Okay," she said and followed him through the open terrace doors. They cut across the lawn toward the parking lot. She didn't speak until he held the door of his car open for her. "Where are we going?"

"Some place we can be alone," he said.

She nodded as if she had known that was what he would say and got into the car. In ten minutes they pulled into the driveway of a small house just off the beach.

He cut the motor and looked at her. "There's no one at home. My father won't be in from New York until tomorrow and the housekeeper's gone home."

She looked at him without comment.

"Don't you have anything to say?"

She looked down at her hands folded in her lap, then back at him. "I'm a little frightened."

"Of what?"

"I don't know."

"Don't be," he said, not knowing her real fears. "No one will know you're here. The nearest neighbor is a half mile down the beach."

She didn't answer.

"There's a heated pool out back," he said. "It's great to swim there at night. Would you like that?"

She nodded. "But I don't have a swimsuit."

He smiled. "That's one of the nice things about swimming at night. It's dark." He got out of the car and walked around to open her door. "Coming?"

She suddenly laughed. "Why not?"

"What are you laughing about?"

"I'm afraid you'd never understand." For the first time in a month she was beginning to feel better. It was almost as if she had always known that this was the way it would happen.

They walked through the house and out the back door to the pool. He pointed to a small cabana. "You can leave your things in there."

"Okay," she said, starting toward it. "Where are you going?" she asked when she noticed he was heading back into the house.

"I'll be back in a minute," he said. "I just want to get a few cold drinks."

Entering the cabana, JeriLee looked at herself in the large mirror over the vanity table. There was a calmness about her face that surprised her because it did not reflect the excitement seething within her. Quickly she unfastened her blouse and her breasts sprang free. The nipples were swollen and distended. Softly she touched them. They still ached but the touch was pleasant. Actually that was why she had not worn her brassiere. It had hurt her breasts too much. Gently she pressed her breasts again and felt the pleasure run down into her groin. She slipped out of her skirt. Her panties were moist and she could see the dark pubic hairs clearly in the wet nylon material. Slowly she stepped out of them and spread them neatly on the bench so that they could dry.

She wondered what he was thinking. She remembered how hard he had been when they were dancing, so hard that it hurt as he pressed against her mound. Twice she had almost stumbled and fallen as she climaxed during the dance. Each time she wondered if he had known what had happened, but there were no signs that he did.

She heard him call from outside. "I'm back. Are you coming out?"

She pressed the light switch, plunging the cabana into darkness, and opened the door. He was spreading some towels on the large chaises near the far end of the pool. He was still dressed, his back toward her. Silently she slipped into the water. He was right, it was warm and soft.

He turned quickly. "That's not fair," he said. "You got in before I could even see you."

She laughed. "You're the one that's not fair. You're not even undressed yet."

He bent over the table and turned on the portable radio he had brought with him. The music drifted softly across the pool. With his back to her, he undressed quickly, dropping his clothes to the ground, then swiftly he turned and, almost before she could catch a glimpse of him, dived in. He came up on the other side of the pool.

"How do you like it?" he asked. "Is the water warm enough?"

"I like it. This is the first time I've ever gone skinny dipping. It feels good. Better than when you have a suit on."

"That's what my father says. He says that if nature meant for us to have clothes we would have been born with them."

"Your father might be right," she said. "I just never thought about it."

"My father has a lot of peculiar ideas. About everything. He says if people would only learn to be honest with themselves it would be the end of most of the problems in the world."

"Are you honest with yourself?" she asked.

"I try to be."

"Do you think you could be honest with me?"

"I think so."

"Why did you bring me here?"

"I wanted to be alone with you. Why did you come?"

She didn't answer. Instead she swam away toward the deep end of the pool. He swam after her. Abruptly she turned under water and came up on the other side of him. He laughed and caught her at the shallow end.

He held her by the arm. "You didn't answer my question?"

Her eyes looked into his. "Because you weren't being honest with me."

"Why do you think I brought you here?" he asked

"Because I thought—" she hesitated a moment and

then, unable to think of another way to say exactly what she meant, she went on—"you wanted to fuck me."

He was startled. "If you thought that why did you come?"

"Because I wanted you to fuck me."

Abruptly he let go of her arm and climbed out of the pool. He picked up a towel and tied it around his waist and made himself a rum and Coke. He sipped it without speaking.

She rested her arms on the edge of the pool ."Are you angry with me? Did I say anything wrong?"

He took another swallow of his drink. "Christ, Jeri-Lee, you sound cheap and vulgar."

"I'm sorry. I was only trying to be honest. I felt you against me while we were dancing and I thought that was what you wanted."

"But girls don't act like that," he protested. "You just don't make it with every guy that gets a hard-on for you."

"I don't."

"But the way you talk. What's a fellow supposed to think?"

"Is that what you think?"

"I don't know what to think. I never had a girl talk like that to me before."

Suddenly the warm feeling left her and she was perilously close to tears. She was silent for a moment. When she spoke her voice was calm. "It's getting late, Walt. I think you better take me home. My parents will be wondering what happened to me."

He let her out of the car in front of her house but made no move to get out of the car himself. "Good night, Walt," she said.

"Good night," he said abruptly. Then he put the car into gear and drove off, leaving her on the sidewalk. Slowly she went into the house.

Her father looked up from the television set as she came in. She kissed his cheek. "Where's Mom?"

"She was tired and went up to bed," he said. "You're home early. Who brought you?"

"A boy named Walt. He's one of the members."

"Is he nice?"

"Yes." She started from the room, then stopped. "Dad."

"Yes?"

"Is there such a thing as being too honest?"

"That's a strange question, darling. Why do you ask?"

"I don't know. It seems to me that whenever I answer a question truthfully my friends get upset with me."

He looked at her thoughtfully. "Sometimes people don't want to hear the truth. They would rather live with illusion."

"Is it always like that?"

"In a way I guess it is. I try to be as honest as I can with people. But there are times when it's not always possible."

"Are you honest with me?"

"I hope I am."

"Do you love me?"

He reached over and turned off the television set. Then he turned and held out his arms to her. "I think you know I do."

She knelt in front of his chair and laid her head on his chest. He closed his arms around her and held her quietly against him. For a long while they did not speak.

Finally in a tight small voice of hurt she said, "You know, Dad, it's not easy growing up to be a woman."

He kissed her cheek and tasted the salty wetness of the tears on her cheeks. A curious sadness came over him. "I know, darling," he said gently. "But then I think that it's not easy to grow up to be anything."

Chapter 9

IT WAS LIKE a storm that had passed. For weeks the pressure of having to know and understand the nature of her sexual being had been tearing her apart. Then one morning she awakened and the urgency was over.

She knew what she did not know. But she was no longer driven by the need to force the knowledge. The things she felt were part of her expanding consciousness and somehow she knew she would experience them all in their own time. She became more herself, more relaxed, more able to enjoy the simple exchange of being with other people.

Once again she and Bernie could be friends. Now when they parked and petted at the Point she was able to respond without having to push further and further into her desires. Sex no longer permeated her every thought. She knew that it would come in time. But it would come when she was equipped to deal with it as a part of her total being.

And it was not with Bernie alone that she had dates. Martin too was a good friend. They would sit on her porch for hours talking about the books they had read and discussing different people in town. Often they shared laughter at the ridiculous postures that some people assumed in order to seem important. Once she even let Martin read a short story she had written.

It was about a mayor of a small town who during the war became depressed because all the towns around him had war heroes and his small town did not. So he made up his mind to make a hero out of the first returning veteran. It happened to be a man who had gotten a medical discharge and had never been near the front.

Nevertheless he was given a welcoming ceremony at which everything went wrong. In a way it was very much like the story of her real father but with a twist. In the midst of the proceedings, two M.P.'s appeared and took the hero away, because it seemed that he had faked his discharge from a psycho ward.

"It's great, JeriLee," he told her enthusiastically after he'd finished it. "I recognize almost everybody. You should send it away to a magazine."

She shook her head. "I'm not ready yet. I still feel there are too many things wrong with it. Besides I'm working on another I think might be better."

"What's it about?"

"It's about a girl like me. About growing up in a town like this."

"Can I read it when you're finished?"

"It may not be finished for a long time. There are too many things I have to learn before I can begin to write about them."

"I understand that," Martin said. "Hemingway says the best writing comes from gut experience."

"I don't like Hemingway. He knows nothing about women. He seems not to care about them at all."

"Who do you like?"

"Fitzgerald. At least he feels for the women characters in his books as much as he does for the men."

"To me, all of his men seem strange, weak sort of," Martin said after a moment. "They seem to be afraid of women."

"Funny. I think that about Hemingway. His men always seem to me more afraid of women because they are always trying to prove themselves as men."

"I have to think about that," he said, getting to his feet. "Now I'd better be getting home."

"Everything all right there now?" she asked. They had long since dropped pretenses and she was openly inquiring about the problems he had with his parents.

"A little better," he said. "At least they're not drinking as much now that Dad's got that job at the gas station."

"I'm glad." She rose from the chair. "Good night."

Martin stood looking at her without moving.

She touched her cheek self-consciously. "Is there anything wrong?"

"No."

"Then what are you staring at?"

"You know I never realized it before. You really are very beautiful."

Another time she might have smiled but there was a sincerity in his voice that moved her. "Thank you," she said simply.

"Very beautiful," he repeated, then he smiled and ran down the steps. "Good night, JeriLee," he called.

Bit by bit JeriLee's popularity was growing. There was something in her that seemed to attract friends. Boys and girls alike. Maybe it was because she dealt with each of them on their own terms and within their own frame of reference. At the same time she was still a very private person. In the end they liked to talk to her because they all felt that she really listened.

Once the season was in full swing, the club stayed open every night for dinner and there was a dance on Wednesdays as well as on Fridays and Saturdays. Since it became impractical for the musicians to return to the city every night, Mr. Corcoran put them up in a small cottage out in the back of the tennis courts. The back of the cottage faced out on the parking lot, so they did not have to come through the club in order to get to the bandstand.

JeriLee, who now worked late on Wednesday nights, was on the terrace railing sipping a Coke and talking to Fred between sets when Walt came out the terrace doors.

"JeriLee," he said, ignoring Fred completely.

It had been more than a month since that night at his house and this was the first time he had spoken to her. "Yes?"

"I have some friends down from school and we're getting up a beach party. I thought you might like to join us."

JeriLee looked at Fred. There was no expression on his face. She turned back to Walt. "Do you know Fred?"

"Yes. Hello, Fred."

"Waltuh." Fred's voice was as expressionless as his face.

"It'll be fun," Walt said. "And if the Sound is too cold, there's always the pool at my house."

"I don't think so," she said. "I have to be here early tomorrow. I'm working lunch."

"Come on, JeriLee. We won't be too late. We'll just have a few drinks and a few laughs, that's all."

"No, thank you," she said politely. "As a matter of fact I was thinking of leaving early. There's still time for me to catch the eleven-thirty bus."

"You don't have to do that. We can drop you off at your house."

"I don't want to trouble you. It's out of your way."

"Not much. Besides it's no trouble."

"Okay."

"I'll get the guys," Walt said and went back into the cocktail lounge.

Fred looked at her. "You got a thing for that boy?"

JeriLee thought for a moment. "I thought I did. But not now."

"He's angry with you," Fred said.

She was puzzled. "How do you know?"

"I feel it. But I could be wrong. He also don't like me much. But that might be because he don't like black folk in general."

"I hope you're wrong. He might be a little spoiled but I wouldn't want to think that about him."

It was time for the orchestra to go back to work. Fred looked at her. "See you on the weekend?"

"Sure." She nodded. "Sing pretty for the people."

He smiled. "I always do."

"Good night, Fred."

"Night, JeriLee."

The sound of music began to drift through the doors just as Walt came out.

"Okay, JeriLee. Let's go." He started down the terrace steps. "We can cut across here to the parking lot."

"What about your friends?"

"They already went to the car with Marian Daley."

She followed him down the steps and they crossed the tennis courts to the parking lot. She could hear the laughter coming from his car. "Sure I wouldn't be spoiling anything?" she asked. "I can still make the bus. I don't mind."

"I said it was okay, didn't I?" He sounded annoyed.

"Okay," she said.

Silently they walked the rest of the way to the car. It was an open convertible. Marian and two boys were already in the back seat. "What took you so long?" one of the boys called as they came up.

"I had to sign the bar check," Walt said. He opened the door of the car. "Fellows, this is JeriLee. JeriLee, Joe and Mike Herron. They're brothers. You know Marian."

JeriLee nodded. "Hi."

Marian seemed cool, but both boys smiled and one of them held a bottle up to JeriLee. "Join the party," he said. "Have a drink."

"No, thank you," JeriLee said.

"I'll have one," Walt said. He took the bottle and held it to his mouth. He took a long swallow, then handed the bottle back to the boy. "That's good rum."

"It should be." The boy laughed. "Your father has nothing but the best."

Walt closed the door and got in behind the wheel. He started the motor and gunned the car out of the parking lot. They turned down the highway in the direction that led away from her house.

JeriLee looked at him. "We're going the wrong way."

"I thought I'd drop them off before I took you home," he said.

She didn't answer. A sound of laughter came from the back seat. She turned around. Both boys were trying to unbutton Marian's blouse and she was giggling while slapping their hands away. "Not fair." She laughed. "It's two against one."

JeriLee turned back in the seat. She glanced at the speedometer. The needle was up around seventy. "Better slow down," she said. "The highway patrol is on the road tonight."

"I can handle them," Walt said grimly.

There was no sound from the back seat now. She glanced into the rearview mirror. Marian seemed to have disappeared. Involuntarily she turned and looked into the back seat. Marian had her head in Joe's lap. It was a moment before she realized what the girl was doing. She was holding Joe's penis in her hand and taking it in her mouth.

She turned back quickly, a curiously sick feeling in the pit of her stomach. Somehow she knew this was not the way it should be. She knew what girls and boys did in cars but this was not at all what she had imagined. She couldn't wait until Walt dropped them off and took her home.

Walt pulled the car into the driveway and cut the motor. "Okay," he said. "Everybody out." He opened his door and came around to her side.

"You said you were going to take me home."

"I will," he said. "What's the big deal? Last time you couldn't wait."

"Last time was different. You were different."

Marian and the two boys were out of the car. "Come on." Marian laughed. "Don't be a party pooper."

"Just one drink, then I'll take you home. I promise," Walt said.

Reluctantly she got out of the car and followed them into the house. They went right through to the pool. With a loud whoop the boys dropped their clothes and dived into the water. "It's great," Mike shouted. "Come on in."

She turned, looking for Walt. She saw a light go on in the house as he went into the kitchen. A moment later music came from the portable radio on the table near the pool. Marian was dancing by herself to the music.

Walt came out with a tray of Cokes and a bucket of ice. He picked up the bottle of rum near the radio and quickly mixed the drinks. He held one toward Marian. She took it and began to drink it quickly. He held one out to JeriLee.

"No, thank you."

"You're not much fun, are you?"

"I'm sorry. I told you I wanted to go right home."

"Well, you can damn well wait until I have a drink," he said angrily, raising his glass.

"Come on, JeriLee," Marian said. "Don't be a pill. You're among friends."

"No, thank you," she said again. She started toward the house.

Walt put a hand on her arm. "Where do you think you're going?"

"I can get the bus on the highway," she said levelly.

"I said I'd take you home," he snapped. "Isn't my word good enough for you?"

Before she could answer him, she felt a pair of hands grab her ankles and her feet went out from under her as she was dragged into the pool. She came up sputtering and angry and striking out at the boy nearest her.

"She wants to play," she heard one of the boys say. Then two pairs of hands grabbed her shoulders and pushed her down into the water again. She tried to wriggle free and she felt her dress rip as their hands caught her. Then she went under again. She came up gasping and held on to the side of the pool.

She looked up at Walt through eyes burning with tears. "Please take me home," she cried.

"I will," he said, raising the glass to his lips. "As soon as your clothes are dry."

Chapter 10

BERNIE CAME UP to Fred on the terrace. "Is JeriLee out here?"

"No."

"If you see her, tell her that her father called. He

wants her to bring home a quart of ice cream." Bernie started back.

Fred stopped him. "When did he call?"

"Just now. I picked it up in the bar."

"That's funny. How long does it take from here to her house?"

"About ten minutes by car, half hour by bus."

"Then she should have been home by now. She left more than an hour ago." A curious feeling of dread came over him. "You know where the Thornton kid lives?"

"On the other side of the Point. Why?"

"He was supposed to drop her off home. But he was higher than a kite and so were his two friends. I saw them inside knocking back rum and Cokes like water. He wanted her to join him at a beach party but she said she wanted to go home."

Bernie stared at him. "I saw Marian Daley leave with those two boys. She was trying to get another girl to go with them but the girl wouldn't."

"I don't like it. JeriLee should have been home by now." He looked at Bernie. "You got a car?"

The two boys stared at each other. "I'll get the keys and meet you in the parking lot," Bernie said.

She was crying, lying huddled and naked on the grass beside the pool, trying to cover herself. She sensed a movement and looked up.

Joe was bending over her. "Stop bawling," he said in an annoyed voice. "It isn't as if you never did this before."

"I never—"

"You did," he said positively. "Walt told us about the time you came here with him."

"Nothing happened," she cried. "Honest, nothing happened."

"You never stop lying, do you?" He turned and shouted at Walt. "You better get over here and do something about this cunt or I'm goin' to belt her."

Walt came up. He still had a glass in his hand and was weaving. "Come on, JeriLee," he said in a placating voice. "We just want to have a little fun. Take a drink of this. It'll make you feel better."

"No."

There was a sound from the other side of the pool. Joe turned around. "Well lookee over there." He laughed.

She looked across the pool. Marian and his brother were coupled on the ground. She could see the frenzied movements of the boy, and the moaning sounds they made echoed in the night.

"Ain't that pretty?" Joe asked. "They're makin' it. How about comin' off your high horse and we can have a real party?"

She didn't answer.

Joe got angry. "Then what the hell did you come out here for, you fucking cockteaser?" he shouted.

"I didn't!" she cried, suddenly realizing that Walt had not told them she was going home, that he never intended to take her home. She turned to Walt. "Tell them, please. I didn't—."

Joe knelt by her side and grabbed her hair. He forced her head back. "Gimme the drink," he snapped. He took the drink from Walt and, forcing her mouth open by bending her head back, poured the drink down her throat.

She began to choke and gasp. The sticky sweet liquid ran down her cheeks spilling across her shoulders and breasts. He didn't stop until the glass was empty. Then he threw it away. JeriLee heard it breaking against the concrete.

He put his face close to her. "Now, you goin' to cooperate an' be nice or am I goin' to have to get rough with you?"

Her eyes widened. She tried to hold her breath. "Please, let me go. Please."

He moved suddenly, throwing his weight against her, pushing her flat on the ground with his body. His fingers sank into her breasts as he tried to kiss her.

She thrashed wildly, trying to turn her face to avoid him. Involuntarily she brought her knee up to his groin.

A grunt of pain escaped him. "Bitch!" he yelled.

Angrily he slapped her face with his open palm. "You hold her," he shouted up at Walt. "No bitch is gonna try to knee my balls an' get away with it."

Walt stood there indecisively.

"Hold her!" Joe snarled. "Time she got what's comin' to her."

Walt dropped to one knee, pinning her arms to the ground. Suddenly she felt a sharp pain on her breast. She cried out.

Joe raised the lighted cigarette. He was smiling. "You didn't like that, did you?"

She stared back at him, unable to speak. He moved swiftly. The scorching pain burned into her other breast. She screamed.

"Yell your head off. Ain't nobody to hear you." Joe held the cigarette to his mouth and dragged on it.

"Walt, please, make him stop!" she implored.

"Maybe, we better—" he began.

Joe cut him off. "You stay out of it! This is between me an' her. When I get through she ain't gonna cock-tease nobody." He straddled her legs with his knees and brutally put his hand on her pubis. With his fingers he spread her open. A strange smile came to his face. "Now, ain't that pretty pink little pussy?"

He bent his face forward and bit her mound. She tried to move but couldn't. He straightened up and laughed. "Not bad. A little pissy, but not bad." Slowly he brought the cigarette down toward her. "Now you'll get a taste of something real hot."

Fascinated, as if she were watching a snake, she stared, her eyes following the glowing tip of the cigarette as it came toward her. Suddenly she felt its approaching heat and she shut her eyes tightly.

They heard her scream as their car stopped in the driveway and were out of the car running through the house almost before the engine had stopped.

Bernie was the first one through the sliding doors. He froze for a moment at the horror of what he saw—the two boys holding JeriLee down and her mouth still open in a scream. His mouth opened. "What—?"

Fred reacted with the reflexes of one used to street fighting. He took one step and kicked Joe in the side of his head, lifting him from the ground and tumbling him backward on to the concrete walk. Walt was trying to get to his feet, but Fred never gave him a chance. Slashing viciously with his fist, he caught Walt flush on the nose and mouth, and felt the crunch of bone and teeth against his knuckles. Walt fell back as if he had been hit by an ax.

Fred knelt beside JeriLee pillowing her head in his arms. She was crying in pain. "Don't hurt me, please. Don't hurt me." Her eyes were tightly shut.

"It's okay, honey," he said softly. "Nobody's gonna hurt you now."

"Fred!" Bernie's voice was sharp.

He turned to see another boy coming toward him and started to get up. But Bernie caught the boy from behind in a tackle and they fell to the ground, rolling over and over. Joe was coming back toward him now and there was something in his hand that looked like a rock.

He rose quickly, his hand making a lightning move under his trouser leg. The knife came to his fingers and at the same time he pressed the switch and the blade flashed forward. He held the knife flat in his hand before him. "One move, white boy," he said quietly, "an' I'll cut your balls off."

Joe froze, staring at him, his hand still in the air. It wasn't a rock that had been in his hand, it was a portable radio.

Fred stepped back on catlike feet so that he could see them all. "Get something to cover her up," he said to Bernie. "And let's get her out of here."

He heard a sound from across the pool. Marian was coming around the walk, staggering drunkenly, a bottle of rum in her hand.

"What'sh happenin' to the party?" she asked.

"The party's over, honey," he said, his voice filled with contempt.

They managed to cover JeriLee with the remnants of her dress and a towel and get her to the car. She sat between them shivering and crying and moaning in pain, her head against Fred's chest, while Bernie drove. She was still crying as the car pulled up in front of her house.

When Fred tried to help her out of the car, she wouldn't move. "I'm afraid," she whispered.

"There's nothing to be afraid of now, JeriLee," he said soothingly. "You're safe now. You're home."

But an instinct told her that this was only the beginning of the horror. And she was right.

Chapter 11

THE LETTERS WERE scrawled in black crayon on the white picket fence:

JERILEE FUCKS. JERILEE SUCKS.

John stared silently at the words. Next to him, Bobby was still holding the wet bloody handkerchief against his nose, although the heavy bleeding had stopped. "I saw them doing it when I came around the corner, Daddy."

"Who was it?" John asked, a sick feeling inside him.

"They were big boys," the twelve-year-old replied. "I never saw them before. When I went to stop them, they hit me."

John turned to his son. "There's a can of white paint in the garage," he said. "Get it. Maybe we can paint it over before your mother and JeriLee get home from shopping."

"Okay, Dad. But why do they say things like that about my sister?"

"Some people are just sick, Bobby. They're stupid."

"It's an awful thing to do. I wanted to kill them."

John looked at his son. The child's face was grim. "Get the paint," John said gently.

The boy ran across the lawn toward the garage and John turned to look down the street. There was no one in sight. He fished in his pocket for a cigarette. It had been less than a month since that night. The night he had opened the door to find the two boys holding a frightened beaten JeriLee between them.

The late show was almost over when the doorbell rang. He rose from the chair in front of the television set where he had been dozing and glanced at his wrist watch. It was one o'clock. "It must be JeriLee," he said. "She probably forgot her key."

Veronica was absorbed in the film. "Tell her not to be so forgetful the next time. We might have been asleep."

He went into the small hallway leading to the front door. The doorbell rang again. "I'm coming, honey," he called, turning the lock.

The door swung open without his touch. For a moment he was transfixed by what he saw. JeriLee stood between the two boys, her clothes torn, blood running down one cheek almost to the top of an exposed breast. Bernie held one arm around her waist to keep her from falling.

There was a look of terror in her eyes as she raised her face to him. "Daddy," she said in a weak voice, taking a stumbling step toward him.

He caught her before she fell. His arms tightened around her, he could feel the frightened flutter of her heart pounding against his shirt. "My God!" he exclaimed. "What happened?"

The black boy whom he had never seen before spoke first. "We'll tell you what happened, Mr. Randall," he said, "but you better get a doctor for JeriLee. She's been hurt bad."

By this time Veronica was behind him. When she saw her daughter she let out a small scream. "John!"

JeriLee turned her face to her mother. "Mother, I—"

A tone of anger and fear came into her mother's

voice. "What trouble did you get yourself into this time, JeriLee?"

"Ronnie!" John said harshly. "Get Dr. Baker on the phone and tell him to come over right away!" Without waiting for a reply, he lifted JeriLee into his arms and carried her upstairs to her room. Gently he placed her on the bed.

She moaned softly. The remnant of the dress which clung to her breasts fell away, revealing the angry burns welting her flesh. "I'm frightened, Daddy," she cried.

"There's nothing to be afraid of now. You're home now. And safe."

"But I hurt all over, Daddy."

"It's okay," he said softly. "Dr. Baker is on his way. He'll stop the pain."

"He'll be right here," Veronica said as she came into the room. She looked down at JeriLee. "What happened?"

"Walt said he was going to take me home—"

Veronica didn't wait for her to finish. "Walt?" she asked angrily. "Who's Walt? That colored boy down there? You know better than to have anything to do with people like that!"

"No." JeriLee shook her head weakly. "He's not Walt. He's Fred. He came with Bernie to get me."

Again Veronica interrupted. "Get you? Where did you go? You were supposed to be at work."

John saw the fear come into his daughter's eyes. "Ronnie!" he said sharply. "No more questions. Let's try to make her a little more comfortable until the doctor gets here. Get a washcloth and some warm water.

"It's okay, baby," he said as Veronica left the room.

"I don't want to wake up Bobby," she whispered. "I don't want him to see me like this."

"Don't worry," he reassured her. "Your kid brother can sleep through an earthquake." The doorbell rang downstairs. "That must be the doctor." His hand brushed some hair away from her forehead. "You're going to be all right now."

"Mother is going to be angry with me."

"No she won't. She's just upset."

Dr. Baker had been around a long time. After forty years of practice, he didn't wait for verbal explanations. Without speaking, he snapped open his black bag. Quickly he administered a shot. "That will take away the pain, JeriLee," he said. He straightened up and turned to her parents. "You two go downstairs while I look after her."

"Will she be all right?" John asked.

"She'll be all right," the doctor said.

They went down the stairs and into the living room where Fred and Bernie were waiting. "How is she?" Bernie asked.

"Dr. Baker said she'll be okay," he said. "Now tell me what happened."

"She was tired and wanted to go home early," Bernie said. "Walt said he would drop her off on his way home. He had some friends with him. When you called and she wasn't home yet, Fred figured something was wrong. That was when we went after her."

"What made you think that?" John asked Fred.

"Walt and his friends were drinkin' pretty good. I thought they were acting mean."

"Who is this boy Walt that you're talking about?" Veronica asked. "I haven't heard JeriLee mention him before."

"Walt Thornton," Bernie said. "He lives out at the house on the Point."

"The writer's son?" John asked.

"Yes."

"What happened when you got there?"

It was Fred who answered. "Walt was holding her on the ground, the other boy was doin' things to her. She was screamin' so loud we could hear her on the other side of the house."

John's face was tight. He picked up the telephone.

"What are you doing?" Veronica asked.

"I'm calling the police," he answered in a tight voice.

"Wait a minute," she said, taking the telephone from his hand and putting it down. "We don't know if they did anything yet."

John stared at her. "You saw what they did. They were like animals. They tortured her. Isn't that enough?"

"Did you see them doing anything else?" she asked Fred in a calm voice.

The black boy's face was impassive. "I don't know what you mean, ma'am."

She flushed. "Did you see them having intercourse with her?"

"No, ma'am." Fred's voice was even. "I don't think they got that far."

"You see?" she asked, turning back to her husband. "They didn't do anything."

"They did enough," John said angrily.

"You call the police and everybody in town will know what's happened," she said. "I don't think Mr. Carson would like that."

"I don't give a damn what Mr. Carson would like."

"Besides, we don't know what JeriLee might have done to provoke them."

"You don't believe that?"

"That's the first thing people will think. I know this town and so do you."

John was silent for a moment. "Okay. I'll wait until the doctor comes down. We'll see what he has to say." He turned back to the boys. "I don't know how to thank you for what you've done. If it weren't for you . . ." His voice trailed off.

The boys stood looking awkward.

"Would you like a cup of coffee or something?" Veronica asked.

Fred shook his head. "No, thank you, ma'am. I have to be getting back to the club. They'll be wonderin' what happened to me. We'll just wait a minute to hear what the doctor says."

"You don't have to wait," Veronica said quickly. Suddenly she wanted them out of the house. If anything more had happened to JeriLee she did not want them to know about it. "I'll call you first thing in the morning."

Bernie hesitated. He glanced at Fred, then nodded.

"Okay," he said reluctantly. They started moving toward the door.

Veronica cleared her throat. "I'd appreciate it if you would keep this to yourselves," she said. "This is a small town. You know how people will talk even if there's nothing to talk about."

Bernie nodded. "You don't have to worry about us, Mrs. Randall. We won't say anything."

The door closed behind them and John came back to his wife. "The doctor's been up there a long time."

"It's only fifteen minutes." She glanced up the staircase, then back to him. "I don't know how JeriLee could get herself into a position like that."

"You heard what the boys said," John replied. "They were supposed to drop her off here."

"Do you believe that?" she said.

He met her eyes. "Yes," he said simply.

"I don't," she said flatly. "I know JeriLee. She's more like her father than I like to think. He never thought of consequences, neither does she. I think she knew exactly what she was doing."

"You're not being fair to her," he said angrily. "JeriLee's a good girl."

How naïve he was, she thought. "We'll see what the doctor has to say," she said noncommittally. "I'll put some coffee on."

She had just put the coffee on the table when the doctor came down.

"She's okay," he said. "She's sleeping. I gave her a shot."

"Some coffee, Doctor?" Veronica asked.

He nodded wearily. "Thank you."

She filled a cup and gave it to him, then handed a cup to John and poured one for herself. "Did they—?" she asked.

The doctor looked at her. "No," he said.

"She's still a virgin?"

"If that's all you're worried about," he answered edgily, "yes, she's still a virgin."

"Then nothing happened," she said in a relieved tone.

"Nothing happened," he said sarcastically. "If you

don't count the violent beating and almost third-degree burns on her breasts and pubis, besides a broken nose and teeth marks that look as if they'd been made by a wild animal."

"I'm going to call the police," John said. "They can't be allowed to get away with it."

"No," Veronica said firmly. "The best thing to do is to forget it. We still don't know what she did to provoke them. And even if she did nothing, you know what people will think. It's always the girl's fault."

"Do you believe that, Dr. Baker?" John asked.

The doctor hesitated. He knew how John felt. He would feel the same way if she were his daughter. But Veronica was right. The best thing was to sit on it. "I'm afraid your wife is right, John," he said. "People are funny about these things."

John's lips tightened. "Then you'd let those boys get away with it completely."

"Maybe you could discuss it confidentially with their parents," the doctor suggested.

"What good would that do?" John asked. "I'm sure the boys will find a way to blame it all on JeriLee."

"That's exactly what I mean," Veronica said quickly. "Either way it will get all over town. I say we just forget about it."

John looked at his wife. It was as if he were seeing her for the first time. She was more frightened and more calculating than he had ever thought. His voice was heavy with pain. "Maybe we can forget about it," he said. "But what about JeriLee? Do you think she will be able to forget?"

Chapter 12

"YOU AN' YOUAH fuckin' college ways!" Jack muttered as he began to throw his clothing angrily into the battered valise.

Fred lit a cigarette without speaking.

Jack straightened up. "Better git youah things together. The man gave us until noon to git out."

Fred got to his feet. "I'm goin' out," he said. He blinked as the morning sun hit his eyes, the sky was clear. It was going to be a scorcher. He cut across the parking lot to the beach and looked out across the Sound.

The water shimmered blue-green, and small white-crested waves broke across the deserted sand. He took off his shoes, rolled up his trouser cuffs to his knees and, holding his shoes in one hand, began to walk along the water's edge. He took a deep breath of the sweet ocean air. Jack was right. It was a beautiful world—if you were white. It was nothing like this back in Harlem.

Less than a week had gone by since that night. The first day had been quiet. JeriLee had not come in to work, and neither Walt nor his friends had shown up at the club. Even Marian Daley had not appeared. Then suddenly in the afternoon the rumors began to fly.

One of the boys who were visiting Walt Thornton had wound up in the hospital at Jefferson, about thirty miles from Port Clare. He had a broken cheekbone, a fractured jaw and several caved-in ribs. It had been reported as an accident, the result of a bad fall. Perhaps it would have escaped notice, except that Walt too had cuts and bruises. It was enough to raise questions.

Meanwhile, Marian Daley's mother had been checking around town among her daughter's friends. Marian had not come home that night. By morning she had begun to worry. She traced her to Walt's house and, when the telephone was not answered, decided to drive out there.

There had been no answer at the front door but when she discovered that it was unlocked she went inside. Finding no one on the main floor of the house, she went out the sliding doors to the pool. The whole areas was a mess of overturned chaises and broken bottles. She stood for a moment, then went back into the house and picked up the telephone to call the police. It was then that she heard a sound coming from one of the bedrooms.

She had reached the top of the staircase just as Marian came out of the room. She was totally naked. As they stood there staring at each other in stunned surprise, a boy she did not know appeared in the doorway behind her daughter. He too was naked.

Mrs. Daley was the first to find her voice. "Get your clothes, Marian, and come with me." Then she turned and went out to the car without waiting for an answer.

A few minutes later Marian came out and got into the car silently beside her mother. Without a word, her mother started the engine and pulled out of the driveway. It wasn't until they were on the street that she spoke. "You've really done it this time, Marian. When your father finds out about it, there's no telling what he'll do."

Marian began to cry. It took only two minutes for her to blurt out her version of what had happened. Her mother did not interrupt her. At the end she glanced at her daughter, "You say JeriLee came with you?"

"Yes," Marian said quickly. "We were only going to go swimming. Then Bernie and Fred suddenly showed up. There was a terrible fight and they took JeriLee away with them."

"Where's Walt and the other boy?" her mother asked.

"He was hurt so badly that Walt took him over to Jefferson to the hospital," Marian said.

"Why was the nigger there?" Mrs. Daley asked.

"I don't know," Marian said quickly. "But JeriLee is very friendly with him. They're always together around the club."

Mrs. Daley's lips tightened. "I told Mr. Corcoran when he hired them that you couldn't trust niggers. They have no respect for people."

"What are you going to tell Daddy?" Marian asked in a small voice.

"I don't know yet," her mother said. "He'll go crazy if he finds out that a nigger was out there and saw you like that. First I better have a talk with JeriLee's mother and find out if she knows what her daughter's been doing. Then I'm going to have a talk with Corcoran. If he wants to keep his memberships he better find a way to get rid of those niggers."

The telephone on his desk rang just as he returned from lunch. He picked it up. "Randall speaking."

"John?" Veronica was clearly upset.

A sudden fear clutched him. "Is JeriLee all right?" he asked quickly.

"Yes, but I just had a call from Mrs. Daley. She told me that boy is in the hospital at Jefferson, he was so badly beaten up."

"Too bad," John said sarcastically. "If it had been me I would have killed him."

"That's not it. She said that JeriLee was very friendly with the colored boy and that they had been running around together and that the reason they went out there was because he was jealous of her."

"That's crazy!"

"She said Marian was there. That she said that JeriLee went with them. Nobody said anything about taking her home."

"The Daley girl's a liar!" he exploded.

"She asked me if JeriLee got home all right."

"What did you tell her?"

"I said she did. Then she wanted to know who brought her home. I told her. She told me that she was going out to the club to talk to Mr. Corcoran about getting rid of the colored orchestra and that I ought to be more strict with JeriLee and not let her associate with people like that."

"We can't let that happen," John said. "The boy deserves a medal for what he's done. You call her back and tell her exactly what happened."

"I can't do that. She wouldn't believe me anyway. She thinks JeriLee went there with her daughter. And even if she does believe me, the story will spread all over town like wildfire."

"Better that than having the boy lose his job for something he's not responsible for."

"Nobody will believe that. They'll all think that it's JeriLee's fault. We won't be able to hold our heads up in this town. And you know how Mr. Carson feels about bank employees. One bad word and they're finished."

"He'll believe the truth if I tell him," John said. "I think I better go in and have a talk with him before this gets any further."

"I think you ought to stay out of it."

"I'm already in it. I can't let that boy suffer for saving my daughter from being raped." He put down the phone and walked to the rear of the bank and knocked on the glass door that partitioned off Mr. Carson's office.

The bank president's voice came through the door. "Come in."

He opened the door and took a half step into the office. "Mr. Carson," he said in a polite voice, still standing half across the threshold, "would you have a moment to spare?"

Mr. Carson looked up. "Of course, John," he said in his nice-guy voice. "Any time. My door is always open. You know that."

John nodded, even thought it wasn't true. He closed the door carefully behind him. "It's a personal matter, Mr. Carson," he said.

"No raises," Carson said quickly. "You know our policy. We review once a year."

"I know that, Mr. Carson. It's not that. I'm perfectly satisfied with my compensation.

Carson broke into a smile. "I'm glad to hear that. People never seem to be satisfied anymore." He waved a hand at the chair opposite the desk. "Sit down, sit down. What is it you want to talk about?"

"It's very confidential."

"You don't have to tell me, John. Anything said in here remains within these four walls."

"Thank you, Mr. Carson. It's about my daughter, JeriLee."

Carson sighed. "You don't have to tell me, John. I have children of my own. Problems, always problems."

John lost his patience. "She was beaten up and almost raped last night!" he blurted out.

"My God!" Carson's shock was genuine. "Is she all right?"

"Yes. Dr. Baker took care of her. He said she'll be fine."

Carson took out his handkerchief and mopped at his forehead. "Thank God. You're very fortunte." He put the handkerchief down on the desk. "I don't know what this world is coming to. I hope you've caught the fiend responsible for it."

"That's just it," John said. "Veronica thinks we shouldn't say anything about it, that it would only expose JeriLee to further public shame."

"There is something to what she says," Carson agreed. "But you can't let a man like that walk around. There's no telling who he might pick on next time."

"That's the way I feel. But now it's even worse than that. One of the boys who helped save JeriLee is going to lose his job because he tried to help her."

Carson was not altogether stupid, and instinct told him that he had better learn more about what had happened. "Suppose you tell me the whole story from the beginning."

He listened quietly while John told him what had happened. "I don't see how the Daley girl is involved," he said at the end of John's story.

"Apparently she was there when it happened. Jeri-Lee said she was still there when they left."

"Did they do anything to her?"

"I don't know."

"How did her mother hear about it?"

John shrugged his shoulders.

The banker fell silent. It would be a simple matter if John were not an officer of the bank. "Did you talk to the police?" he asked.

"I was going to, but Veronica told me to wait. Perhaps I'd better do that now."

"No," Carson said quickly. "I think things like this are better handled privately."

"How do I do that?" John asked. "I can't just go over to Mr. Thornton and say, 'Your son tried to rape my daughter,' or to Mr. Daley and tell him that his daughter is a liar."

"No," Carson said thoughtfully.

"Meanwhile that poor boy is going to lose his job."

"Ordinarily I wouldn't say this but I think it might be better for all concerned if you followed Mrs. Randall's advice and just let the matter slide. As an officer of the bank, you must realize that Mr. Thornton maintains huge balances here and that Mr. Daley, as a home builder, steers us a tremendous amount of business. Something like this could very well lead them to place their business elsewhere."

"That would be stupid."

"Of course it would," Carson said smoothly. "But you know customers. We've lost them for flimsier reasons. And these two are very important to us."

"But what about the boy?"

"I'll have a quiet talk with Corcoran at the club and see what I can do." Carson got to his feet and came around the desk, placing his hand on John's shoulder. "I know how you feel, but take my word for it. There are some things that are better left unspoken. The boy is only here for a few weeks anyway. But we have to continue to live in this town."

John didn't answer.

Carson dropped his hand from John's shoulder. His

voice took on a more businesslike tone. "By the way, I've heard via the grapevine that the state bank examiners might be paying us a surprise visit. I'd like you to review all the accounts just to make sure that everything's in tiptop order."

John got to his feet. "I'll get on it right away, Mr. Carson."

"Good," Carson said. "The main thing is that your daughter is all right. Don't worry about anything else. Things have a way of working themselves out."

"Thank you, Mr. Carson," John said. He went back to his desk and sat down, a strange futility in him. Carson would do nothing. He knew that. It had all been spelled out very clearly. The bank's business was the primary consideration. As usual.

It took Mrs. Daley only four days to get Fred fired.

Chapter 13

JeriLee was sitting on the porch when Dr. Baker came up the walk. He thought as he looked at her that the healing powers of the young never ceased to amaze him. The swelling around her nose had almost gone, and the puffy black and blue under her eyes had vanished completely. "I didn't expect to find you out here," he said.

"I got tired of staying in my room."

He came up the steps. "How are you feeling?"

"Much better. Will I have any scars on my . . . ?" She didn't finish the question.

"No. You'll have white marks where you were burned for a while, but eventually they'll blend in and disappear."

"Good," she said in a relieved tone. "I was beginning to worry. They looked so bad."

"You are getting better." He laughed. It was good to see her vanity returning. "Come inside and let me have a look at you."

They went up to her room. She undressed quickly without self-consciousness and wrapped a towel around her. He put his reflector on even though he really didn't need it. He felt somehow that it made his examination seem more professional. She stretched out on the bed while he removed the dressings. Carefully he wiped away the ointment and studied the burns. After a moment he nodded with satisfaction. "You're doing okay. I think we can leave the dressings off now. Just don't wear anything that will be irritating."

"You mean a brassiere?"

He nodded.

"I can't do that."

"What not? No one can see anything under your blouse."

"That's not it," she said. "I bounce too much. It's embarrassing."

He laughed. "Walk slower, it will be all right." He got to his feet. "I don't have to come here anymore. Suppose you come down to my office in about a week and we'll see how you are getting on."

"Okay," she said, sitting up. "Can I go back to work?"

"Do you want to?"

"Yes."

"You might run into those boys out there."

"I'm not afraid of them. They're not going to try anything again. Besides I can't hang around the house all the time."

"You can go back if you want to," he said. "But don't push it. You still haven't got all your strength back."

"I thought I'd wait over the weekend and go back on Monday. It's easier at the beginning of the week."

"Okay," he said, "but don't hesitate to call me if there's anything you need."

"Thank you, Doctor." She watched the door close behind him, then got out of bed. She felt vaguely troubled. Bernie and Fred had been telephoning every morning but this morning there had been no calls. She slipped into a robe, went downstairs and on a hunch decided to call Bernie at home.

When he answered he said, "I was just going to call you."

She looked at her watch. It was after eleven o'clock. "Why aren't you at work?" she asked.

"Corcoran fired us," he answered.

"You and Fred?" Surprise raised her voice. "What for?"

"I don't know. But Marian's mother has been making a big stink. God knows what kind of story Marian told her."

"Where's Fred?"

"He's out at the club packing. They fired the whole group."

"I have to see him," she said. "Will you run me out there?"

He hesitated a moment. "He's pretty upset."

"So am I," she said. "Will you?"

"Okay. When?"

"Right now. I'll be ready in ten minutes."

"Fred! Fred!" Her voice floated on the wind across the dunes.

She was standing at the crest of the small hill that separated the beach from the clubhouse. He raised his hand and waved, then stood waiting as she ran down the hill. There was, he thought, something simple and animal-like about the way she moved. He came out of the water to join her on the beach.

Without speaking, she took his hand. He stood very still for a moment, feeling the warmth in her fingers. Then, still holding hands, they began to walk along the water's edge.

"It's not fair," she said finally.

His eyes sought hers, his voice was soft. "Nothing ever is, little girl."

"Why do you call me that?"

"That's what you are. A little girl just growin' up. Trying being a woman on for size."

"Maybe you're right. I feel like that sometimes."

They were silent again for a few minutes and then she said, "They can't do this to you."

He smiled. "They done done it."

"They won't do it if they learn the truth," she said. "I don't know what Marian's mother said, but when I tell Mr. Corcoran what happened he'll hire you back. You'll see."

"You're not goin' to tell that queer bastard nothin'!" His voice was almost savage.

She looked up at him, startled by his tone.

He hadn't meant to frighten her. But she hadn't heard the stories that had been circulated by Mrs. Daley and Mr. Corcoran. Suddenly JeriLee had become the villain of the piece while Marian had grown an instant halo. "I'll find another job," he said more softly.

She stopped. "But where will I find another friend like you?"

Her words seemed to reach into his heart and suddenly his eyes burned with tears. "You're a lovely lady, JeriLee. You'll find many friends in your lifetime." He turned and stared out over the water, fearing that if he looked at her, he would take her into his arms and lose something he never really had. "It's beautiful here," he said. "So peaceful."

She didn't speak.

"I guess that's what I'll miss. Walkin' on the beach barefoot in the mornin' before anyone's awake an' there's no people aroun' to spoil it." He deliberately lapsed into black talk. "Black folk got nothin' lak this back in Harlem."

"Won't you ever come back to see me?"

He let go of her fingers. "I got no business here. Besides I'll be busy. Workin' all summer an' back to school in September."

"You're bound to have a day off sometime."

There was an agony in his voice. "JeriLee, leave me be!"

He saw the tears spring suddenly to her eyes but held himself away from her. "I got to get back an' finish packin' or we goin' to miss the bus to New York."

She nodded, regaining her self-control. "I'll walk back with you."

They didn't see the policemen until they crested the dune. The two uniformed men stopped in front of them. The bigger man looked at Fred. "You Fred Lafayette?"

Fred glanced at JeriLee before he spoke. "Yes."

The policeman took a paper from his pocket. "I have a warrant here for your arrest."

Fred took the warrant without looking at it. "What's it for?"

"Assault and battery with a deadly weapon against the person of one Joseph Herron on the night of July tenth. Will you come quietly or do we have to put the cuffs on you?"

"I won't make any trouble," Fred said.

"Good boy." For the first time the policeman relaxed. "Let's go."

JeriLee found her voice. "Where are you taking him?"

"County jail at Jefferson."

"I know Chief Roberts," she said. "Can I talk to him?"

"You can talk to anyone you like, lady, but he's got nothin' to do with this case. We're out of the county sheriff's department."

"Don't worry, Fred. I'll talk to my father. He'll get this straightened out."

"You keep out of it, JeriLee, I'll make out okay."

"How can I keep out of it?" she asked. "I'm already in it."

Chapter 14

JUDGE WINSTEAD looked at the large old-fashioned gold pocket watch his father had given him fifty years ago when he had come into the law office. "It's twelve-forty-five," he announced, snapping the case shut and returning the watch to his pocket. "First time since the war that Carson's been late."

Arthur Daley nodded. "Must be something important to hold him up."

The monthly luncheon had become more than a ritual. On the third Friday of each month the three men would meet and review the concerns of the town. Together they formed the core of power that moved Port Clare. Nothing could be accomplished without their stamp of approval, and though none of them had ever been elected to office it was understood by everyone, even the politicians, that the only way to get things in Port Clare was through them.

"Another drink?" the judge asked.

"No, thanks. I'm due out at the construction site at two. I want to have a clear head."

"I'll have one." The judge signaled the waiter. "How's it going?"

"Okay. I should have the first ten houses ready by September."

"That's not bad."

"Still haven't got county approval on the water lines and sewers yet though."

"Township approval okay?"

Daley nodded.

"No problem then," the judge said. "I'll have the state D.W.P. get on it."

"That will be a help."

"V.H.F. mortgages?" the judge asked.

"I don't know yet. I wanted to talk to Carson about it. Thirty thousand is a high price for V.H.F. If I price the houses cheaper we won't get the kind of people we want in there."

"We can't have that. We have a responsibility to the community not to lower the standards."

"Yeah," Daley said dryly. They understood that one of the most effective ways of keeping out undesirables was to price them out of the market.

The judge looked up. "Here he comes now."

Carson was walking quickly toward them. His face was red and flushed. He dropped into his chair without apologies. "I need a drink," he said.

Wisely the others said nothing until after he had taken a good swallow of his scotch. He put his glass squarely on the table. "We've got trouble," he announced.

He didn't wait for them to ask questions. "Your wife started the damned thing, Daley," he said angrily. "Why didn't you check with me before you let her go off half cocked?"

Daley was genuinely bewildered. "I don't know what you're talking about?"

"That thing that happened out at the Thornton house last Sunday night."

"What thing?"

"You don't know?"

Daley shook his head.

"Your daughter and JeriLee Randall went out there from the club. Apparently two of the boys tried to rape JeriLee and were beating her up when two of her friends showed up. Murphy's kid and a nigger from the club orchestra. The nigger put one of the boys in the Jefferson hospital."

"I don't see what my wife had to do with it," Daley said.

"Apparently your wife found out about it and went after the nigger's ass. She didn't stop until she got Corcoran to fire the Murphy kid and the nigger. If she had stopped there it wouldn't have been so bad. I could still have controlled it. I'd already talked Randall into not doing anything. But then your wife convinced the boy's parents to sign an assault charge against the nigger. The county police took him in this morning. Now JeriLee says she's going into court and file charges against the Thornton boy and his two friends. She also said she'd testify for the nigger. If she does that, Port Clare will get the kind of publicity we're not looking for. Nothing like a juicy attempted rape charge against the son of one of the country's most important writers to make headlines."

"Any way of talking her out of it? Maybe her father—"

Carson interrupted the judge. "None. He's just as upset as she is. He would have preferred charges the next day if I didn't talk him out of it. But he's heard the stories going around town making his daughter out to be a tramp and he's boiling about it." He looked at Daley. "You knew nothing about your daughter being out there?"

"No." Daley's voice was flat. "My wife never said anything to me."

"Then you have to be the only man in town who hasn't heard about it." He turned to the judge. "You?"

"I heard some stories."

"What do we do now?"

The judge thought for a moment. "If the charges were dropped we could probably keep it quiet without too much trouble. But someone will have to talk to the boy's parents and to Randall."

"I can take care of Randall," Carson said. "But someone's got to talk to the parents." He turned to Daley. "Your wife got us into it, maybe she can get us out of it."

"I don't see how," Daley protested. "If the boy was really hurt—"

"You better find a way. Don't forget your daughter was involved in this too."

"She had nothing to do with it."

"How do you know?" Carson asked, his voice cold

and blunt. "She and the boys were drunk when they left the club that night. Your wife found her and one of the boys naked when she went looking for her the next morning."

"Oh, Jesus!" Daley groaned. "I kept telling Sally she was letting the kid get away with murder."

Carson looked at him coldly. "Maybe you're lucky after all. It could very well have come to that."

Daley got to his feet. "I'd better skip lunch and go right home and talk to Sally."

Carson watched the builder walk out of the restaurant, then turned to the judge. "You get on to the county prosecutor over in Jefferson and tell him to sit on it. That you have word that the charges are going to be withdrawn."

"What if he already has impaneled a grand jury?"

"Tell him to stall then."

"Okay," the judge said.

"He'll listen," Carson said confidently. "Without Port Clare's votes he never would have been elected. He won't forget that."

"Why the hell didn't you tell me what was going on?" he yelled. "I felt like a damn fool. I was the only man in town that didn't know."

"I didn't want to upset you, Arthur," Sally said placatingly. "You had enough on your mind with the new construction."

"God damn it, woman, how many times do I have to tell you to check with me if there are any problems? Have I ever refused to talk with you?"

She was silent.

"Now we got a real mess on our hands. Bad enough our daughter was fucking her brains out with those boys, now it's going to be all over the papers."

"Nobody will believe JeriLee's story," she said. "Who's going to take the word of JeriLee and a nigger against Marian and those three boys?"

"Enough people. Especially when they bring in Dr. Baker to tell how badly JeriLee was beat up."

"I didn't know about that until today."

"Of course you didn't," he said sarcastically. "You should have had brains enough when you found Marian bare-assed with that boy to leave well enough alone. Why weren't you satisfied with getting the nigger canned? What made you push the kid's parents into signing a complaint?"

"I didn't push them," she protested. "What could I say to them when they called me to check on their son's story? Especially after I had been yelling at Corcoran to fire him for what he did."

"But you said you would back their complaint."

"I had no choice. It was either that or admit that I knew what Marian had done. I didn't think it would go this far."

"That's the trouble. You didn't think. You never think. You're stupid."

She began to cry.

"Stop bawling," he snapped. "That ain't going to solve anything." He paused for a moment. "Where are they now?"

"Who?" she sniffled.

"Who the hell do you think I'm talking about? That kid's parents. Where are they?"

"They're staying at the Thornton house."

"Call them up and tell them we have to see them. It's important."

"I can't do that. I don't know them well enough."

"Oh, Jesus!" he groaned in despair. "Tell them your daughter's been fucking one of their sons or maybe both. That makes us practically in-laws. That should be reason enough."

"Why do you have to do everything Carson tells you? Can't you once do anything on your own?"

"Because I owe him two hundred and ninety thousand in building loans, that's why. If it weren't for him I'd still be a carpenter building one house at a time. Now get on that phone." He walked to the door. "I don't care what you say to them, but get an appointment."

"Where are you going?"

"Upstairs to see that little cunt we call our daughter,"

he said harshly. "If she won't tell me the truth about that night, I'll beat it out of her."

He slammed the door violently. She heard his heavy footsteps on the stairs as she reached for the telephone. She began to dial the number but stopped when she heard her daughter shout in pain. Her fingers froze over the dial. There were no more sounds from upstairs. Slowly she began to dial again.

As he pressed the doorbell, he automatically cast an appraising eye around the property. Prime beach-front land. At least forty thousand an acre. The house was worth a good seventy thousand too.

The door was opened by a slim tired-looking man of about fifty. "I'm Walter Thornton," he said. "Come in."

He put out his hand. "Arthur Daley," he said. "My wife and my daughter, Marian."

Thornton shook his hand and nodded at the other two. "Mr. and Mrs. Herron are in the library."

"I'm sorry to be bustin' in on you like this," Daley said after having been introduced to the Herrons, "but I feel we have something important to talk about. It concerns all of us here in this room."

"I think everything has been taken care of," Mr. Herron said. "The police have that boy in custody."

"I'm not too sure we all did not act kind of hasty."

"I'm not sure I understand you, Mr. Daley," Thornton said.

"What I mean . . ." Daley hesitated a moment, embarrassment creeping into his voice. "We did not get the true story of what happened that night."

"My son was beaten severely," Mrs. Herron said. "I don't need to know any more than that."

"Mrs. Herron, you might not like to hear what I have to tell you, but did you ever stop to think maybe your son brought it on himself? Maybe he was doin' something he shouldn't?"

The doorbell rang. Thornton looked surprised.

"That must be Judge Winsted and John Randall," Daley said quickly. "I took the liberty of asking them to join us. John maybe knows more about this than any of us, an' the judge is a good friend of mine. We may need his advice."

Thornton went to the door and returned a moment later with the two men. "Now, Mr. Daley," Thornton said, "supposing you continue."

"I asked John Randall to come because his daughter is involved in this."

Mrs. Herron's voice was cold. "She certainly is. It was her friend that attacked my son."

John slowly got to his feet. His voice was calm but he was shaking inside. "I'm going to say this once and I'm not going to repeat it. Your son, Mrs. Herron, and your son, Mr. Thornton, attempted to rape my daughter. They beat her severely and savagly burned her breasts and body with a live cigarette after bringing her here under the pretense that they were going to take her home from work. We were persuaded by friends not to bring charges in view of good community relations but we cannot stand idly by and see the boy who saved my daughter go to jail. Despite the fact that none of us want public attention, my daughter and I are planning to file these charges against your sons first thing in the morning."

Thornton was the first to break the heavy silence. "Obviously you must believe this story, Daley, because you brought Mr. Randall here. What I don't understand is why you are so convinced."

Arthur cleared his throat. "My daughter was there. She corroborates JeriLee's story."

"They're both lying!" Mrs. Herron burst out. "What was she doing while it was going on? Standing idly by?"

"Tell her, Marian," Arthur said harshly.

Marian began to cry.

"Tell her!" he repeated.

"Mike and I were makin' out on the other side of the pool while Joe and Walt were with JeriLee." She sniffled.

"Didn't you see what was happening?" Thornton asked.

"We couldn't see in the dark too good. Besides we

thought they were only fooling with her. Just before that they pulled her into the pool with her clothes on."

"I still don't believe you," Mrs. Herron said stiffly. "Neither of my boys would do things like that."

"Sally," Arthur said. "Tell Mrs. Herron what you found when you came the next morning to get Marian."

"They both came out of the bedroom upstairs. They were naked," she said in a hushed voice.

Thornton walked to the door that led to the back. "Walt," he called. "Mike back there with you?" He didn't wait for an answer. "Both of you come in here a minute."

A moment later the boys came into the room, and stopped when they saw Marian and the others.

"You didn't tell me the whole story about what you tried to do to JeriLee that night, did you?" Thornton asked his son in a pained voice.

The boy looked at the floor. "We didn't mean to hurt her, Dad." His voice broke. "It all started as a joke."

"It seems a terrible mistake has been made," he said. "Now what can we do to make it right?"

"That's why I asked the judge to come along," Daley said. "He'll tell us what to do."

Chapter 15

JACK AND AN OLDER man Fred had never seen before were in the sheriff's office when the policeman brought him from the cell. "You're being released, boy," the sheriff said. "The charges have been dropped."

The sheriff took a heavy manila envelope out of the desk and pushed it toward him. "Your things are in there. Would you please check them?"

Fred opened the envelope and took out the contents. His ten-dollar Timex was still there, so was the small gold ring his mother had given him when he graduated high school and the silver-plated I.D. chain bracelet with his name engraved on it that had been a gift from his sister. Two single crumpled dollar bills and seventy cents in small change made up the rest of the envelope's contents. He put the watch, ring and bracelet on and the money in his pocket.

"Is it all there, boy?" the sheriff asked.

"Yes."

The sheriff held a paper out to him. "Sign that. It's a receipt for your property."

Quickly he took the pen and signed the inventory sheet. "Everything's okay now," the sheriff said. "You can go."

Jack pumped his hand enthusiastically. "I'm glad you're out. I jes' spoke to the agent. He got us a gig up in Westport."

Jack saw Fred look questioningly at the older man with the white hair and mustache. "This is Judge Winsted," he said quickly. "He got things straightened out fer us."

The judge held out his hand. "Glad to meet you, Fred."

"Thank you, Judge."

The judge turned to the sheriff. "Peck, do you have a room where I can talk to my client?"

"Sure thing, Judge," the sheriff said, pointing. "Through that door there. The room is empty."

Fred and Jack followed the judge into the other room. The judge pulled a chair up to the small table and sat down heavily. "The older I get, the hotter it gets. I wonder if it's a sign of something."

The judge gestured for them to sit down. "In case you're wondering what I'm doing here," he said, "I'm representing JeriLee and her father."

Fred nodded.

"When they came to me early this afternoon, I could see there might be a terrible miscarriage of justice. I couldn't permit a thing like that."

"Lucky for me," Fred said. "They were going to throw the book at me."

"Couldn't happen," the judge said definitely. "I must admit that things get fouled up sometimes but in the end justice manages to win out."

Fred didn't believe the statement any more than he thought the judge believed it, but he didn't say anything.

"You have a real friend in JeriLee. You know that. Despite what it would do to her, she was ready to go into court to prove your case."

"JeriLee's a very special lady."

"She sure is," the judge agreed. "She's got much more sense than most girls her age. Anyway, soon's I heard her story I went right out and saw that boy's parents. It didn't take me long to convince them of their error. Then I went over to the club to see Corcoran but it was too late to get him to take you back. He had already hired another orchestra. I didn't think that was right, because you were still out the money you would have made if you had continued working there. I didn't think that was the way to reward a hero."

"I'm glad to get out of jail," Fred said. "I don't care about the job. Or the money."

"It still isn't right. Somebody ought to be made to pay for the anguish you went through."

"Yeah," Jack agreed. "That po' boy went through a lot jes' for doin' right."

"Exactly how I felt. I had another discussion with those concerned and they have agreed to reimburse you for the loss of employment. Figuring that you all lost five weeks' work at the club at two hundred dollars a week plus board, which was worth another two hundred, we came to a total of two thousand dollars." He reached into his pocket and pulled out an envelope from which he removed a package of bank notes that he spread fanwise on the table in front of him.

Fred looked at the twenty hundred-dollar bills. "I don't want their damn charity money!" he snapped.

"It's not charity, son. It's justice."

"Man, the jedge is right," Jack said. "That's four

hundred dollars fer each of us. Take it, boy. That's gravy money."

"You knew about it?"

"Sure I did. That there money is for all of us. We all lost our jobs along with you."

"You take it, son," the judge advised. "It's the right thing to do. After all, there's no reason why your friends should suffer because of what happened."

Fred thought for a moment, then nodded. "Okay," he said.

The judge smiled. "That's good thinking." He took another paper from his pocket and put it on the table in front of Fred. "This piece of paper is a release by which you and the people who pressed charges against you mutually agree that you won't hold each other in further liabilities. It's just a form thing. When you sign it the money is yours."

Fred signed the paper without reading it.

"I have to be getting back to Port Clare," the judge said as he placed the paper in his pocket. "It's a pleasure to have met you. And I'm glad I was able to be of service to you."

Fred shook his hand. "Thank you, Judge. Don't think I don't appreciate what you've done. I'm very grateful."

When the door closed behind the judge Fred turned to Jack. The drummer was grinning from ear to ear.

"What is it, Jack?"

"That judge is the shittiest character I ever met. He was goin' to try to get you to sign that piece of paper fer a hundred dollars. But I knew you had them by the short hairs." He picked up the money and fingered it lovingly. "Oh, baby, don' that look pretty? The easiest day's work any of us ever had."

She was waiting at the foot of the steps when he came out of the building. And suddenly he realized that without knowing it he had been looking for her.

He stopped on the bottom step. "JeriLee." His voice was soft.

She looked into his eyes. "Are you okay?"

"I'm fine. Actually they were very nice. One of the best jails I've ever been in."

There was a startled expression on her face. "Have you ever been in jail before?"

"No," he laughed. "I was jes' foolin'. You didn't have to come all the way over here. I would have called you."

She looked at him skeptically.

"I mean it. I had to thank you for what you did."

Jack tugged at his arm. "It's goin' on seven o'clock, Fred. We better git a move on if'n we goin' to make the last bus to the city."

"You got transportation back to Port Clare, JeriLee?"

"Yes. Bernie loaned me his car. He's working tonight."

"Cocoran give him back his job?"

"Yes."

"Are you going to go back to work there?"

"I was going to, but now I don't think so."

"What are you going to do?"

"I don't know. Catch up on my reading. Maybe try to finish the story I've been writing."

"Man, we better hurry," Jack said.

"You go on ahead, Jack. I'll catch up to you."

"You know where the bus station is?"

"I'll find it."

"The bus leaves at seven-thirty."

"I'll be there."

They watched Jack hurry off. "Where you parked, JeriLee? I'll walk you over."

"Not far, just the next block."

"What are you going to do?" she asked.

"Jack's got another job lined up in Westport."

"I'm glad," she said. "Bernie asked me to give you his regards and wish you luck for him."

"Your boy friend's okay."

"He's not my boy friend really. We just sort of grew up together."

"That'll do it every time."

"Do you have a girl friend?"

"Yes," he lied.

"Is she pretty?"

"I guess so."

"What kind of an answer is that?"

"It's kind of hard for me to tell. You see, we sort of grew up together."

She looked at him quizzically for a moment. "That'll do it every time," she said finally with mock seriousness.

They both laughed. "Here's the car," she said. "I'll drop you at the bus station."

A few minutes later she pulled the car to the curb in front of the bus terminal and looked across the seat at him. "I would like for us to be friends," she said.

"We are."

"I mean . . . to see each other again."

"No, JeriLee," he said after a moment of silence. He opened the door and started to get out.

She put a hand on his arm. "Thank you, Fred," she said gently. "For everything."

"JeriLee."

"Yes?"

"I lied, JeriLee. I have no girl friend."

She smiled. "You didn't have to tell me. I knew that."

"Goodbye, JeriLee." He didn't wait for her reply but moved quickly into the bus terminal. He didn't turn to look back until he was inside the building. And by then she was gone.

Chapter 16

SHE CAME OUT of the five-and-ten, walked to the corner and waited for the light to change. A car pulled up to the curb. "Can I give you a lift, JeriLee?"

It was Dr. Baker. "I thought you were coming in to the office," he said as she got into the car.

"I've been feeling all right. I didn't want to bother you."

"It's no bother. I'm your doctor."

When she didn't answer, he said, "I thought you were going back to work."

"I changed my mind," she said shortly.

He stopped for a light and turned to her. "What's wrong, JeriLee?"

"Nothing."

The light changed and he put the car into gear. "Cigarette?" he asked, holding the pack toward her after coming to a stop in front of her house.

She shook her head but made no move to get out of the car.

"You can talk to me," he said, lighting a cigarette.

She turned away from him. He reached out, turned her face toward him and saw the tears in her eyes. "You can talk to me," he repeated gently. "I've heard the stories too."

She began to cry then. No sounds, just the tears running down her cheeks. He opened the glove compartment, took out a Kleenex and gave it to her. "You don't know how they look at me."

He dragged on his cigarette without speaking.

"There are times when I wish that I just let those boys do what they wanted. Then nobody would have said anything."

"That's not true and you know it," he said.

"Everybody believes that something happened," she said. "And that I wanted it."

"No one who knows you, JeriLee, would believe that."

She laughed bitterly. "They wouldn't believe the truth if I told them. I don't understand it." She looked at him. "What do I do now, Doctor?"

"You pay no attention. It will pass. Tomorrow they will have something else to talk about."

"I wish I could believe that."

"You can believe me," he said confidently. "I know this town. It will happen."

"Mother said that Daddy might lose his job if Mr. Thornton takes his account away from the bank. She said that's why she didn't want me to do anything."

"Has Mr. Thornton said anything about it?"

"I don't know. I only heard that he hasn't come into the bank since."

"That doesn't mean anything."

"Daddy is worried," she said. "I can tell. His face is very drawn. And he's been working late every night."

"Maybe there's another reason," he said. "Did you ask him?"

"No," she answered. "And if I did, he wouldn't tell me."

"Put it out of your mind for tonight," he said. "And come into the office tomorrow. I want to check those burns. We can talk some more then."

"Okay." She opened the door. "Thanks, Doc."

He smiled. "Tomorrow. Don't forget."

"I won't." He watched her walk toward the house before putting the car into gear. He drove off thoughtfully. The maliciousness and stupidity of people never ceased to amaze him. Given the choice of believing good or bad about others, they always chose the bad.

"How about a soda?" Martin asked as they came out of the movie.

"I don't feel like it," she answered.

"Come on," he urged. "It'll be fun. The whole crowd will be there."

"No."

"What's the matter, JeriLee?" he asked. "You're not the same."

She didn't answer.

"Let's have a soda," he said. "I'll spring for it. We don't have to go dutch this time."

A reluctant smile came to her lips. "Be careful, Marty. You're becoming a big spender."

He laughed. "You don't know me. A dime here, twenty cents there." He snapped his fingers.

She looked thoughtful for a moment. "Okay," she said finally.

Martin was right. Pop's ice cream parlor was jammed. The juke was blaring in the corner but they managed to spot a table in the back. She walked through the crowd, her eyes fixed straight ahead.

When they found that there was only one chair. Martin reached for a vacant chair at the crowded table next to them. "Anyone using this?"

"No." The boys glanced up at him, then at JeriLee. There was a long silence. Then one of the boys leaned over and whispered something to the others. They all laughed and turned to look at JeriLee.

She felt her face flushing under their stares and buried her face in the menu as the waiter came up. He was a pimply-faced boy she knew from school. "What'll it be?" he asked, then he saw her. "Hey, JeriLee," he said. "Haven't been around much lately, have you?"

She heard the burst of laughter at the next table and one of the boys remark raucously, "Not much, she's been around."

She looked at Marty. "I really don't feel like anything."

"Have something," he urged. "How about a chocolate pineapple float?"

"No," she answered. There was another shout of laughter from the next table. She didn't hear what they were saying but she was very conscious of their stares. "I'd better go," she said, suddenly standing up. "I don't feel too well." Without giving Martin a chance to reply she almost ran from the ice cream parlor.

He caught up to her halfway down the block and fell silently into step with her. They turned the corner before she spoke.

"I'm sorry, Martin."

"It's okay," he said. "But you're not handling it right."

"I . . . I don't know what you mean."

He stopped under a streetlight and turned to her. "I may not know much," he said, "but I'm the world's greatest expert on people talking about me. I grew up on it."

She didn't speak.

"With parents like mine, people never stopped. It's not easy being the kid of the town drunks." He stopped suddenly, his voice tightening.

"I'm sorry, Marty," she said.

He shook his head, blinking his eyes. "I learned when I was very young how to deal with it. You know what you are and you have to hold your head up no matter what people say. That's what I always did. After a while it got so that they didn't matter anymore. I knew I was doing right."

"It's different when you're a girl," she said. "No one comes right out with anything. You don't have a chance to fight back."

"It's the same with me," he said. "Do you think anyone comes right out—Hey, your father's the town drunk? Nohow. Instead they whisper and look until you wish they would come out with it so that you could say something instead of having to sit there and pretend that nothing is going on."

She nodded, remembering what her mother had said about his coming from the wrong kind of people the first time he had come to see her. "I can't get used to it," she said. "I always have the feeling that they're looking right through my clothing. I just know what they're thinking."

"But you know what you've done," he said. "That's more important."

"I haven't done anything," she said. "That's what makes it so terrible."

"No," he said with knowledge beyond his years. "That's what makes you right and all the others wrong. And when you know that, ain't nothing anybody can do to take it away from you."

She turned the corner in front of the drugstore. The boys standing around the door suddenly fell silent but separated to let her pass. She could feel their eyes following her to the counter.

Doc Mayhew came from the back. "Afternoon, Jeri-Lee," he said. "What can I do for you?"

"Toothpaste, mouthwash, deodorant," she said.

He nodded and quickly placed the packages in front of her. "We have a one-cent sale on Love-Glo cosmetics," he said. "Buy one lipstick and get the second for only a penny."

She shook her head. "I don't think so."

"It's very good," he said. "You ought to try it. Just as good as Revlon or Helena Rubinstein or those other fancy labels."

"Maybe next time," she said. She took out her list. "Aspirin too, please."

He picked up the bottle from the shelf behind him. "Love-Glo has eye shadow and nail polish too. Same deal goes."

"No, thank you, Doc."

"Sale's on only till the end of the week."

She nodded. "I'll mention it to my mother. Maybe there's something she might want."

"Do that," he said pleasantly. "Charge or cash?"

"Charge, please." She walked over to the magazine rack while he was writing up the sales slip and picked up a Hollywood magazine. There was a picture of Clark Gable on the cover. Idly she leafed through it. Out of the corner of her eye she could see the boys outside still watching her.

"All ready now, JeriLee," the druggist said.

She put the magazine back on the rack and picked up the package from the counter. The boys parted again to let her go by. She acted as if she didn't even see them. She was almost at the corner when they caught up to her.

"JeriLee," one of them said.

She stopped and looked at him coldly.

"How you doin', JeriLee?" he asked.

"Okay, Carl," she answered shortly.

"Not workin' out at the club no more?"

"No."

"Good." He smiled. "Now, maybe, you'll have some time to give a local guy a break."

She didn't return his smile.

"Never could understand why the town girls all run after those city people."

"I don't see anybody running after them," she said.

"Come on, JeriLee. You know what I mean."

Her eyes were steady. "No, I don't."

"They ain't the only ones who know how to have fun. We don't do so bad, do we, fellas?"

There was a general chorus of agreement from the other boys. He looked at them, smiling. Emboldened by their support, he turned back to her. "What do you say, JeriLee? Suppose we take in a movie one night? Then maybe take a ride out to the Point? I got wheels."

"No," she said flatly.

He stared at her, suddenly deflated. "Why not?"

"Because I don't like you, that's why," she answered in a cold voice.

He grew angry. "What's the matter, JeriLee? You like niggers better?"

Her slap took him by surprise. He caught her hand angrily and held it so tightly she felt the pain shooting up her arm. "You got no right to be so snooty, JeriLee. We know all about you."

She stared into his eyes, her face white. "Let me go!" she said through clenched lips.

He dropped her hand abruptly. "You'll be sorry," he said.

She pushed her way past them and managed to hold her head high until she turned the corner. Then she felt herself begin to tremble. She put a hand against the wall of the building to steady herself. A moment later she drew a very deep breath and began to walk again. But she could hardly see where she was going. She was almost blinded by her tears.

It was the next day that the graffiti began to appear on the fences and walls near her home: JERILEE FUCKS, JERILEE SUCKS.

Chapter 17

JERILEE AND HER MOTHER turned the car into the driveway just as her father and brother finished painting the fence. They got out of the car. Veronica looked at her husband. "The fence didn't need another coat," she said.

"Some boys painted dirty words on it, Ma," Bobby said.

Veronica looked at John. He didn't speak. His eyes squinted against the sun. She heard JeriLee come up behind her. "Let's go inside," Veronica said quickly. "I'll make some coffee."

He nodded. "Bobby, put the paint back in the garage," he said. "And don't forget to rinse out the brush."

"Okay, Pop." The boy picked up the can of paint and cut across the lawn to the garage.

"What happened?" JeriLee asked.

"Nothing," John said.

She looked at the fence. The paint had not yet dried and the letters beneath the white were still faintly visible. Her face tightened.

"Come inside, dear," her mother said.

JeriLee stared at the fence. "Did you see who did it?" she asked tautly.

"No," John answered. "Lucky for them that I didn't." He took her arm. "A cup of coffee wouldn't do any of us harm."

Silently she followed them into the house. "I don't think I want any coffee," she said. She looked at her father. "Could I have the car for a while?"

He glanced at his wife. "Sure," he said.

"I left the keys in the dash," Veronica said. "Be careful. There's a lot of maniacs on the road today."

"I will, Mother." She went to the door. "I just want to go out to the beach for a while."

They heard the car pull out of the driveway. John looked up at his wife. "They're crucifying her."

Veronica did not answer. She put the coffee on the table and sat down opposite him.

"I don't know what to do anymore," he said.

"There's nothing you can do," she said. "Nothing anyone can do. It will just have to pass."

"If just once we could catch them at it. We could make an example of them."

"Anything you do will only make it worse," she said. "We'll just have to be patient."

"I can wait. You can wait. But what about JeriLee? How much more of this do you think she can take before she breaks down completely? Already she's stopped seeing her friends. She won't go out anymore, won't do anything. Bernie says she won't even go to the movies with him. School opens in four more weeks. What do you think will happen then?"

"By that time it should be over," Veronica said.

"And if it's not?"

The question went unanswered as they both silently sipped their coffee.

She stopped the car at the far end of the Point overlooking the Sound and walked down to the beach. It was a deserted rocky section, much too rough for swimming. She sat down on a rock at the edge of the water and stared out at the sea.

A sailboat was tacking into the wind, its snow-white sail billowing against the blue of the water. Idly her eyes followed it until it disappeared around the Point.

"Beautiful, isn't it?"

The sound of the voice behind her made her jump. She turned around.

"I didn't mean to startle you," the man said. He paused, staring at her. "Do I know you? You look familiar."

"We met once, Mr. Thornton," she said. "On a bus."

"Oh, yes." He snapped his finger, remembering. "You were the girl who wanted to be a writer."

She smiled. He did remember.

"Do you still take the same bus?" he asked. "I haven't seen you on it recently."

"School's out," she said. "It's vacation time."

"Of course." He looked at her. "How's the writing coming on?"

"I haven't been doing much lately."

"Neither have I." He smiled. He looked out at the water. "Do you come out here often?"

"Sometimes. When I want to think."

"It's a good place for thinking," he said. "There's usually no one around." He fished in his pocket for a cigarette and took one without offering the pack to her. He lit the cigarette, inhaled deeply, then coughed and threw it away. "I'm trying to give up smoking," he said apologetically.

"That's a funny way to do it," she said.

"I figure if I light one and inhale very deeply, I cough. That makes me realize what it's doing to me and I throw it away."

She laughed. "I'll have to tell my father to try that one."

"Does he smoke much?"

"Too much," she said.

"What does he do?" he asked.

"He works in a bank," she answered.

He nodded absently, his eyes looking beyond her to the sea. She turned following his gaze. The sailboat was coming back.

"Walter!" The sound wafted down on the wind.

They looked back. There was a woman standing at the edge of the road on the crest of the hill overlooking the beach. She waved.

He waved back. "My secretary," he explained over his shoulder. "What is it?" he yelled.

"London is calling," the woman shouted back. "I came out in the car to get you."

"Okay." He turned to JeriLee. "I have to go. Will you be out here again?"

"Probably."
"Maybe we'll see each other."
"Maybe," she answered.
He looked at her peculiarly. "I hope so." He hesitated a moment. "I have a strange feeling that I intruded on your thoughts. That you wanted to be alone."
"It's okay," she said. "I'm glad I saw you."
He smiled and held out his hand. "So long."
His hand was firm and warm. "So long, Mr. Thornton," she said.
He turned and stared up the dunes toward the road, then stopped and looked back. "You never told me your name," he said.
She looked up at him. "JeriLee. JeriLee Randall."
He stood for a long moment registering the name. "Tell them I'll call back," he shouted up the hill, then he turned and came back down on the beach.
"Why didn't you tell me who you were?" he asked.
"You didn't ask me."
"I don't know what to say."
"You don't have to say anything."
"You're not angry with me?"
"No."
"What my son did was unforgivable," he said. "I'm sorry."
She didn't answer.
"If you don't want to speak to me," he said, "I'll understand."
"You had nothing to do with it," she said. "Besides I like talking to you. You're the only real writer I know."
He fished out a cigarette and lit it. "You really want to become a writer?"
"Yes," she said. She looked at him. "This time you didn't throw it away."
He looked at the cigarette. "That's right. But this time I didn't cough."
"It's not going to work," she said. "You won't give them up."
He smiled suddenly. "I know." He sat down on the edge of a rock. "You said you come out here to think. What about?"

"Things."
"This time, I mean?"
She looked at him. "About going away."
"Where?"
"I don't know," she said. She looked out at the sea. "Anywhere. Just away from here."
"Have you always felt like that?"
"No."
"Only since . . . since it happened?"
She thought for a moment. "Yes." She looked into his eyes. "Port Clare is a funny town. You wouldn't know unless you grew up here. You see, everybody makes up stories."
"About you?"
She nodded. "They think that I . . ." She didn't finish.
He was silent for a moment. "I am sorry," he said.
She looked away but he could see the tears on her cheeks. He reached for her hand and held it. "JeriLee."
She raised her head.
"I want to be your friend," he said. "You can talk to me."
The tears were flowing freely. "No," she said. "I can't talk to anyone. There's nothing they can do to help."
"I can try," he said earnestly. "At least I owe you that for what my son did."
"You don't owe me anything."
"Talk to me, JeriLee. Maybe it will help."
She shook her head silently.
Still holding her hand, he rose to his feet and drew her close to him. "Come here, child," he said gently, placing her head against his chest. He felt the sobs shaking her body. For a long time he stood there holding her. After a while the tears stopped.
She drew back and looked into his face. "You're a very nice man," she said.
Without answering, he took out his pack of cigarettes. This time he offered one to her. She took it and he lit their cigarettes. He inhaled with pleasure. "I really like smoking," he said. "I think I'll give up giving it up."
She laughed. "You are funny."
He smiled at her. "Not really. I'm just being realistic."

"Do you really want to help me?" she asked.

He nodded. "I said I did."

"Would you read something I wrote if I gave it to you?"

"Yes."

"And you'll tell me the truth about it? If it's bad, I mean. You won't be polite."

"I respect writing too much to be phony about it. If it stinks I'll tell you. But if it's good I'll say so."

She was silent for a moment. "There's something else you can do."

"What's that?"

"If you have time, that is," she said hesitantly. "It would be nice if you went into the bank and let them know that you're not angry with them because of my father."

"Is that what they think?" he asked, the surprise plain in his voice.

She nodded.

"That's really stupid!"

"I told you that you don't know this town unless you grew up here," she said. "That's exactly how they think. My mother is worried that Dad will lose his job if you take your account away. That's why she didn't want to do anything about what happened to me. Dad was angry. He wanted to press charges, but she talked him out of it."

"Then what made him speak up finally?"

"We couldn't let Fred go to jail for something that wasn't his fault," she said.

He nodded soberly. He was beginning to realize that she was right about this being the kind of town you didn't understand unless you grew up in it. "Is your father from here?"

She shook her head. "No."

He nodded. It made sense. "I'll make time to go down to the bank," he said.

Her face brightened. "Thank you."

Suddenly he wanted to meet her father again. "I'd like to have lunch with him if that's all right with you."

"That's up to you. Just going there will be enough."

"I'd like to know him," he said. "He sounds like a nice man."

She looked into his eyes. The words came from a feeling deep inside her. "He's the gentlest, kindest man in the whole world."

Chapter 18

BEFORE THE SUMMER was over, Port Clare had a new topic of conversation. JeriLee and Walter Thornton. At first they met at the beach, where they'd sit and talk for hours. He was fascinated by her curiosity and insights into people. Her instincts led her to a subtle understanding of motivations that was far beyond her years.

When the weather grew too cool for the beach she began to drive to his house once or twice a week. He read her work and made some suggestions. She rewrote and he explained to her what worked and what did not. Then one day he gave her a copy of the play he was writing.

She asked if she could read it somewhere alone, and he allowed her to take it with her when she left. He didn't hear from her for three days. Then late one afternoon after school she appeared with the play under her arm.

She gave him the script without comment.

"What did you think?" he asked. Suddenly it was important to him that she like it.

"I don't know," she said slowly. "I read it twice but I don't think I understand it."

"In what way?"

"Mainly the young girl. She doesn't work. I think you tried to make her like me but she's not. I'm not that smart. And she's too smart to be that naïve."

Hearing those words from her, he felt a new respect. The one thing he had not surmised was her awareness of her own naïveté.

"But if she doesn't maneuver the people around her we don't have the story," he said.

"Maybe there isn't any," she said bluntly. "I don't see how a man as bright as Jackson could fall in love with a girl less than a third his age. There's nothing really there to attract him outside of her youth."

"And you don't think that's enough?"

"Not just physical attraction," she said. "And certainly not cunning. That would repel him. It would have to be something more. Now, if she were a woman, a real woman, I could understand it. But she's not."

"What do you think it would take to make her a real woman?" he asked.

She looked at him. "Time. Time and experience. That's the only way people grow up. And that's the way I'll grow up."

"Do you think he might have fallen in love with what she could be?"

"I hadn't considered that," she said. "Let me think about it." She was silent for a few minutes, then she nodded. "It's possible. But there would have to be more of a hint of what she could be, something that would let the audience feel there is more to her than they now see."

"You've made your point," he said. "I'll take another look at it."

"I feel silly. I'm like a child trying to teach an adult how to walk."

"We can learn a great deal from children," he said. "If we would only listen."

"You're not angry at me for what I said?"

"No. I'm grateful. You made me look at something that could very well have made the whole play invalid."

She smiled, suddenly happy. "I've really been of help?"

"Yes," he said, smiling. "Really." He reached for his cigarettes. "Tonight's the cook's night off. Do you think your parents would object if I took you out to dinner?"

She was suddenly silent, and there was a troubled expression on her face.

"What is it?" he asked.

"I don't think my parents would object. Dad likes and respect you. But do you think it's wise?"

"You mean—?"

She nodded. "This is still Port Clare. People will talk."

He looked at her. "You're right. I don't want to cause any more unhappiness for you."

She met his gaze. "I'm not thinking about myself," she said quickly. "I'm thinking about you. The way they think, there's only one reason a man like you would go out with a girl like me."

He smiled. "That's very flattering. I didn't know they thought that way about me."

"You're a stranger," she said. "You're rich. You're divorced. You go to Hollywood and Europe and all those wild places. Only heaven knows what goes on there and what you do."

He laughed. "I only wish they knew how dull it really is. I go there just to work, that's all."

"That may be the truth," she said. "But you'll never get them to believe it."

"If you're up to it," he said, "I'd like to take that chance."

She looked at him for a long moment, then she nodded. "Okay," she said. "Let me check home first."

They went to dinner at the Port Clare Inn. The next morning, just as JeriLee had predicted, the news was all over town. And for the first time since they were children she and Bernie had a bitter quarrel.

It was Bernie's night off from work and they had gone to a movie. Afterwards they had gotten in his car and driven out to the parking place at the Point.

He switched on the radio and music filled the car. He turned and reached for her.

She drew back, pushing his hands away. "No, Bernie, I'm not in the mood right now."

He looked at her. She was staring out the window at the sea which shimmered in the moonlight. He reached for a cigarette and lit it. They didn't speak. Finally, the cigarette finished, he flipped it out of the window and started the engine.

She looked at him in surprise. "Where are we going?"

"I'm taking you home," he said sullenly.

"Why?"

"You know why."

"Because I'm not in the mood to neck?"

"Not only that."

"What else then?"

He glanced at her, his voice filled with resentment. "I was coming home from the club after work last night and I saw you with Mr. Thornton. You were driving."

She smiled. "Of course. He doesn't drive."

"But he had his arm along the seat behind you. You were laughing. You never laugh with me anymore."

"He was probably saying something funny," she said.

"It wasn't only that. I saw the way you were looking at him. Real sexy like."

"Oh, Bernie." Suddenly she felt her face flushing. She hoped he would not see it in the dark. It was not until then that she realized how excited she'd been. She knew she had not been able to sleep until she had eased the feeling inside her, but she had not related it to Mr. Thornton.

"Don't give me that 'Oh, Bernie' crap," he said, annoyed.

"You're jealous," she said. "You have no right to be jealous. Mr. Thornton and I are good friends. He's helping me with my writing."

"Oh, sure. A man like him's going to bother with a kid writer."

"That's true," she said heatedly. "He thinks I'm pretty good. And he even talks to me about his work."

"Does he tell you about all those wild parties in Hollywood?"

"He doesn't go to any wild parties," she said. "He just goes there to work."

"Oh, yeah?"

She didn't answer.

"I might have figured it," he said, bitterly. "First you

had the hots for the son, now the old man. Maybe he's the one you wanted all along. I remember that time you met him on the bus. You were wetting your pants even then."

"I was not!"

"You were too," he insisted. "Too bad I didn't know then what I know now. Maybe people ain't so crazy after all. Everybody in town sees the way you go around teasing—not wearing a brassiere and all that. In a way I don't blame Walt for what he thought."

Now she was angry. "Is that why you see me?"

"If that's what you think, I won't see you."

"That's okay with me," she snapped.

"It's okay with me too," he muttered. He stopped the car in front of her house.

She got out without a word and slammed the door. "JeriLee!" he called after her. But she went into the house without looking back.

Her father looked up from the television set as she came in. "Was that Bernie?" he asked.

"Yes."

He saw the expression on her face. "Is there anything wrong?"

"No. He's just stupid, that's all. I'm not going to see him anymore."

He watched her march up the steps to her room, then turned back to the television set. But his mind wasn't really on the late show. He had a real problem to solve. The state bank examiners were due any day and somewhere in the maze of accounts there was almost three hundred thousand dollars missing, most of it from Walter Thornton's account.

Chapter 19

MR. CARSON looked down at the sheet in front of him. "Did you check all the transfer vouchers?"

"Yes, sir," John said.

"What about bank cable advices?"

"They balance. We have all the receipts posted."

"I don't understand it," the bank president said.

"Neither do I," John said. "I've been worried sick ever since I discovered it."

"When was that?"

"A few days ago."

"Why didn't you come to me right away?"

"I thought I might have made a mistake," John answered. "So I went through the whole thing over again. But the answer was the same."

Carson looked up at him. "Don't say anything about this to anyone. Leave it with me for a few days. I want to think about it."

"Yes, sir. But if the auditors should come in—"

Carson didn't give him a chance to finish. "I know, I know," he said testily. "But I want to check the figures myself before we do anything about it."

He waited until the door closed behind the cashier before he reached for the telephone and dialed. A guard voice answered. "Hello."

"Mr. Gennutri please. Carson calling."

The voice became less cautious. "This is Pete, Mr. Carson. What can we do for you today?"

"I don't know," Carson said. "How do we stand?"

"You did good yesterday. That filly paid six ten. You got your marker down to eleven grand."

"What about the other two?"

"They ran out." The bookie's voice was sympathetic. "They shouldn't have. I was sure you were going to hit me big."

Carson was silent for a moment. "I'm in trouble, Pete," he said. "I need money."

"You're a good customer, Mr. Carson. I could let you have ten grand."

"I need more than that," the banker said. "Big money."

"How much?"

"About three hundred thousand."

The bookmaker whistled. "That's too rich for me. You have to go to the big boys for that."

"Can you get to them?"

"Maybe." Caution returned to Gennutri's voice. "What you got to give them for the money?"

"You mean collateral?"

"Yes. I guess that's what you bankers would call it."

"Nothing much that's liquid. My house. The shares in the bank."

"The shares in the bank," Gennutri asked. "What's that worth?"

"Five, maybe six hundred thousand," the banker said. "But it's non-negotiable."

"You mean you can't sell it?"

"Not without the consent of the bank's board of trustees."

"Would you have any trouble getting them to do that?"

"I would have to tell them why," he said. "And I can't do that."

"It won't be easy then."

"Would you try them for me? I'd appreciate it."

"I will, Mr. Carson," the bookmaker said.

Carson's eyes fell on the newspaper lying next to the report on his desk. The page was turned to racing charts. "Pete," he said.

"Yes, Mr. Carson?"

"Put a thousand across the board on Red River in the fifth at Belmont."

"Gotcha."

Carson put down the telephone cursing himself. It was stupid, and he knew it. But he couldn't help himself. The horse had a chance and the odds were long enough to make it a good bet. He stared down at the newspaper, a sinking feeling coming into the pit of his stomach. Somehow no matter how good they looked they never won when you need them. He promised himself that if he straightened out this time he would never allow himself to get into the same trap again.

JeriLee came out of the warm pool. Walter put down his newspaper, picked up a large bath towel and draped it around her shoulders.

"Thanks." She smiled.

He returned her smile. "The October air has a way of getting to you."

She looked up at him. "In a way I'm sorry that winter is coming. There'll be nothing for us to do."

"You can always come over and sit by the fire."

"That would be nice." She hesitated. "But you'll be leaving soon. The play will be going into rehearsal in a few weeks."

"Yes," he said. "That is, if we can get it cast."

"I thought it was all set."

"It is. Except for the girl." He looked at her. "Do you know of a seventeen-year-old actress who could play a child as if she were a woman?"

"I never thought about it. I would think there must be several."

"Not really," he said. "The director should be here any moment to talk about it. We're going over some possibilities."

"I'll dry and get out of your way then," she said.

"No hurry," he said quickly. "You won't be in the way."

"Sure?"

"I wouldn't say so if I weren't."

"I'll get out of the wet bathing suit then," she said.

He watched her walk into the cabana, then picked up his newspaper again. But he wasn't reading. He was thinking. The play was one thing. There he was in complete control. The characters did only what he let them. But life was different. Very different.

He heard the cabana door open and looked up. She was wearing faded blue jeans and a bulky knit sweater. She caught his glance and smiled. "Would you like me to get you something to drink?"

"Yes, please," he said. A tight hard knot suddenly gathered in the pit of his stomach. "Scotch and water."

"Okay."

He watched her disappear into the house. The surge of feeling left him almost trembling. It was the first time he realized he had fallen in love with her.

"All right, Guy," he said. "If we don't find the girl we don't open in November. We'll go for next spring."

"Can't do it," the director said. He was a slim lanky man with large horn-rimmed glasses and an air of quiet confidence. "We lose Beau Drake if we wait. He has a film commitment in May. And without him we'd have to begin all over again. We'll just have to take a chance and go with the girl we think is best."

Walter shook his head. "The play is chancy enough," he said. "If the girl lets us down it won't work."

"I've never steered you wrong, Walter. There are ways to get around her."

"I'm not rewriting," Walter said stubbornly. "If I wanted it to be something else I would have written it that way."

Guy made a gesture of futility. "It's your baby, Walter." He glanced through the glass sliding doors at the pool. JeriLee was sitting there reading a newspaper. He turned back to Walter. "Who's the girl? A friend of Junior's?"

Walter felt his face flushing. "In a way."

Guy was sensitive. "That's a funny answer," he said, probing. "Sure she's not a friend of yours?"

"Come on, Guy. She's just a child."

"How old is she?" He took a stab. "Seventeen?"

Walter stared at him.

"Can she act?" Guy asked.

"You're crazy! She's a high school kid who wants to be a writer."

"Has she any talent?"

"I think so. There's something extraordinary about her. If she keeps on the way she's going she's going to make it someday."

"You have doubts?" Guy asked shrewdly.

"There's only one thing that could stop her."

"And that is?"

"She's a girl and there's something very physical about her. She's really not aware of it but I have the feeling that a tigress is in there waiting to be unleashed."

"You've just given me a perfect description of our girl," Guy said. "Now, if she could only act."

Walter was silent.

"Ask her to come in here."

As she came through the door, Guy played a hunch. Without waiting for an introduction, he spoke the opening lines of the play. "Your father just called. He wants you to come home right away and said that he doesn't want me to see you anymore."

His hunch was right. She had read the play. She answered him from the script. "My father is insane. If he can't have me, he doesn't want anyone else to."

"Anne! That's no way to talk about your own father."

She looked at him with a demurely innocent smile. "Don't act so shocked, Mr. Jackson. Didn't you ever have any incestuous thoughts about your own daughter?"

Guy turned to Walter, who had been watching with fascination. "What do you think?"

Walter was looking at JeriLee.

"She is the girl, Walter," the director said.

JeriLee was bewildered. "What's he talking about?"

Walter found his voice. "He wants you to play the girl."

"But I am not an actress."

Guy smiled at her. "All it takes to be one is to be one."

"It's not that easy," she said. "I've never really been on stage before except for a few school productions."

Guy turned to Walter. "It's up to you to convince her."

Walter was silent and there was a strange expression on his face as he looked at her.

Guy walked to the door. "I'm going back to the city. Give me a call when you decide what you're going to do."

Walter didn't answer him.

JeriLee saw Walter staring at her. "Are you angry with me?"

He shook his head.

"Then what is it?"

He found his voice. "Suddenly I find out I'm like the father in my own play. I'm jealous of you."

Carson looked at his watch. It was four o'clock. They should have the results of the fifth race my now. He dialed the bookmaker's number.

Gennutri answered the telephone with his customarily cautious voice. "Hello."

"Pete? What happened in the fifth?"

"Tough luck, Mr. Carson. Your horse ran out of the money."

Carson was silent for a moment. "Did you get in touch with your friends?" he asked.

"I did." Gennutri's voice was expressionless. "They're not interested."

"But surely they understand. I'm not just the usual horseplayer. I'll pay them back."

"Nothing personal in it, Mr. Carson, but that's what they all say."

He looked down at the newspaper still on the desk. There was a horse in the eighth race that could help out. "Okay, Pete," he said. "Give me two thousand across the board on Maneater in the eighth."

"Can't do it, Mr. Carson." Gennutri's voice was cool. "You're into me for twelve grand right now and I can't give you any more markers until that's cleaned up."

"But I've run more than that before," he protested.

"I know," the bookmaker said flatly. "But things were different then. You weren't hurtin'."

"A thousand then," Carson said. "You got to give me a chance to get even."

"Sorry." The bookmaker went off the line.

Carson stared at the dead phone in his hand for a moment, then slowly put it down. He sat there for almost an hour until he was sure everyone had gone home. Then he opened the small drawer in the bottom of his desk. He took out the revolver, put the muzzle in his mouth and blew the top of his head all over the wall under the picture of President Eisenhower.

Chapter 20

WEARILY JOHN RANDALL glanced up at the big clock on the wall. Three o'clock. The bank guard was looking at him. He raised his hand, the guard nodded and turned to lock the door. At the same time the two tellers dropped the windows closing their cages.

Frustrated, the crowd of people still in line in front of the teller's windows surged toward him. He got to his feet. The news of Carson's suicide had hit Port Clare like a shock wave.

He glanced over his shoulder. The door of the president's office was closed. Behind it the state examiners were still going through the records. Several other large discrepancies had been found but the total had not yet been reached. Carson had been thorough. Transfers and approvals had been carefully forged. No one could understand how he had slipped up this time.

"When do we get our money?" an irate customer shouted at him from the crowd. "Why are you closing the doors on us?"

"It's legal closing time," he said patiently. "And you

will get your money. Whatever losses there have been are completely covered by insurance."

"How do we know that?" another customer shouted. "I remember they told us the same thing when the Bank of the United States failed back in thirty-two."

"Things were different then," John explained. "Savings accounts are protected by the F.D.I.C. up to ten thousand dollars. The bank carries insurance against fraud and theft. Every penny will be replaced."

"That's what you say," the man replied. "But you don't have the cash to give us back our deposits right now, do you?"

"No," John said. "But no bank has all the cash on hand to return to its depositors. Banks have the same problem as people. Cash comes in and goes out all the time. Like when you pay up your mortgage we have the money to lend to someone else or to give them a mortgage. Multiply that by hundreds and you understand how it works. It's really simple common sense."

"I'm not stupid," the man said. "If I don't make the payment on the mortgage, the bank takes my house away. If the bank doesn't make our payment, what do we do?"

"The bank will make the payments."

"What if you close?"

"We won't close," John said stubbornly. "We have assets enough to cover all our liabilities. All we need is time to convert them. And if you give us that time, I can promise that not one of you will suffer."

"Mr. Randall, why should we believe you after what happened?"

John looked the man squarely in the eyes. He spoke slowly and clearly so that they could all hear him. "Because like you, Mr. Sanders, I've worked for a living all my life. And I have every penny I've managed to save in the world in this bank. And I'm not worried about it."

The man was silent for a moment, then turned to the others. "I'm goin' along with Mr. Randall. How 'bout you?"

There was a murmur among the crowd. Their hostility was dissolving. This was something they could understand. The word of one man.

"We'll go along too!" a man in back of the crowd shouted.

Sanders held out his hand to John. "You'll keep your promise to us?"

John nodded. He didn't trust himself to speak. Several of the others grabbed at his hand and then he watched the crowd silently leave the bank as the guard opened the door for them.

As he returned to his desk, John saw that Arthur Daley and several other members of the board of trustees had come out of the president's office, where they had been closeted with the examiners, and were looking at him. Arthur nodded and they went back into the office.

Three days later John was elected president of the Port Clare National Bank.

John looked up from the breakfast table as JeriLee came into the room. "You're early," he said. "Especially today."

"What's so special about today? I'm always up early."

"On Saturdays? When there's no school?"

She blushed. "I wanted to get to the stores."

He raised an eyebrow. "You? I thought you hated shopping."

"It's Mr. Thornton's birthday tomorrow," she said. "I wanted to get him something special."

"How old will he be?"

"Forty-eight."

Surprise came into John's voice. "I thought he was older."

"Many people do. I guess it's because his first play was produced on Broadway when he was only twenty-three."

"He's still older than I am," John said. He was forty-three.

"Not much," JeriLee said. "The funny thing is that he doesn't seem old." She looked at her father. "You know what I mean."

John nodded. He picked up his coffee cup. "He was in the bank yesterday. We had a long talk."

She took some coffee and sat down. "What about?"

"Business mostly," John said. "He's been very nice about what happened. If he had wanted to, he could have made real trouble for us. If he had taken away his account, it could have started a run that would have closed the bank."

"But he didn't."

"No," he answered. It was curious how things happened. He wondered if she knew that if it weren't for Walter Thornton he might never have been president of the bank.

It had happened the night the bank examiners had finished. The board of trustees had gone to see Mr. Thornton. He had been the hardest hit of any individual. More than two hundred thousand dollars. They had asked him for time to replace the loss and to show his confidence in the bank by not taking the account elsewhere.

His agreement had been immediate. But conditional. Later Arthur Daley had told John the exact words Mr. Thornton used. "I will stay under one condition only. That is, if John Randall is made president of the bank."

As Arthur had put it, the board was relieved. They had already come to that decision on their own so it was a simple matter of them to agree.

He watched her take some toast and butter it. "We also spoke about you," he said.

"Yes?" She waited until she swallowed. "What did he say about me?"

"He said you really can write. And that you should take special care about what college you go to after graduating Central."

"He told me that too."

"Do you really want to become a writer?" John asked curiously. "What happens if you get married and have a family?"

"Oh, Daddy!" She flushed. "That's a long way off. I still haven't met a boy I would want to settle down with. And besides, writing is the one thing you do on your own. Many women writers are married and have families."

"He says you should start making applications to college now. After all, you'll be graduating soon."

"He promised to get me some information. Then I'll be able to make up my mind."

"He mentioned that too. He said he would keep in touch with us."

"In touch?"

John nodded. "He's going to be gone for a long while. Hollywood, Europe, then back to Hollywood."

She was silent for a moment. "Did he say anything about a play on Broadway?"

"No," her father replied. "He never mentioned anything like that at all."

She pressed the doorbell. Inside the house, chimes rang softly. The door was opened by his secretary. "Oh, JeriLee!" she exclaimed. "I didn't expect you. We're in the midst of packing. I'll tell him you're here."

The woman went into the library, closing the door behind her. After waiting a moment in the foyer, JeriLee walked through the living room and out onto the terrace. The pool was already covered for the winter and the cold November wind was tearing off the Sound. She shivered and pulled her jacket around her.

"JeriLee." His voice came from the doorway.

She turned. "It's really getting cold now," she said.

"Yes," he answered. "Come back inside where it's warm."

She followed him into the living room. "I didn't expect to see you today," he said.

"It's your birthday tomorrow," she said, handing him the small gift-wrapped package. "I wanted you to have this."

He took it awkwardly.

"Open it," she said. "I hope you like it."

Quickly he undid the wrapping. It was a small pocket memo and telephone book bound in black pinseal leather. And in a loop along the side was a small gold pencil. "It's lovely," he said. "What made you think of it?"

"You're always looking for telephone numbers."
He nodded.
"Happy birthday," she said.
"Thank you." He forced a smile. "I'm getting old."
"You'll never get old, Mr. Thornton," she said. "The things you've written will keep you young forever."
He felt a tightness inside him. "Thank you. Really thank you. That's the nicest thing anyone ever said to me."
She stood awkwardly for a moment, then she said, "I guess I'll be going, Mr. Thornton. I'm expected home for dinner."
"JeriLee," he said, without moving.
"Yes, Mr. Thornton."
His eyes were on her face. "I'm going away tomorrow."
"I know. My father told me."
"I'll be gone a long time."
"My father told me that too."
After a moment he said, "I've withdrawn the play. I don't think it's ready."
She was silent.
He smiled. "You're a writer," he said. "You'll find things like that happen sometimes."
She nodded.
"You go off on the wrong track and suddenly you find that you don't know what you're talking about."
"Or that you know too much. And you don't want to say it."
His eyes fell. "I'm sorry, JeriLee."
Her voice suddenly broke. "So am I, Mr. Thornton," she said and went out of the house.
He moved over to a window where he could watch her as she got into the car and drove away.
His secretary called from the library. "Walter, do you want me to take your notes on the Chicago story?"
Unshed tears burned his eyes.
He didn't answer. JeriLee's car was at the corner and turning out of sight.
"Walter, do you—?"
"I'll be right there," he said.

Chapter 21

IT HAD BEEN so long ago and yet not that long really. Seventeen years. What was that? Half her life to date. So much had happened since and still, if she pushed the right button in her memory bank, it all came back.

She glanced up at the clock on the wall over the hospital bed. It was four o'clock and the other women had long since gone home. She was the only patient left.

The doctor came to the side of the bed and looked down at her through his glasses. He smiled. "How do you feel?"

"Bored," she said. "When do I get out of here?"

"Right now. I'll sign the discharge." He picked up the chart from the foot of the bed, made a note and then pressed the button for the nurse.

The big black lady came in. "Yes, Doctor?"

"Miss Randall can go now," he said. "Help her with her things."

"Yes, Doctor." She turned to JeriLee. "They's been a gen'mum waitin' downstairs in reception for you since twelve o'clock."

"Why didn't you tell me?"

"He said he'd wait. He didn't want to disturb you." The nurse went to a small closet and took out JeriLee's clothes and put them on the chair next to the bed. "You let me he'p you out of bed, honey."

"I'm all right," JeriLee answered. But when she was on her feet she felt strangely weak and reached for the hand the nurse held out to her. "Thank you."

The nurse smiled. "You'll be okay in a few minutes, honey. Takes that long fo' you to git yo' legs back."

She went to the bathroom and when she came out the

doctor was still waiting for her. "I want to see you in a week," he said.

She nodded.

"And no sex until after I check you out," he added.

She looked at him and smiled. That had been the furthest thing from her mind. "Can I give head?" she asked.

He laughed. "That's out of my area," he said. "Check with your dentist."

"Okay, Doc."

"Take it easy for a few days. Don't push things."

"I will, Doc. Thank you." He left and she began to dress. By the time she finished, the nurse was back with a wheelchair. JeriLee looked at it dubiously. "Do I have to go in one of those things?"

"Regulations. Right to the door."

"Let me put some lipstick on first," JeriLee said. She looked in the mirror. A little color in her cheeks wouldn't hurt either. Hospital pallor didn't take long to set in.

At first she didn't recognize him. Dark mirror glasses, a false brown mustache and a wig covered his normally clean-shaven face and curly black hair. She almost laughed aloud. He looked so ridiculous.

"How are you, JeriLee?" he piped, trying to disguise his deep voice.

"Just fine."

"The car's right outside, Nurse," he said.

The nurse nodded and rolled the chair to the car entrance and down the ramp. He had a rented Continental instead of using his own Corniche convertible. He opened the door and the nurse helped her into the front seat.

"Goodbye," JeriLee said. "Thank you."

"You're welcome, honey. Good luck."

He took out a twenty-dollar bill and gave it to the nurse. "Thank you," he said.

The nurse looked at the twenty then at him, her shining dark face breaking into a big grin. "Thank you, Mr. Ballantine."

He stood with his mouth open, then turned to JeriLee. "How did she recognize me?"

JeriLee was giggling. "You may be a star, George," she said, "but you still don't know a damn thing about makeup."

He walked around the car and got in behind the wheel. "I didn't want anyone to recognize me."

"Don't worry about it. She's seen 'em all. Coming and going. She won't talk."

"I can't afford any more talk," he said, putting the car into motion. "The studio's on my back enough as it is."

"Don't worry."

He looked at her. "How do you feel?"

"Okay."

"Just okay?"

"Okay."

"Don't you feel better now that it's over?" he said.

She looked at him. "Do you?"

"Much. It was the right thing to do."

She reached for a cigarette.

"Don't you think so?" he asked.

"If you think so," she said.

He reached across and patted her hand. "I'm right. You'll see. Tomorrow morning you'll wake up and you'll see that I was right."

"Tomorrow morning I'm going to wake up so stoned that I won't even remember what happened today," she said.

"What's the matter with you, JeriLee? What do you want from me?"

"Nothing," she said. "Absolutely nothing." She shrank down into her seat.

What was wrong with men that always made them feel you wanted something from them they were not prepared to give? Especially when you asked nothing and wanted nothing. That they could not understand at all.

There had been only two men in her life who had not felt like that. Her father and Walter Thornton. All they wanted was to give to her. And maybe that was why she failed them. She did not know how to take.

"He's too old," her mother said. "He's older than your father. And what about his son? You'll have to see him."

"No, I won't have to. He's moved to England with his mother," she said. "Besides it doesn't matter. I love him."

Veronica looked at her. "What do you know of love? "You're still a child. You're not even eighteen yet."

"What is love, Mother?" she asked. "I like him, I admire him, I respect him, I want to go to bed with him."

"JeriLee!"

"If that isn't love, then tell me what it is," JeriLee said.

"It's not what you think it is," Veronica said. "Sex. You saw what almost happened with those boys."

"Was that supposed to make me afraid of love?"

"That's not what I'm talking about," her mother said. She turned to John for help. "Tell her, John. Make her understand."

John shook his head. "I can't," he said. "Love is what each individual person thinks it is. Love is what two people agree it is. And it is different for every person who loves."

"But she's still a child," Veronica said.

"Then you don't know your own daughter. JeriLee stopped being a child a long time ago."

"He'll be fifty before she's eighteen," Veronica said.

"If that turns out to be a problem, it will be their problem. I'm sure they have both thought about it and they will have to solve it."

"She still needs my signature on the marriage license," Veronica said stubbornly. "And I won't sign it."

"Then it will be too bad. Because I will."

Veronica grew angry. "You can't. She's not your daughter!"

JeriLee could see the hurt on her father's face. But his voice was calm and quiet. "Yes, she is," he said. "As much mine as her real father's. I love her and I adopted her. That's enough to satisfy the law."

"Then you're willing to let everyone believe that what they've been saying all this time is true?"

"I don't care what people say, or think, or believe. What I care about is my daughter's happiness."

"Even if you know she's making a mistake in the long run?"

"I don't know that and neither do you. But if she has made a mistake, I will still love her and try to help."

Veronica turned to her daughter. "For the last time, JeriLee. Please listen to me. There will be younger men, closer to your own age. You can grow up together, grow old together, have children together. Those are things you won't be able to do with him."

"For God's sake, Mother," JeriLee said, exasperated. "He's not a cripple! I've already been to bed with him and he's a wonderful lover."

"So that's it. Then the stories were true."

The tears sprang to JeriLee's eyes. "No. Only if you believe them." She turned and ran from the house.

Wearily John looked at his wife. "Veronica," he said hopelessly, "sometimes I wonder what I ever saw in you. You're such a goddamn fool!"

George pulled the Continental into the driveway of her house.

"Would you like to come in for a drink?" she asked.

He shook his head. "I promised my agent I would meet him for a drink at the Polo Lounge at five."

"Okay." She opened the door and got out. "Thanks for coming to pick me up."

"It's okay. I'm sorry. I didn't mean for it to become such a big deal."

"It's not a big deal," she said. "Haven't you heard? It's easier than curing a cold." She walked around to his side of the car. "Sure you don't want to come in?" she asked, playing with his false mustache. "We can't fuck but I can give you head. The doctor said so. And you always say I give the best head in town."

"Well," he said, "maybe. I can always be a half hour late. My agent won't mind."

She laughed and pulled the false mustache from his lip and stuck it in the center of his forehead. "Oh, George," she said. "Why do you have to be such a shit?"

Then she turned and, half laughing, half crying, walked up the driveway to her house. Locking the door behind her, she leaned back and let the tears run down her cheeks. What was there about her that always seemed to attract the shits?

It hadn't always been like that. Walter was not a shit. Not really. He was just weak. He needed even more reassurance than she did.

She walked through the house to her bedroom and fell on the bed with her clothes on. She stared up at the ceiling, her eyes dry once again. The telephone began to ring but she lay there making no move toward it. After three rings the answering service picked up.

She reached for the cigarette box at the side of the bed and took out a rolled joint. Slowly she lit it and inhaled deeply. The sweet calm went down into her lungs and spread through her body. She pressed a button and the tape deck went on, the music filling the room. She took two more tokes from the joint, then placed it in an ashtray, rolled over on her stomach and covered her face with her hands. Once again the picture of the little girl sitting at the top of the stairs and crying flashed before her eyes. Then it was gone. Abruptly she sat up on the bed. She was no longer that little girl. And she had not been for a long, long time.

Not since the day she and Walter were married and he had taken her down to New York and up, up, in the elevator to the apartment at the top of the building which looked out over the city.

Book Two

BIG TOWN

Chapter 1

IT WAS SPRINGTIME in New York. The young green of the new leaves on the trees in Central Park fluttered in the gentle wind and the children were playing in the first flush of May warmth. We walked past the benches filled with idlers. We neither spoke nor looked at each other, together yet not together, each thinking our own silent thoughts.

He didn't speak until we came out at the Avenue of the Americas exit at Fifty-ninth Street. We stood waiting for the light to change. As usual the traffic was backed up on both streets. "You can take your time about moving," he said. "I'm making the ten o'clock flight to London tonight and I won't be back for a month."

"It's okay. They told me the apartment would be ready."

He took my arm as a truck making a turn came uncomfortably close, then as quickly let it go as we stepped out of the gutter. "I just wanted to know," he said.

"Thanks, Walter, but I'm going home over the weekend. By Monday I'm sure everything will be in."

The doorman who held open the door looked at us strangely. "Mr. Thornton," he said. "Mrs. Thornton."

"Joe," I said. I was sure he knew about it. By now the whole world had to know. It had been in all the columns. The Thorntons were getting a divorce.

We were silent up in the elevator to the penthouse. We stepped out into the corridor. "I have my key," Walter said.

His bags were already packed and in the foyer. He

closed the door and stood silently for a moment. "I think I could use a drink," he said.

"I'll fix it for you," I said, automatically starting for the bar in the living room.

"I can do it."

"I don't mind. Matter of fact I can use one myself."

I threw some ice in the two glasses and poured the scotch over it. We faced each other across the bar. "Cheers," he said.

"Cheers."

He took a long swallow, I just took a sip. "Six years," he said. "I can't believe it."

I didn't speak.

"They went so fast. Where did they go?"

"I don't know."

"Do you remember the first time I brought you here? It was snowing that night and the park was white in the darkness."

"I was just a child then. A child in a woman's body."

There was a bewildered expression in his eyes. "When did you grow up, JeriLee?"

"It was happening a little bit every day, Walter."

"I didn't see it."

"I know," I said gently. That was it. More than anything else. To him I would always be the child bride.

He finished his drink and put the empty glass on the bar. "I'm going upstairs to try to get a nap. I never could sleep on those night flights."

"Okay."

"The car's picking me up at eight-thirty," he said. "Will you be here when I come down?"

"I'll be here."

"I wouldn't want to go without saying goodbye."

"I wouldn't want that either," I said. Then the dam broke and my eyes filled with tears. "Walter, I'm sorry."

His hand touched mine for a brief moment. "It's all right," he said quickly. "It's all right. I understand."

"I loved you, Walter. You know that."

"Yes."

There was nothing else to say. He left the room and I heard his footsteps going up to the bedroom. A moment later the sound of the closing door echoed through the silent rooms. I dried my eyes with a Kleenex and went over to the window and looked down at the park.

The leaves were still green, the children were still playing, the sun was still shining. Spring was here. Damn! If that was true why was I shivering with the cold?

The apartment was empty after he left. I was on my way from the door to the kitchen to get myself something to eat when the telephone rang.

It was Guy. "What are you doing?"

"Nothing. I was just going to fix myself some dinner."

"Walter gone?"

"Yes."

"You shouldn't be alone tonight," he said. "I'll take you out to dinner."

"That's sweet of you." I really meant it. Guy was a good friend to both of us. He'd directed me in my first play—Walter's play, the one he had been writing when we met. "Can I get a rain check? I really don't feel up to it."

"It'll do you good."

"No, thanks."

"Then let me bring up some sandwiches. I'll stop off at the Stage," he said quickly.

I hesitated.

"Besides I have some ideas for the rewrite on your play," he added. "We can talk."

"Okay."

"That's better. I'll bring a bottle of wine and some grass. We'll have a nice quiet evening. Half hour okay?"

"Fine." I put down the telephone and went up to the bedroom. I started for the closet to get a pair of jeans when the telephone rang again.

It was my mother. "JeriLee?"

"Yes, Mother."

"When did you get back?"

"This afternoon."

"You could have called me," she said in a peeved voice.

"I didn't have time, Mother. I went to the lawyer's office right from the airport. Walter and I still had some papers to sign."

"Then the divorce is final," she said disapprovingly. "I didn't think Mexican divorces were legal in New York."

"It's legal."

"You should have called me. I'm your mother. I'm entitled to know what's happening."

"You know what was happening. I explained all that to you before I went to Juarez. Besides I'll be there all weekend and I'll tell you all the gory details."

"You don't have to tell me anything if you don't want to," she said stiffly.

I tried to keep from getting angry. I don't know what it is but she always had the ability to get me on the defensive. I looked around for a cigarette but couldn't find one. "Damn," I muttered.

"What did you say?"

"I can't find the damn cigarettes."

"You don't have to swear," she said. "And you smoke too much."

"Yes, Mother." I finally found one and lit it.

"What time will you be out here?"

"Some time in the morning."

"I'll have lunch for you. Don't eat too much for breakfast."

"Yes, Mother." I changed the subject. "Is Daddy there?"

"Yes. Do you want to speak to him?"

"Please."

His voice was warm and gentle on the telephone. "How's my little girl?"

That did it. I could feel the tears start to my eyes again "Big and hurting," I said.

All the sympathy in the world was in the one word "Rough?"

"Yes."

"Hold your head up. You've got us."

"I know."

"It'll be all right. Takes time. Everything takes time."

I was under control again. "We'll talk tomorrow. I can't wait to see you."

I had just enough time to take a quick shower and dress before Guy came.

He stood in the doorway with a silly smile on his face, a shopping bag in one hand and a bouquet of flowers in the other. He pushed the flowers into my hands and kissed me on the cheek. Even before he spoke I could tell from his breath that he was smashed. "Happy, happy," he said.

"You're crazy," I said. "What are the flowers for?"

"Celebrate," he said. "It's not every day that a man's best friends get divorced."

"I don't think that's funny."

"What do you want me to do? Cry?"

I didn't answer.

"I cried at your wedding," he said. "For all the good it did me. Now you're divorced and you're both happy. I guess that's worth a celebration."

"You do everything backwards."

"What the hell?" he said. "It's just as good." He walked into the living room and took a bottle of champagne out of the shopping bag. "Get the glasses," he said. "Dom Perignon. Nothing but the best."

Raising his glass, he said, "Drink up to better times."

I sipped. The bubbles tickled my nose.

"All of it."

I emptied my glass and he refilled it. "Again."

"You're trying to get me drunk."

"Right." He nodded. "And it won't hurt you one bit."

It went down like champagne was supposed to. I began to feel warm. "You're really crazy," I said.

He looked at me out of those pale blue eyes and I suddenly realized that he wasn't as drunk as I thought. "Feel better?"

"Yes."

"Good. Then we'll eat. I'm starved." He began emptying the bag on the bar. In a moment I was surrounded by the wonderful odors of hot corned beef and pastrami and garlic pickles. My mouth began to water.

"I'll set the table."

"Why?" He picked up a sandwich and bit into it. He mumbled with his mouth full, "You don't have to impress nobody."

I stared at him. With Walter everything had to be in place. We never once had eaten in the kitchen.

He refilled my glass. "Eat, drink and be merry."

I picked up a sandwich and took a bite. Unexpectedly my eyes began to moisten.

He picked up on it right away. "No. Please. No."

There was a lump in my throat. I couldn't swallow. I couldn't speak.

"Don't cry," he said. "I love you." Then he smiled and his face took on a mischievous look. "That is, I love you as much as any queen can love a girl girl."

Chapter 2

I WAS A LITTLE BIT smashed, a little bit stoned and there was a pleasant buzz to my high. I sprawled back on the couch and looked down at Guy, who was stretched on the floor at my feet. "Why don't you get up?" I asked.

He rolled over on his back and reached up to take the joint from my fingers. "I don't know whether I can," he said, taking a drag.

"Try. I'll help you."

"What for? I'm happy here."

"Okay. What were we talking about?"

"I don't remember."

"The play. You had some ideas for the rewrite."

"I can't talk about it now. I feel too good."

I looked toward the windows. The night sky over Central Park was gray with the reflected light. "Do you think the plane took off already?"

"What time is it?"

"Almost midnight."

"It's gone," he said.

I got to my feet and went over to the window. I held up my hand and waved at the sky. "Goodbye, Walter, goodbye." Then I began to cry. "Have a nice flight."

Guy struggled to his feet and weaved toward me. "Hey, this is a celebration," he said. "Don't cry."

"I can't help it. I'm alone."

"You're not alone," he said, putting an arm around my shoulders. "I'm here."

"Thank you. That's very nice."

He led me back to the couch. "Have another glass of champagne."

I took a sip from the glass he put in my hand. Suddenly it didn't taste good anymore. I was coming down. I placed the glass on the cocktail table. It made a small wet ring on the polished surface. I stared at it. Usually I would wipe it quickly and place the glass on a coaster. Walter hated drink stains on his precious antiques. Now I didn't give a damn. "I think I'll go to bed," I said.

"It's early," he protested.

"But I'm tired," I said. "It's been a long day. I was in court in Mexico at eight-thirty this morning. By eleven I was on the plane on my way back. I haven't had any rest in two days."

"What did you do with your wedding ring?" he asked.

"I'm wearing it." I held out my hand. The tiny gold band glimmered in the light.

He shook his head solemnly. "That's bad. You have to get rid of it."

"Why?"

"It's a symbol. You won't be free until you get rid of it." He snapped his fingers. "I've got it. In Reno there's a little bridge over a stream. When the women come out of the courthouse, they stand on the bridge and throw their rings in the water. That's what we have to do."

"But we're not in Reno."

"It doesn't matter. I know just the place. Get your coat."

A few minutes later we were downstairs getting into a

taxi. "Central Park Lake," he told the driver. "The dock near the boathouse."

"You crazy, mister?" the cabby asked. "They don't rent out boats at night."

"Drive, my good man," Guy said with a lordly wave of his hand. He sank back into his seat as the cab started off with a jerk, made a U-turn and went into the park at the Avenue of the Americas entrance. He stuck his hand into his pocket and came up with another joint, which he promptly lit. He blew the smoke out contentedly.

Abruptly the taxi slowed down. The driver looked back at us. "You better cut that out, mister," he warned. "You want to get us all busted?"

Guy smiled and held the cigarette toward the driver. "Relax. Have a toke. Enjoy life."

The driver reached back and took the joint. He took two good long hits, then passed it back. "That's good grass, mister. You get it locally?"

"Brought it all the way from California last week. Can't get shit like that around here." He passed me the joint. "Here, baby."

I sucked on it. It did make me feel good. Walter never really approved of my smoking grass except when we were alone. But it never made me any higher than he got on whiskey.

The taxi slowed down and came to a stop. "We're here," the cabbie announced.

"Hold the clock," Guy said, opening the door. "We'll only be a minute."

"This place ain't safe at night," the cabbie said.

Guy gave him the joint. "Drag on that. We'll be right back."

The cabbie took the joint with one hand and with the other picked up a tire iron from the floor. "Okay," he said. "But God better help any spic or nigger that comes near."

We went up the walk onto the dock, then stopped and leaned on the railing to look out over the water. It was absolutely still, not a ripple marred its surface.

"Take your ring off," Guy said.

It wouldn't budge. My fingers were swollen. I looked at Guy helplessly. "What do we do now?" I asked.

"Leave it to me." He cupped his hands around his mouth and yelled at the taxi driver. "Do you have a file there?"

In the night the sound of his voice was like an explosion.

The cabbie's voice echoed back. "What the hell do you think I'm drivin'? A plumber's shop?"

Guy turned back to me. "Cabs aren't what they used to be," he said. He took my hand and led me off the dock and across the damp ground to the water's edge. "Put your hand in it," he said.

I knelt and stretched out my hand. I looked up at him. "I can't reach it."

"Give me your hand. I'll hold you."

He gripped my hand firmly and I leaned forward. The water was cold against my fingers. "Okay?"

"Okay." After a few minutes my fingers began to numb. "This water is freezing," I said.

"Good. That should do it," he said and let go of my hand.

It wasn't deep, but it was wet and cold when I stood up the water came just below my knees. I took his hand and climbed out.

All the way back to the cab he apologized. I was so angry I couldn't speak.

The cabbie stared at us as Guy opened the door. "You're not getting into my cab like that."

"There's an extra ten dollars in it for you."

"Got any more of that grass?"

"A couple of joints."

"Ten bucks plus the grass," the cabbie said quickly.

"Okay."

We got into the taxi and he pulled away with a roar. "We better get out of here," he said with a glance in the rearview mirror. "They pull you in for swimming in the lake."

Guy had his jacket off and around my shoulders. I looked down at my hand. The ring was still there. Suddenly I began to laugh so hard that tears came to my eyes.

Guy didn't understand it. "What's so funny? You're liable to wind up with pneumonia."

I couldn't stop laughing. "We were supposed to throw the ring in the water. Not me."

I came down from the bedroom wrapped in a heavy terry cloth robe. He was sitting on the edge of the couch and got to his feet. "You okay?"

"Fine." I looked at the bar. "Any sandwiches left? Swimming always makes me hungry."

"Plenty. I made some coffee too."

We were both sober now.

"I'm sorry," he said.

"Don't be," I answered. "I enjoyed every minute of it. If you hadn't come over I probably would have spent the night being miserable and feeling sorry for myself."

He smiled and picked up his own coffee cup. "Good." He looked at me thoughtfully.

"What are you thinking?"

"About you," he said. "About how things are going to change." I was silent.

"They are going to change. You know that, don't you?"

"I guess so, but I don't know exactly how."

"For one thing," he said, "you're not Mrs. Walter Thornton anymore. And that will make a difference. Doors won't open as easily."

I nodded. "I kind of figured that. I used to wonder whether people liked me for me or because I was Walter's wife."

"Both," he said. "But being Walter's wife made it practical."

"I'm still the same person," I said. "I have the same talents as I did when I was married to him."

"True."

"You're trying to tell me something," I said. "What is it?"

He didn't answer.

I had an intuitive flash. "Fannon still likes my play. He is taking an option on it, isn't he?"

"He still likes it, but now he won't option until after the rewrite."

I was silent for a moment. Earlier in the week Fannon had done everything except force the check into my hands. Now it was a different story. The divorce had been in the morning papers. "Did he think Walter would rewrite the play for me?"

"Not exactly, but he probably thought that Walter would be there to help out if he was needed."

I felt the resentment rising. "Shit! Now he won't get the play even if he wants it."

"You listen to me, because I'm your friend and I love you. I also happen to believe in you. So, lesson number one, Fannon happens to be the best producer in town for your play, and if he wants it you're going to give it to him."

"He's a dirty old man. He makes me feel slimy the way he undresses me with his eyes every time we meet."

"That's lesson number two. You're in a business that is controlled by dirty old men and fags. You'll have to get along with them."

"Isn't there anything in between?" I asked.

"Bridgeport," he said.

"I've been there."

"Then you know what I mean. This is the Big Town. You make it here and you make it anywhere in the world."

"I'm beginning to get scared." I said. "Somehow Walter made everything seem so easy."

He reached over and took my hand. "Don't be. You'll make it all right. You've got the talent. Now you've got to fight."

"I don't know how," I said. "I've never had to before. I went right from my parents' home to Walter. And he never wanted to let me grow up."

"That was always one of Walter's problems," Guy said. "He tried to rewrite life like he did his scripts. But things had a way of getting away from him and he never could understand why. Proof. You grew up in spite of it, didn't you?"

"Now I'm not so sure."

"Well, I am," he said, getting to his feet. "It's after three. I'd better let you get some sleep." I followed him to the door. "You come to my office at ten o'clock Tuesday morning. We'll go over the play and then I'll buy you lunch."

"Thank you, but you don't have to take me to lunch if you have something more important to do."

"Lesson number three. When a director or a producer offers to take you to lunch you say, 'Yes, sir.' "

"Yes, sir."

He laughed and kissed my cheek. I closed the door behind, went back into the apartment and looked around the living room. Somehow it all seemed strange and foreign to me now. Suddenly I realized why.

I didn't live here anymore.

Chapter 3

MY FATHER'S CAR was blocking the driveway so I pulled to a stop in front of the house. I had just cut the motor when my brother came out of the house and down the walk toward me. For a moment it was hard to believe that it was Bobby.

He was tall, over six feet, and slim. Somehow the gray-blue Air Force uniform made him look older and taller than his twenty years. He came around the car and pulled open the door. "Holy cow!" he said, sticking his head inside the car and looking at the wood-paneled dashboard of the Jaguar.

"You could say hello first."

"A sister is a sister. But a new car is a joy forever," he said, kissing me on the cheek.

"What are you doing in that uniform? R.O.T.C.

comes home with you now?" I asked as I got out of the car.

"Nope," he said. "I'm in. They accepted me for pilot training so I decided, Why wait? If I did, the war might be over before I graduated. I leave Monday for San Antonio."

"What did Mother say?"

"You know." He made a face. "She hollered a lot."

"She was right this time," I said, opening the trunk.

He reached over and took out my small suitcase. "Don't you start in," he said. "I got enough from Mother."

I snapped the trunk lid shut and followed him up the walk. "We have no business being in Vietnam," I said. "But as long as they can get kids like you to go, it will never end."

"You're beginning to sound like all those other New York commies."

"Shit, Bobby, I just don't like the idea of my kid brother having his head shot off in some stupid jungle."

"I wouldn't worry about it," he said. "The President says it'll all be over by Christmas, and I'll be in school for two years so I'll probably miss it all anyway."

He stopped on the front steps of the porch and turned to look back at the car. "I didn't know you had a new car."

"It's almost a year old."

"Looks new."

"Can't drive a car much in the city."

"It's smooth," he said. "Expensive?"

"Five thousand."

He whistled. "Whose is it? Yours or Walter's?"

"Mine. I paid for it with my own money. Walter thinks anything other than a Cadillac isn't worth buying."

"That means you get to keep it."

"Of course."

He looked at me. "I'm sorry about the divorce. I liked Walter."

I met his gaze. "So did I. But we just weren't making it. The divorce was the best thing for both of us."

He pulled open the door. "You planning to go out tonight?"

I knew what he was getting at. "You want to borrow the car?"

He nodded. "I got a heavy date tonight. Sort of good-bye thing."

I handed him the keys. "Just be careful with it. It's a hot car."

A grin crossed his face and for a moment I saw the little boy I had always known. "Thanks, Sis. I'll handle it with kid gloves."

Mother didn't really start in on me until after dinner, when she followed me out to the porch.

We were silent while I lit a cigarette. I saw the disapproving look in her eyes. "Is your apartment ready?" she finally asked.

"Yes. I'm moving in on Monday."

"I hope it's a safe building. I read stories in the paper every day about things happening."

"It's safe."

"Do you have a doorman?"

"No. Doorman buildings are too expensive. I can't afford it."

"I'm surprised Walter allowed you to do that."

"It's not his responsibility. We're divorced, remember?"

"I'm sure he would have given you more money if you had asked him for it," she said.

Now I knew what she was getting at. "Why can't you come right out and ask what's on your mind, Mother? Do you want to know how much alimony Walter is paying me?"

"You don't have to tell me. It's really none of my business."

"I don't mind telling you," I said. "Nothing."

"Nothing?" she echoed, disbelief in her voice. "How could he do a thing like that? I think it's terrible."

"I don't. I didn't want any."

"But you told me about all the money he was paying to his ex-wife. Why shouldn't you get any?"

"I said I didn't want it, Mother."

"But you were married for six years," she protested. "How are you going to live?"

"I can work, Mother. I've got a play that might be produced and I'm up for several parts in shows."

"But if nothing happens what are you going to do for money then?"

"I have some money. Walter would never let me touch a penny of the money I earned. It's all in the bank."

She was silent, waiting.

"Would you like to know how much I have?"

"You don't have to tell me. It's really none—"

"I know, Mother," I said sarcastically. "It's really none of your business but I'll tell you anyway. I should have about eleven thousand dollars."

"Is that all? I thought you were getting seven hundred and fifty dollars a week while you were in the play. What did you do with all that money?"

"Taxes took a big part of it. Walter is in a top bracket and we filed a joint return. The car, clothes and furniture took the rest."

"Maybe you ought to sell the car. I don't see why you need a car in the city at all. Especially an expensive car like that."

"But I like it. I wouldn't have bought it if I didn't."

"I wish you had spoken to your father and me before you did anything."

I was silent.

"Walter was a good man. You shouldn't have left him like that."

"I discovered I didn't love him anymore, Mother. It wouldn't have been fair to stay on with him, knowing that."

"Are you in love with someone else?"

"No."

"Then you shouldn't have left," she said emphatically. "You don't break up a good marriage on a whim."

"It was not a whim," I explained patiently. "And if I had stayed on we would have wound up hating each other. This way we're still friends."

"I'm afraid I'll never understand you, JeriLee. Do you know what you're looking for?"

"Yes, me."

She was genuinely puzzled. "What kind of an answer is that?"

I was tired and went up to bed early. But as soon as I lay down I was wide awake. I got out of bed and sat near the window with a cigarette. I wasn't even thinking. I remembered sitting in this same window staring at the same street ever since I had been a little girl.

The picture flashed through my mind. The little girl sat at the top of the stairs and cried. The little girl was me. But I was no longer a little girl, so why was I crying?

There was a soft knock. "Are you still awake, honey?" my father whispered.

I opened the door. His face, framed by the hall light, was a little thinner and a little more lined than I remembered. "Can't sleep?" he asked.

I shook my head.

"I can make you some hot milk."

"I'll be okay."

"I hope Mother didn't upset you. It's only that she worries about you."

"I know. She didn't."

"She has a lot on her mind. Bobby's signing up upset her more than she admits."

"And now me. I guess it doesn't make things any easier."

"We'll manage. All we want is for you both to be all right." He hesitated a moment. "You know that if there's anything you need, anything, all you have to do is call us."

I leaned over and kissed his cheek.

He patted my hair gently. "I don't like to see you hurting."

"It's my fault," I said. "And I'll have to work it out myself. But it will get better now that I have the chance."

He looked at me silently for a moment, then nodded.

"I'm sure it will," he said. "The last thing in the world you needed was another father."

My surprise showed in my eyes. He didn't wait for me to speak. "Walter's problem was the same as mine. Neither of us wanted to believe that you were growing up." His smile suddenly warmed his face. "I knew that the moment I saw you in his play. He would like nothing better than to keep you that girl forever. But the difference between life and the play is that life changes and plays don't. That girl in the play is still the same age today that she was five years ago. But you're not."

I felt the tears running down my cheeks. He pulled my head against his chest. A thoughtful tone came into his voice. "Don't feel bad, JeriLee. It could have been worse. Some people just never grow up at all."

Chapter 4

I WATCHED MY FATHER walk down the hall into his room before I closed the door. I lit another cigarette and went back to the window.

The girl in the play never grew up at all. But I had been the girl in the play. Was I still the same girl? Was the growing up I thought I did an illusion? I still remembered that afternoon, the second week of rehearsals, when my growing up began.

I didn't want to do it. I kept saying I wasn't an actress. But Walter and Guy kept pressing and finally I gave in. At first I felt strange and awkward. An amateur among professionals. But I learned bit by bit. By the end of the first week they could hear me in the balcony. Everyone was so nice, so considerate, I began to feel more comfortable, more sure. Until that afternoon when it came at me from out of the blue.

Beau Drake had come from Hollywood to make his first appearance on the New York stage since he had left fifteen years before. He was a star and he knew it. He was a professional and never let anyone forget it, especially me. He knew and pulled all the tricks. Half the time I found myself playing the scene with my back to the audience, other times I would be hidden by his broad shoulders or upstaged and left hanging while the attention of the audience was directed to another portion of the stage.

In the beginning I didn't know enough to be bothered by it, but as I began to realize what he was doing I started to get angry. I didn't want more of a role than the play gave me, but I felt I was entitled to what I did have. I began to fight back in the only way I could. By this time I recognized that he was a stickler for cue lines. The slightest variation in the reading would throw him off. And so I began to change the lines that Walter had written into my own language.

It was the second run-through of the afternoon and we were at the climax of the second act, the scene just before curtain, when he blew. "God damn it!" he suddenly roared.

We froze. Dan Keith, who played my father, stared first at him then at me. Jane Carter, in the wings waiting for her entrance, stood with her mouth agape while Beau marched angrily down to the center of the stage and leaned over the footlights.

"I'm not getting paid enough money to be Stanislavsky," he shouted at Guy and Walter. "If I wanted to run an acting school for stage-struck girls I could do better in Hollywood. If you can't get Mrs. Thornton to say the lines that were written for her, you can find yourself another actor for my part. I'm walking!"

He turned and stalked off the stage. There wasn't a sound or a movement until we heard the door of his dressing room slam shut backstage. Then everybody began to speak at once.

"Quiet!" Guy's voice was firm as he came up on the stage followed by Walter. He looked at Dan and Jane. "We'll break for a half hour."

They nodded and left the stage silently. Guy and Walter looked at me without speaking. I remembered feeling just at that moment like a child defying her parents.

"You saw what he was doing," I accused. "It wasn't right. He was doing everything to make me look stupid."

I had nothing more to say so I began to cry. "Okay. I never said I was an actress. I'll go."

Guy's voice was quiet. "No. I'll decide that. I'm the director."

"It's the best thing for the play," I sobbed. "He hates me. You won't have any trouble with another girl."

"Beau is right," Guy said. "You were changing the lines on him. Why?"

"He had no right to do what he was doing."

"You didn't answer my question."

"You didn't answer mine," I retorted.

"I don't have to. I wasn't tampering with the author's lines."

"If you objected to it, why didn't you say something?"

"Because it wasn't time. What I want to know is why you did it."

"It was the only way I could get him to let me play my part."

Guy and Walter exchanged a communicative glance. "That's not a good enough reason," Guy said.

Suddenly I was no longer intimidated. "Then how about this one? There was no way I could get myself to say those lines and still be the seventeen-year-old girl you want me to be. Those lines are written for a thirty-year-old woman. I don't know any kids who talk like that."

For a moment there was silence, then I caught a glimpse of Walter's set and guarded face. "Oh, Walter, I'm sorry. I didn't mean it like it sounded. I—"

"It's all right," he said stiffly. Abruptly he turned and walked off the stage.

I started after him but Guy held out a hand. "Let him go."

"What are you talking about? That's my husband walking out."

"Not your husband. The playwright."

"I hurt him. I'm going after him."

"No, you're not. He's a pro, he'll get over it."

"I don't understand."

"Someone had to tell him. The lines weren't right. It was becoming more obvious every day. If the dialogue were right, Beau would not have had the chance to do what he did. He'd be too busy working on his own part."

Over Guy's shoulder I saw Beau coming out of the wings. He seemed relaxed as he approached us. "Everything okay?" he asked in a casual voice.

"Fine, now," Guy answered as if nothing had happened.

Suddenly I understood and I felt the anger surging within me. "You set me up for this," I accused. "Because none of you had the nerve to tell him the truth."

"You were the only one he would take it from," Guy said. "Now he'll go back and rewrite until he gets those lines right."

"You're a shit!" I snapped.

"I never said I was a saint."

"The truth," I said. "Can't any of you tell the truth? Do you always have to manipulate others into doing your dirty work for you when the truth is so much simpler?"

"That's show business," Guy said glibly.

"I don't like it," I said.

"You better get used to it if you're going to stay in it."

"I have no intention of doing that either."

"If you plan to stay married to Walter, you'll get used to it whether you like it or not. Because he's going to be around for a long time. This is the only life he knows or wants." He started for the wings without waiting for a reply. "Rehearsal at two o'clock tomorrow," he called back over his shoulder.

Beau and I were left alone on the stage. He smiled slowly. "Just you and me, baby."

"I don't think that's funny."

"I'm sorry. I didn't mean for it to get so rough."

When I didn't answer, a look of contrition came over

his face. "I couldn't help it. I guess I'm a better actor than I thought."

That broke the ice. I began to smile. "You're pretty good," I said. "But you're also a prick."

He grinned. "I've been called worse. But it's all for a good cause. Can I buy you a drink just to show there's no hard feelings?"

"I don't drink," I said. "But you can buy me a cup of coffee."

It all worked the way they had planned it. By the time I got home that night Walter was working on the rewrite. He didn't come to bed at all and the next morning when I came down for breakfast there was a note on the table.

Dearest,
Have gone to Guy's for breakfast to go over the new lines. See you at rehearsal. Love,
Walter.

P.S. Please forgive me but I had to use your lines. They were better than anything I could dream up.
W.

I felt the warm glow of approval, and later in rehearsal I noticed that the changes had already been incorporated. For the first time we were all together.

It wasn't until long afterward that I realized what that afternoon had cost me. By that time Beau and I had already picked up our Tonys for best actor and supporting actress, even though the award for the best play had gone to another writer. It happened the week the play closed on Broadway after a year's run.

I had a suggestion to make to Walter about his new script and went into his study to give it to him. He listened to me impassively. When I finished he reached for the script I still held in my hand.

"You weren't supposed to read this," he said.

"I didn't know that, Walter. I picked up the copy in the bedroom."

"I forgot it."

"I was only trying to help."

"When I want help I'll ask for it."

It was not until then that I really believed they had found the only way to get him to make the changes. He didn't care any more for the truth than the others in the business. All they were really interested in was their own egos.

"I'm sorry," I said stiffly. "It won't happen again."

"I don't mean to sound harsh. But you can't know what it is until you do it yourself. You have some idea how difficult it is. You tried to write once yourself."

"Then I'll find out," I said. "Now that the play is closed and I have the time to spare, I have an idea of my own that I want to try."

"Good. If you have any problems you can talk to me about it."

I didn't answer. But when I left the room my mind was already made up. He was the last person in the world I was going to go to for help.

That had been four years ago and the beginning of the end of our marriage. After that in a thousand subtle ways I became aware that he felt challenged. Now it was over. I hoped that he was no longer threatened.

I heard the telephone begin to ring downstairs and glanced at my watch. It was after two in the morning. I had been sitting at the window for over an hour. An impulse made me go downstairs to answer it. My parents were old-fashioned enough to believe that extension telephones were a needless extravagance.

The voice on the phone was harsh and strangely familiar. "Veronica?"

"No. This is JeriLee."

"JeriLee, I didn't know you were home. This is Chief Roberts. Do you own a blue Jaguar?"

My heart began to pound but I tried to keep my voice calm. "Yes."

"There's been an accident."

"Oh, no!"

My parents had suddenly appeared behind me. My father reached and took the telephone from my hand. "This is John Randall."

He listened for a moment, then his face went white. "We better get dressed," he said as he put down the phone. "There's been an accident and Bobby's in the hospital at Jefferson."

Chapter 5

MY BROTHER never went to Vietnam. The car went off the road on the same curve that killed my father fifteen years before. He lived only long enough to apologize to my mother.

"I'm sorry, Ma," he whispered through the maze of tubes that ran in and out of his body. "I guess I had too much to drink." Then he turned his head away and went to sleep. And never woke up.

Mother seemed to turn to stone. For her it must have been like a nightmare revisited. No matter what we said or tried to do we received no response. The only question she addressed to Chief Roberts. "Was he alone in the car?"

"Yes, Veronica. He dropped Anne off at her house fifteen minutes earlier. She said she asked him to stay and have a cup of coffee before he went home but he said he wanted to get JeriLee's car home so that she wouldn't worry about it."

She nodded without speaking.

"Anne said they were planning to get married before he went off to training camp," he said. "Did you know she was pregnant?"

My mother stared at him.

"He hadn't said anything to us," my father said.

"She said he was going to tell you this morning."

"You spoke to her?" my father asked.

The chief nodded. "The accident went out on the one

o'clock news flash on the Jefferson radio station. She called here and I spoke to her. She's pretty broken up."

"The poor kid," I said. "She's got to be scared to death."

My mother turned on me angrily. "Don't feel sorry for that slut! I warned Bobby that she would do anything to trap him."

"I don't know the girl," I said. "But it can't be—"

"I do," my mother cut in in an icy voice. "I'm almost glad that he's beyond her reach."

I felt my heart swell up and almost choke me. Suddenly I realized something I had never known before. I had never seen my mother cry. Never. Not even now. I couldn't stop the words. "Don't you know how to cry, Mother?"

She looked at me for a moment, then turned to my father. Her tone was almost normal. It was as if I had said nothing. "We'll have to make arrangements for the funeral, John . . ."

I couldn't stand it. I forced myself between them and looked deep into her eyes. The tears were running down my cheeks. "Bobby's dead, Mother. Your only son is dead. Can't you spare him any tears?"

Mother's voice was cold and calm. "You have no right to speak like that, JeriLee. It's your fault this happened. You shouldn't have given him the car."

It was too much for me. In tears, I turned and walked down the short flight of stairs to the main floor, then out of the front door.

The dawn was breaking in the east. The morning air was cold. I shivered but it wasn't from the cold. I fished a cigarette from my purse and was about to light it when a large callused hand held a burning match for me. It was Chief Roberts.

"I'm sorry, JeriLee," he said. There was genuine sympathy in his voice.

"I know."

"I don't like to bother you at a time like this, but there are certain questions that have to be answered."

"I understand. Go ahead."

"The car registered and insured to you?"

"Yes."

"You'll have to notify your insurance company. I ordered it towed to Clancy's garage on Main Street."

I looked at him.

"It's totaled. There won't be anything they can do with it."

I was silent.

"I can come by the house later and you can sign the accident report. You don't have to come down to the station."

"Thank you."

"Chief Roberts," I called as he started to turn away.

"Yes?"

"That girl, Anne?"

He nodded.

"Tell her to call me. Maybe there's something I can do."

"I'll do that, JeriLee," he said. "I've known her as long as I've known you. Since she was a baby. She's a right nice girl."

"She has to be if my brother loved her."

He nodded again, then looked up at the sky. "It's going to be clear today."

"Yes," I said and watched the pudgy figure in the baby-blue uniform walk away from me.

He was right, I thought as I looked up. It would be a clear day. There wasn't a cloud in the sky.

The funeral was on Tuesday. Walter sent flowers from London and Guy came to hold my hand. When we came home afterward, Mother went right up to her room and closed the door. "I guess I'll pack," I said to my father. "Guy offered to drive me back to the city."

"I guess so," he said. He look tired. It had not been easy for him. He loved Bobby too.

"If you want me to stay, I will."

"No. We can manage. It will be all right."

"But will you be all right?" I asked pointedly.

He got the nuance. "I'll be fine." He hesitated a moment. "Don't be angry with your mother. She's gone through a great deal."

"I'm not angry. I just don't understand."

"Then be charitable. Don't push her away. You're all she has left now."

"I can't get through to her, Daddy," I said. "You know how many times I've tried. We don't think or feel alike about anything."

"Keep trying," he said. "That's what love is about."

I went over and put my arms around him. "You never stop trying, do you, Daddy? You must love her very much."

"I do. I see her faults. But they don't matter. I also see the good things about her. The strength and courage she had to go on with you two children after your father died. Do you know she said she wouldn't marry me unless you approved? That she would never do anything that would make you unhappy?"

"I didn't know that."

"Your aunt and uncle wanted to take you both off her hands so that she could be free to make a new life for herself. She wouldn't do it. She told them that you were her children, her responsibility, and that she was going to take care of you. The first thing she asked me about when I proposed was how I felt about the two of you."

I kissed his cheek. He was lovely. And naïve. But then he loved her. He said so himself. So how could I expect him to see that all these wonderful things she said and did were not because she loved but because she thought they were the right things to do? I kissed his cheek again. "I'll try to remember what you said, Daddy."

The telephone rang. He picked it up, then held it out to me. "For you."

I took the phone from his hand. "Give Guy a drink, will you, Daddy? I have a feeling he's dying of thirst."

"I'm okay," Guy said quickly.

Father took his arm and led him into the living room. "I think I could use a whiskey myself," he said.

"Hello," I said into the phone.

The voice was soft and young and tired. "Mrs. Thornton?"

"Yes."

"Anne Laren. Chief Roberts gave me your message. I wanted to call and thank you."

"I meant it. If there is anything I can do . . ."

"No," she said quickly. "Nothing." She hesitated a moment. "Was everything all right? My flowers get there?"

"Yes. They were lovely." I remembered. A blanket of yellow roses with just the small card and her name on it.

"I wanted to go, but the doctor wouldn't let me get out of bed."

"Are you okay?"

"I am now," she said. Again the moment's hesitation. "I lost the baby, you know."

"I'm sorry."

"Maybe it's for the best," she said. "At least that's what everyone says."

"I guess so," I said.

She began to cry softly. "But I wanted his baby. I really loved him."

"I know."

She stopped crying. I felt the control in her voice. "I'm sorry. It's bad enough for you. I didn't want to make it any worse. I just wanted to thank you."

"Anne," I said, "when you're feeling better, give me a call and come into the city. We'll have lunch. I'd love to meet you."

"I'd like that," she said. "I will."

My mother was standing at the foot of the stairs when I put down the telephone. "Who were you talking to?" she asked.

"Anne."

Her lips tightened slightly. "Did you thank her for the flowers?"

"I thought you would do that."

"If she loved him as much as she said she did, why didn't she come to the funeral?"

"Why didn't you ask her?"

Mother's eyes met mine. "I called. But she wouldn't speak to me. I guess she was too ashamed of what she had done."

"That wasn't the reason, Mother."

"Then what was the reason?"

"She was probably too sick. She lost the baby."

My mother's face suddenly went white and she seemed to stagger. I put out a hand to steady her. "I'm sorry, JeriLee, I really am."

I didn't speak but I could see the color slowly coming back into her face. A very strong lady, my mother. "Now he's really gone," she said.

We looked at each other for a long moment, then she took a tentative step toward me. I opened my arms. She came into them as if she were the child, and the tears finally came.

Chapter 6

IT WAS WEDNESDAY, matinee day, and Sardi's was already crowded with ladies from the suburbs.

The bar was crowded too, but mostly with regulars. I nodded to several of them and the maitre d' came up to me. "Mrs. Thornton." He bowed. "So nice to see you again. Mr. Fannon is expecting you."

I followed him to Fannon's usual table. It was back against the wall separating the restaurant from the Little Bar—the most important location in the place. Everyone coming in or going out could see or be seen. I had heard he hadn't missed a weekday lunch there for fifteen years, except when he had been in the hospital, and then they had catered his meals.

He was sitting on the banquette. As I approached he tried to rise but his potbelly pressing against the table forced him to remain in a half crouch until I sat down next to him. He sank back into his seat with a sigh and kissed my cheek.

"You look beautiful, my dear," he said in his hoarse voice.

"Thank you, Mr. Fannon."

"Adolph, my dear," he said. "Call me Adolph. After all, we're old friends."

I nodded. We had known each other almost two years. That was a long run on Broadway, even for friendship. "Thank you, Adolph."

"A champagne cocktail for Mrs. Thornton." The waiter went away and he turned to me beaming. "Nothing but the best for you."

I liked champagne, but champagne cocktails made me nauseous. Nevertheless I smiled. "Thank you, Adolph."

"Taste it," Fannon urged when the waiter returned with the cocktail.

I began to raise the glass toward my lips.

"Wait a minute, we must have a toast." He picked up his own glass, which was supposed to look like vodka on the rocks but which everyone knew was nothing but water. Ulcers had taken away his liquor license. "To your play," he said.

I nodded and took a sip. The sickeningly sweet cocktail turned my stomach but I manage a smile. "Very good," I said.

A serious look came over his face. "I have a very important announcement to make," he said, putting his hand on my knee

"Yes, Adolph," I said, my eyes on his face.

"I've decided to do your play." His hand was now halfway up my thigh. "We'll go into rehearsals in August. I'd like to bring it to New York in October."

Suddenly I forgot about his hand on my thigh. "You mean it?"

"Yes. I loved the rewrite. I've already sent the script to Anne Bancroft."

"You think she'll do it?"

"She should. She'll never find a better part. Besides she always wanted to do a play with Guy."

"Is he going to direct?"

"Yes. I called him in California this morning and he's agreed." His hand went the rest of the way up.

"Adolph, I never knew anyone who moved so fast," I said pointedly.

He cleared his throat. "When I like something, I like it. I don't believe in playing around."

"Neither do I," I said, looking into his eyes. "But I'm soaking wet already and if you don't take your hand away, I'll come right here."

He flushed and put his hand on the table. "I'm sorry. In my enthusiasm I forgot myself."

"It's okay. I just happen to be very excitable. And I've never known a man quite like you before."

"No?" he asked in a questioning voice.

"You're something else. In a business full of wishy-washy people you have the strength of your convictions."

"I make decisions," he said, looking pleased. "Like I told you, I know what I want."

"That's what I admire about you."

"We're going to be seeing a lot of each other. I'm not the kind of a producer who leaves it all up to the director. I get very involved with my plays."

"I know. That's why I'm glad you're going to do it."

"There's still work to be done on the script. We'll have to get started soon. I would like you to have my ideas before Guy gets back from the Coast."

"You let me know when. I'll make myself available."

"Good," he said, obviously delighted with the way things were going. I had calculatedly told him everything he wanted to hear. His hand was on my knee again. "My office is drawing up the contract. I thought a ten-thousand-dollar advance would be very fair. It's more than twice what I give anyone else for a first play."

I believed him. Both Guy and my agent told me not to expect more than thirty-five hundred. "That's very fair. Thank you, Adolph."

"You deserve it," he said, smiling. "Besides from what I have heard you could use the money. I understand Walter didn't give you any alimony."

"I didn't want any," I said quickly.

"Most girls in this business don't feel like that."

"That's their bag. I can work. I can take care of myself."

His hand began to travel. "That's what I respect about you."

"I'm getting hungry," I said, trying to divert him. "I haven't had any breakfast."

"Let's order then."

But before he could signal the waiter, Earl Wilson of the New York *Post* came in and spotted us. His round face broke into a smile. "Adolph, JeriLee, what are you two cooking up?"

"You've got a scoop, Earl. I'm putting on JeriLee's new play."

"What kind of a part are you playing this time, JeriLee?"

"She's not acting in this one, Earl," Fannon said. "She wrote it."

Earl whistled enthusiastically. "That is a scoop." He smiled at me. "Did you have any help from your ex?"

"Walter had nothing to do with it," Fannon said quickly. "JeriLee was a writer before she was an actress. She only went into acting because Walter wanted her to do his play."

"You got someone in mind for the lead?" the columnist asked.

"Anne Bancroft."

Earl looked at me. "How do you feel about it?"

"I'm thrilled," I said and almost jumped out of my seat to prove it. Fannon's hand was on my cunt again.

The story was the lead item in the New York *Post* the next day.

> Adolph Fannon, noted Broadway producer, confided to us at Sardi's yesterday that he is planning to present a new play on Broadway next season by Thornton's ex-wife. He also told us that Anne Bancroft is penciled for the lead.

That was it. Walter Thornton's ex-wife. Although it had been two months since the divorce he never even mentioned my name.

I left the paper on the kitchen table and went into the living room just as the telephone began to ring.

It was Guy returning my call from California. "Congratulations," he said.

"I wanted to thank you. If it weren't for all the work you did on the play, Fannon would never have bought it."

"I just made suggestions. You did the writing."

"I'm glad you're going to direct it."

"So am I."

"He sent the script to Anne Bancroft."

"He told you that?" Guy's voice was skeptical.

"Yes. He even told Earl Wilson, who ran it in today's column."

Guy laughed. "Don't you believe it. I'll give you ten to one she never got it."

"Then why would he say something like that?"

"It's a flyer. He's smart. He figures she'll hear about it and be curious enough to ask her agent to get her a copy. That way she's asking him, he's not asking her."

"Oh, Jesus," I said.

"Did you get the contract yet?"

"My agent called this morning. He's got them. By the way, I'm getting a ten-thousand advance."

"That's great. How are the payments scheduled?"

"I don't know. Why?"

"He never pays more than thirty-five hundred until the play opens on Broadway. What you'll probably get is a thousand on signing, a thousand when we go into rehearsal, fifteen hundred when we go on the road and the balance when and if we open in New York. Just don't spend it until you get it."

"I don't know," I said. "He said a ten-thousand advance."

"Everything you get before the show opens on Broadway is considered an advance," he said. "Check it with your agent."

"I will," I said. "When are you coming back?"

"I should wrap up here in about a month."

"Please hurry, Guy. I miss having you around."

When Guy hung up I called my agent. The payment spread was exactly as Guy had explained it to me. Apparently I still had a lot to learn.

I sat down again at the kitchen table and took out my checkbook. Even with the thirty-two hundred I had gotten from the insurance company for my car I only had about a four-thousand-dollar balance. Furnishing the apartment had taken much more than I had figured.

I did some quick arithmetic. The apartment cost me about eleven hundred a month, including gas, electricity, telephone and a maid two days a week. Food, clothing and cabs came to another four hundred at least. With five months to go before we opened on Broadway, I'd be shaving it pretty close. And if the play didn't make it to Broadway, I'd be broke.

There was no getting away from it. I couldn't sit around and wait for the play to come through. I needed an acting job to get me through the summer. And I needed it right away.

Chapter 7

I WAS ON TIME for my appointment at George Fox's office at ten o'clock the next morning and was ushered in almost immediately. George was senior vice president of Artists Alliance, Inc., and Walter was his personal client.

He was a short dapper man with gray hair and an easy smile. He came around the desk and kissed me on the cheek. "Congratulations," he said. "Fannon's really high on your play."

"Thank you," I said, taking the seat in front of his

desk. "I am disappointed about the payments though. I had hoped that it would all be paid in advance."

"They never do that," he said quickly. "Believe me, I personally went over your contract. You've got a very good deal for a first play. And more important, you have the hottest producer in town."

"I know that. But I have money problems. I have to find some work if I want to make it until the play opens."

"I can lend you some money," he said quickly.

"There's no need for that. I can get by. What I need is some work."

"Have you anything in mind?"

"Not really. I though maybe I could pick up some work in summer stock."

He looked doubtful. "I shouldn't think so. All the shows are already packaged. They begin casting in January."

"Some writing jobs then," I said. I knew they were shooting next fall's TV programs.

"Pretty late for that too," he said. "They're usually wrapped up by January too."

"Maybe there's an acting job in one of the pilots. After all, I have had stage experience. I saw in last week's *Variety* that they're short of new faces for TV."

"They always say that but whenever possible they go with the tried and true. They like to play it safe. Besides all the action is out on the Coast and they would never pay your fare out even if they wanted you. In addition to everything else, they're cheap."

"If there was a chance of my getting a few things, I'd pay my own way out."

"I don't know. I'm really not up on the situation." He thought for a moment. "Let me put you together with a young man in our office who is into these things. I'm sure he'll find something for you." He picked up the telephone. "Ask Harry Gregg to come up here."

A few minutes later Harry Gregg arrived. He was tall and thin with tousled hair and wore the black suit, white shirt, black tie and reserved expression that were standard issue in the agency.

"Harry, let me introduce you to one of the agency's most important new talents as well as a close personal friend of mine, JeriLee Thornton . . . er, Randall. JeriLee, Gregg, one of the agent's brightest and most up and coming young men."

Harry smiled and we shook hands.

"I want you to do everything you can for her," George continued. "I'm making you personally responsible. We've already made a deal with Fannon to produce a play that she has written but I want you to explore other areas in which we might be of service."

Before I knew it, I was out of George's office and sitting in Harry's tiny cubbyhole. "Would you like some coffee?" he asked, pushing a pile of papers to one side of his desk.

I nodded.

"Two coffees," he said into the phone. "How do you take it?"

"Black. No sugar."

A minute later his secretary came into the office with two plastic cups of coffee. It was very different from George's office. There the coffee was served from an elaborate silver set in genuine Wedgwood cups.

"Did George make the deal with Fannon for you?" Harry asked.

"No. I worked on it myself but mostly it was Guy Jackson. Without him it never would have happened."

"I thought so."

"What do you mean?"

"George is not a negotiator. He picks up packages." He took a swallow of coffee. "Is Guy directing?"

"Yes."

"That's good. I like him," he said. "Are you friendly with your ex?" He saw the expression on my face. "I don't mean to pry into your personal affairs, but it's important that I know how we stand."

"Why?"

"Walter is one of the agency's most important clients. If he's down on you, the agency will bury you, no matter what bullshit they hand you."

Suddenly I liked this young man. At least he was honest. "We're friendly," I said.

"Does George know that?"

"I don't know."

"It would be helpful if he did. It would make my job easier. Right now, he probably doesn't know how things are between you."

"Is that why I'm down here?"

"Don't quote me. But . . . yes."

"I see." I got to my feet. "Is there any point in us talking then?"

"Sit down, sit down," he said quickly. "There's no point in going off half cocked. You've already got the play with us, you might as well go the rest of the way. We could get lucky."

I returned to the seat and took a sip of coffee. I had always hated the taste of coffee in plastic cups.

"What are you looking for?" he asked.

"Work," I said. "Anything. Acting, writing."

"Why?"

"I have to support myself."

He was silent for a moment. I didn't know whether he believed me or not. "Okay," he said in a businesslike voice. "We have to start somewhere. Do you have a portfolio?"

"Sort of." I took a brown envelope out of my script case. "Not very good though. They were all taken when I was in the play four or five years ago."

He skimmed through the photographs. "We're going to need new pictures. You looked like a kid then."

"That was the part."

"I'll need a complete layout. Face, character, cheesecake. Do you have a photographer?"

"No. But I know quite a few."

"Do you think one of them would do it for you?"

"I don't know. I could ask."

"If not, I know a very good one that would do exactly what we need for two hundred. And if you let him do a magazine layout on you, it could wind up costing you nothing and even making you a few dollars."

"What kind of a layout?"

"You know. *Playboy*. You get fifteen hundred dollars."

"I'd have to think about that," I said. "Wouldn't something like that screw up my career?"

"Your guess is as good as mine. Attitudes are changing. The studios aren't as uptight as they used to be."

"Will he do the portfolio for the two hundred even if I don't go for the magazine deal?"

"Yes."

"Then let's use him. I can afford that."

"Okay. I'll set it up. Now, do you have a copy of the play that I can read?"

I took out a copy of the script and gave it to him.

"Is there a part in this for you?" he asked.

"The lead, but Fannon wants Anne Bancroft."

"I'll read it," he said. "It will give me an idea of how you write."

"I told George that I could go out to the Coast if you can line up a few guest spots on some of the pilot shows."

At that moment the telephone rang. Listening, he said, "Put him on," then, "Hello, Tony."

He was silent for about two minutes. Finally he spoke. "How old is this girl as you see her?"

The voice crackled on the other end. "We may be in luck, Tony," he said. "I've just picked up a new client. Remember JeriLee Randall? Walter Thornton's ex-wife. She did a year on Broadway in his play and she's just the right age. Twenty-three, that's right. And she looks sensational. We got just one problem. I don't know whether she'll do a part like that. She's a very classy dame."

He listened for a few more minutes, then interrupted. "Send me the script, Tony. I'll talk to her and see what I can do.

"No, Tony," he said into the phone. "I told you she's a very classy dame. She doesn't do cocktail interviews. That's not her style." He paused for a moment, then looked over at me. "What's she look like?" he echoed. "She's sensational. Stacked like you would not believe, but very classy. Sort of a combination Ava Gardner and

Grace Kelly. She's the kind who when she comes into your office you want to bend down and kiss her pussy out of sheer reverence. So send me the script and I'll get on it right away."

He put down the telephone. "I'm sorry I had to talk like that," he apologized. "But that's the only language that son of a bitch understands. He thinks he can fuck every actress who comes into his office."

"Who is he?"

"Tony Styles. He's got a part open in a picture that starts shooting in New York next week and the girl he was counting on for the part got a job on the Coast.

I had heard about him. I thought I might have met him once at a party in Hollywood with Walter. A vulgar little man with a dirty mouth. But he and his brother made pictures that made money. The Styles Brothers. "What kind of a part is it?"

"Two weeks' work. A high class New York call girl who runs through the picture getting in and out of her clothes. He said she had some good lines but I'll know more when I see the script. He's desperate though and he might go as high as twenty-five hundred for the two weeks."

"Can I read it after you get through?" I asked.

"Of course." He looked at his watch. "My God, it's lunchtime. Do you have a date?"

"I'm free."

"Good. I'll buy you some lunch and we can talk some more."

And lunch was different too. We had sandwiches in his office.

Chapter 8

THEY WERE TWINS but you wouldn't believe it looking at them. Tony Styles was five four, pudgy and vulgar, while his brother John was six one, slim, esthetic-looking and quiet. Tony's own description was perhaps the best. "John's the artist in the family. He's got everything. Good taste, good manners and class. Me, I'm the hustler. But we go good together. I shoot all the shit. John shoots the picture."

I sat on the couch in his office with Harry next to me. Across the room Tony was seated behind the desk while John leaned against the wall. Beyond the standard greeting, John hadn't said a word, but his eyes were watchful.

"Did you like the script?" Tony asked.

"She loved it," Harry said quickly.

John spoke for the first time. "Really?"

I didn't like the tone in his voice. It was as if he doubted that anyone with good taste could like it. Unfortunately, he was right. I met his eyes. "Not really," I said.

Harry was silent at my side.

"What did you really think of it?" John asked.

I consoled myself with the thought that I wouldn't have gotten the job anyway. "It's a piece of shit. Commercial shit probably. But shit anyway."

Tony looked at his brother with a triumphant smile. "See? I told you she'd like it."

I laughed. He had to be completely crazy. I could see John's eyes smiling with me.

Tony turned back to me. "Do you think you could do the part?"

I nodded, knowing that any girl with a good body would do just as well.

"We could add some dialogue. You know, give you some business. Make it interesting."

"That would be nice."

"Would you mind standing?"

I got to my feet.

"Would you take off your shoes, please?"

They weren't high heels but I slipped out of them. He turned to his brother. "Not too tall, you think?"

John shook his head.

"Those tits real?" Tony asked. "You're not wearing falsies?"

"I'm not wearing a brassiere, period," I said.

Tony met my gaze without smiling. "I had to ask, you know."

"I know," I said. My basic costume for the picture consisted of a brassiere and panties.

"Do you have a bikini with you?"

I nodded.

"You can change in there," he said, pointing to a small door at the far side of the office.

It was a little private john. I changed quickly and went back into the office. I walked in front of the desk. He was watching me. I turned around slowly and stopped.

"Okay," he said. "One other thing. We shoot a few scenes separately for the foreign version. They ain't got the same hangups we Americans have. Would you object to a little nudity?"

I looked at him silently.

"Nothing vulgar," he added quickly. "Discreet. Good taste. But sexy. You know. Like Bardot and Lollobrigida. Quality."

Harry was suddenly on his feet. "That's out," he said. He turned to me. "Get dressed, JeriLee. We're leaving."

I started back to the john. Through the closed door I could hear Tony protesting. By the time I came back into the room it had all calmed down. "It's okay," Harry said. "You don't have to do the nude scenes."

"I changed my mind," I said. "I don't want to do the picture at all."

Harry stared at me, his mouth open.

I looked down at Tony. "Nice meeting you both. Good luck with the picture." I picked up my bag and walked out.

Harry caught up to me at the elevator. "I don't get it," he said, bewildered. "I had you locked in for thirty-five hundred and you walk out."

"I'm not a piece of meat," I said. "Let him go to the nearest butcher shop if that's what he's looking for."

The doors opened and he followed me into the elevator. "Okay. Now what do we do?"

"You tell me," I said. "You're the agent."

"I'll try to think of something."

By the time I got home there was a message on the answering service. Call John Styles. I hesitated for a moment, then dialed the number.

John Styles answered.

"This is JeriLee Randall," I said. "You asked me to call."

His voice was quiet. "I'm sorry if my brother upset you, Miss Randall. I'd like you to do the part. I wish you would reconsider."

"What for? You know how I feel about the screenplay."

"That's the script, Miss Randall. But films are a director's medium. The script can be changed. And I'm the director."

My voice was skeptical. "You mean that you'd rewrite for me."

"No, Miss Randall," the gentle voice replied. "For myself."

"But my part isn't important enough for that."

"Right. But within the context of the film it can be valid. And I think that you're the one that can make it work."

"Do I have time to think about it?"

"Not much. We'll have to have your answer by tomorrow morning. We go on the floor Monday."

"I'll call you in the morning."

"Thank you, Miss Randall."

"Thank you, Mr. Styles." I put down the phone and called Harry on his direct line.

"John Styles just called me," I said.

"I know. He called me first. I let him talk me into giving him your number."

"Why'd you do that?"

"Two reasons. One, it's now five grand for the two weeks' work. Two. John says you'll be treated right and I believe him. He's got a good reputation."

"Then what do we do now?"

"We take the job."

"Right," I said. And we did.

John Styles did something special with what began as a stereotyped role. Suddenly the hooker developed into a frightened desperate girl trying to survive in society with the only talents at her disposal. Still it was a small role and since I didn't have that much to do, I spent a good part of my time just hanging around the set.

John was good. In his own low-key manner he kept everything moving and under control. There were no flaps, no panic, no pressure. He just moved from shot to shot putting together his film. He came over to me after I had finished my last scene.

"You were very good, JeriLee. Thank you."

"You made it possible," I said. "Thank you."

He smiled. "You were right for the part. I couldn't let my brother frighten you away."

"I'm glad you didn't."

"How about dinner tonight?" he asked. "No shooting tomorrow."

"Okay," I said, surprised. He had given no sign of any special interest while we had been working.

"I can pick you up about eight o'clock."

"Fine."

"Twenty One, okay?" he asked when I got into the cab.

"Lovely." I hadn't been there for dinner since my divorce.

Chuck greeted us at the door as we came in. "Mr.

Styles," he said. Then he saw me and his eyes widened. "Hi, Mrs. Thornton." He beckoned to a maitre d'. "We have a table for Mr. Styles in the main dining room upstairs."

"But I reserved in the bar," John said.

Chuck flushed with embarrassment. "It's a bit crowded in there," he said quickly. "You'll be more comfortable upstairs."

"Okay, Chuck," I said. "Out with it."

"Your ex is in there, Mrs. Thornton. And the only table open is right opposite his."

John looked at me.

"I don't mind if you don't," I said.

The bar was crowded. We followed the waiter to our table. Walter was with George Fox. He didn't see us until after we sat down. When he did, he rose and came over to our table.

I held up my cheek for his kiss, then I introduced him to John. They shook hands with a display of show business cool but my legs were trembling.

Walter smiled. "George told me how well you were doing. I'm pleased."

"I've been lucky."

"You've got talent. I always said that." He looked at John. "How's the picture coming?"

"Good. We've wrapped up here and move back to the Coast over the weekend."

"Are you going out too, JeriLee?"

"No. I finished today."

"Maybe we can have lunch one day next week then?"

"I'd like that."

"I'll call you." He smiled. "Enjoy your dinner."

I thought as I watched him walk back to his table that he looked a little tired. But then he was always a little tired. It seemed to be a condition of his existence.

"Why don't you?" John's voice interrupted my thoughts.

"Why don't I what?"

"Come out to the Coast with us."

"That's ridiculous. What on earth for?"

"To get away. I think you need a change of scene."

"Maybe I do. But I can't afford it. I have to stick around here and look for another job."

"There's work out there too."

"My agents thinks I have a better chance here. He doesn't want me to go out there except for a film job."

"Agents like to keep clients under their thumb."

"I'd need a better reason than that."

"Okay. How about this one? Because I want you to."

I was silent, looking at him.

"No strings," he said quickly. "I'm not my brother."

I shook my head. "Not yet." I took a sip of water. My mouth had suddenly gone dry. "Maybe later. When I'm sure I can handle things."

"Like what?"

"Myself."

"I think you do very well."

"I don't know yet."

"Chuck is smarter than we are," he said. "It would have been better if we had gone upstairs."

I felt the pressure of the tears behind my eyes but I managed a smile. "You know something? You're absolutely right."

Then we both laughed and it wasn't as bad after that.

Chapter 9

It was about one o'clock in the morning when the telephone rang. I had just dozed off, and I reached for the phone still in the fog of early sleep.

"Are you alone?" It was Walter.

I came out of the fog. "Yes."

"I had to call you." He paused for a moment and I could hear the wheeze deep in his chest. He was still smoking too much. "There were so many things I wanted to say to you when I saw you in the restaurant."

I fished for a cigarette and lit it. The lighter made a loud rasping click.

"Are you sure you're alone?"

"I'm alone."

"I thought I heard something."

"It was my cigarette lighter." I was getting annoyed. One of the most difficult things in our relationship had been his insatiable desire to know everything I had done and thought every minute of the day. "I'm tired. You woke me. What was so important that you had to call me tonight?" I knew he had been in town almost a month.

"I just wanted to know one thing. Are you sleeping with John Styles?"

"No," I answered without thinking. Then I got angry. "Besides what difference would it make to you if I were? What I do is none of your business."

"It would make a difference. I don't want to see you used."

"Nobody's using me. Just because I had dinner with him doesn't mean that I'm sleeping with him."

"That's not the talk around town. They said he paid you double the money they offered anyone else for that part."

"Who is they?" I asked sarcastically. "George Fox?"

He didn't answer.

"George is a prick. He's trying to make points with you. It could be that he can't get it through his head that maybe John thought I was worth twice as much as anyone else."

"I know John Styles. That's not his reputation."

"You've got him mixed up with his brother Tony."

"No, I haven't." he said. "I've heard he's worse, in his own quiet way."

"I'll believe that when I see it. He's been a perfect gentleman with me." I ground out the cigarette. "And if that's the only reason you woke me up, let me go back to sleep. I'm tired."

"I'm sorry," he said.

"Okay."

"Can we still have lunch next week?"

"Yes, call me after the weekend."

"Goodbye," he said.

I hung up and rolled back on my pillow. There was no use trying to sleep now. I was wide awake. I got out of bed and went to the medicine cabinet in the bathroom. I was looking for a Librium or a Valium but there weren't any. Then I remembered.

The last time Guy had been here working on the play he had left me a joint. I went back into the living room and took it out of the drawer under the coffee table. It was a big one. Guy called it a bomber. Two tokes were guaranteed to put you away.

I carried it back into the bedroom and got into bed. I leaned back against the headboard, lit the joint and took the first hit deep into my lungs. I did it again, holding my breath for what seemed almost half an hour. I felt the warm easy feelings come over me. I took one more toke, then carefully pinched it out before I floated away on the tide. No sense wasting it. I already had a beautiful high.

I looked across the empty king-sized bed. Instinctively I put my hand out to where Walter would have been, then took my hand away quickly. Walter would never be there anymore.

Still I couldn't help remembering how it was when we were together and had a joint and got a little high. Sex was better than when we were straight. Walter didn't seem uptight and he lasted longer. Without it, he either came almost as soon as he entered me or he had problems getting hard. It got so that most of the time he either brought me off orally, manually or mechanically with the aid of a little vibrator. But even then it hadn't mattered. I had loved him and been perfectly happy. And if I got too uptight, I helped myself. It was something I could rely on, something I'd been into since I was fifteen.

Again I looked at the empty bed. There had to be something the matter with me. Other girls were getting it. They had no trouble. But not me. I had even gotten a new birth control pill that had come out last year, thinking it would free me of inhibitions. But it didn't help.

I looked good, I knew that. Everybody told me that I was sexy, but nobody made a move, nobody touched. Something in me was putting them off. Even Beau Drake, who fucked everything that came his way, never laid a hand on me.

I remembered one afternoon when, over coffee between the matinee and evening performance, he'd gone into a vivid description of what he would do to me if we were alone. It was so vivid that when I got back to my dressing room my panties were soaking wet. I eased my tensions while taking a shower but went through the whole evening performance in a state of sexual excitement.

By the time I got home that night I thought my cunt was on fire. The note from Walter on the night table said he was having a late dinner at Twenty One with George Fox and a producer.

I couldn't wait. I took off my clothes, stretched out naked on the bed and reached into the drawer of the night table for the little "Green Hornet"—our name for the vibrator. I slipped my hand through the strap so that the motor rested on the back of my hand and plugged it in. The soft familiar sound filled the room and I put my hand between my legs.

I don't know how long I lay there riding the waves but suddenly I became aware that Walter had come into the room. I opened my eyes. He was standing looking down at me with a curious expression on his face.

"Walter . . . I—"

"Don't stop," he said.

"I . . . want . . ." I couldn't finish, as another orgasm flowed through me.

He knelt beside the bed, his face very close to me, but not touching me. "What turned you on?" he asked.

"I don't know. Thinking of you. I . . . wanted—"

"What did you want? A big stiff prick?"

"No."

He ignored my answer. "A big stiff prick? One like Beau Drake's?"

At the mention of the name, I came again.

He didn't miss the reaction. "So that's it," he said softly.

"No, no. I want you. Give me your cock, Walter, please."

He got to his feet slowly and stood looking down at me.

I pulled at his zipper and took him out. His penis was soft and fragile. I kissed it gently and took it in my mouth. But no matter what I did nothing happened.

After a moment he took my head between his hands. "I'm sorry," he said. "I'm tired and I drank too much."

I didn't speak.

"Sometimes I feel I'm too old for you," he said. "I wouldn't blame you if you took another man."

"No, Walter, no!" I buried my face against his trousers. "I only want you!" I began to cry.

Absently he stroked my hair. "It's okay," he said. "I understand."

But he really didn't. He only knew enough to manipulate my own sense of guilt. And in the end even I came to understand that. Shit. I looked at the empty bed, then touched myself, feeling the tiny nerve endings. My buddy the Green Hornet called to me from the night table: Hey, baby! I'm always ready, whenever you are.

I spoke aloud. "But you're not real. You're not alive."

Don't quibble, baby. You can't have everything.

"Why not?" I asked. "I want everything."

That ain't human either, baby.

I shook my head. I had to be going around the bend, holding a conversation with a vibrator. Suddenly I was alone. The apartment was empty. Maryjane had left me.

I got out of bed, lit a cigarette and went to the living room. I looked out the window but there was nothing to see except the apartment houses across the street. It was not anything like Central Park South, where I had a view of the park and the city stretching out into the night.

I looked at the clock. Two in the morning. The trouble with being alone was there was no one to talk to. I wondered if the darkened windows of the city held other people like me. Alone with no one to talk to.

It was eleven o'clock on the Coast. Guy would still be awake. I put in a call. But his room didn't answer. He had not returned from dinner.

I sat there with the telephone in my hand and without thinking further dialed a number. By the second ring I had changed my mind and was about to hang up.

"I'm sorry," I apologized. "Did I wake you?"

"No," John said. "I was reading."

"Your offer still open?"

"Yes."

"You don't think I'm crazy, do you?"

"No."

"I suddenly felt as if I had to get out of the city."

"I'm glad," he said quietly.

"When are we leaving?"

"The noon flight on Sunday," he said. "If you'll be downstairs I'll pick you up at ten-thirty."

"Will you make a reservation for me at the Beverly Hills Hotel?"

"What for?" he asked. "You're staying with me."

"I don't want to put you to any trouble."

"It's no trouble at all. I've got a big house and a housekeeper that has nothing to do."

When I put down the telephone my heart was pounding as if I had just walked up five flights of stairs. But when I went back into the bedroom and lay back on the pillows I slept like a baby.

Chapter 10

THE HOUSE WAS on a hill in Malibu a few miles north of the more exclusive colony. A narrow staircase, cut into the rocks, led to the beach a hundred-odd feet below. The beach itself was a narrow cove between two rock formations, making it almost inaccessible to the wandering bather. A pool surrounded by flowers was built into the small garden which hung out over the ocean. Once in the pool, it felt as if one were swimming in the sky.

A studio car met us at the airport and drove us to the house. We were greeted at the door by his housekeeper, a small smiling broad-faced woman of Mexican-Indian descent. She showed no surprise at my arrival. He said something to her in Spanish; she nodded and led me to my room.

A corner room with an ocean view on two sides, it was decorated in Mexican Mediterranean. The bed was Hollywood king sized and looked as if it were intended to sleep six people. She placed my suitcase on a small table against the wall and said something to me which I didn't understand.

As soon as she had left, John appeared in the doorway. "Do you like it?"

"I love it. It's just beautiful."

"It's simple," he said, sounding pleased. "But I did it all myself. It's just what I always wanted."

"Have you had it long?"

"Two years. Since my separation. My wife and the children have the house in Bel Air."

I looked at him.

"I had to tell you that. I wanted you to know how things are."

I appreciated his honesty. "Thank you."

"The telephone, radio and remote TV control are on the side of the bed." He stared toward a small door at the side of the room. "The bathroom is over here."

I went through the door he opened for me. It was a large bathroom, double sink, sunken tub with built-in Jacuzzi, shower stall and bidet. I eyed the other door which was opposite the one we entered.

"That leads to the other guest room," he said. "But for all intents and purposes it's yours. I had it built this way because the kids share it when they stay over."

"How many do you have?"

"Three. Two boys and a girl. The girl is fourteen, the twin boys are twelve. You're in her room."

I nodded and followed him back into the bedroom. He turned to me. "I suggest you take a nap before dinner. The time change is always tiring."

"I don't feel tired," I said.

"You will. It always hits me at dinnertime." He walked to the door. "We'll have dinner at eight o'clock if that's okay with you."

"Perfect."

He smiled. "I'll see you then."

When I opened my eyes the room was bathed in purple and violet light. I checked my watch. It was still set on New York time. Ten o'clock. I reset it and got out of bed. He had been right. The time change had caught up to me.

I went into the bathroom and turned on the water in the tub. I stared at the water, pale and sparkling green, spilling from the spout and put some lemon-scented Vitabath into the water. I stripped and got into the tub just as the automatic Jacuzzi went on.

I gave myself up to the currents. One of the jets seemed aimed right between my legs. It was lovely, even better than the Green Hornet.

Suddenly I was aware of the phone buzzing in the bathroom. I reached out of the tub and took it. "Hello."

"Are you awake?"

"Yes, I'm in the tub."

"No rush. Dinner will be ready when you are."

I laughed. "I may decide to have dinner in the tub."

"You like it?"

"The Jacuzzi is too much. I may decide to marry it."

He laughed. "Enjoy. See you in a little bit."

I put back the phone but by then the water had turned cool so I got out. I took one of the giant-sized towels and rubbed myself briskly. Everything in California was large—the beds, the tubs, even the towels. I wondered if it signified anything. I gave up thinking about it, got into a pair of slacks and a shirt and went downstairs.

The table with a salad in a large wooden bowl in the center was already set next to the open patio door. Outside a charcoal fire was glowing in the barbecue.

I stopped in the center of the room, sniffing. "What's that?"

"Baked potatoes in charcoal. I hope you like them."

"Roast mickeys?" I said. "I love them."

He smiled and went to the bar. He turned on the Osterizer. "I have two specialties," he said. "I make the best Margaritas and the best steaks in the world." He pulled the cocktail glasses from the ice bucket and quickly rimmed them with salt, then stopped the machine and filled the glasses to the brim.

"Welcome to California," he said as I took the glass from him.

The Margarita went down like liquid fire, sending a warm glow through me. "Unbelievable," I said. He couldn't know I had never drunk a Margarita before.

"I'll put the steaks on," he said. "By the time we finish two of these, they'll be ready."

As if on cue, the housekeeper came into the room carrying two huge steaks on a wooden platter which she handed over to John. "Buenas noches," she said.

I smiled and nodded as she left.

"She usually has Sunday off," he said. "She only stayed to see that everything was right."

I followed him out to the barbecue and watched him

put the steaks on the grill. There was a hissing sound as the fat hit the coals.

"The steaks have been marinated in oil, vinegar and garlic," he explained. "Gives them a special flavor. Like it rare?"

I nodded.

"Good. So do I."

By the time the steaks were ready I felt good, light-headed but good. I sighed with relief as I sat down at the table.

I watched him solemnly as he lit the candles and poured the wine. The wine glass was almost too heavy for me to lift. After the tequila the red wine was soft to the taste. "Lovely," I said, putting the wine glass down carefully.

"I think I overdid the Margaritas," he said.

"No."

"Are you all right?" he asked.

"I'm okay," I said quickly. "Just a little drunk."

"You'll be all right after you eat something," he said.

He was right about that. The steak, salad and baked potatoes were delicious and by the time we got to the coffee my head was clear.

"Do you smoke?" he asked after we'd finished our coffee.

I nodded.

"I have some great grass. Acapulco Gold. It goes great with cognac." He looked at me. "Feel up to it?"

"Lead on. You've already seen me drunk, you might as well see me stoned."

I followed him to the couch. He opened a wooden cigarette box on the coffee table. "I've got a few J's already rolled," he said.

He lit the joint, then passed it to me while he went to get the brandy snifters and the bottle.

I took a big hit and let the smoke slowly out. I nodded. "Mellow."

"The best," he said, taking it from me. He hit it again and gave me my brandy. I watched him chase the smoke down his throat with the cognac. "Try it like that."

I followed his example. It was dynamite. In a second I was up there. Suddenly it all seemed very funny. I began to laugh.

"Que pasa?" he said.

"I still don't believe it."

"Believe what?"

"I'm here. You. Me."

He took the J from my fingers. Hit, sip, back to me. "It's not hard to believe," he said.

"I've never gone anywhere with a man before except my husband," I said. "And here I've flown all the way across the country with you."

"Are you having second thoughts?"

"No."

"I don't want you to."

"I don't have any." I passed the joint back to him and giggled. "I'm high as a kite already."

He laughed. "Feelin' good is how to say it."

"I'm feelin' good." I leaned against the back cushions. "You sure know how to treat a girl."

He didn't speak.

"I'm so relaxed," I said. "I feel all loose and lazy."

"Whenever you're tired, you can go to bed. Don't worry about me."

"You're a nice man, John Styles."

"Thank you."

"A perfect gentleman."

He didn't speak.

Suddenly I was warm. I looked outside at the pool and got to my feet. "Can I go for a swim?"

"Anything you want. There are bikinis in the small cabana. I think you'll find one that fits."

I met his eyes. "Do I have to?"

He shook his head silently.

I went outside, got out of my clothes at the side of the pool and dived in. The water was cool and refreshing. When I came up, he was still inside sitting on the couch. "Come on in," I called. "It's great."

He came out, the joint still in his mouth, undressed and slipped into the water.

"Isn't it great?" I asked. Without waiting for an answer I took the J from his lips and put in my mouth. Then I went over on my back, sucking the smoke into my lungs. The sky above was diamond-studded velvet. "Hey! This is really floating."

Inside the house the telephone began to ring. I treaded water and looked at him. The phone rang again. He started to lift himself from the pool.

"You don't have to answer it," I said.

"I've been expecting the call," he said. "It's my A.D. to give me the schedule for tomorrow."

I watched him get out of the pool and run dripping to the telephone in the cabana. He was on the phone almost fifteen minutes. When he came back I had finished the joint. But it didn't seem to matter. My high was almost gone.

"The call is for six o'clock tomorrow morning," he said.

I stared at him. "You want to go to bed?"

"I'd better," he said. "Or else I'll be in a fog all day."

I got out of the pool and into another one of those giant California towels, which he wrapped around me as carefully as if I were a baby. I picked up my clothes while he wrapped a towel around his waist, then followed him up the stairs.

I stopped at my door and turned to him. He leaned forward and kissed my cheek. "Sleep well," he said. "I left the keys in the convertible for you. Anything else you want just ask Maria. I'll be leaving about five o'clock so I'll see you when I get home in the evening."

I stood in the doorway, watching him walk down the hall to his room and close the door behind him.

I went back to the bathroom, dropped the towel, lit a cigarette and stared at myself in the mirror. There had to be something wrong with me. I didn't understand it. Cool was cool but his cool was too much. It had to be me.

"Damn!" I said angrily to myself in the mirror as I dragged on the cigarette and noticed that my hand was shaking.

I went back into the bedroom and took the Green Hornet from my suitcase, then looked around the bed for an outlet. I finally found it behind the giant headboard. There was no way I could get to it. That did it.

I threw the vibrator on the bed and walked out of my room and down the hall. I opened his door without knocking. He came out of the bathroom, the towel still around his waist, and stared at me.

In the mirror on the far wall I caught a glimpse of myself standing naked in his doorway. "Is there anything wrong with me?" I demanded. I didn't wait for him to reply. "Or am I supposed to believe that you flew me three thousand miles across the country in order not to fuck me in California?"

Chapter 11

INSIDE THERE WAS a small light glowing from the lamp in the far corner of the room. Outside there was the blackness of the night and the quiet pounding of the surf. I was on the side of the bed near the open window; he was toward the wall, half hidden in the shadow.

"What time is it?" I asked.

"Four o'clock." The tip of his cigarette glowed in the dark. "Time for me to get up."

"I'm sorry."

"What for?"

"I kept you awake. And you have to go to work."

He was silent for a moment. "I'll be okay. A shower and a red can work wonders."

"Funny thing, I don't feel sleepy. I was so tired when we got off the plane. And now I'm not tired at all."

He smiled. "Youth."

"Is that all it is?"

"I don't know."

"Is it always like this?"

He looked at me but I couldn't see the expression in his eyes. "What do you mean?"

"The first time. All night."

"No."

I reached and took the cigarette from him, then I laughed and gave it back.

"Why did you laugh?" he asked.

"Habit. I really didn't want the cigarette but I used to take Walter's away from him pretending that I did because he wasn't supposed to smoke."

"Oh."

"He had emphysema."

He got out of bed without speaking.

"You're not angry with me because I spoke about Walter, are you?"

"No."

I sat up in the bed. "Are you sorry that I came out with you?"

"Are you sorry that you did?"

"No. But you didn't answer."

"I'm not sorry."

"Was I okay? I mean was it good for you?"

He smiled. "You don't hear me complaining."

"I mean it. I want it to be as good for you as it is for me."

The smile grew broader. "If it got any better I'd wind up in a hospital in less than a week."

"I never knew it could be so good. I didn't want to stop."

"I kind of thought it had been a long time for you. How long since your divorce?"

"Going on five months."

"That can be a long time for a girl as sexual as you are. There's been no one else during that time?"

"No." I didn't tell him there hadn't been much during my marriage either. Walter had his own routines. And I didn't know any better.

"I'd better get started," he said, going toward the bathroom.

"I'll go downstairs and make coffee."

"Know where the kitchen is?"

"I'll find it."

I went back to my room, put on a robe and went downstairs. The housekeeper was gone. The kitchen was as neat as a pin and the coffeepot was ready to be plugged in. I opened the refrigerator and by the time he came down I had bacon and eggs and toast on the table.

"You didn't have to do that," he said.

"I wanted to."

He didn't eat very much but I ate like a truckdriver. I was famished.

"What are you going to do today?" he asked.

"I don't know. Sleep a little. Get some sun maybe."

"Do you want to eat out or in?"

"Let's eat in and go to bed early."

He smiled.

I felt myself blush. "You'll have to get some rest. Living on reds isn't the best idea in the world."

"Okay." He got to his feet. "I should be back about eight. I have to look at the rushes tonight."

"I'll be here." I started to get up.

"Stay there. I'll see you later."

I watched him leave, then finished my coffee, stacked the dishes in the washer and went up to my room to bed. I crashed the moment my head touched the pillow.

The telephone beside the bed was buzzing, buzzing, buzzing. I rolled over, opened my eyes, then closed them against the burning sunlight. The telephone kept on buzzing. I looked at the flashing light and finally I picked it up. "Yes."

"Señorita, para usted." The housekeeper's voice was pleasant.

"Thank you." I stared at the phone for a moment, thinking it must be Mother who couldn't wait for me to call her. I pushed the button down.

It wasn't my mother. It was Harry Gregg. "What are you doing out there?" he asked abruptly.

"Sleeping when you woke me up," I said sarcastically. "How'd you get my number?"

"For Christ's sake! It's three o'clock in the afternoon out there. What the hell were you doing all night?"

"Fucking, if it's any of your business!" I snapped. I was beginning to feel that everything they said about agents was true. Once they got you a job they felt they owned you. "How'd you find out where I was?"

"Your service told me you were out of town but they didn't know where, so I called your mother. She told me." His voice dropped to a conspiratorial whisper. "I just got a call from Fox's office. He wanted to know where you were. Your ex is looking for you."

"So?"

"I didn't tell him. Do you think your mother might?"

"No." Not my mother. She wasn't about to admit that her little girl would go off across the country with a man. And even if she did, what difference did it make? Walter had no claims on me. "Is that why you called?"

"No." His voice returned to normal. "I got you another job. Just as well you're in California."

"I don't get it."

"Got you a guest shot on *The Virginian*. They want to see you over at Universal this afternoon. Thirty-five hundred for the week."

"How did that happen?"

"They saw some of the film you did in New York last week."

"It's late," I said. "I'll have to do the whole works. Hair. Makeup. Everything. I won't make it. How about tomorrow?"

"They insist on today. They called me early this morning to get you on a plane. They said they'll wait at the studio until eight o'clock for you."

I was silent.

"It's a good shot. Universal does a lot of film. If they like you, they'll keep you working."

"Okay. Who do I have to see?"

He gave me the information and when he was finished his voice became conspiratorial again. "What do I tell Fox? By morning he'll know you've been to Universal."

"You think of an excuse. I don't give a damn what he tells Walter."

"You better. George will make it rough for you if Walter gets angry."

"Tell him the studio got to me before you did and that I was on my way out there." I put down the phone and then got angry. I didn't like being intimidated. I decided to call him back. "Is there anything wrong?" he asked as he came on the wire.

"Yes. I don't like being pushed. By Walter. George. You. Or anybody. And I don't owe any of them explanations."

"Wait a minute! Don't get mad at me. I'm on your side."

"Okay. Then tell them the truth. And if they don't like it, they can go fuck themselves!"

I felt better when I put down the telephone. I got dressed and was at the studio by six-thirty.

In the course of the next three hours about seven men came into the producer's office to talk to me. At the end of that time the only thing they didn't know was that I had a beauty mark high on my left buttock. Finally they all sat around the office in a semicircle looking at me.

The big man whose office it was finally spoke. "I think she'll do. What do you think, fellers?"

There was a chorus of agreement.

"What kind of a part is it?" I asked finally.

"A very good part," the big man said. "Exciting, if you know what I mean. A real acting part."

"Can I read it?"

"Of course you can. We'll give you a script first thing in the morning."

"I'm supposed to start work in the morning."

"That's right."

"How am I supposed to learn my lines?"

"You'll have time. Your first setup isn't until the afternoon. You can read it while you're in Costume and Makeup."

"Why can't I have it now?"

An uncomfortable look crossed his face. "I don't think we have the final scripts back from mimeo."

"I can read one of the others. At least I'd get an idea of the character I'm supposed to play."

"It's a good part," he said defensively. "Don't you take my word for it?"

"I take your word for it."

"That's a good girl." He got to his feet. "Now you be here at seven tomorrow morning for Costume."

"No."

His chin dropped. "What do you mean?"

"What I said. No. I think I'm entitled to read the part to see if it is something I can and want to do before I agree to it."

"Of course you are, but we have an emergency here. We have to go on the floor tomorrow and it has to be settled tonight."

"Then get me a script. I read quickly."

His eyes hardened. "You're pretty independent, aren't you, Miss Randall?"

"Not at all. I just feel I'm entitled to the same consideration that you demanded. You wouldn't agree to give me the part until I came out here and gave you all a chance to look me over. Well, I'm here because I understand that. As I see it, it's a matter of common courtesy."

He stared at me for a moment, then smiled and turned to the man next to him. "Okay, Dan, get her a script.

"Okay, fellers, the meeting's over," the big man said.

As they filed from the room I looked at the man behind the desk and said, "I can go outside to read if you have work to do."

"It's okay."

I read it quickly. My instincts had been right. The part was for that of an Indian girl and I would be all wrong for it. It was one of those roles with a lot of scenes but very little dialogue. As a matter of fact I didn't know why they even needed the girl in the script at all. She served no real purpose and it would have been better if they had left her out.

"I don't think so," I said, getting to my feet.

He stared up at me challengingly. "It's not much of a part but you're on camera a lot."

"I don't even have black hair or black eyes."

"No problem," he said. "A wig and contact lenses will take care of that."

"No, thank you."

"Think of the exposure. Twenty million people will see you in one night."

"I wouldn't be comfortable in the part."

"It's a great opportunity. Don't pass it up. There's a lot of work out here. Do you know how many girls would give their ass to be standing where you are?"

"I have an idea. And I'm willing to bet that many of them would be more right for the part than I am."

"But I want you. I backed myself into a corner to get you for this. I think you could give it something special."

"Thank you. I genuinely appreciate that."

"Look, it's late. Why don't we have a bite of dinner and talk it over?"

"I'm sorry. I have a date."

"Then you won't do it?"

"No."

I placed the script on the desk in front of him. "Can I get a taxi?"

He looked at me as if he had already forgotten that I was there. "Yes. Just ask my secretary. She'll call one for you."

"Thank you. Good night."

He nodded silently and I left the office.

I didn't get back to the beach until ten o'clock. By that time everything had gone wrong.

Chapter 12

THE A.D. who had been on the picture with us in New York answered the door. "Hello, JeriLee," he said.

I looked at him. In New York it had been Miss Randall. "Hello," I said, trying but failing to remember his name. I went into the house and started down the steps to the main floor.

"Go easy on him," he warned. "The boss had a rough day."

There was something about his voice that implied that we understood each other, that we were allies.

"Everything was a shambles. I don't think we got two minutes of film today. Then when he came home and you weren't here he hit the roof."

"What for? I left a note saying where I went."

"I don't know whether he got it," he said.

"I'll explain it to him." I glanced at him. "Coming down?"

"No. I was just on my way home."

"Okay. Good night."

John was seated on the couch with a drink in his hand. He looked up as I came into the room.

I bent over and kissed his cheek. "Hello," I said. "I'm sorry I'm so late."

"Where the hell were you?"

"Universal. I left a note."

"I never got it," he snapped. "What the hell were you doing out there?"

"I explained it in the note. They called me for a job."

"Here?"

I was becoming annoyed by his childishness. "No. They sent a carrier pigeon."

"Who else did you give my number to?"

"I didn't give your number to anybody. My agent figured it out for himself."

"Then how come the whole damn world has it?" he demanded. "In the two hours I've been home I've gotten half a dozen phone calls for you. Your mother, your ex-husband, your agent twice and Universal twice."

"I didn't give it to anybody," I repeated.

"Then how come everybody has it?"

"I don't know. I'm sorry. I didn't mean to be a bother."

"Fuck it!" He got up and went to the bar and refilled his glass. "This is all I needed."

I watched him take another belt of the drink without speaking. I had never seen him like this.

"By now it will be all over town that you're out here with me."

"What difference does it make? Nobody has any strings on us."

"On you maybe. But you forgot that I'm still married."

"You said you were separated."

"That's not divorced. I've always been careful not to give my wife a chance to nail me."

"I'm sorry. I didn't mean to put you on a spot."

"You weren't thinking. I told you what the score was."

"Sure you did. After I got here. Why didn't you tell me in New York?" I answered without waiting for his reply. "Because you knew damn well I wouldn't come."

"I didn't expect the whole world to be calling you."

I stared at him for a moment. "I think you ought to call me a cab," I said. "It would be better for both of us if I checked into a hotel."

Just then the telephone rang. John picked it up, then handed it to me. "For you."

It was Harry. "What the hell did you do out there at Universal? They're boiling mad."

"I did nothing," I said. "I just told them I never heard of a blue-eyed Indian."

"They want you anyway. They're changing the part

so that you're the adopted daughter of the chief, the only survivor of a wagon train who has been brought up as his own."

"The part still stinks."

"They got the hots for you. They also promised to give you some other jobs if you do this."

"Sorry."

"What the hell's got into you?" he shouted in exasperation. "Just a few weeks ago you were begging for a job. You said you needed the money. Now that you've worked two weeks, you're suddenly nigger rich!"

"I'm not going to do it just to satisfy some producer's ego. They can find some other girl to run around in a torn Indian shirt with her boobs hanging out."

"It's half past one in the morning here and I'm bushed," he said. "I'm going home to bed. You think about it and I'll call you in the morning."

The moment I put down the telephone it rang again. "Hello," John barked. Then his voice changed abruptly. "How's it goin', Chad?"

He listened, then glanced at me before he spoke. "You're absolutely right, Chad, she's quite a girl. A good little actress too."

I realized he was talking about me and listened to the rest of the conversation with a kind of stunned fascination. It was almost as if I were his property.

"I don't blame you one bit. She sounds perfect for the part. . . . Of course I'll talk to her, but you know these New York actresses. They have their own ideas. . . . Sure, she's right here. I'll put her on." He held the phone out to me.

"Who is it?" I asked.

"Chad Taylor."

"Who is he?"

"For Christ's sake, you spent the afternoon in his office at U.I."

I took the telephone. "Yes?"

"Did you talk to Harry Gregg, JeriLee?"

When I left his office I was still Miss Randall. Apparently we were now old friends. "Yes, Mr. Taylor."

"Did he tell you how we solved your problem?"

I hadn't known it was my problem. "Yes, Mr. Taylor."

"It's a hell of an idea. What do you think?"

"I still think the part stinks, Mr. Taylor."

"JeriLee, what makes you so difficult?"

"I'm not being difficult, Mr. Taylor. I just know what I can and what I can't do."

"If you'll keep an open mind about it," he said almost pleadingly. "I'll have a revised script for you to read in the morning."

Suddenly I was tired. I had enough hassling for one day. "Okay."

"Can you come in around eleven o'clock? I'll send a car out for you."

"Don't bother. I can get a cab." I put down the telephone.

"You ought to do it," John said.

"Why? Did you read it?"

"No, but the exposure would be good for you. The public will get to know your name. Maybe that way I can get my brother to increase the size of your billing."

Another lesson. I was learning a lot today. Exposure is good because it helps the marketability of other products. Since there was nothing more for me to say, I turned to leave.

"Where are you going?" he asked.

"To pack."

"Wait a minute. What's the rush?"

"I don't want you to get nailed," I said sarcastically.

He made a deprecatory gesture. "I was just a little steamed. Debbie and I have an understanding. She doesn't expect me to lead a virginal life."

"Oh, shit." I said disgustedly.

"God, what a bitch day I had," he said. "Nothing went right."

I didn't answer.

"I'll make us a couple of Margaritas and we'll take off our shoes and relax." He went back to the bar. "Maria's made arroz con pollo. You never tasted anythink so good in your life."

I still didn't speak.

He turned on the blender. Its soft hum buzzed through the room. "You don't know what I went through."

"It's not easy."

He missed the sarcasm. "We'll have dinner and go right to bed."

"Will I have time for a bath first?"

"Of course, but that's a funny question. Why do you ask?"

"I feel dirty," I said.

He didn't understand that either.

He came into my room about an hour after I had gone to bed. "I've been waiting for you," he said.

"You have another early call in the morning," I said. "I thought it would be better if you got some sleep."

"I can't sleep, I'm too uptight."

"I'm sorry."

He came into the room and closed the door behind him. He sat down on the edge of the bed. "What are you doing?" he asked.

"Nothing," I said. "Just lying here. Thinking."

"About what?"

"Things. Nothing special."

"You don't want to talk, do you?"

I reached for a cigarette and saw in his eyes the reflected light of the match. "Do you?" I asked.

"You're angry with me."

"No."

"What is it then?"

"Things just aren't right. It's not going the way I thought it would."

"You shouldn't have gone out. We were okay yesterday."

It was exactly the kind of thing Walter would say. I didn't answer.

"Yes, I would have had a chance to absorb it. I wouldn't have been taken by surprise."

"I didn't think I was doing anything wrong."

"After all, you are my guest. I brought you out here."

I was beginning to understand. It made some kind of sense. Not real sense. But crazy sense. It had something to do with property rights. Because he had paid the freight, I belonged to him. He was more like Walter than I had thought.

"Do you understand what I mean?"

"Yes."

"Good," he said in a satisfied voice. He got to his feet. "Now, let's put it all behind us and go to bed."

"I am in bed."

An edge of anger crept into his voice. "I don't like to be used."

"I'll leave you a check for the plane ticket before I go in the morning," I said, thinking that I'd been more used than he.

"Don't bother," he said in a cutting voice. "I've given more money to a whore for a one-night stand."

The door slammed behind him. I fought back the tears, too hurt to be angry. It wasn't fair. It just wasn't fair. Why did it have to be like this?

I didn't go to Universal in the morning. Instead I took the red eye back to New York that night.

Chapter 13

HARRY SAW ME through the glass partitions that enclosed his office and rose to his feet. He shook his head. "You did it. You really did it."

"I thought it over," I said. "I didn't want the job no matter what they said."

"You fucked yourself. In only two days you managed to do what would take most people a lifetime to accomplish." A curious note of wonder entered his voice. "You really fucked yourself."

"All I did was turn down a job. I even called the studio and left word that I wasn't coming in."

"Jesus," he said. "Universal's putting out the word that you're impossible to deal with and then I get a frantic call from Tony Styles that you screwed up his picture."

"Tony Styles? I never even saw him!"

"He says you fucked up his brother's head and he had to close down the picture for two days so that John could stay in bed. He says he's going to cut your part down to nothing even if he has to shoot some of the scenes over with another girl."

"I don't get it."

"What happened between you two?"

"We just didn't agree, so I left."

"Jesus," he repeated. He picked up a sheet of paper. "This memo got here just before you did. George wants to see me about you."

"If George wants to talk to me all he has to do is say so."

"You don't understand. You're not his direct responsibility anymore. You're mine. He tells me whatever he wants to do or say and I tell you."

"What does that mean?"

"George doesn't like to make waves," he said. "George is Mr. Nice Guy with everybody—Universal, Styles, your ex, even God himself."

"So?"

"So we're in trouble. George must have picked up some of the flap and he doesn't want anybody mad at the agency."

"Does that mean he's going to drop me?"

"I don't know," he said. "But if you have any friends he will listen to, now is the time to get to them."

"But we have a contract."

"Read the fine print. They can drop you any time they want."

I was silent.

"Your ex. Would he put in a good word for you?"

"I don't want to go to him," I said. "It took me too long to get out from under."

"Any other friends?"

I thought for a moment. "Guy Jackson?"

He shook his head. "George hates him. He signed with another agency after George broke his ass to get him."

"Then there's nobody."

Slowly he got to his feet. "I might as well get it over with."

"Do you want me to wait for you?"

"What the hell." He shrugged. "Might as well get it hot from the oven."

By the time he got back half an hour later I had gone through the rest of my package of cigarettes and was beginning to work on his. He closed the door, went behind his desk and collapsed in his chair. "Jesus," he said. It seemed to be his favorite remark of the day.

"Okay," I said. "Let's have it."

"They're dropping your acting contract but they're keeping you for writing even though I tried to get him to drop that one too."

"I thought you were my friend," I said sarcastically. "Half a loaf is better than none."

"You got a lot to learn. If they let you out of the writing contract, you would have a lever to get another agent. You have the play, which could bring him some income. But this way we keep all the money and you got no muscle."

I stared at him. "That's not fair."

"I didn't say it was."

"I'll go up and see him."

"It won't do any good. You'll never get past his secretary. George has that down to a fine art."

"Is there anything I can do?"

"Only one thing I can think of, but you won't like that either."

"What's that?"

"Eat humble pie," he said. "Call Chad Taylor out at Universal. Tell him it was that time of the month or something female like that and that you thought it over and decided you would do it. I happen to know they haven't cast that part yet."

"You're sure?"

"Sure as I'm sitting here."

"Is that your idea or is that what George told you to tell me?"

I could see the flush creep over his face. "George's."

"And if I don't do that, I'm finished here?"

He nodded silently.

I felt trapped. They were playing a game and all of them were on the same team. There was no way I could win. "Okay," I said finally. "Get him on the phone for me."

I was a better actress than I thought. I not only ate humble pie, I rubbed my face in it. And all the way to the Coast on the plane that evening I had a sick feeling in my stomach to prove it.

They had a car to pick me up at the airport and take me to the hotel. Even before I'd got my baggage the driver gave me a note from Taylor.

> Dear JeriLee,
>
> Keep dinner open. Will be by at eight-thirty with the script. Dress for Chasen's. Regards.
>
> Chad.

Short and to the point. There was no mistaking who was in charge. By now it didn't matter. I was so tired all I wanted to do was to get into bed and sleep.

The driver took me to a hotel-motel called the Regency on Hollywood Boulevard between Fairfax and Laurel Canyon. I had a small two-room suite on the second floor overlooking the pool.

"We put lots of New York people out here," the driver explained. "There's a short cut to the studio over Laurel Canyon."

I thanked him as he placed my luggage on a small rack. As soon as he left I took off my clothes and closed the drapes to the sun. Then I turned down the big king-sized bed and called the operator to leave a wakeup call for seven-forty-five.

I was just drifting off when the telephone rang. It was Chad Taylor. "Everything all right?"

"Perfect."

"Good." He sounded pleased. "Dress up tonight. There'll be some important press people there."

"Okay."

"See you about eight-thirty." He rang off.

I turned over and closed my eyes when the telephone rang again. I reached for it wearily. "Hello."

"JeriLee? This is John." There was no sign of anger in his voice. It was as if nothing had happened.

"Yes."

"I'm glad you came to your senses. I was beginning to worry about you."

"I'm okay."

"I thought we might have dinner. I remembered you liked the steaks on Sunday."

"I have a date. Mr. Taylor is bringing the script over this evening."

"What are you doing afterwards?"

"Going to sleep. I'm wiped out." Flying back and forth across the country wasn't my idea of fun.

"I have to see you, even if it's just for a minute."

"We're going to Chasen's. He said there will be press there. I don't know what time I'll get back here."

"We have to get some things straightened out."

"It'll keep until tomorrow. If I don't get some rest, I'll die."

"Okay," he said finally. "Meanwhile is there anything I can do for you?"

"No." Then I changed my mind. "Yes, there is one thing. Tell your brother to stop bad-mouthing me all over the country."

I put down the phone but by that time I was too keyed up for sleep. I popped a Librium and waited for it to slow me down. Meanwhile I ran the tub and got into it. I felt the lassitude come back. Quickly I dried myself and jumped back into bed. This time I slept. But not for long. In less than an hour the telephone rang with my wakeup call.

In a fog, I popped a red and stood under an ice cold

shower. Then I began the slow job of getting myself together.

The doorbell rang at exactly eight-thirty. I opened the door in a robe. "Come in, Mr. Taylor. I'll be just a few more minutes."

"I brought the script with me."

"Make yourself comfortable," I said, heading back to the bedroom.

He followed me to the door. "My flowers get here yet?"

"I haven't seen them."

"They should have been here when you arrived. Damn secretary. Mind if I use your phone?"

"Help yourself."

He disappeared back into the living room while I went into the bathroom. I put on two pair of false eyelashes, penciled in the liner quickly and checked the mirror. Not bad for a quick job.

He was standing in the doorway when I returned to the bedroom. "She says she ordered them."

"Don't worry. They'll get here. Thanks anyway."

"Nobody does anything right these days. You gotta keep on their ass." He didn't move from the doorway and something told me he was not about to. I opened the closet door and stood behind it while I slipped into my dress. It was the long black silk that clung to my body. When I came out from behind the door he gave a long low whistle.

"Not bad."

"I feel a mess."

"You don't look it."

"Thanks." I pulled the white angora stole from my bag and put it around my shoulders. "I'm ready now."

He looked at me critically.

"Anything wrong?" I asked.

"Do you have a fur?"

"I have, but I like the look of the white angora with the black silk."

"Wear the fur. This is Chasen's."

I stared at him for a minute, then took off the stole and put on the short chinchilla jacket.

"That's better," he said. "Class."

I noticed the script on the table in front of the couch as we went to the door.

"Do you want to take it with us?" I asked. "We can discuss it during dinner."

He shook his head. "Too many people there. We'll go over it when we get back." He didn't give me a chance to answer. "The car's right in front."

"How do you like it?" he asked as he opened the door for me.

"Beautiful."

He smiled. "It's a classic. A fifty-five Bentley Continental convertible. They only made fifteen like this. There are only five that are still in use. This is one of them."

"It's really something," I said.

It was Tuesday night and Chasen's was jumping. But we had a large table near the door where everyone coming in or leaving could see us. I noticed there were only two places set.

"I sort of expected other people from what you said," I said as I sat down.

"The restaurant is loaded," he said. "No place to talk shop. People will be stopping by. You'll see."

He was right about that. He couldn't have displayed me any better if he had put me in Macy's window.

"Deviled ribs is the best thing on the menu. But since they always run out I ordered some in advance, along with a side dish of chili. How does that sound?"

"Good to me," I said. By that time I would have eaten the tablecloth.

He signaled the waiter. First we had the cracked Dungeness crab with the mustard and tomato side sauces, then the ribs. Between the wines and the red I had popped my head was spinning. Somehow I managed to keep my conversation halfway intelligible, but it probably wouldn't have made any difference if I had gone totally dumb. He never stopped talking about his career and the fact that Universal would never have made it without him.

For dessert we each had three Irish coffees and by the time we got up to leave at one o'clock in the morning I could hardly manage to stand straight. As soon as we got back to the suite, he plopped himself down on the couch and picked up the script. "Now we can go to work," he said.

I couldn't believe my ears.

"We improved it," he said. "But that's not the important thing. I have other plans for you. Big plans. Do you understand?"

I could only shake my head. I didn't understand.

"The minute you walked into that office I knew you were the girl I had been looking for." He paused to let the importance of his statement sink in. "You know, I'm not staying on this show. I'm preparing a feature. A big picture. The deal's already closed."

"Congratulations," I managed to say.

He nodded. "And you're the girl. The lead. Today's girl. Feisty. Tough. Sexy. Intelligent. That's why it was important that I get you for this show. I had to show them what I could do with you."

I didn't speak. My head was beginning to buzz.

He opened the script. "Now, let's go over this."

The hammers were really beating my scull now. "Chad," I said. "Mr. Taylor."

He looked up at me with a puzzled expression.

"It's not that I'm not grateful, I really am," I said, speaking as clearly as I could. "But if you don't let me get to bed, I'm going to pass out right here."

His expression cleared and he rose with a rueful smile. "Of course. I forgot the kind of a day you've had."

I followed him to the door. "I'll see you in the morning," he said.

I was beginning to feel dizzy.

"Don't worry about getting to the studio. I'll have a car and driver here for you at seven o'clock."

I managed to nod.

He gave me a quick peck on the cheek. "Good night,"

he said, then drew back and looked at me. "The next time we go to dinner don't wear a dress with so much decolletage. I had a hard-on all night and half the time I didn't know what the hell I was saying."

I closed the door and felt the nausea rising. I just about made it to the bathroom. Then, still dressed, I threw myself across the bed and passed out.

Chapter 14

I WAS NAKED and they were all staring at me as if I were a piece of meat. I tried to hide behind my hands but no matter which way I turned I couldn't escape their eyes. The white merciless spotlights tore at me from all sides.

Somehow, of all the men there, I didn't seem to mind the strangers as much as those that knew me. I didn't even seem to mind the way the men all were dressed in football uniforms, helmets, face guards, bright red sweatshirts with black numbers. And they were all wearing the same number—One. Perhaps the strangest thing about the uniform was that the heavy padded pants had no fronts and their huge cocks hung out almost to their knees.

Abruptly they all went into a huddle. I tried to hear what they were whispering but the words were lost. Then they broke from the huddle and went into a playing formation. The only man I recognized in the line was the center, Harry Gregg. Behind him I could see the faces of the backfield. George Fox as quarterback, halfbacks Chad and John and, not too far behind, Walter as fullback.

George straightened up and gestured violently toward me, then pointed at Harry. Responding to a compulsion

I did not understand, I walked toward the line, got down on my knees and crawled between Harry's legs. Curling myself into a fetal ball, I hugged my knees close to my chest and pressed my face into my thighs.

I heard Harry grunt as he crouched even lower and forced his large hands between my arms until each one was firmly locked on my breasts. He nudged his knees against my buttocks and I raised myself slightly. He grunted again and I felt his long tool ram into me from behind. It was strange, but I felt nothing. Neither surprise, nor resentment, nor excitement. Then he exploded inside me and I felt his semen dripping down my legs as George shouted "Hup!" in a strange hoarse voice.

Abruptly I was flung backward between his legs into George's hands. They felt rough and callused, not at all like the soft manicured hands I knew he had. Still locked in the fetal position, I felt his heavy hands pressed down on my breasts forcing me onto his cock. Then he was running, his cock moving in and out of me with his strides. A moment later I heard Walter's voice shouting "Get rid of her! God damn it! Ged rid of her!"

George's orgasm splashed into me, firing me into the air like a rocket. I felt myself spinning sideways, over and over, and the air was cold against my skin.

I was floating over them now and suddenly I felt free.

There was something about soaring high like a bird. Nothing could touch you except the wind. And the wind loved you. You were safe. Then I began to fall.

I looked down. Chad and John were running toward the center of the field.

I felt the fear knotting my stomach. I could hear myself screaming inside my head but no sound came out. I willed the wind to keep me up. But I kept falling, falling toward them until I could see their faces grim with power behind their masks.

The scream finally tore from my throat. "No! No! This is not a game. I am not a football!"

Then I woke up cold, sweating and shaking, with tears running down my cheeks. For a moment I lay staring into the darkness. Then, still trembling, I reached across and turned on the lamp.

The ghosts of my dream fled before the light. I looked down at myself. My dress was totally crushed and the long skirt was ripped on one side where it had caught on the heel of my shoe while I was asleep.

I checked the time—almost five o'clock. Another two hours and the car would be here to take me to the studio. My mouth felt dry. I got out of bed and went into the bathroom.

The first thing I did was brush my teeth and rinse out my mouth. Then I looked at myself in the mirror.

My eyes were puffy and my face white and drawn. I stared at myself in disgust. It would take at least two hours to make myself presentable. I started the water running in the tub and I opened a jar of cream to begin removing my makeup.

I noticed my hands were still shaking and without thinking reached for a tranquilizer. Then I stopped. Between the pills and the drinking, I had really done a job on myself. There was no other explanation for that crazy nightmare.

I put the pill back in the bottle. There had to be a better way to keep going.

I spent two hours in Makeup and Hairdressing, where they toned down the blond in my hair and eyebrows and covered my body with a dark makeup that turned my skin to a dull copper. Then came the selection of my costume—a short loose-fitting chamois dress with a few touches of colored beads They called it the Debra Paget. She had worn it last while playing the mother of Cochise in an old Jeff Chandler film. By ten o'clock I had been driven to the back lot where they were doing the filming.

Chad came over to the car as I got out. He kissed my cheek. "You look sensational," he said. "Sleep okay?"

I nodded.

"Good," he said. Chad then introduced me to the man who had ambled over to us. "This is your director. Marty Ryan. JeriLee Randall."

Ryan was wearing a faded blue shirt and cowboy

jeans. His grip was firm. "Glad to meet you, JeriLee," he said with a Western twang.

"My pleasure," I said.

"Ready for work?"

I nodded.

"Good," he said. "We're ready for your first setup."

I felt a moment of panic. "I just got the script last night," I said quickly. "I haven't had a chance to read it yet. I don't know my lines."

"No problem," he said. "You don't have any dialogue in these scenes anyway. Come with me."

I followed him down to the camera and sound truck, which was standing in front of the Indian camp set. A number of men in Indian costumes were seated around a wooden crate playing cards. Near the corral two wranglers were tending to the horses.

"Hey, Terry," the director shouted, "bring her horse over here."

The smaller wrangler cut a large white horse out of the pack and started toward me. The director turned back to me. "It's a simple shot," he explained. "You come from the tent over there, look around for a moment, then run to the horse, jump up and ride away."

I stared at him, too dumbfounded to speak.

He mistook my silence for confusion. "It sounds more complicated than it really is," he explained gently.

I shook my head. "Somebody made a big mistake."

He was puzzled. "What do you mean?"

"The script I read had no scenes of me on horseback."

"We rewrote the script to give you more to do," he said. "We've given you a key part now. You're practically the chief of the tribe. You're in charge because your father has been wounded."

"Sounds great," I said. "Except for one thing. I can't ride."

"What did you say?"

"I can't ride," I repeated.

He stared at me dumbly. Chad came up to us, sensing something was wrong.

"What's the matter?" he asked.

The director turned to him. "She can't ride."

Chad stared at me. "You can't ride?"

I shook my head. "I've never even been on a horse."

"Holy shit!" Chad exploded. "Why the hell didn't you say something?"

"You never asked me," I said. "Besides the script that I saw didn't have any riding scenes."

"What do we do now?" the director asked him.

"We use a double," Chad said.

"No chance," the director said firmly. "This is television. Every shot is in close. There's no way to fake it."

Chad turned toward the wrangler. "How much time do you think it would take you to teach her?"

The little wrangler looked at me with slitted eyes, then shifted a wad of tobacco in his cheek and spat into the dirt. "If she learns fast, about a week to do what's called for in the script."

"We're fucked!" the director said in a disgusted voice and walked off.

"I knew it," Chad said. "I knew it. The first minute you walked into my office, I smelled trouble."

"Don't blame me," I said angrily. "I didn't want the damn part to begin with. But you couldn't take no for an answer."

"How the hell was I supposed to know you couldn't ride?" he snapped.

"The only horses I even saw were outside the Plaza Hotel in New York hitched to a carriage," I said.

"I'm jinxed," Chad said.

"What do you want me to do with Queenie here?" the little wrangler asked.

Chad gave him a look which left no doubt as to what he would like him to do. I turned to the wrangler. "Is the horse gentle?" I asked.

"She's like a baby," he said. "Loves evvabody."

"Help me up," I said. "Let me see how it feels."

He squatted at the side of the horse, making a clasped cup of his two hands. "Put your left foot in here," he said. "An' swang your right foot over."

"Okay." I followed directions and everything was going fine until the horse moved as I crossed my leg over her back. I kept right on going and wound up in a puddle of mud on the other side.

"Are you all right?" Chad asked in a frightened voice.

I raised myself up on one elbow. The mud was all over my face and dress. I stared up at them. "Sorry, fellers," I said. Then the absurdity of it all got to me and I began to laugh.

Thinking that I was becoming hysterical, they quickly helped me to my feet. "Get a doctor!" Chad yelled. Then he turned to me. "Don't worry, don't worry, everything will be all right."

But I couldn't stop laughing and by that night I was off the picture.

Chapter 15

CHAD DROVE ME BACK to the motel. On the way he stopped off at a package store and bought a bottle of scotch. Within an hour after we got to my room, he had put away half the bottle. It was almost eight o'clock when he finally got to his feet, weaving unsteadily. "We better get something to eat."

He was in no condition to drive. "Maybe we ought to get something from room service," I suggested.

"They don't have any. Do you think the studio's going to put you somewhere where you can run up room service charges?"

I didn't answer.

"We'll go out for something."

"I don't want you driving," I said.

"We can walk. There are a few places down the block on Sunset."

"Okay," I said.

We went to a restaurant on the north side of the

street opposite Schwab's Drug Store. The place was dimly lit like most California restaurants and there was a piano player sitting in the bar area near the entrance. A few people sat around the piano nursing their drinks. We walked past them and a headwaiter escorted us to a table.

"The prime ribs are extra good tonight," he said.

Chad looked at me and I nodded. "Make it two," he said to the headwaiter. "But first bring me a double scotch on the rocks."

The ribs were as good as the man promised but Chad left his untouched while he drank his dinner.

"You're not eating," I said.

"Don't be a woman," he said.

I was silent. The waiter brought coffee and Chad took a sip. "What are your plans now!" he asked.

"I'll probably go back to New York tomorrow."

"Anything special doing back there?"

"I'll start climbing on my agent's back again."

"I'm sorry about what happened," he said.

"The luck of the draw," I said.

"I want to thank you for trying to get on that horse," he said. "If you hadn't done that, I could have blown my job."

I didn't understand but I kept silent.

"It gave us a perfect out. The doctor called it an accident. Insurance took over the delay in shooting. It didn't cost the studio one penny and this way everybody's happy."

I still didn't speak.

He looked at me. "Except me. I felt we could have done great things together."

"Maybe we will someday," I said.

"No." He shook his head dolefully. "It doesn't work like that. The pressure's too great. Each week there's another show. You got to go forward."

"But what about the feature you were telling me about?" I asked. "We can still take a shot at that."

"Maybe, but that's why I wanted you in this show. The studio likes to go with people out of their own productions."

"I'm sorry," I said.

"Not your fault," he said. "You tried."

The waiter came and refilled our cups.

"Have you ever been to Vegas?" Chad asked.

"No."

"Why don't you stay then?" he asked. "A gang of us are going down tomorrow night to catch Sinatra's opening. We'll have a few laughs and you can fly back from there."

"I don't think so," I said.

"There won't be any heat. You'll have your own room."

"No, thanks. I'm not up to it. I'm going home and spend the next few days in bed."

He was silent for a moment. "Anything serious between you and John?"

"No."

"You didn't have to answer that," he said quickly. "It wasn't any of my business."

"I already did," I said.

"I don't want you to leave," he said.

"Why?"

"If you go, I'll feel I've failed. And I don't like failing."

I was beginning to get irritated. "You mean you don't want me to leave until you fuck me, is that it?"

"Not exactly. Well, maybe. I really don't know."

"Why can't you say exactly what you mean?" I asked. "Or is that the way the men here play the game?"

"I'm not playing any game," he said defensively.

"What's on your mind then?"

"Look," he snapped, "I don't see any reason why I should have to be cross-examined like this. I went out on a limb for you."

"You're absolutely right," I said. "I apologize."

He relaxed and smiled. "Don't apologize," he said. "You were absolutely right. I do want to fuck you."

When I didn't answer, he signaled for the check. Back at the motel he followed me into the room and began to take off his jacket.

I stopped him. "Are we friends?"

"Yes."

"Would you understand it if I told you my head isn't ready for you yet? I've got too much shit goin' on in there that I have to get rid of before we can make it."

He was silent for a moment. "You're not putting me on?"

"It's straight. You're okay. I like you. I'm just not up there yet."

He slipped his arm back into his sleeve. "They'll think I'm crazy but I believe you."

"Thanks, Chad."

"Can I call you if I come to New York?" he asked.

"I'll feel bad if you don't," I said.

I followed him to the door. "I'll see you then," he said, kissing me quickly.

The phone began to ring almost the moment I closed the door.

It was John. "I've been calling all night," he said.

"I've just got back from dinner."

"I know, but I've got to see you."

"I've got to pack," I said. "I'm going back on the first plane in the morning."

"I heard what happened out at the studio," he said. "But all I want is a few minutes. You can't go without giving me a chance to explain."

I thought for a moment. "How long will it take you to get here?" I asked.

"One minute," he answered. "I'm in the motel office downstairs."

He was there as soon as I put down the phone. "Come in," I said.

He followed me into the room. I gestured at the half empty bottle of scotch that Chad had left. "Would you like a drink?"

"Yes, please."

I took some ice cubes from the refrigerator and gave him a healthy drink. He looked drawn and tired. He took a good belt and some of the color seemed to come back into his face. I gestured at the couch and sat down in the chair opposite him.

"I don't know what got into me," he said. "I'm not usually like this."

I didn't answer.

"I want to apologize," he said.

"Don't. It's as much my fault as it is yours. I didn't know the rules of the game."

"It wasn't a game," he said. "I care for you. I really do."

There was nothing I could say.

He took another sip of his drink. "I don't want you to go back tomorrow. I want you to come back to the beach with me so we can start over. This time it will be right. I promise."

"It won't work," I said gently. "I know that now."

His voice grew more earnest. "It will. I know it will. Remember how beautiful it was that night? It will be like that again if you just give it a chance."

Looking at him, I thought there was so much he didn't understand. All he could remember was the way he felt then. By some strange quirk he seemed to have erased everything that happened afterward.

But I could not. Everything that had happened between us came together in the way I viewed him now. And the way I felt about him had changed. But seeing him so abject, I knew that there was no way of telling him the truth without bringing him down further. So instead I lied.

"I have to go back," I said. "Fannon and Guy have some ideas they want me to work on right away. They're going to try to get the play on a month earlier than they'd planned."

He took a deep breath. I could see some of the tension leave his face. This was the kind of rejection he could cope with. It was business, not personal. "Was it beautiful for you too?" he asked.

I got to my feet. "It was beautiful."

He rose from the couch and reached for me.

I put a hand on his arm, stopping him. "No."

He looked at me questioningly.

"I'm exhausted," I said. "I wouldn't be any good tonight." I remembered the nightmare. "I've been going back and forth so much the last two days I feel like a football."

He didn't speak.

"Do you understand that?" I asked. "I'm not a machine. I'm human. And I have to get some rest."

He nodded. "I keep forgetting. Women don't adapt to the time changes as well as men."

I stared at him. That made no sense at all. But all I wanted to do at this point was to go to bed, so I agreed.

"I'll let you get some rest then," he said.

He kissed me. I felt nothing but he didn't seem to be aware of it. "We'll be in touch," he said.

"Yes."

He smiled. "I'm glad we were able to have this talk."

"So am I."

"Call me when you have time," he said.

He kissed me again and I closed the door behind him. I walked back into the room and stared at the whiskey bottle. I picked it up and dropped it in the wastebasket. Then I went into the bedroom and undressed. I crawled naked between the sheets and closed my eyes. I remember the last thought I had before drifting off.

Oh, shit.

Men.

Chapter 16

THE SNOW was still falling heavily as we came out of the darkened theater. Max, the fat little company manager, came hurrying toward us through the lobby.

"Mr. Fannon took the limo back to the hotel. He had some important calls to make. He said that he'd send the car right back." He was puffing with exertion. "It won't be long," he added.

I glanced at Guy. "Feel like walking?" I asked.

"The snow will be up to our ass," he said.

"What the hell. It's only three blocks. Besides I think it will do me some good."

"Okay." He looked at Max. "Hold the car for the cast."

"Yes, Mr. Jackson."

Heads down, we walked stolidly for two blocks before exchanging a word. A plow moved past us spraying snow to the sides of the street. We paused at the corner to let it go by.

The whole performance was running through my head. The echo of the actors' voices in an almost empty theater, the laughter that never came, the lines that fell flat, the critics' averted faces as they left. "The play stinks," I said.

"You're not being fair to yourself. Look what we had to open against. The worst fucking snowstorm in five years."

"It wasn't snowing inside the theater," I said. "Nothing worked. And the cast kept blowing their cues. One after the other."

"They were nervous," he said. "Tomorrow night they'll be better. That's why shows go on the road. To work out the kinks."

We were almost at the hotel. "We ran too long," I said. "I think if I took about five minutes out of each act it would help."

"Ten minutes out of the first," he said. "That's where our big problem is. We don't hook them early enough."

We pushed open the door and were hit by the blast of warm air from the lobby. "Feel up to working tonight?" he asked as we went to the desk for our keys.

"That's what I'm here for."

He grinned. "Your room or mine?"

"Yours," I said. "I'll bring the typewriter." Directors and stars got suites. Authors were the low end of the totem and got small singles. Unless they happened to be my ex-husband.

We walked to the elevator. "I'll order some sandwiches and coffee," he said.

"Give me a half hour to shower and change into dry clothing," I said.

"Good enough," he answered.

The first thing I saw when I entered my room was the giant basket of flowers on the dresser. I read the card.

Love and success.
We're very proud of our little girl.
Mother and Daddy.

I looked out the window at the falling curtain of snow, then back at the flowers and began to cry.

We had been working almost three hours when the knock came at the door.

"I'm sorry to bother you, Mr. Jackson," Max said apologetically, "but Mr. Fannon wants to see you up in his suite right away."

"Tell him I'll be right there," Guy said.

"What do you think he wants at this hour?" I asked.

"I don't know. Probably wants to tell me the play needs fixing and what to fix." He slipped into a cardigan. "Finish off that bit on the first act. I think we've helped it a lot. I'll be right back."

It was a half hour before he returned. By that time I had finished the first act rewrite and was working on the second. I took one look at his face and knew it was bad news.

"He wants to close it down," he said.

"He can't do that," I said. "We're entitled to more than one night."

"He's the producer; he can do whatever the hell he wants. He controls the money."

"Why?" I asked. "We haven't even seen the reviews yet."

"He's got them all," he answered. "He has spies at the newspapers. He's got slugs of every one just as they'll be in the papers tomorrow morning."

"What did they say?" I asked.

"Slaughter. Every one of them. Bloody slaughter."

"Did you tell him what we were doing?"

"I did," he answered. "He said we should have thought of that before we opened. I did manage to get one thing out of him though. I asked him not to make his final decision until after he talks to you. After all, it's your play."

"He wants to see me now?" I asked.

He nodded.

"What am I supposed to tell him?"

"Explain to him again what we're doing. You got to convince him that the play has a chance. You know what we're doing is right. Don't let him cut us off at the pass. We got to get this play into New York."

I got to my feet. "What if he won't listen to me?"

For the first time in all the years I'd known him I saw the bitch come out. His lips drew back over his teeth in a contemptuous smile, and unconsciously his voice went a register higher. "For Christ's sake, Jeri-Lee! If he liked boys I'd suck his cock to get this play on Broadway. It's got to be worth that to you. You're a woman. Just this once try using your cunt instead of your head!"

All the way up to the Presidential Suite where Fannon was staying Guy's words kept running through my head. For me it wasn't only the money. If the play went on I would be alive at the agency. Without it I was dead.

He opened the door, wearing a red velvet robe that I thought existed only in old movies. "Hello, my dear," he said.

I bent slightly so that he did not have to stretch to kiss my cheek. "Adolph," I said.

"I have a cold bottle of champagne. I find it always helps to have a little lift when you're facing the facts of life."

I followed him into the room without answering. The wine was in a bucket next to the window. Solemnly he filled two glasses and gave me one. "Cheers," he said.

We drank.

"Dom Perignon," he said. "Nothing but the best."

I nodded.

"Guy told you about the reviews?"

"Yes, but I don't think it's fair to go on them. Comedy doesn't play in an empty house. That's why TV shows have laugh tracks. Too bad we can't do the same thing in the theater."

He refilled the glasses. "That's not being realistic. Believe me, my dear, I've had years of experience with these things. They never go right after a start like this."

"But it will work, Mr. Fannon," I said. "I know it will. Guy and I have been rewriting. We have got all the problems out of the first act and we can lick the others."

"Cheers," he said again and took another sip of champagne.

I wondered if he'd even heard me. "You've got to give us the chance," I said. Then in spite of myself I began to cry.

He led me to the couch, took some Kleenex from the desk and pressed it into my hand. "There, there, my dear. You mustn't take it so hard. You must think of it as experience. After all, this is your first play. There will be others."

I couldn't stop crying. "It will work," I said. "I know it will work."

He sat down on the couch beside me and drew my head to his chest. He stroked my hair gently. "Listen to the words of a man almost old enough to be your father. I know how you feel. After all, I feel just as bad. I don't like to lose eighty thousand dollars. But it's better than going into New York and losing seventy thousand more. A man has to learn when to cut his losses. And, in a way, that's what you're doing. Nobody will remember the reviews you get in New Haven when it comes time to get your next play produced. But if you get bad reviews in New York they never forget it."

"I don't care," I cried. "I know the play will work."

He continued stroking my hair while the arm around my waist moved up toward my breasts.

I turned and let my breast fill his hand. "Adolph," I said, "you don't know how much I've always admired your courage as a producer. You were the one man I felt would never quit on me."

"I'm not quitting." He cleared his throat. "I'm just trying to be practical."

This time I let him feel both breasts. A curious flush blotched his face.

Then abruptly he got to his feet. He picked up the champagne glasses and gave one to me. "Drink it," he ordered.

There was something in his voice I hadn't heard before. And I suddenly realized that this little monster was really a man. I drained my glass.

"I want to fuck you," he said. "And I know you're ready to fuck me. But, would you still be willing if I close the show?"

"No," I said, looking into his eyes.

He stared at me for a moment, then emptied his glass. Suddenly he smiled and patted my cheek. "I like you," he said. "At least you're honest."

"Thank you," I said. "What about the show?"

"I'm closing it. But I promise you this. If you write another play, bring it to me. We'll take another crack at it."

I rose to my feet. Suddenly I didn't feel cheap anymore. "Thank you, Adolph," I said. "You're a gentleman."

He held the door open for me. I bent my cheek for his good-night kiss, then went down to my room. There was no reason to see Guy.

The show closed in New Haven.

Chapter 17

"MODERN FURNITURE is a drug on the market," the man said.

I didn't reply. Every used-furniture dealer who had come to look at the apartment made the same remark.

"The rugs belong to you?" he asked.

I nodded.

He looked down disapprovingly. "White and beige. Bad colors. Hard to keep clean." I had heard that before too.

The telephone rang. I answered, hoping that it was my new agent calling about an interview he was trying to arrange for me with an Italian producer.

It was the telephone company about their bill, which was already two months overdue. They were apologetic but said they would have to disconnect my service if a check was not in their office by the following morning. I told them it was in the mail and hung up. It wasn't but it didn't matter. By tomorrow I wouldn't live here anymore.

The furniture dealer was coming out of the bedroom. "You moved some furniture out," he said in an accusatory voice. "I could tell from the marks on the rug. And I didn't see any silverware, dishes or pots and pans."

"What you see is what's for sale," I said. I wondered if he thought I was going to live in a suitcase. The things I needed were already in the small studio apartment I had rented on the West Side.

"I don't know," he said doubtfully. "It's tough merchandise to move."

"It's practically new. Only about a year old. And I bought the best. It cost me over nine thousand dollars."

"You should have come to us," he said. "We could have saved you a lot of money."

"I didn't know about you then."

"That's the trouble with people. They never learn until it's too late." He gestured toward the couch. "How much do you want for that?"

"Five thousand dollars."

"You'll never get it."

"Then make me an offer."

"A thousand dollars."

"Forget it," I said, walking toward the door. "Thanks for coming up."

"Wait, you got a better offer?"

"Yes. Much better."

"How much better? A hundred, two hundred?"

I didn't answer.

"If Hammersmith was here, he wouldn't give you more than twelve hundred," he said.

He knew the competition. That was exactly the amount I had been offered.

"I'll take a chance," he said. "I'll give you thirteen hundred. That's my top offer."

"No, thanks," I said, looking at him steadily, holding open the door.

He appraised the room again quickly. "How fast can I get the merchandise?'

"You can take it with you right now as far as I'm concerned."

"This afternoon?"

"If you like."

"No mortgages, no time payments due? It's free and clear? You'll sign a paper?"

"Yes."

He let out a reluctant sigh. "My partner will think I'm crazy but I'll give you fifteen hundred. And that's absolutely my top offer."

That was three hundred more than any offer I had received so far. And he was the fourth dealer I'd seen. "Cash," I said. "Not a check." A check wouldn't clear my bank in time to cover the rent and deposit check I had issued for the new apartment.

"Of course," he said.

"Sold," I said, closing the door.

"Can I use your phone?" he asked. "I can have my truck in an hour if you'll wait."

"I'll wait," I said.

I made it to the bank just before three o'clock. After making the deposit I came out into the mild May afternoon and decided that since I hadn't heard from my agent I would go to see him. On the bus I did some calculating. I figured that after paying all my bills I would have about eight hundred dollars left.

Lou Bradley's noisy offices in the Brill Building were nothing like the elaborate offices of Artists Alliance.

And Lou wasn't exactly the kind of agent I would have preferred but I didn't have much choice. I had been to all the big ones—William Morris, A.F.A., C.M.A.—before coming to him. They were polite but not interested. It was as if I had suddenly become an untouchable. I tried to look at it realistically. After all, no one wanted to associate themselves with failure. And whether or not it was my fault, I had three good ones to my credit. Despite what John had told me, his brother had cut down on my part in the film, then there was the episode at Universal and, last but not least, the play.

It was the play that had hurt most, not only because it closed but because I began hearing all over town that Guy was dumping on me, saying that I had been uncooperative and had refused to make the changes he wanted. I tried to call him, convinced that I could make him stop, but I could never get him on the phone. Then after I had gotten back I received the notice from Artists Alliance canceling my contract.

I was bewildered. Harry Gregg had said nothing about it.

I picked up the phone and called him. His voice was guarded. "Yes?"

"There has to be a mistake," I said. "I just got a

notice that the office dropped my contract, and you never said anything about it."

"That's not my job," he said. "That's upstairs."

"But you knew about it?"

He hesitated. "Yes."

"Then why didn't you say something? I thought you were my friend."

"I am. But I also have a job here. I don't mess in affairs that aren't my concern."

"But we talked about plans, things you were going to do," I said. "And all the time you knew you weren't going to do any of them."

"What did you expect me to say? 'Don't bother me, baby, you've had it'?"

"You could have said something."

"Okay. I'll say it now. Don't bother me, baby, you've had it." The line went dead in my hands.

I was hurt and angry but I had no time for tears. I needed another agent and another job fast.

But I found neither quickly as I had hoped. The money from the last payment on the play had run out before I knew it. I guess my parents must have sensed something was wrong, because on my twenty-fifth birthday they sent me a check for twenty-five hundred dollars. Then I cried.

I had to wait half an hour for Lou to get off the phone. In that way he was no different from any other agent. They were all telephone freaks. Finally his secretary gave me the signal to go into his office.

He looked up at me, his eyes pale blue and watery in his thin face. "Hi, baby," he said quickly. "I been thinkin' about you. I haven't been able to get the son of a bitch on the phone yet." He yelled through the open door. "Hey, Shirley, try DaCosta again for me."

Then his voice dropped to a confidential whisper. "I think he's with the boys."

I was puzzled. "Who?"

His voice went even lower. "You know who I mean. The boys. Big Frank. Joe. Where do you think those guinea producers get their money from?"

"You mean the rackets?" I asked.

"Shh!" he said quickly. "We don't use that word around here. The boys are all good guys. Friends. You know what I mean." The phone buzzed.

"Hey, Vincenzo," he said jovially, "how's it going?"

He listened for a moment, then spoke again. "That sounds real good. By the way, I got that girl I was talking to you about right here in my office and I was wondering if you could set an appointment to see her?"

He looked over at me and nodded into the phone. "Would I steer you wrong? She's a real good looker, you know what I mean? Lots of experience. Broadway, films, Hollywood, everything."

He covered the mouthpiece with his hand. "He says he's all tied up the next two days, then he's going back to Italy. You free for dinner tonight?"

I hesitated.

"You don't have to worry about this guy. He's a perfect gentleman."

I nodded. Even if I didn't get the job, dinner out was better than eating a hamburger alone.

"She says she's free," he said into the phone, then covered the mouthpiece again. "He wants to know if you got a friend?"

I shook my head.

"She says she hasn't. But don't worry. I'll send somebody up." He nodded. "Gotcha. Eight o'clock. Your suite at the Saint Regis."

"You're lucky," he said solemnly as he put down the phone. "A guy like him don't usually go out of his way to see anybody. He's got his pick of all them Italian actresses. Loren, Lollobrigida, Mangano. Only trouble is their English ain't no good."

"What kind of a part is it?" I asked.

"How the hell do I know? You don't ask foreign producers and directors for a script. They would think you were crazy or something. Half these guys make their pictures with no script at all. An' they win all the awards."

"Maybe I'm not the type he's looking for," I said.

"You're American, aren't you?"

I nodded again.

"You're an actress?"

I nodded again.

"Then you're perfect for the part. Exactly what he asked me for. An American actress." He got to his feet and, taking my arm, steered me to the door. "Now you go home, take a hot bath and make yourself up real pretty. Wear a long sexy dress. These guys wear black tie for dinner every night."

He held open the door to the outer hall. "Don't forget. Eight o'clock at his suite in the Saint Regis. Don't be late. These guys are very prompt."

"Okay," I said. "But you forgot one thing."

"What's that?"

"To tell me his name."

"Oh. DaCosta. Vincent DaCosta."

DaCosta. The name was vaguely familiar but I couldn't recall where I had heard it before.

Chapter 18

As I WALKED down the carpeted corridor to the suite, the shouting grew louder. The noise was vulgar in the faded gentility of the Saint Regis halls. I stopped in front of the double doors and knocked at the wooden panels. The shouting continued. I could hear a woman's voice. But I couldn't understand what she was saying because she was speaking Italian. Thinking that they hadn't heard me, I knocked again.

The door was opened almost immediately by a tall, good-looking, dark-haired young man dressed in a conservative dark suit, white on white shirt and white tie. There was no sign that he was expecting anyone.

"Mr. DaCosta?" I asked.

He nodded.

"JeriLee Randall," I said. "Mr. Bradley asked me to be here at eight o'clock."

His face cleared. "Luigi sent you." He smiled suddenly, revealing white even teeth. "Come in." There was no trace of accent in his English.

I followed him through the small entrance hall into the large living room. There were two men sitting on the couch, but they didn't glance in my direction. They were looking up at the woman in the flimsy short chemise who was shouting at the bald older man.

I stood in the doorway for a moment, not knowing whether or not to enter. Suddenly I recognized the woman. Carla Maria Perino. Just two years before, she had won an Academy Award for her performance in *Remnants of a War*. Then I recognized the bald man on the couch. It was her husband, Gino Paoluzzi, who had produced and directed the film.

Suddenly Paoluzzi's eyes glittered and he rose to his feet. He was a head shorter than she but there was a strange sense of power in him that made him seem larger than anyone in the room. His hand moved swiftly. There was the sharp sound of the slap across her face and the harsh guttural sound of his voice. *"Putana!"*

Abruptly she was silent, then she dissolved in tears. He turned away from her and crossed the room toward me. The other man rose from the couch and followed him.

DaCosta came between us. "This is Mr. Paoluzzi, the famous director," he said to me. "He doesn't speak any English." He looked at the director. *"Io presento JeriLee Randall."*

Paoluzzi smiled and I held out my hand. He gave a short half bow and kissed my hand in such a way that his lips seemed to brush on his own hand, which covered mine.

Looking at me, DaCosta snapped his finger. "I know you!" he said excitedly. "Didn't you get a Tony award about five years ago?"

I nodded.

"I saw that play. You were fantastic." He turned to

Paoluzzi and began to speak rapidly in Italian. I could pick up only a few words. Broadway. Tony, Walter Thornton.

Paoluzzi nodded and looked at me with an expression of respect. He said something in Italian.

DaCosta translated. "The Maestro says that he has heard of you. He is honored to meet you."

"Thank you."

DaCosta introduced the other man, who was tall, gray-haired and paunchy. "Piero Guercio."

Again the strange hand kiss. "How do you do," he said in a strongly accented English.

"Signor Guercio is the Maestro's consigliere," DaCosta said. He saw the puzzled expression on my face. "Lawyer," he added.

"Gino." Her voice was a small plaintive cry.

It was almost as if they had forgotten that she was in the room. Her husband said something to her. She nodded her head and looked at me appraisingly.

Paoluzzi spoke again. This time I gathered he was telling her about me. After a moment she came toward us. *"Mia sposa,"* he said to me.

We shook hands. I was surprised at the strength in her slim fingers. I turned to DaCosta. "Tell her I'm a fan. I loved her performance in the film."

Da Costa translated and she smiled. *"Grazie."* Then she left the room.

"She was upset because the maid burned a hole in her dress while she was ironing it," DaCosta explained to me.

If that was all it took to bring on an outburst like that, I wouldn't have wanted to be around when something really went wrong.

"How about a drink?" he asked. "We have everything."

"A glass of white wine?"

"You got it."

I took the glass from him and sat on the couch where he indicated. The men sat on chairs in a semicircle around me.

DaCosta translated for Paoluzzi. "Are you working right now?"

"No, but I'm considering a few things."

Paoluzzi nodded as if he understood. "Do you prefer theater to films?" DaCosta asked, translating for Paoluzzi.

"I can't tell," I said. "I've never really had a film role that I felt was rewarding."

Paoluzzi nodded, then spoke again. "The Maestro says that Hollywood has destroyed the American film industry with their emphasis on television. At one time they led the world but now the leadership has passed to Europe. They are the only ones to make films that have any artistic or real values."

I sipped my wine and we sat in awkward silence for a moment until there was a knock at the door.

DaCosta jumped up and hurried out into the foyer. He returned with a tall red-headed woman wearing a beaded green evening dress and a long black mink stole. The men got to their feet and kissed her hand as they were introduced. Then DaCosta looked at me. "Marge Small, JeriLee Randall."

There was an antagonistic look in the girl's eyes. "Hi," she said.

"Hi," I replied.

"You're with the consigliere," he said, pointing at Guercio.

She nodded casually. "Okay."

The attorney smiled at her. "Would you like something to drink?"

"Yeah," she said. "You got some champagne?"

He nodded and she followed him to the bar, where he filled two glasses, one for her and one for himself. They stayed there, talking in low tones. I wondered what they were saying.

DaCosta interrupted my thoughts. "The Maestro wants to know if you ever thought of working in Italy?"

"Nobody ever asked me," I said.

"He says you would do very well there. You're the type they're looking for."

"Tell him I'm available."

Paoluzzi smiled, got to his feet, then vanished into the next room. DaCosta picked up the phone. "Front door," he said. "Tell Mr. Paoluzzi's chauffeur that we'll be down in ten minutes."

"How long have you been with Lou?" he asked as he hung up the phone.

"A week now."

He nodded, smiling. "I don't know how the little bastard does it. He always comes up with a winner."

"I'm a little confused," I said. "Mr. Bradley told me you were a producer."

He laughed. "He never gets anything right. I'm a producer's rep. Paoluzzi's the producer."

"I see," I said, although I really didn't. "What's the picture about?"

"Damned if I know. Every meeting we go to he tells a different story. I'm willing to bet that none of them are what he's going to make. He's afraid that if he tells the real story someone'll steal the idea. It doesn't make my life any easier, I tell you."

"Why?"

"I'm supposed to raise American financing for him and our money people don't work that way. They want to know what they're getting into."

"You're Italian?" I asked.

"American. My parents were Italian."

"You come from New York?"

"Brooklyn. My father and brothers are in business out there."

Suddenly I remembered why his name was familiar. The DaCosta family. They certainly were in business out there. They owned the waterfront. One of the five families that divided up New York. Now I understood what Bradley meant.

He smiled, as if he had read my mind. "I'm the black sheep of the family," he said. "I didn't want to go into the business. They all think I'm stupid for beating my brains out in show business."

Suddenly I liked him. There was something disarmingly honest about him. "I don't think you are," I said.

The bedroom door opened and the Paoluzzis came

out. I couldn't help but stare at her. None of the pictures I had seen of her had done her justice. Without a doubt she was the most beautiful women I had ever seen.

I saw her swift appraising glance of Marge Small. In a moment she turned to me, and I knew the girl had been dismissed from her mind as if she never existed. "I'm sorry I took so long," she said in a soft pleasantly accented voice.

"It's all right," I said.

DaCosta led the way to the car and opened the door. In the limousine he sat up front with the driver. The lawyer and Marge were on the jump seats and the Maestro sat between his wife and me. We went to Romeo Salta's, a restaurant only two blocks from the hotel.

At dinner there was no mistaking who the star was. We had the best table and Carla Maria the best seat. She got the same kind of treatment at El Morocco, where we went after dinner. Mysteriously, photographers appeared everywhere we went, and in a curious way it felt good even if it wasn't for me. It had been a long time since I had been around this kind of show business excitement.

"Dance?" DaCosta asked.

We went out onto the small crowded dance floor. The music was sedate. It was not until after one o'clock that they went into any rock. He held me closely as we moved slowly to the Sinatra record on the stereo system.

"Enjoying yourself?" he asked.

I nodded. "It's fun."

"Do you really have some jobs on the fire?"

"No."

"I didn't think so."

"What makes you say that?"

"You wouldn't be with Luigi if you did. He's generally a desperation area." His eyes were serious as he looked down at me. "You have talent, real talent. What went wrong?"

I hesitated. "I don't know. Everything. It's like— One day it was all there and, the next day—nothing."

"It's the breaks," he said. "It happens like that sometimes."

I didn't answer.

"Carla Maria likes you," he said.

I was pleased. "I like her too. She's really a fantastic lady. You can tell her I said so."

"The Maestro also likes you."

"Good. He must be a great talent."

He found an opening and steered me to a corner of the dance floor near the wall. "He was wondering if you would be interested in doing a scene with Carla Maria."

"I would," I said quickly. Then I looked at his face and knew we weren't talking about the same thing. I felt myself turning red. I didn't know what to say.

"It's okay," he said finally. "You don't have to."

"I'm surprised," I said. "I just didn't expect this."

"They have their own ideas of fun," he said. "I'm just delivering the message."

"Is that part of your job too?"

"That and a lot of other things."

When we got back to the table Guercio and the other woman had gone. I caught the signal that passed between Paoluzzi and DaCosta, then the producer got to his feet and said something in Italian.

DaCosta looked at me. "The Maestro apologizes but it's time to leave. He has appointments early in the morning."

We all rose and almost caused a collision between captains and waiters rushing to move the table out of the way. Carla Maria and her husband led the way out of the club, DaCosta and I brought up the rear.

The limousine rolled up as we came out the door. "The Maestro wants to know if we can drop you off on the way back to the hotel?" DaCosta said.

"No, thanks. I live over on the West Side. Tell him I'll grab a cab. And thank him for a lovely evening."

DaCosta repeated it in Italian. Paoluzzi smiled,

bowed and kissed my hand again. Then he looked into my eyes and said something.

DaCosta translated words. "He says that he hopes he has the good fortune to work with you someday."

"I do too," I said.

I held out my hand to Carla Maria. She smiled. "That is not the way we say good night in Italy." She leaned forward, pressing her cheek against both of mine and making kissing sounds. "Ciao," she said.

"Ciao."

They got into the limousine. DaCosta escorted me to my taxi and pressed a bill into my hand. "Cab fare," he said.

"No," I said, trying to push it away.

"Take it. It's on the expense account." He closed the door of the cab before I could protest again. "Good night."

"Good night," I said as the taxi moved away from the curb.

"Where to, lady?" the driver asked.

I gave him the address.

"Was that Carla Maria Perino getting into that limo?" the cab driver asked.

"Yes."

"Gee." His voice was filled with a whispering wonder. "She's really something else, ain't she, lady?"

"She really is," I said, and I meant it. Then I remembered the bill I had in my hand. For a moment as I looked down at it I couldn't believe my eyes.

I had never seen a real five-hundred-dollar bill before.

Chapter 19

I CALLED HIM on the house phone at nine o'clock the next morning. He sounded sleepy.

"JeriLee Randall," I said. "I didn't mean to wake you."

"It's okay," he said.

"I just want you to know that I left the money you gave me in an envelope at the desk in your name," I said. "Thank you anyway."

"Wait a minute!" He sounded wide awake now. "Where are you calling from?"

"The lobby."

"Don't go away. I'll be down in a minute. We can have a cup of coffee or some breakfast."

"I don't want to be any trouble."

"I want to see you."

I put down the phone. In less than three minutes he came out of the elevator. He hadn't been asleep as I had thought. He was already shaved and dressed. He didn't speak until after we had gone into the restaurant and the waiter had brought us some coffee.

"You didn't have to do that," he said.

"Neither did you."

"You don't understand. It's all part of the business."

"But it's not my business," I said.

"You really are an old-fashioned girl, aren't you?"

"No. New-fashioned. I don't believe in taking money I haven't earned."

"What are you going to do for a job?" he asked.

"Keep on looking," I said.

"I'll talk to Luigi about you. I'll make sure he doesn't hustle you."

"I'm not going back to him." I hesitated. "Is Paoluzzi really going to do a picture in which he needs an American actress?"

"Paoluzzi is only interested in doing pictures with his wife," he said.

"Then there wasn't really a job?"

"No."

"That's what I finally figured out. I guess I'm really stupid."

"It's a stupid business. There are millions of girls and very few jobs. Even those with talent rarely make it."

"I'll make it," I said. "I did it once."

"Weren't you married to Walter Thornton?" he asked.

I knew what he was getting at. "They gave me the Tony for acting, not because my husband wrote the play.'

"But everybody needs a friend," he said. "At least that gets you past the secretaries."

"What are you getting at?"

"Paoluzzi kept me up half the night talking about you. He says you can get more work than you can handle in Italy—with the right kind of a sponsor."

"Meaning himself?" I asked.

He nodded.

"No, thanks," I said. I started to get up.

He put a hand on my arm to stop me. "Don't be a fool. I could name a half dozen stars who made it that way including Carla Maria. And she was only seventeen when he found her in Naples a dozen years ago."

"It's not my style. I came close to it once and it left me feeling like half a human being."

"Independence isn't what it's cracked up to be," he said. "Most independent people I know are broke."

"What about you? I notice you didn't go into the family business."

He reddened slightly. "That's different."

"Why is it different?"

"Because I'm a man and you're a girl. I can take care of myself better than you can."

"Maybe you can right now, but I'll learn. And when I do, there'll be no difference."

"The world won't change. If you're smart you'll find some nice guy, get married and have a couple of kids."

"Is that the only answer you have for me?"

"That. Or the other. And you already said you're not interested in the other."

"You mean either I become a wife or a whore. There's no other way for me to make it?"

"Outside chance," he said. "One in a million."

"My kind of odds," I said. "Thank you for the coffee."

He took my hand. "I like you. I'd like to see you again sometime."

"I'd like to see you too. But on one condition."

"What's that?"

"No business. No bullshit."

He grinned. "You're on. How do I get in touch with you?"

I gave him my number and we walked out to the lobby. "I'll give you a call next week when I get these people out of town."

"Okay," I said. We shook hands and I went out into the street. The sun was shining, the day was warm. I didn't know why, but suddenly I was feeling up.

I didn't see him again for three months. And by then things were very different for both of us. My father died that summer and for the first time in my life I found out what it really meant to be alone.

There had been no work that summer, not even in summer stock. I made the rounds every day, read *Casting News* and answered every call. But without an agent I wasn't getting anywhere. Even for television commercials you needed an agent to get you inside the doors of the advertising agencies.

Every night I would return to my small apartment exhausted, but after only a few hours' sleep I would wake up and be unable to go back to sleep. I worked on my new play but it wasn't coming together. Everything I wrote seemed forced and artificial. Then, after a while, I didn't write at all. I would sit by my typewriter staring out the window at the night-darkened street, not even thinking.

Somehow my father sensed what was happening. And one day, without a word, I received a check for one hundred dollars. And from then on, the check came regularly every Monday. Without it I couldn't have managed.

I tried to talk to him about it one day. But he would say nothing except that it was something both he and Mother wanted to do because they loved me and had faith in me. When I went to thank Mother, she looked at me coolly. "It's your father's idea," she said. "I think you should come back home and live with us. I don't hold with a young girl living alone in the city the way you do."

After that I was even more determined to show her. I attacked my typewriter with new ferocity. But it didn't matter. Nothing good came of it.

I felt so totally alone. I had no friends—male or female. Show business camaraderie didn't seem to exist on the level on which I lived, at least not for me. And then suddenly one day I became brutally aware of something else—the fact that I was no longer young.

I had answered a cattle call for girls who were to play bits and extras in a beach scene for a film that would be shooting on Long Island. The audition was held in a large hall over the Roseland ballroom on Broadway and we all had to appear in bathing suits and bikinis. I was almost last in a line of about thirty girls. I stood waiting to walk past the casting director and the producer, hoping that all the jobs would not be filled before I got my turn.

My figure had always been good. I knew that. And I made sure that I kept it that way by spending a half hour every morning doing exercises. I heard my name being called and walked out across the small stage.

In the center of the stage I paused, turned around slowly as we had been instructed, and then walked away from them, swinging my hips suggestively. I had almost reached the end of the stage when I heard the producer whisper, "No."

"But she's got a great figure and a sensational ass," the casting director rasped.

The producer was trying to whisper, but I could hear him. There was a tone of finality in his voice. "Too old. She has to be at least twenty-five."

I went around behind the stage to get my clothes. The other girls chattered as they dressed, but none of them seemed to have anything to say to me. The producer's words were beginning to sink in. Too old. They were all younger than I—seventeen, eighteen—bright and fresh and untarnished.

Suddenly I wondered what I was doing trying to live in a world I had outgrown.

Broadway was sweltering in the July heat, but I decided to walk back uptown to my apartment.

By the time I got to my street I was perspiring and exhausted. I decided to go into the liquor store, where I bought a cold bottle of white California wine. Then I went up to my apartment and began to drink. Within an hour I was smashed. The wine worked better on an empty stomach and I had not eaten that morning because I did not want my stomach to bulge when I got into my bikini.

I sat at the window, staring out at the hot streets. Shit. What was the matter with me?

The telephone began to ring, but since I was expecting no calls I decided not to answer. But when it continued to ring I finally picked up.

It was my mother. From the steely control in her voice I knew it was something bad. "JeriLee? Where have you been all day? I've been trying to get you."

I was angry, yet somehow frightened. "For Christ's sake, Mother! I was out looking for a job. What do you think I've been doing?"

The steel was still there. "Your father had a heart attack this morning. He died before they could get him to the hospital."

The pain seemed tightened around my heart. Then I found my voice. "I'll be home right away, Mother."

Chapter 20

IT SEEMED as if the whole town turned out for his funeral. Many stores closed during the morning and the crowd at the church spilled out into the street. The words of the minister were carried to them by loudspeaker.

"John Randall was a good man. He gave freely of his life and time for the welfare of his neighbors. Many of us here today have been enriched by his aid and kind advice. We shall miss him. And we shall always remember him."

Then the flower-laden coffin was carried out to the hearse and borne to the cemetery, where he was laid to rest. Later after the neighbors had all gone home, Mother and I were alone.

"Let me make you a cup of tea," I said.

She nodded. "He hadn't been feeling well that morning before he went to work," she said, sipping her tea. "I wanted him to stay home and rest. But he said he had too much to do. His secretary said he was dictating a letter when he suddenly slumped over his desk. She called for help right away. But there was nothing anyone could do."

"Try not to think about it now," I said.

Her eyes met mine. "Sometimes I think I did not give him enough. He might have wanted a son of his own. But he never said anything. He knew how busy I was with the two of you."

"He loved you," I said. "He was happy."

"I hope so," she said. "I would not like to feel that I cheated him of anything he wanted."

"All he ever wanted was you, Mother," I said.

We were silent for a long itme.

"You know many things will have to be changed now," she said finally. "Without Father's income, we'll have to cut back."

I didn't speak.

"I was thinking it might be a good idea if you came back home to live."

"What would I do, Mother?" I asked. "There's no work for me here."

"I won't be able to continue sending you the hundred dollars a week."

"I can understand that, Mother. I'll manage."

"How?" she asked directly.

"I'll get something soon," I said. "And I'm almost finished with my new play. Fannon promised me that he would put it on."

"What if it fails like the other one?" she asked.

"Then I'll try again," I said.

She rose from her chair. "I think I'll go up and lie down," she said. She started from the room, then turned back. "You know there's always a room for you here if things don't work out."

"Yes, Mother. Thank you."

I watched her slowly climb the stairs to her room. She was still a good-looking woman. Her back was straight and she held her head high. Suddenly I had a feeling of admiration for her. I wished I could be like her. She always seemed to know exactly what she had to do.

My apartment was hot and musty. I threw open the windows. Even with the noise of the traffic it was better than the dank dead smell of the closed-up rooms.

I picked up the mail that had accumulated in the week I'd been away. It was mostly bills.

Idly I opened the latest copy of *Casting News*. I went through the casting calls and open auditions. There was really nothing for me. Then an ad caught my eye.

WANTED! ACTRESSES, MODELS, SHOW-GIRLS! WORK IN YOUR SPARE TIME. MEET

IMPORTANT PEOPLE. If you are between assignments, over twenty-one, not less than 5′5″, good figure and conversationalist, and can give us at least four nights out of the week, we have a job that might interest you.

STARTING SALARY $165 per week, including all Social Security and Unemployment Insurance Benefits plus Costume and Tips. Increases after three months. Based on a forty-hour work week.

IF INTERESTED APPLY:
TORCHLIGHT CLUB, EAST 54TH STREET OFF PARK AVENUE, MONDAY THROUGH FRIDAY THIS WEEK BETWEEN 2 P.M. AND 5 P.M.

*IMPORTANT—NO HUSTLERS! ALL EMPLOYEES WILL REQUIRE N.Y.P.D. AND N.Y.S.A.B. LICENSES AND APPROVALS.

I reread the ad slowly, thinking that it must be a new club. The only two I knew of were the Playboy and the Gaslight. In my financial condition, a hundred and sixty-five dollars a week sounded good, and they had to be legitimate. They did require police department and state liquor board licenses. The hours seemed right for me too. It would leave me time to write and follow up any other jobs that might turn up.

I checked my watch. It was almost noon. And it was already Thursday. The ad had been in all week. If I wanted to get a crack at it I had to move quickly. Having made up my mind, I went into the bathroom, dumped a whole bottle of bath salts into the tub and turned on the water. While the tub was running I lined up all my makeup including the false eyelashes on the shelf over the sink. I was determined to look my best.

It was a wide gray stone building with black-painted double doors. On either side of the door were heavy brass coach lamps that matched the brass plate on the door. The letters etched into the brass read simply, "Torchlight."

I tried the door but found it locked. I checked my watch. It was after two o'clock. Then I saw the small buzzer almost concealed under the brass plate.

When I pressed it the door opened automatically and I stepped inside. There was a smell of new paint and in some of the rooms off the entrance hall I could see workmen hammering and tacking draperies on the walls and over the windows.

One of the workmen saw me. "Upstairs," he said, pointing. "The front room."

The girl sitting behind the desk looked at me with a bored expression.

"I came in answer to the ad," I said.

Her expression didn't change. "All the jobs are filled."

"The ad said interviews all week."

"I can't help that. We had over four hundred girls here in the first two days." She reached for a piece of paper. "The place was a madhouse. You can leave your name and number if you like. We'll get in touch with you if there's an opening."

The telephone on her desk buzzed. "Yes, Mr. DaCosta. Right away, Mr. DaCosta," she said. After putting down the phone, she looked up at me. "Do you want to leave your name or not?" she asked impatiently.

I played my hunch. "Tell Mr. DaCosta that JeriLee Randall is here."

The expression on her face changed suddenly. "Why didn't you say so? I've heard him mention your name," she said, picking up the phone again. "Mr. DaCosta, JeriLee Randall is here to see you." She listened for a moment, then looked at me. "Next floor up, first door on the right."

He was standing in the open doorway waiting for me, a smile on his face. "How did you know I was here?"

"I didn't," I said. "But I heard the girl downstairs say the name DaCosta and I took the chance it was you."

"I've thought of calling you many times," he said. "But something always came up."

"It's okay," I said.

"How's it been going?"

"Not good. I came in answer to the ad. But the girl says that all the jobs are filled."

His face grew suddenly serious. "Do you have any idea of what the job is?"

"Only what I saw in the ad."

He walked around behind his desk. "It's a kind of superexpensive Playboy Club with extras—sauna, swimming pool, massage—as well as a cocktail lounge and restaurant. There'll also be a discotheque in the basement."

"Sounds like quite an operation."

"It is," he said. "We have eight hundred people who have already laid down six hundred dollars apiece for membership. We've been looking for some very high class girls to act as hostesses. They have to be very special type girls because they will set the tone of the place. Just as the Bunnies do over at Playboy."

"How will your hostesses be different?" I asked.

"First, they won't have to wear those silly costumes. Each hostess will wear a gown especially designed for the room in which she works. Second, they have to be able to talk, to be friendly without being pushy. They must make the members feel comfortable, almost as if they were in their own home."

"Sounds like a good idea," I said.

"It is," he said. He looked at me. "Would you like to see some of the gowns?"

I nodded.

He went to a closet in the corner of the room and took out two gowns. One was Grecian, soft and flowing and very decollete. The other was granny dress of flowered chiffon with a square deep-cut peasant neckline. He held them in front of the window. They were almost transparent. "The girls wear these," he said. "And nothing else."

I was silent.

"No bras, no panties, nothing but high-heeled shoes." He put the gowns back in the closet and returned to his desk. "What do you think?"

"I didn't think I was applying for a job in a kindergarten," I said.

There must have been something in the expression on my face that made him come suddenly toward me. He put his hands on my arms and looked down into my eyes. "What happened?" he asked.

"My father died," I said. Then the tears came and I buried my face against his jacket. "And for the first time in my life I'm frightened."

Chapter 21

I LOOKED UP at the wall clock. It was after eleven. The ten o'clock changeover should have been completed by now. It was time to begin the check. I stopped and looked in the full-length mirror on the door of my small office.

The sheer floor-length granny clung smoothly. I was satisfied. The first few days I had felt very self-conscious about wearing it, but I'd since learned that no one seemed to pay any attention, so I'd stopped thinking about it.

I took the elevator down seven floors to the disco in the basement. It was my job to see that all the stations were covered and make sure that there was always someone to replace the absentees, as well as to arrange work schedules. The club had been Vincent's idea and it had succeeded even beyond his expectations. Now, six months after the opening, membership applications were backed up for two years. It wasn't what Vincent really wanted to do but his family had been on his back after allowing him two years to chase film deals that always seemed to evaporate into thin air. And when the Paoluzzi business fell apart his father had drawn the line.

Vincent was offered two choices. Either he got into what they considered a proper business or he had to come in with them. Vincent chose the lesser of the two evils. It cost his family more than two million dollars to open the club but they didn't seem to mind. The money was insignificant. The important thing was that their son was making something of himself.

The loud music echoed in the partially filled disco. It was still a little early for any action there.

Dino, the stocky little maitre d', came over to me. "Everything's cool," he said. "Come down later. We're trying out a new D.J. He's supposed to be terrific."

"I'll try to make it." He gave me the checklist of the girls that were working and I went up to the cocktail lounge on the ground floor. Angelo was at the desk in the corner. "It's good tonight," he said.

I collected his list and went up another flight to the restaurant. The dining room was just beginning to thin out. Carmine hurried over to me. "I'll need a couple of extra girls Saturday night," he said. "I'm just about making it now."

"I'll take it up with Vincent."

"Do it for me, baby. We got to keep up the standards. We can't afford to fuck up."

All the floors above the third were reserved for members only. I decided to look into the health club. There were a few men lolling about in the raised swimming pool and some girls sitting around the edge looking bored. They paid absolutely no attention to the fact that the men were nude.

Tony came out of his little office. "Quiet," he said. "There's nobody in the steam or sauna."

The gym and massage parlor floor above was just as empty. Only one of the little booths had the curtain drawn. "It's dead tonight," Rocco, the trainer, said. "Nobody's got a hard-on. They're all staying home with their wives."

I laughed.

His face was serious. "It's not funny. The girls are beginning to practice on each other. I caught Joan giving Sandy a massage."

"You can't let that happen," I said with a straight face. "You'll have to make some sacrifices and let them practice on you."

He stared at me in disbelief. "My wife'll kill me!"

I laughed and went upstairs. There was absolutely nothing happening on the sixth floor, which had private rooms for guests who wished to stay the night. Gianni and his two girls were playing gin. I waved and went up to the office.

I put the checklists in a time box for the bookkeepers, lit a cigarette and went to Vincent's office. He hadn't come in yet. That was strange. When I had left his apartment just before eight o'clock he had said he would be in by ten. Since there was nothing else for me to do at the moment, I thought I might go down to the disco and check out the new D.J. A hip D.J. made all the difference. The right music for the right crowd kept the room jumping.

But I made no move to go. I really wasn't in the mood. I didn't feel like talking to anyone. It wasn't easy having to smile at people all the time, pretending to be interested in what they were saying.

I ground out my cigarette. What I really wanted to do was get stoned. But I couldn't do that either. The rules were very strict. No grass, no coke, no drugs on the premises. "We take absolutely no chances," Vincent said. "Everybody'll be looking to bust us if we make it. We make sure we don't give them a handle."

But at his apartment it was different. He had everything from grass and angel dust to poppers, which he loved to use while we were balling. But there was never anything on him. I used to wonder sometimes how the stuff got there but I didn't ask. There were some things I just didn't talk to him about and that included his family.

I remembered the only time I had seen his father and his two older brothers. They had come in one night shortly after we opened. There were two other men with them. Vincent took them right up to the office. About a half hour later they came down and Vincent gave them a tour of the club.

I happened to be at the entrance as they were on their way out. Vincent saw me but made no move to introduce us. His father was a thin gentle-looking little man with iron-gray hair and black, impenetrable eyes. Vincent bent over him and kissed him on each cheek.

The old man smiled, gently touched Vincent's face and nodded. "It is good, my son," he said. "We are proud of you." Then he turned and left, followed by the others.

Vincent glanced at me and, without a word, took the elevator up to his office. A few minutes later I followed him.

There was a bottle of scotch on his desk and he was refilling his glass as I came in. I had never seen him take a drink at work before. "It's okay," he said quickly. "It's okay."

But I noticed that his hand was shaking as he carried the glass to his lips. He took a swallow of the drink. "I want to fuck you," he said.

There was a strange expression in his eyes. Somehow I knew he was afraid of what my answer would be. "Okay," I said.

"Right away."

"Shall I lock the door?"

"Not here. At my place. Change your clothes."

Minutes later we were on our way. We didn't say a word until we walked into his apartment, which was only a few blocks from the club on Sutton Place, overlooking the river.

He turned on the light and crossed to a built-in bar. "Do you smoke?" he asked.

I nodded.

He lit a joint for me and another for himself. It was sweet stuff. Very easy. Usually it took only two tokes for me to get stoned but this time it didn't seem to be working.

"Come on," he said.

I followed him into the bedroom. He turned toward me, taking off his jacket. "Strip."

I put the joint in an ashtray and began to undress. I bent down to unfasten my shoe straps, and when I straightened up he was naked. He stared at me for a moment, then opened a drawer in the night table beside the bed. He brought out a yellow box, a small white vial of powder and an tiny gold spoon. He came toward me with the vial and spoon.

He took the cap off the vial and spooned out some white powder. Then he held it to his nostril and snorted. Afterward he took a deep breath and repeated the process under his other nostril. His eyes began to lighten. "Bang," he said, holding out a spoonful of powder to me.

"What is it?" I asked.

"Coke," he said. "Take it. It won't hurt you."

He held the spoon to my nose. I snorted. The powder made me sneeze. He laughed and held the spoon under the other nostril. I snorted again. This time is only stung a little.

"How is it?" he asked.

"I don't feel anything."

"You will." He laughed. "Takes a few minutes."

He was right. Already my nostrils were numbing and there was a dryness in my mouth. Suddenly I was up there. He had been watching me. "Good?"

"Way out."

He put down the vial and pulled me toward him. His mouth was rough and bruising and I could feel his hands gripping hard into my arms. We stumbled and almost fell across the bed. I felt his teeth biting into my breasts, hurting my nipples. I moaned in pain and he raised his head.

His eyes stared into mine. "I'm crazy about you. Do you know that?" he said, almost angrily.

I shook my head. My pain seemed like nothing compared with his. His world of pain was far beyond me.

He reached across to the little yellow box and pulled out an amyl nitrite capsule. Holding it in his hand, he pushed my legs back in a jacknife position against my chest and rose to his knees, poised over me. His entire body seemed like a tense steel spring.

There was a strange faraway glaze over his eyes. Then, before I had the chance to be frightened, he fell forward across me. I could feel the length of him pushing into me and at the same time he broke the popper.

My head seemed to explode with the rush of blood and heat to my brain and at the same moment his orgasm began. He raised himself away from me suddenly, digging his arms into the mattress on either side of me. His eyes were closed and his face contorted.

"No! Oh, Christ! No!" he almost screamed, trying to control his spasms. "No, no, no!"

I pulled him down to me. "Don't fight it, don't hold it back. Let it come."

He shivered for a moment more, then it was over. He lay very still, his chest heaving against me. Then abruptly he began to cry. Hard, racking sobs.

I held his head to my breasts and stroked his hair. "It's all right," I said. "It's all right."

He raised his head to look at me. His eyes were wet with tears. "You don't understand," he said. "Damn them!"

I waited for him to go on.

"They finally got what they wanted," he said. "They wanted me in the family business, and like it or not I'm in it."

"Don't talk about it," I said. "It will be all right."

"No. The club was supposed to be mine. They loaned me the money for it. But now they don't want the money back. We're all partners. After all, aren't we family?" he asked bitterly.

"Is that why they were at the club tonight?"

He nodded. "I would have been better off if it had bombed. At least that way they would have forgotten the whole thing. It would have been just another of Vincenzo's crazy ideas."

"I didn't know they were like that. From everything I've heard, Italian families always kept their word to each other. No matter what happened."

"Except when it comes to money and power. Cosa nostra is just a word for the newspapers. My father got rid of his brother in order to become the head of the family, and when he's gone my brothers will kill each other to take his place."

I was silent for a moment. "What happens now?"

"Nothing," he said. "I run it just the same as before. Only now we cut the profit four ways."

"What happens to the money they loaned you? The two million dollars. Do you have to pay it back?"

"Of course not. It's the family business now. The business will pay it back out of their share."

"Then you're ahead," I said, looking at him. "My father was a banker and I remember he once told me that any loan you did not have to repay personally was a clear profit. You just made yourself a half million dollars clear."

Finally he began to smile. "You're a strange girl," he said. He swung his legs off the bed. "Care for a drink?"

"No, but if you have another stick I'd like it."

He came back into the bedroom with a cigarette box full. I lit one and leaned back on the pillows inhaling gently. This time it worked. I began to feel very mellow.

He was standing at the side of the bed looking down at me. I passed him the joint. He took a few tokes then I reached up for him.

"Come here," I said. "You owe me one."

He came down into my arms and this time we made love. The next day I moved everything except my typewriter and papers into his apartment. I didn't give up the apartment, because I always wanted a place to go to where I could work.

Chapter 22

BY THE TIME I went back down to the disco it was jammed. There was just about enough room on the floor to move up and down in time with the beat. The rest of the room was filled with people huddled around tiny tables without an inch of space between them.

Dino came over to me, a wide grin on his round face. "The new boy's good," he said. "He keeps them movin'."

I looked across the dark room to where the D.J. was working at two turntables which were raised on a platform slightly above the floor. He was a tall slim black boy, dressed in an outlandish costume—safari wide-brimmed hat, hand-made chamois shirt and wide bell-bottomed chinos. He held an earphone to his ear while he placed a new record on the second turntable and marked the disk. When he finished he put the headset down, looked at me and smiled.

There was something vaguely familiar about his smile. I nodded and made my way through the crush of people to the turntable. When I stopped in front of the stand, he smiled again. "Hello, JeriLee," he said shyly.

I couldn't keep the surprise from my voice "Fred! Fred Lafayette!"

He grinned. "You remembered."

I held out my hand. "I can't believe it," I said.

"Yep. Here we are. Right back where we started. Me up on the stand, you down there on the floor, workin'."

"But your singing," I said. "What happened?"

"You know, girl. Mellow singers like Nat King Cole just ain't cuttin' it today. The world is rock happy." He let go of my hand. "How long has it been? Ten years?"

"Just about."

"I used to read about you in the papers," he said. "Then I sort of lost touch. You divorced that man, didn't you?"

I nodded.

"You look real good," he said. "You grew up pretty."

"I feel old."

"That's no way to talk. You're still a kid."

"I wish it were true," I said. "My father died."

"I'm sorry to hear that. He was a nice man."

"Yes."

"I saw you when I came into work an' thought I recognized you."

"Why didn't you talk to me?" I asked.

"When I checked to see if I was right I was told to keep off. That you were the boss's lady." His eyes searched mine.

"That's true. But you should have said something anyway. After all, we're old friends."

Before he could answer, Dino was at my side. "Vincenzo just came in. He wants to see you right away."

"Okay," I said. I looked up at Fred. "I hope you like it here. Maybe we could get together for a cup of coffee sometime."

"Sure," he said. He picked up the earphone and began placing another disk. "You let me know when."

I pushed my way back to the door and went up to the office. Vincent was on something. The expression in his eyes was too bright. His voice was angry. "What the hell were you doing holding hands wtih that nigger?"

"We were shaking, not holding hands," I said. "He's an old friend. He saved my life once."

"I don't give a shit what he did. I'm going to fire the cock-sucker!"

"You do," I said, "and you fire me too." Fred had been more right than he knew when he said we were back where we started. It looked as if I were going to cost him another job.

Vincent suddenly calmed down. "He really saved your life?"

"Yes," I said. "A couple of kids were beating me and trying to rape me. He got me away from them just in time."

Vincent was silent for a moment. "How old were you?"

"Sixteen."

"I guess it's all right then," he said. "You really are old friends."

I didn't answer.

"Change your clothes," he said. "We're gettin' out of here."

"Where are we going?"

"Over to El Mo. I'm onto something. We're goin' to meet some people there."

"About what?"

"About a movie," he snapped. "How long do you think I can stand a stinking joint like this before going crazy?"

"Does your family know about it?"

"No. And I don't give a damn! Now change your goddamn dress and stop asking so many damn questions."

We walked into El Morocco and it was like a rerun of the first time we had met. The Paoluzzis were at the best table. Only one thing was different. Instead of the Italian lawyer there was a hard compact medium-sized man in a dark suit who was introduced only as Frank.

Paoluzzi kissed my hand in that strange way he had and Carla Maria pressed her cheek to mine.

"Everything settled?" Vincent asked as we sat down.

Frank nodded. "You'll have my check for a million dollars in the morning."

Vincent suddenly smiled. "This calls for a drink. Another bottle of champagne," he said to the headwaiter.

Frank got to his feet. "It's already past my bedtime. I'd better get going." He shook hands formally with the producer and Carla Maria, then said something in Italian to which they responded with smiles and nods. "Good night, young lady," he said to me. "Nice meeting you."

"Nice meeting you," I replied.

"Good night, Vincent. Don't forget to give my regards to your father."

Vincent got to his feet. "I won't, Uncle Frank. Good night."

I watched him walk toward the door. There was something about the man that radiated power. Even the headwaiters seemed to bow more deferentially than usual. He went up the few steps to the entrance to the street and I saw two men come from the little bar and join him. They walked out together.

"To the film," Vincent said, raising his glass of champagne.

"And you're going to be in it," Vincent said to me. "The second lead next to Carla Maria."

"You've got to be joking."

"I'm not. It's part of the deal."

"How did you manage to do it?"

He laughed. "Simple. I couldn't get the money anywhere else so I put it up myself."

"Where did you get it?" Then it dawned on me. "Is that the money your Uncle Frank was talking about?"

"I put up my share of the club as security."

"Does your father know?"

"What difference does it make? I have the right to do what I like with my share."

I was silent.

He refilled my glass. "Stop thinking about it and drink up. You're going to be a star, baby."

It was a little after three o'clock when we came out of El Morocco. Vincent pushed me toward the limousine. "You go to the hotel with them," he said. "I'll run over to the club, make sure that everything is okay and then join you."

"I'm tired," I said. "I'd just as soon go home to sleep if it's all right with you."

He was smiling but I could tell from his eyes that he was angry. "It's not all right with me. You go with them. I have some things to settle with Dino and they have to be settled tonight."

I knew better than to argue with him when he was in that mood. I got into the car. He waved his hand and started walking up the street as the limo moved down to First Avenue.

Carla Maria smiled at me. "It's like a dream come true. Making a picture with the two of you."

She reached across her husband and patted my hand. "You Americans are so funny." She laughed. "I mean tonight." She read the expression on my face. "Didn't Vincent tell you that we were going to spend the night together?"

I shook my head. "He said that he would meet us later."

She said something to her husband in Italian, then

spoke to me. "We will call Vincent from the hotel and straighten this out."

"No." I reached across to the front seat and tapped the driver on the shoulder. "Could you stop the car here, please?"

The car pulled to the curb. Neither of them said a word as I got out. I flagged a cab and went to the apartment.

I had just finished undressing when Vincent came storming in. He stood in the bedroom doorway shouting at me. "You goddamn stupid cunt! After all I went through just to get them to agree to let you have the part."

"You should have told me what you had in mind," I said.

"Well now you know, so get yourself dressed and haul your ass over there!"

"No. I told you once before it wasn't my game."

"You like going around town begging for jobs and starving better?"

I didn't answer.

"Remember what it was like the day you came into the club? You were on your ass when I took you off the streets. Now you think you can shit on me!"

"I'm not dumping on you."

"Yes you are!" he yelled. "We can blow the whole deal just because you won't go along with it."

"No you won't," I said. "The million dollars you're getting for him is the important thing. Not me."

"You're part of the deal too!" he shouted.

"You had no right to do that without asking me."

"I had no right to commit the money either," he yelled. "But I did it. Now don't you fuck it up or I'll wind up in a sewer someplace."

I stared at him.

He suddenly slumped into a chair and covered his face with his hands. After a moment he looked up at me. There were tears in his eyes. "The only thing my family respects is success. If the picture goes over, everything will be all right."

I didn't speak.

"Please," he begged. "Just this once. Afterward you can do anything you want. It's the only chance I have to get out from under them."

I didn't move.

"They'll bury me if this deal doesn't go through. My father and Uncle Frank haven't spoken in years. I don't dare give him a chance to get that share of the club."

"You already have," I pointed out.

"Not if the picture is made. Uncle Frank promised to keep it quiet if he gets paid back." He put his hands over his face again and began to cry.

I stood looking at him for a long minute, then I slowly began to get dressed. As I walked past him to the door he stopped me.

He went to the night table, took out a few joints, the vial of coke and a box of poppers. He put them all in my handbag. "This might help," he said.

I didn't speak.

He bent and kissed my cold lips. "Thanks. I love you," he said.

I turned and went out the door. Even then I knew I would never come back.

Ten minutes later I was at their hotel suite. Carla Maria opened the door with a smile. "I am so glad you have coming," she said.

I laughed suddenly. It wasn't only her English. The whole thing just was beginning to feel ridiculous. I immediately lit a stick, then I took a double hit of coke and chased it down with two glasses of champagne.

By the time we made it to the bedroom I was as high as a kite and nothing seemed to matter. Much to my surprise I even began to enjoy it. I never dreamed that a woman's touch could be so delicate and so exciting. And the tricks Carla Maria could do with her tongue made the Green Hornet seem like a child's toy. It was as if a whole new world were opening up for me.

And when I woke up in the morning beside her and saw how beautiful she really was, I knew I had loved every moment of it.

Chapter 23

I WAITED UNTIL after noon, when I thought he would be at the club for the morning accounting, before going back to the apartment for my clothes. I let myself in and went through to the bedroom. I had guessed wrong. He was in bed, still asleep.

I started to back out of the room quietly but he awakened and sat up in bed rubbing his eyes. "Good morning," he said, smiling.

I didn't answer.

"Come on now," he said. "It wasn't so bad, was it?"

"No."

He was wide awake now. "Did she eat your pussy?"

"Yes."

"Did you eat hers?"

"Yes."

I could sense he was getting excited. "What did Gino do all the time you were together?"

"Once he came in the room and watched us."

"Did he fuck her?"

"I don't know."

"Did he fuck you?"

"I don't know," I repeated. "I remember he fucked one of us but I don't remember which one."

"What did he do afterward?"

"He went back to his own room to sleep."

"And what did you do?"

"We snorted the rest of the coke, popped a few more ammies and kept on balling."

"Jesus!" he exclaimed. He got out of bed. I was right. He was excited. "I wish I had been there. It must have been something to watch."

I didn't speak.

"Let's ball."

"No." I let a moment pass. "I'm all fucked out."

"There's always room for one more."

"No." I went to the closet and took down my suitcases.

"What are you doing?" he asked.

"Packing."

"What for?" He seemed genuinely puzzled.

"Because I'm moving out. Why the hell do you think I would be packing?"

"For Christ's sake, you don't have to be so pissed off about it. You said you had a good time, didn't you?"

"That has nothing to do with it," I said. "I don't like lies, and you lied to me."

"Shit, baby," he said. "That was an important deal. You might have blown it for us."

"You mean I might have blown it for you. There never was anything in it for me."

He stared at me without speaking.

"All that crap you gave me about being in the picture was just that. Crap. Carla Maria told me this morning that she didn't know what you were talking about last night. There isn't any part in the picture for me. Why couldn't you have told me the truth?"

"I wasn't lying about my family. My father would—" He stopped when he saw the expression on my face.

"You were lying about that too," I said. "Carla Maria told me that Frank and your father are partners in the deal, that each is putting up half the money."

"Aw Christ, honey," he said, coming toward me. "It's over. Everything worked out. You know I love you."

"You're right. It is over. You can stop lying now." I began to take my clothes out of the closet and put them in the suitcases. "Just let me pack."

"Where are you going?" he asked.

"To my apartment."

"Jesus, you're not going back to that dump?"

"Would it make more sense if I told you that I was going to Italy with Carla Maria?"

"I wouldn't believe you," he said.

I opened my bag and handed him the airline ticket. "Would that convince you?"

"Well I'll be a son of a bitch."

"You're beginning to tell the truth," I said, taking back the ticket.

He shook his head. "To think you turned out to be a goddamn dike."

I laughed. "Little boys shouldn't play with fire. They might burn their fingers. But don't worry about it. I already told her I wasn't going. I don't intend to be a whore for either one of you."

Relief crossed his face. "You've had a rough time," he said. "Why don't you just hop into bed and get some rest. You can even have the night off."

"I'll do that. Just as soon as I get to my place. And don't worry about giving me the night off. I've just quit."

"Don't be stupid," he said. "We can still be friends."

"Maybe you can. But I can't."

"What are you going to live on?" he asked after a few minutes.

"I've saved some money," I said. "And I have a play to finish. I haven't had much time to work on it lately."

"You haven't got that much money," he said.

"When it runs out I'll find another job," I said. "But I'm not going to stop writing. Not ever again."

Two nights later my doorbell rang. I got up from the typewriter and answered the door.

"Hi," Fred said. "I just happened to be in the neighborhood so I thought I'd take a chance and see if you were in."

"How did you get my address?"

"From the girl in the office."

"Aren't you supposed to be at work?"

He smiled. "I got fired. I was just hoping that I wasn't the reason you got fired too."

"I wasn't fired. I quit." Then realizing that he was still standing in the hall, I said, "Come on in."

I saw his eyes moving around the room.

"Excuse the mess," I said quickly. "But I've been working."

"I didn't mean to disturb you."

"No, it's okay. I'm glad you came. I needed a break and I have some cold white wine in the fridge." I offered to take his jacket but he made no move to take it off.

"I thought if you hadn't eaten we could go out and get some chink's."

I grinned. "You just talked me into it. Give me one minute to get into some other clothes."

"Don't pick out anything too fancy," he said. "I got a rich man's taste but a poor man's pocket."

"Jeans okay?"

"Fine," he said.

I slipped into the jeans and a clean shirt behind the closet door. "How's that?" I asked.

"Perfect."

"Now if you give me another minute to brush my hair and put on my face." Ten minutes later I came out of the bathroom, and found him still standing where I had left him.

"You could have sat down," I said.

"I didn't think of it. I was happy where I was."

The cold night air felt good. I had been inside all day. "Do you know a good Chinese restaurant around here?" he asked.

"There's one over on Seventy-second near Broadway. We can walk."

We chattered all the way through our meal of egg rolls, spareribs, won ton soup and lobster Cantonese with fried rice. Back at my house he stopped at the outside door.

"I still have the wine in the fridge," I said.

"I don't want to put you out none."

"Come on," I said.

It was two o'clock in the morning when Fred got to his feet. "I'd better let you get some sleep," he said. "I feel guilty enough about keepin' you from working."

"It was fine," I said, opening the door for him. "Thank you." I stood on my toes to kiss him good night.

His lips touched mine gently, and suddenly something

happened. A warmth rose between us and I moved into his arms. I pulled him back into the apartment and kicked the door shut.

Later, much later, when we lay quietly in each other's arms, his soft voice whispered in my ear. "You know, JeriLee, I've always loved you. Even way back then."

"You don't have to say that if you don't mean it, Fred. I'm happy enough just being with you."

"But I do mean it, JeriLee."

"I don't want you to lie to me. I'm tired of people saying things they don't mean."

"I'm not lying to you, JeriLee," he said patiently. "I loved you then. I love you now. And, in a way, I guess I always will."

Because I could feel the truth in him I began to cry. Two days later he moved into the apartment with me.

Book Three

ANY OLD TOWN

Chapter 1

THE DREAM was there. It was always there. The little girl at the top of the stairs. But in the split second between sleeping and waking it was gone. JeriLee heard the soft gentle humming of a song through the closed bedroom door and rolled over sluggishly. A sharp pain much like the headache after a hangover knifed through her temples.

It was, as the doctor had told her to expect, the aftereffect of the anesthetic.

After a moment the pain subsided and she got out of bed. She made her way to the bathroom, quickly swallowed two Bufferin and sat on the toilet. She felt congested and swollen, as if she needed to have a bowel movement. But after a moment when nothing happened she gave up and simply decided to change the tampon.

She looked at it curiously before discarding it. It wasn't as bloody as she thought it might be, no more so than an ordinary period. So far the doctor had been right.

Angela's voice was soft through the closed bathroom door. "JeriLee. Are you all right in there?"

"I'm fine."

"The coffee is made," Angela said. "I'll have breakfast ready by the time you come out."

"Thank you. But I'll be a few minutes. I want to shower first."

"It's okay. Take your time."

JeriLee realized as she stepped into the stall shower that it had been more than a month since Angela had been to see her, and she wondered why she had chosen to come today of all days.

Coffee and orange juice were waiting on the night table when JeriLee emerged from the bathroom. The sheets felt cool and crisp against her skin and she realized that Angela must have changed them while she was showering. She propped the pillows behind her, drained the glass of orange juice and had just finished pouring her first cup of coffee when Angela came back carrying a tray laden with scrambled eggs, bacon and toast.

"I didn't think I'd be hungry," JeriLee said.

Angela's gentle eyes smiled. "Eat then. If you want more I can make it."

Angela sat on the chair next to the bed and poured herself a cup of coffee. "Aren't you eating?" JeriLee asked.

Angela shook her head. "I just want some coffee."

"What made you come today?" JeriLee asked after a moment.

Angela's eyes were steady. "I thought you could use some help."

"You knew?"

Angela nodded. "Everyone knows. George can't keep his mouth shut and your agent wasn't much better."

There were no secrets anywhere, she thought, taking another bite of egg. "You're not working today?"

"No. We've taped all our shows for the week. I'm not due back in the studio until Monday."

Angela was the ingenue on a daily television show, *The Stars Never Fall.* Every afternoon at two o'clock housewives all over the country turned on their sets to watch it. It was probably the most successful soap in history. In the five years Angela had been on the show it had always been number one in its time slot.

JeriLee wiped up the plate with a piece of toast. "That was good," she said.

"Food always helps," Angela said.

JeriLee smiled. "My mother always said that."

Angela picked up the tray and started for the door. "If there is anything else you want," she said, "I'll be here."

"Angela," JeriLee called.

The girl looked back.

"Thank you, Angela," JeriLee said.

Angela's eyes filled with tears and she turned, closing the door behind her with her foot.

JeriLee stared at the closed door. Angela cared about her. She had always known that. She cared about Angela too. But there was a difference. The difference was that she loved Angela but Angela was in love with her.

Angela—tall, slim, beautiful—so cool on the outside but so frightened and fucked up on the inside. Why had it happened? It should have been so easy for her. But nothing ever brought her any real satisfaction. Her search for love was endless and unrequited.

Still it had to have begun somewhere for Angela, just as it had to have begun somewhere for her. But it was difficult to tell exactly where. We are the sum total of our experiences to any given point. And the point was always changing.

For JeriLee it had started somewhere between Port Clare, New York and Los Angeles and all the way stops and towns in between—Pittsburgh, Gary, Chicago, Des Moines, Phoenix, Las Vegas. She'd been to all of them. And she'd had them all—all the way to the madhouse.

Strange that that should come back to her now. A cold shiver of fear ran through her. Did it mean she was sliding back, back into that world of fear where everyone was a stranger?

No! she thought. She was not going back. It would never be like that again. Never would she let herself be used, not by anyone, not for any reason, even love.

She would give only what she could give. Too many times she had tried to be what others wanted her to be. And it hadn't worked. She could not be all things to all people. She could not even be all things to one person. And it was not until she recognized that in herself and saw the limitations of her own capacities that she began to be able to accept herself and give up some of the guilt.

She knew she couldn't run the mile in four minutes, or soar like a gull in the morning wind. And there were mornings when the day seemed to stretch into disaster.

But there would always be those times, those days, and if she recognized them not as signs of failure and weakness, but as part of her basic humanness and right to be imperfect, she would never have to be afraid again.

That was the one thing she had learned and it had helped. At least now she could stand alone without the need to clutch and cling for support. Still it would be good if there were someone. It was not fun to be alone.

She lit a cigarette and leaned back against the pillows. That was the heart of it. Aloneness. All of it, all of them, the men, the women. When it was over and they were gone you came back to being alone. Still she knew that just outside the window there was a world filled with people.

What was it Angela had said to her one morning while they were lying on the bed together, the Sunday papers spread between them. "You never seem to want anything, JeriLee. You never ask anyone to do anything for you, not even to get you a cup of coffee. Just once I would like you to ask me to do something. At least that way I would feel needed."

"Is that what you want—to be needed?"

Angela nodded. "How else can I tell that I mean something to you?"

"Isn't it enough that we're together, that we've been balling all night? Doesn't that mean anything?"

"That's sex. I know I'm not the only one you sleep with and there's nothing you can do with me that you don't do with others. But I want more. I want to be important to you."

"Would you feel better if I couldn't function without you?" JeriLee asked.

Angela didn't answer.

Suddenly she was angry, more with herself than with Angela. "I haven't lied to you, have I?" she demanded. "I told you exactly where it would be with us, didn't I?"

Angela nodded, misery in her eyes. "Yes," she answered in a small voice.

"Then what more do you want from me?"

"I want you to love me."

"I can't love you the way you want me to. I can only love you the way I do."

"Don't be angry with me, JeriLee."

She walked over to the window and looked out into the bright California sunshine. Down below them the traffic on the Strip was beginning to come alive. "There's a whole world out there, Angela," she said. "And somewhere there is someone who will love you the way you want to be loved. All you have to do is give that world a chance."

Angela came to the window and stood beside her. "Is there someone out there for you too, JeriLee?" she asked.

A sudden sorrow flooded JeriLee, a knowledge of her own and Angela's pain. It was as if they were sisters, even more than sisters. Suddenly they moved toward each other and their tears mingled.

"I hope so," JeriLee said softly. "I should hate to think there wasn't."

Then they had gone back to bed and made love and in the sweet agony of their sex they had rediscovered their sameness and their separateness. But by the time Sunday had gone they knew that the affair was over, even though a residue of their love would remain with them.

The next morning when Angela had gone to work she had taken her small suitcase but she had not returned JeriLee's key. Suddenly she realized how Angela had come into her apartment this morning. But right now she was tired. The pain throbbed in her pelvis, a reminder of yesterday.

The telephone rang and she picked it up. "How are you feeling?" the doctor asked.

"Okay," she answered. "The pain just started up again but I'm not bleeding as much as I thought."

His voice was matter-of-fact. "You'll bleed a little but don't be frightened, and keep taking some aspirin to kill the pain. Stay in bed if you can. If you need someone to take care of you I can send over a practical nurse."

"That's okay. A friend of mine is here."

"Good. I'll look in on you this afternoon on my way back from the hospital."

"Thank you."

A moment later the door opened. "Everything all right?" Angela asked.

"Yes. It was the doctor. He's coming by this afternoon."

"Is there anything I can do?"

"Nothing, thanks. He just told me to stay in bed and rest." She leaned back against the pillows. "I think I'll try to sleep."

JeriLee stared at the closed door. Which, she wondered, was the stronger—needing, or the need to be needed? She didn't know the answer. Probably never would.

Suddenly she remembered what Fred had said many years ago: "We're good for each other, baby, because we need each other."

She had agreed with him. But neither of them had really known what their needs were. And in the end it turned out that she had been feeding on herself.

Chapter 2

THE CHATTER of the typewriter keys stopped. She sat at the small table staring at the words on the page, their sound still echoing in her mind.

"I love you. I don't love you. How the hell do I know how I feel?"

She rose from the chair and went to the window. The city street was dark and deserted except for a garbage truck that was collecting refuse from the restaurant across the street. The radio clock told her it was two-thirty in the morning. She went back to the table, took a deep drag on the cigarette and ground it out in the ashtray already littered with broken butts. Without sitting down, she hit the keys, forming the final word: CURTAIN.

Almost angrily, she tore the page from the typewriter and put it in the box on top of the rest of the neatly typed pages. It was finished.

The momentary anger passed and now she felt drained and empty. Tomorrow, with the realities she had put off day after day while clinging to her writing, loomed in front of her. Tomorrow she would have to think about money, about paying bills. Tomorrow she would have to go beyond her own walls, back into the world of people, back into the marketplace which sat in judgment upon her work.

She felt the nervousness rise within her, and she started to tremble. What are you afraid of, JeriLee? she asked herself. You've done nothing wrong. You've been working. You had a reason not to leave the cocoon.

But her hands were shaking to the point that she couldn't hold them still. She went into the bathroom and took the vial of Valium from the medicine cabinet, then popped a ten-mg blue, which she flushed down with a swallow of water.

She looked up at the clock. Two-thirty-five. It would be an hour and a half before Fred got home. He had a weekend gig at a bar on West Forty-ninth Street and wouldn't be out until after three o'clock. The tightness began to disappear from the pit of her stomach. She was beginning to feel better now. Her confidence was returning.

It was done. The play was finished. Tomorrow she could get on with her life. There was nothing to be afraid of, except what was in her head.

The first thing she had to do was get the play to Fannon. He had promised that he would do it. The next thing she had to do was to go to a beauty parlor. No, first she would go to the beauty parlor, then she would take the play to Fannon. She wanted to look her best when she walked into his office.

She began to separate the originals and the carbons. In a few minutes she had them all neatly together, each copy in its own ring binder. It wasn't a bad job. The typing service couldn't have done better—and they charged more than a hundred dollars for five copies. Quickly she stacked them on the shelf, put the cover over the typewriter and wheeled it into the closet. The room looked strangely empty. It was the first time in almost six months that the typewriter wasn't the main fixture.

A feeling of elation came over her. This was an important moment. A time to celebrate. This was a night for champagne and caviar. She opened the cupboard—Gallo chablis and Planter's peanuts. That wasn't so bad either.

She put the bottle of wine into the freezing compartment, placed a tablecloth and two candles on the small table and emptied the can of peanuts into a glass bowl. Quickly she straightened the rest of the room, even emptying the wastebasket of all the rejected pages. Now there was no messy trace of work. She lit the candles and turned off the lights, then stepped back to observe the effect. The warm yellow glow flickered through the room.

Satisfied, she went into the bathroom and stripped off her shirt and jeans. She still had time to shower and do something with her hair before Fred came home. After all, it was a special night and she wanted to look special.

Despite the efforts of the conditioners, the air was still heavy with the smell of cigarettes, beer and sweat. Fred looked at his watch. A quarter to three. Only fifteen minutes to go. He looked down at the white keyboard of the piano. There was a nothing feeling to playing and singing. Nobody listened, and if they did they couldn't hear over the noise.

From his perch near the back of the room he looked down the bar. The bar girls were hustling. It was a good night. Maybe fifty per cent of the men were in uniform. Now he knew why the owners fought so hard to keep off the armed services' banned list. Without servicemen there was no business.

"Fred." He turned and saw Licia standing behind him. She was a big honey-colored girl with a lustrous Nancy Wilson wig. The unofficial chief bar girl, she had a quiet air about her that belied her inner toughness. And for whatever reason, nobody fooled with her, neither the girls nor the customers. She talked with them, had drinks with them, but when the bar closed she left alone.

"Got a request for the piano player?" he asked, hitting an opening chord.

"Yeah. The man wants you to stay on till four o'clock."

"Shit," he said, continuing with the song. "I'm beat. I been up here for five solid hours."

"You get double for the extra hour," she said.

That was ten dollars. He was getting twenty-five dollars for the five hours of regular work. "How come the man's suddenly so big?"

"Look at that crowd," Licia said. "He knows they see you get down from that piano they figure the night's over and begin to leave."

Fred wondered if JeriLee was waiting up for him. Chances were that she had already gone to bed. "Okay," he said. The extra ten dollars looked good. It was his first gig in more than three weeks.

JeriLee looked up at the clock. It was half past three. He should have been home by now. She began to feel the tightness gather inside her again.

It was stupid. She would have to get a better grip on herself. There was nothing to be nervous about. She'd finished the play.

A joint would help. She went into the bedroom and took the small cellophane bag full of grass from the table next to the bed. They liked having a joint before sex. A few tokes made everything easy.

Sitting on the couch concentrating intently on rolling the joint gave her something to do. She licked the paper carefully and looked at her handwork. The joint was smooth and neat, the ends tightly rolled. She struck a match and lit up.

She took the first toke deep into her lungs and held it there. There was something reassuring about its smarting sweetness. She took another hit and could feel the tension ease. This was better. She looked up at the clock again. Three-forty-five. It wasn't so bad.

Suddenly she felt dry and thirsty. Grass always did that to her. She took the wine from the refrigerator and poured a glass. She was beginning to feel a little high. Fred would be surprised when he came in and saw her like this.

Usually she was either sleeping fitfully or hunched tensed over the typewriter. It couldn't have been that good for him but only once had he complained. "Baby, looks like you forgot how to have fun. You can't always live uptight like this."

It had been a bad day. "What the hell do you know?" she had shouted. "You get a gig, you don't get a gig, you don't get a gig, you don't have to dig something out of yourself when you don't even know whether it's worth anything or not, whether it's good or bad, right or wrong. You go to work if you have a job. If you don't, you sit around here drinking beer and smoking grass and staring at me night and day. Fuck it. Nothing bothers you."

He stared at her for a moment, then went into the bathroom, closing the door behind him. A little while later she heard the sound of the shower. By the time he came out, her temper had gone and she felt contrite.

"I'm sorry," she said. "I didn't mean to yell like that."

He nodded and without speaking went into the bedroom and came out with a joint already rolled. He lit it and passed it to her. "You'll be okay," he said. "Once you've finished the play."

Well now it was finished and she was feeling good. She took another toke and chased it down with some wine. Feeling good and free for the first time in a long while. She felt the warmth growing inside and touched herself with a sense of excitement. She was wet. This hadn't happened for a long time. God, she was horny. She couldn't wait for him to come home. He didn't know it but he was about to get the most mind-blowing sex he had ever had.

Chapter 3

AT FOUR O'CLOCK the bar closed. In less than ten minutes all the customers and most of the bar girls had gone. The bartenders wasted no motions. Any customer that showed signs of lingering over his drink suddenly found it missing from the bar in front of him.

Fred wearily gathered up his sheet music and placed it in his leather folder, then made his way to the front cash register to collect his pay. The bartender had his back toward him, counting out the cash. Fred stood patiently, waiting until he was finished. He knew better than to interrupt him.

Licia suddenly appeared at his shoulder. "The man wants to buy you a drink," she said.

"Okay, bourbon and water," Fred said gratefully.

"Jack Daniel's and water," she called out. "The bar whiskey is piss," she said. "It's cut by fifty per cent."

"Thanks."

The bartender put the drink in front of him and went back to the register. "Right on," he said, taking a sip.

"The man likes you," she said. "He says you know your music."

"Thank him for me," Fred said. It had been a long time since anyone had said something nice to him about his music.

"What are your plans?" she asked suddenly.

"What do you mean?"

"Work," she said.

"Find another gig."

"You don't have a job during the day?"

"No, there's only my music. I don't know anything else."

"How do you keep busy?"

"Lookin' for gigs," he said. "And there's some songs I been workin' on."

"You write songs?"

He nodded. "Only trouble is I can't get anyone to listen to them. The publishing companies are all locked up with big names an' the only thing they're interested in is rock. Shove a guitar on some kid dressed in hippie clothes an' a beard an' they fall all over themselves to sign him."

"Maybe the man can help you," she said. "He's got connections with a few music companies."

"I'd appreciate it," he said.

"Let me go talk to him," she said.

He watched her walk to the back and disappear into the office between the men's and the ladies' toilets. He was sure that nothing would come of it but he was grateful that she'd shown an interest. In all the time he had been with JeriLee, the subject of his writing had never come up. She was too into her own work. There was no room in her head for anything else.

When Licia came back, she said, "He told me to tell you he has a piano up at his place. If you want to come up there, he'll listen to your songs."

"Now?" he asked. "It's after four o'clock."

"The man is night people," she said. "This is the middle of the afternoon for him. He don't get out of bed until seven o'clock."

Fred thought for a moment. JeriLee was certainly asleep by now. He didn't really expect anything, but any chance was better than no chance at all. "Okay," he said.

"Give Fred thirty-five dollars," she said.

The bartender quickly counted out the money and Fred put it in his pocket. "Thanks," he said.

"Come on then," she said. "I got my car parked up

at the Radio City garage. The man tol' me to bring you up to his place."

The car was a silver Cadillac convertible with black leather and a black top. He sank back into the seat beside her and took a deep breath. Two things always turned him on. The smell of a new car or a new pussy. Somehow they always came together in his head, and this car smelled new.

She hit the tape deck as they moved onto Forty-ninth Street. It was Nat King Cole singing "Too Young"—one of his biggest hits. "There'll never be another like the King," he said.

"The King is dead," she said quietly.

She cut expertly into the Avenue of the Americas going uptown. She had the lights timed perfectly. They were in the park before he knew it.

"Nice car," he said.

"I like it," she said tonelessly.

They left the Park at Seventy-second and Fifth and went across town to York Avenue. She turned in at one of the new buildings on the corner of York and went down the ramp into the garage. She pulled to a stop and got out without waiting for an attendant. "The elevator's over here," she said.

The elevator operator seemed to know her. He touched his hand to his forehead. "Good morning," he said.

"Good morning," she answered.

He knew where they were going. The car stopped at the seventeenth floor without her saying a word. Fred followed her down the carpeted corridor. She had to be pretty thick with the man. They hadn't even called up to announce her the way they usually did in this kind of building. He watched her come to a stop in front of one of the doors and take a key out of her purse. He nodded to himself. Yeah. She was thick with the man. Real thick. She even had her own key.

The lights in the apartment were already on and he followed her through a large entrance hall into an even larger living room. Windows surrounded the room, allowing a view of the East River, the Triborough Bridge uptown and the Queenboro Bridge at Fifty-ninth Street. A white baby grand piano stood in an alcove near the corner windows. He stood in silent admiration. The only time he had ever seen anything like this was in the movies.

"Quite a place the man has here," he said.

She glanced at him without comment. "Jack Daniel's and water?" she asked.

He nodded.

She fixed his drink and waited while he tasted it. "Okay?" she asked.

"Fine." He nodded, then turned in response to the sound of footsteps.

A white girl with long brown hair and blue eyes came into the room wearing a white dressing gown. "I was asleep," she said to Licia, "but I heard voices."

"Sorry we woke you, honey. But Fred here came to play for us." She turned to him. "Fred, this is Sam. Short for Samantha. Sam, this is Fred—" She looked at him questioningly.

"Lafayette," he said quickly.

"Fred Lafayette," Licia repeated.

The girl held out her hand. "Nice to meet you."

"Nice to meet you," he said. Her touch was cool. He turned back to Licia. "The man here yet? I can start any time he's ready."

Licia looked at him steadily. "You can start now."

He stared at her. Suddenly it all made sense. He had worked the bar at least four times and had never seen the man.

"You?" There was a note of wonder in his voice.

She nodded.

He put his drink down on a small coffee table. "I think I better go," he said. "I don't like being put on."

Licia's voice was steady. "Nobody's putting you on. You said you can't get anybody to listen to your music. Well, I can, if I think it's worth a shot."

He met her eyes. "You do this often?"

"First time."

"Why me?"

"I studied music in college," she said. "But I have no talent. I can fake it but that's not the real thing. And I know the real thing when I hear it. I heard some of the things you did in the bar. You have a style all your own. You made those songs sound like you wrote them."

He was silent for a moment. "You manage the Green Bar?"

"I own it," she said simply. "An' just in case you have any wrong ideas about my being interested in your fat black dick, get them out of your head. I'm happy the way I am. I just happen to dig your music, an' if you got what I think you have we can all make a buck out of it."

He looked first at her, then at the girl, and realized he had been very slow on the uptake tonight. "What do you like?" he asked. "Fast, slow, ballad, pop, country or blues?"

"You just play what comes into your head," she said. "I'll listen."

"I'm going back to bed," the girl said suddenly.

Lucia's voice was easy. "Okay, honey."

The girl left the room without saying good night. "I can come back tomorrow if you like," Fred said.

"No reason to. I brought you up here to play. You play."

Licia followed him to the piano. He smiled, responding to his charged-up feelings. It had been such a long time since all he had to do was play the music that was in his own head.

He hadn't gone more than eight bars into his first song when Licia knew that her hunch had been right. It was magic. Sheer magic.

Chapter 4

JERILEE HAD FALLEN asleep on the couch but the sound of his key in the lock woke her up quickly. The room, now flooded with sunlight, reeled for a moment and she had a buzzing sensation behind her temples.

She looked at the empty wine bottle standing between the two burned-out candles. She couldn't believe she had drunk the whole bottle of wine herself.

Fred stood in the open doorway, surprised to see her on the couch. "I didn't think you'd be awake," he said.

"I tried waiting up for you but I fell asleep. What time is it?"

"Almost nine o'clock," he answered. He saw the wine bottle and the candles. "You've been celebratin'. What's the occasion?"

"I finished the play."

He was silent for a moment digesting the news, then he smiled suddenly. "Congratulations, honey. That's worth a celebration."

"You didn't tell me you'd be out all night." She didn't mean it to sound reproachful but it did.

"I didn't know. It was unexpected."

"You could have called me."

"I thought you might be asleep." He bent over the couch to kiss her. "I got some good news too."

She caught the scent of Jack Daniel's on his breath. "You've been drinking."

"A little," he admitted.

"What's the good news?"

"I auditioned for the lady that owns the Green Bar. She's goin' to help me find a publisher and record company for my songs."

"What songs?"

"I got a few numbers I been doodlin' with for years," he said.

"You never said anything to me."

"You never asked me. Besides you always had so much on your mind. And nothin' was happening anyway. At least not until tonight."

She felt a twinge of jealous. "A lady owns the Green Bar?"

He nodded.

"You stayed down there and played for her?"

"No. She took me up to her place. She had a baby grand up there."

"Oh." She got to her feet. There was a sour taste in her mouth. Suddenly she was depressed. The excitement of finishing the play had disappeared. "I'm going to brush my teeth and go to bed."

He followed her to the bathroom door. "Ain't nothin' like you're thinkin'," he said.

She looked at him in the bathroom mirror. "How do you know what I'm thinking?"

"It was straight."

"Sure," she said sarcastically. "You spent six hours after work in her apartment just playing the piano."

"That's right."

She squeezed the toothpaste carefully from the tube. "You don't have to lie to me. You don't owe me any explanations."

"I'm not lying."

"I don't want to talk about it," she said and began brushing her teeth.

"What do you do now?" he asked when she returned to the bedroom.

"Take a copy of the play over to Fannon." She got into bed, reached for the alarm clock and set it for noon. "But first I want to get over to the beauty parlor and get my hair washed and cut."

"It looks okay to me."

"It's not. It's been months since I had it cut." She leaned back against the pillows. "I have to get some sleep."

He left the room, closing the door behind him. The heavily draped room was suddenly dark and she lay in the bed staring at the wall. She didn't like the way she was acting but she couldn't seem to help it. He had no idea how uptight she was, how important her writing was to her. He had never seemed curious enough to want to read what she had written, and she had the feeling that as far as he was concerned her work had nothing at all to do with him. The only communication they had between them was sex.

The alarm aroused her from a deep sleep. The sound jangled her nerves and she groped with shaking hands to turn it off. After putting on the bedside lamp, she lit a cigarette and took a few drags. She was feeling somewhat calmer when the telephone began to ring.

It was a woman's voice. "May I talk to Fred, please?"

"Just a moment."

Fred was asleep on the couch. She touched his shoulder. "Phone call for you," she said.

"Who is it?"

"I didn't ask."

He picked up the telephone beside the couch as she went back into the bedroom. She closed the door behind her and hung up the extension. In the bathroom she stared at herself in the mirror and didn't like what she saw. Her face had an indoor pallor and there were tension lines around her mouth and eyes that she had never noticed before.

She thought about the sound of the voice of the woman on the telephone. Whoever she was, there was no doubt that the lady was in control. She wondered what the woman looked like, how old she was, then suppressed an impulse to eavesdrop on the extension.

What was the matter with her? These were not her kind of thoughts, that was not the kind of thing she would do. There were no strings between her and Fred; he didn't own her, she didn't own him. They were together only because they wanted to be. Any time either one wanted to leave, they were free to do so. But for six months they had been cooped up with each other, and that kind of togetherness sometimes played funny numbers on your head.

She wished now that she hadn't answered the telephone. But then Fred wouldn't have answered it either. He never did—because of her mother.

Her mother had gotten very angry when she discovered they were living together. She hadn't approved of JeriLee's way of life before but living with a black man was going too far. And she made no bones about telling them exactly how she felt. There was no doubt in her mind that Fred had completely destroyed JeriLee's life.

At one point she threatened to have JeriLee committed until JeriLee pointed out that she no longer had the power. Since then communication between them had completely broken down. It had been four months since JeriLee had seen her and weeks since they had spoken on the telephone.

Maybe what she needed was a shrink. But even if she had one, there was no way she could pay him.

She scanned the shelves of the medicine chest. Pills weren't as expensive as a psychiatrist. She took down the vial of Quaalude 500 mg. Just what she needed. Librium relaxed her muscles, Valium helped her sleep, but Quaalude did a double trick. It both calmed her and made her feel good at the same time. She popped the pill and stepped under the shower, turning the cold water on full blast.

Wrapped in a bath towel, she sat on the edge of the bed and dialed Fannon's office.

"Adolph Fannon Productions," a woman answered.

"Mr. Fannon, please. JeriLee Randall calling."

"Just a moment, please." Suddenly she felt her heart begin to hammer inside her chest. It had been more than a year. She wondered if he would remember her or his promise.

There was a click, then his voice. "JeriLee. So good to hear from you."

She made her voice light and casual. "It's good to talk with you, Adolph."

"It's been too long," he said warmly, then he became more businesslike. "You finished the play?"

"Yes," she said, relieved that he had remembered.

"When do I get to see it?"

"I can bring it by whenever you want."

"That isn't the way old friends do business. You come to dinner with me. We'll talk about it first. Then I'll take it home and read it."

She smiled to herself. She knew that the play would be read by his entire staff before he looked at it, but even so it was nicer than just dropping it off at the office. "I'd like that," she said. "When do you want to have dinner?"

"How about tonight?" he asked. "Are you free?"

"I can be."

"Good. Sardi's at eight-thirty. The theater rush should be over by then and we'll be able to talk."

"Eight-thirty," she repeated. "I'll be there."

It wasn't until she put down the telephone that she realized how nervous she had been. Her hands were shaking again. She would need another Quaalude before going to dinner. It was very important that she hold herself together.

Chapter 5

WHEN SHE LET HERSELF in after dinner the apartment was empty. It was almost eleven o'clock. The note on the table was brief and to the point. "Have gone to a meeting. Should be back around midnight."

JeriLee felt a twinge of annoyance. She had not left for dinner until eight and Fred had said nothing to her about a meeting. She crumpled the note and threw it into the wastepaper basket. Restlessly she went into the bedroom and changed into shirt and jeans. Now that the play was finished, the apartment suddenly seemed confining.

She roamed aimlessly through the living room, then went to the kitchen and poured herself a glass of white wine. She had to start thinking about getting a job.

"I'll have to go back to work, I guess," she had told Fannon when he asked about her plans. "Do you have anything for me in any of your shows?"

"I don't think so. It's been a bad season. I don't have any shows on the road this summer."

"I'll have to look around then," she said.

"Who's your agent now?"

"I don't have any," she said quickly. "I sort of let everything drop while I was working on the play."

He had looked at her without speaking. She knew that he knew what had happened. "Now that I finished the play I thought I might go over to William Morris."

"You can tell them that I'm interested in the play if that would be of help," he said.

She looked at him gratefully. "Thank you, Adolph," she said sincerely.

"Anything I can do," he said, moving his hand along her thigh, "just call."

"I will," she said.

He put her into a taxi in front of the restaurant. When the cab turned the corner on Broadway she told the driver to drop her at Forty-second Street. She took the subway uptown from there. Taxis were too expensive these days.

Strange how things had changed. For a long time cabs had been her only way of getting around town. But that seemed like a long time ago. Sardi's too was different now.

A little more than a year ago when she walked into the restaurant it seemed as if everyone knew her.

This time the maitre d' had looked at her with a blank expression even after she had asked for Fannon's table. She wondered if she had changed that much.

"Mrs. Thornton, of course," he answered with a professional smile when Fannon asked if he remembered

Miss Randall. "I thought it was you. But you've changed your hair style. I wasn't sure. Welcome back."

Welcome back? Where was she supposed to have been, the Arctic Circle? "Nice to be back," she said, hating the words as she spoke them.

It was the same with other people who stopped by the table to talk to Fannon. In each case she had to be introduced and she could tell by their expressions that her name rang no bells. Broadway didn't have a long memory, that was for sure.

She had almost finished the wine when the telephone rang.

Fred's voice sounded happy in her ear. "How'd the dinner go?" he asked.

"Fine," she said. She could tell that he had been drinking.

"He goin' to do the play?" he asked.

"I don't know yet," she said. "He's got to read it first."

"We're havin' a celebration up here," he said. "I just signed a management contract with Licia and she broke out a bottle of real champagne. Hop in a cab and come on up."

"Maybe I'd better not," she said hesitantly. "It's late."

"Come on, honey," he said. "There's just Licia, her lawyer an' me." She heard another voice in the background. "Change of plan, honey." He laughed. "You wait there, we comin' to get you. Goin' to do a little finger popping tonight."

Then he clicked off. Maybe it was just as well, she thought. Without work the apartment was depressing.

Arthur's was jammed. The music reverberated from the speakers over their heads and they had to shout in order to be heard. There had been a long line at the door when they had pulled up but, without hesitating, Licia had gotten out of the car and left it for the doorman to park. Then, as if by magic, the door was opened and a good table found for them. She seemed to know everyone in the discotheque.

It wasn't until they got out of the car that JeriLee realized how tall Licia was—at least five ten, she guessed. There was something statuesque about her, a composed strength that revealed itself in the way she moved and walked. By comparison, the girl Sam with her selfish petulant look seemed soft. Marc, the lawyer, was a young man with a shrewd Jewish face which created immediate feelings of distrust.

As soon as they had reached their table and the waitress had taken their order, the lawyer and Sam got up to dance. In a moment they were lost in the press of people on the dance floor.

Fred, sitting between Licia and JeriLee, smiled. "You two are goin' to like each other," he said. "You're both very independent ladies."

Meeting Licia's eyes, JeriLee had the feeling that she and Licia already knew each other. There was a kind of recognition that went beyond the spoken word. She felt herself flushing.

Licia smiled. Her voice was casual. "I know we will."

"Yes." JeriLee nodded.

When the waitress came with their drinks, Licia picked up her glass of orange juice. "To the music man," she said.

Fred laughed as they clinked glasses. "I hope neither of you will be disappointed," he said.

"I don't think we will," Licia said, looking at JeriLee.

JeriLee felt herself flushing again. "We won't be," she added.

"Why don't you two dance?" Licia suggested. "Don't worry about me. I'm okay here."

Fred looked at JeriLee. "How about it, honey?"

She nodded and got to her feet. The floor was crowded with bodies and after a moment JeriLee gave herself up to the pulsing beat. She loved to dance, especially to rock. There was something exhibitionistic about it that appealed to her. It was a form of dancing that seemed to have been made for her alone.

Fred leaned toward her. "What do you think of Licia?"

"She's a very special lady."

Fred nodded, his body moving with the beat. "Smart too. She's got interests in a lot of things besides the Green Bar. Record stores, music companies and some clubs in other cities."

"Sounds good," she said.

"Real good," he said. "At least we don't have to scratch for dough no more. She's guaranteeing me a hundred and fifty bucks a week for the next year at least."

"And what does she get for it?"

"We'll be fifty-fifty partners. We're putting all my songs into a publishing company and everything else, including records and club dates, will spring from that."

"What does she put in besides the money?" JeriLee asked.

"Her contacts. She knows everybody in the business, and with the things she's into she's got a lot of muscle. People are goin' to try to please her."

"Sounds good."

"It is good."

She met his eyes without answering.

"They ain't nothing between us but business. Sam's her friend."

Suddenly it was beginning to fall into place. JeriLee had known there was a quality about Licia that reminded her of someone else. Now she knew who it was. It wasn't a physical resemblance, it had more to do with the way Licia looked at her when they met. Carla Maria had given off the same subtle vibrations. Perhaps it was that experience that had given her a new kind of awareness. Through a break in the crowd she saw Licia glance at her meaningfully and she felt her face flush.

Licia knew just as Carla Maria must have known. Could it be that she was telegraphing a message without realizing it? Was it possible that there was a latent lesbian crawling around inside her skin waiting to get out?

She had been so into her own thoughts that she hadn't heard Fred. She brought herself into focus on him. "What?" she asked. "So much noise I couldn't hear."

"She wants me to get some new threads. She's advancing the bread. She wants me to have a superhip Sam Cooke kind of look."

She nodded without speaking.

"We're goin' to get a few tapes together, then Marc and me are goin' out to Detroit to see some of the biggies at Motown. She thinks we can swing there."

For the first time she realized how young he was—not in age, he was older than she—but in naïveté. His dreams were dreams she had had many years ago.

Suddenly she felt old and depressed and in need of a drink. She touched Fred's shoulder and they left the floor.

As they reached the table, Sam returned alone. "Marc left me on the floor." She pouted. "There was someone he wanted to talk to and I still feel like dancing."

"That's Marc, always hustling." Licia smiled. "Why don't you dance with her, Fred?"

"Sure thing."

JeriLee slid into her seat, carefully reserving Fred's seat between her and Licia.

"Fine bunch of freaks here tonight," Licia said.

"Half of them are stoned. The other half are showoff smartass freaks who are here because this is the in place to be."

"Which club are you in?"

"Neither. One, I really like watchin'. Two, I'm working."

"You have a piece of this place?"

"I have an idea for opening a place like it when the time is right."

"When will that be?"

"A year or two. When this place is gone. There's only room for one of these places at a time."

JeriLee didn't answer.

"Fred tell you about our plans?"

"Yes."

"What do you think?"

"I'm happy for him. He deserves a break."

"You're not in love with him, are you?"

"No."

"He's in love with you. He wants to marry you."

"Did he say that?"

Licia nodded.

"Shit." JeriLee picked up her drink. He was not supposed to go that far.

"Sister," Licia asked, as if she had tuned in to her head, "what is a woman like you doin' messing around with a boy like that?"

"It's better than being alone. And besides there are no real men around."

Licia reached across the table and pressed JeriLee's hand.

In the same tone of voice and without moving her hand away JeriLee said, "Sister, why is a woman like you messing around with a girl like that?"

Licia's eyes widened in surprise, then she laughed as she withdrew her hand. "It's better than being alone. And besides there are no real women around."

Suddenly there was an easiness between them. JeriLee laughed. "I like you," she said. "At least you're honest."

"I like you too."

"But there's one thing I don't understand. Why are you doing all this for him?"

"Partly the money, but that's not all of it." Licia hesitated.

"What's the rest of it?"

"You wouldn't understand."

"Try me."

Licia's voice was soft but with an undertone of toughness. "This is a man's world and I've gone about as far as a woman can go alone and still be tolerated. Men don't like women who want to go all the way by themselves."

"I still don't see what Fred has got to do with it."

"I'm going to make him a success because we both need it for our own reasons. With him in front, ain't nobody goin' to stop me. I'll go all the way."

"I still don't see it. What do you mean with him in front of you?"

Licia reached for JeriLee's hand again. "I'm sorry. I didn't mean to be obscure," she said quietly. "You see, I'm going to marry him."

Chapter 6

JERILEE FOLDED the last shirt and placed it carefully in the suitcase. The new and expensive luggage, a gift from Licia, looked out of place on the bed. "That should do it," she said.

"Yeah."

"Finish dressing. Marc should be here any minute now."

"Okay." He buttoned the collar of his shirt and went over to the mirror to put on his tie. When he had finished he slipped into his jacket and turned to her with a smile on his face. "How do I look?"

"Great."

He came over and kissed. "It's only the beginning. When I come back Licia wants us to get a better apartment. One where we can have a piano."

She snapped the last bag closed without speaking.

"Hey, don't be down," he said. "I won't be gone that long. Detroit, Nashville, Los Angeles. Just a week in each place."

He didn't understand.

"While I'm gone you start lookin' for another place. That way by the time I get back—"

"No," she interrupted him.

A puzzled expression came over his face. "What is it, honey?"

"I'm not moving."

"Come on. It's time we got out of this dump."

"I'm not moving," she repeated.

"We can afford it, honey."

"You can afford it."

"What difference does it make? We never fussed about the bills here." He put his arms around her. "Besides, baby, it's time we got married."

She buried her face against his shoulder. "No," she said, her voice muffled against his jacket.

He held her away from him. There was genuine bewilderment in his voice. "Why not?"

She blinked back her tears. "Because it wouldn't be right."

"Is it because I'm black?"

"You know better than that."

"I don't know. There are girls who'll make it with black guys but won't marry them." There was a subtle edge in his voice.

"You know that's not it."

"What is it then? I know it was okay with you for me to move in here. We were good for each other."

"That's right. Then. But that was not forever. Now it's different."

"The only difference is that now I'll be bringin' home the bread. And I can take care of you proper."

She chose her words carefully. She cared too much for him to want to hurt him. "I'm glad you're making it. You deserve everything you get. But don't you see, I've got to make it too. I've got to do my own thing."

"I won't be stopping you. I jus' want to make it easier for you. Take the nickel and dime heat off."

Her eyes were dry now, her voice steady. "If that was what I wanted I would never have divorced Walter."

"I don't understand you."

"Sometimes I don't understand myself. I only know that I want to be free."

"If you loved me you wouldn't feel like that."

"Maybe that's it. I love you but not in the same way you care about me. It's like we're very close and we're friends and everything is good between us—the vibes, the sex, everything. It's great as far as it goes but it's not enough for me. Something is still missing. Maybe it's inside me, something I may never find, but until I do I won't be ready to give myself up to a relationship. And I won't be able to do that until I feel free and whole."

"If we get married, we can start a family," he said. "That'll get you together."

She laughed. That was the ultimate male answer. A baby made everything right. Maybe it did. For them. But that was not what she wanted. "That's not exactly what I meant by freedom. I don't know if I ever want a family."

"It ain't natural. Every woman wants a baby."

"I don't. Maybe I will someday. But not now."

The buzzer sounded from downstairs. He went over to the window. "Marc is double parked," he said.

"You'd better get going."

"I'm not takin' no for an answer."

"Don't fight it. You have your own life and your own career. Leave me to mine."

The buzzer sounded again.

"You mean you don't want me to come back?"

Her eyes fell, then she raised her head and nodded. "I think it would be the best thing for both of us."

When the buzzer sounded again, insistently, he erupted with anger and frustration. "I'm coming! God damn it! I'm coming."

He stood in the doorway. Anguish altered his voice. "JeriLee."

She reached up and kissed his cheek. "Good luck, Fred. Sing pretty for the people."

He put down the bags and took a step toward her. She drew back. His voice grew thick with pain. "Fuck you, JeriLee," he said. "An' fuck your bullshit honesty or whatever you call it. It's just your excuse for the fact that you don't give a shit for nobody but yourself!" Then he was gone, leaving the door open behind him.

Abruptly she covered her face with her hands.

He was right about what he said. She knew enough

to recognize the truth when she heard it. Her own mother had said the same thing.

There had to be something wrong with her. Why else couldn't she be satisfied with the same things as other people? Why did she always want more, why did she always feel incomplete?

When the doorbell rang she swore to herself and checked her watch. She had just an hour before she was due at Fannon's office. "Who is it?" she called.

"Mr. Hardy, the super."

Shit, that was all she needed. She put an expectant expression on her face and opened the door. "Mr. Hardy." She smiled. "I was just about to call you. Come in."

"I came about the rent," he said in his peculiar thin voice.

"That's what I was going to call you about," she said quickly.

"You got it?"

"That's what I wanted to explain," she said. "You see—"

"It's the twentieth of the month already," he interrupted. "The office is on my back."

"I know, but I'm waiting for a check. I was going out just this minute to see the man who's going to produce my play. Adolph Fannon, the famous producer. You've heard of him, I'm sure."

"No. The office wants me to give you an eviction notice."

"Come on, Mr. Hardy. What are they worried about? They have a month's security."

"They'll apply it to this month's rent if you leave."

"I've always paid. You know that."

"I know it, Miss Randall, but I don't make the rules. The office says the rent ain't paid by the twentieth, serve the notice. That way you're out by the end of the month and nobody's the loser."

"I'll pay you by Friday."

"That's three days from now. They'll have my ass."

"I'll make it up to you. Be a nice guy, Mr. Hardy."

He looked around the apartment. "I ain't seen your boy friend around the last few weeks. He split?"

"No," she said. "But he's gone."

"I'm glad, Miss Randall. I never told the office that you had someone here with you. You know your lease calls for only one person, and besides they find out you got a Negro in here they'd a gone through the roof. They don't have no spics or Negroes living in this building. They don't want the place run down."

She had taken all she could. "Mr. Hardy," she said in a cold voice, "why don't you just go back and tell your office to go fuck themselves!"

He stared at her with an expression of shock. "Miss Randall, what kind of language is that for a nice girl like you to use?"

"Mr. Hardy, the office may own the building but they don't own the tenants. Nobody has the right to tell me how or who to live with. The only thing they have a right to is the rent, which I said I'll pay you on Friday."

"Okay, if that's how you feel about it," he said, taking an official-looking piece of paper from his back pocket and pressing it into her hand.

She looked down at the words printed boldly across the folded page: EVICTION NOTICE. "Why give me this?" she asked. "I said I would pay you on Friday."

He went to the door. "You can always give it back to me with the rent," he said. "That's just in case you don't."

Chapter 7

THE MOMENT she saw Fannon she knew it wasn't going to be good.

"I wanted to get back to you sooner," he said after kissing her on the cheek. "But things have been hectic."

"That's all right. I understand."

"Cigarette?"

"No, thanks."

"You look tired."

"I haven't been sleeping too well. The nights have been hot and the air conditioner broke down."

"You should get out of the city. What you need is some country air."

She looked at him without answering. There was no point in telling him that she didn't have the money.

He picked up the copy of her play and stared at the cover. "I like you," he said abruptly.

She tried to keep her voice light. "But you don't like my play?"

His eyes seemed to bore into her. "Do you like your pills sugar coated?"

"I'll take it straight."

"I don't like your play." He cleared his throat. "I wanted to, believe me. I think you can write. But this doesn't work. It's an emotional exercise, a series of scenes that don't go together, a story that doesn't work. But I haven't given up on you. I think someday you're going to write a play that will turn this town on its end."

"But not this time," she said tightly.

"Not this time."

"Not even if I rewrote it?"

"It still won't work. There's no real story, no focus.

It's all open and spread out, like a kaleidoscope. Every time you turn it you lose the picture. By the time I finished reading it I was too confused to understand what I had read."

"Then what do you suggest?"

"I'd put this on the side. Maybe in time it will straighten itself out in your head. Then you can go back to it. Right now it won't work. I think you ought to start on something else."

She didn't answer. It was easy enough to tell someone to do something else as long as you didn't have to do it.

"Don't get discouraged," he said. "Every successful playwright has had plays that don't work. The important thing is that you keep writing."

"I know," she said, meaning it.

"I'm sorry," he said, getting to his feet.

She looked up at him, realizing the meeting was over. She managed to keep her voice steady. "Thank you anyway."

He came around the desk, gave her the script and kissed her cheek again. "Don't be a stranger," he said. "Keep in touch."

"I will."

"Call me next week, we'll have lunch."

"Yes." She hurried through his secretary's office, fighting back the tears. She didn't want anyone to see her. All the way down in the elevator she was fighting back the tears.

When she reached the street, she saw a trash basket at the curb. In a fit of rage and self-pity she flung the script into the wire basket.

She had gone almost a block before turning and running back to retrieve the script from the bottom of the basket.

Maybe she had unconsciously thought that it should have been discarded, even while she was working on it. But there was no way she could have stopped herself. She was too much into it. She had to write it out.

Now it was over and she would have to begin again. But where? And how? There were other things she had to take care of first. Like the rent and the bills. She would have to get some money to carry her over until she could find a job. Then maybe everything would fall into place.

"Hello," her mother answered.

"Mother, I need help." There was no point in wasting time on the preliminaries. The moment her mother heard her voice she would know the reason for the call.

"What is it this time?"

JeriLee kept her voice calm. "I need two hundred and fifty dollars to get me past this month's bills. I'll pay you back as soon as I get a job."

"Why don't you ask your friend? I'm sure he can give you something."

"He's gone, Mother," she said, controlling her voice. "We broke up almost a month ago."

Her mother was silent for a moment. "It's about time you came to your senses," she said finally.

JeriLee didn't reply.

"What about your play?" her mother asked. "Did you finish it?"

"Yes," JeriLee answered. "It's not good. I took it to Fannon. He won't do it."

"There are other producers."

"It's not good, Mother," she repeated patiently. "I reread it. Fannon was right."

"I don't understand it. Couldn't you have seen that while you were working on it?"

"No," JeriLee answered.

"I don't know, JeriLee," she said, sounding discouraged. "Why can't you be like other girls? Get a job, get married, have a family."

"I'm sorry, Mother. I wish I could be. It would be a lot easier all around. But I'm not."

"I can let you have a hundred dollars," her mother said finally. "The market went down and there isn't much money coming in."

"It won't be enough. The rent alone is a hundred and seventy-five."

"That's all I can spare this month. If things pick up, maybe I can give you a little more next month."

"At least give me the money for the rent. They gave me an eviction notice today." JeriLee was angry with herself for pleading but she felt she had no choice.

"You can always come home to live."

"What would I do? There's no work for me."

"You're not working anyway."

JeriLee lost her patience. "Mother, either you're going to give me the money or you're not. There's no point in our going around in a circle."

"I'll put a check in the mail for a hundred dollars," her mother said coolly.

"Don't bother!" JeriLee said, slamming down the phone. It happened every time they spoke to each other. There seemed to be no way they could communicate.

She went back to the couch and started flipping through the pages of *Casting News*. Nothing. The business was dead and the few things that were going were all locked up by the agents.

On the last page was another ad for the Torchlight Club. It was in the paper all the time now. The turnover in girls was obviously tremendous. On an impulse she picked up the telephone and dialed the club.

"Torchlight Club," a woman's voice said.

"Mr. DaCosta please."

"Who is calling?"

"JeriLee Randall."

"Just a moment, please." There had been no sign of recognition in the woman's voice.

There was a click, then he came on. "Hello," he said cautiously.

"Vincent, this is JeriLee."

"How are you, baby?"

"Okay," she said. "You?"

"Never been better," he said. "How come the call?"

"I need a job."

He was silent for a moment. "You still got that nigger living with you?"

The question took her by surprise. She had not known that he knew about Fred. "No."

"It's about time you came to your senses," he said. "A guy like that is nothing but bad news."

She didn't answer.

"What about the play you were writing?"

"It didn't work. I'm junking it."

"Too bad," he said, but there was no sound of sympathy in his voice. "What kind of a job are you looking for?"

"Anything," she said. "I'm busted."

"Your old job is filled. We got a guy doin' it."

"I said anything," she replied. "I know the whole setup. I can fit in anywhere."

"Okay. Come on over an' we'll talk about it."

"What time?"

"Just a minute, let me check my book. I'm locked in tight all afternoon," he said. "How about seven o'clock at the apartment? We can have a drink and talk there without anybody bugging us."

"Okay," she said. "I'll be there."

She got up and went into the bathroom. There was one Valium left in the bottle. She swallowed it and looked at herself in the mirror.

Her eyes looked strained and red but a few drops of Visine would clear them up. Maybe things weren't so bad after all. If she did get a job she was sure that Vincent wouldn't mind giving her an advance on her salary.

Chapter 8

A WOMAN LET HER into the apartment. "Vincent's in the shower," she said without introducing herself. "He'll be out in a minute."

"That's okay," she said.

"Would you care for a drink?"

"Thanks. Vodka and tonic."

The woman nodded and went behind the bar. JeriLee watched her. She was very pretty in a showgirl way—heavy eye makeup, lots of false eyelashes and carefully styled shiny black hair that fell to her shoulders. "Okay?" she asked as JeriLee tasted her drink.

"It's fine." JeriLee smiled.

The woman went back to the bar and picked up her own drink. "Cheers," she said, raising her glass to her lips.

"Cheers," JeriLee replied.

"Sit down," the woman said, gesturing to the couch. She climbed up on the bar stool and swung around facing JeriLee.

The telephone began to ring. Automatically the woman made a gesture toward it, then checked herself. It rang again, the sound cutting off in the middle. "He doesn't like anyone to answer his private phone for him," the woman explained.

JeriLee nodded.

"He's crazy. You know that, don't you? His whole family is crazy."

JeriLee didn't answer.

"His brothers are worse."

"I don't know them," JeriLee said.

"Consider yourself lucky then." She took a bottle of

scotch from the bar and refilled her glass. "Jesus, what a family."

They fell silent, the woman staring morosely into her glass. Through the closed door there was the faint sound of Vincent's voice on the telephone. Then abruptly the bedroom door opened.

He was wearing the white terry cloth bathrobe that she remembered. "You're here," he said.

"Yes."

"I thought I told you to tell me when she got here," he said to the woman in a harsh voice.

"You were in the shower," she said. "Then you got on the phone."

"Stupid cunt," he said. "Fix me a drink."

Silently the woman got down from the stool and poured some scotch over the rocks. He took the drink and walked over to JeriLee. "You don't look so good," he said abruptly.

"I'm tired."

"The nigger fuck you out?"

She didn't answer.

"Everybody knows about them," he said. "All their brains are in their cocks."

She put down her drink and rose from the couch. "I don't have to listen to that shit," she said.

His hand gripped her arm tightly. "You want a job, you listen whether you like it or not."

It was not until then that she saw the glittering brightness in his eyes and knew he was coked to the ears. He had probably taken a few snorts before he came out. "What about the job?" she asked.

He let go of her arm. "I told you you'd come crawling back."

She didn't answer.

"What makes you think I'd give you a job?" he asked. "What can you do better than anybody else?"

She kept her silence.

"Maybe the nigger taught you some new tricks." Abruptly he pulled at his belt and the robe fell open. "Show me," he said. "Get it hard. I got room for a good cocksucker up in the massage parlor."

"I think I'd better go," she said.

"What's the matter? Isn't it big enough for you anymore?" He laughed harshly. "Everybody knows they're hung like horses."

She turned and started for the door. He caught her arm. "Maybe I was all wrong. Maybe you'd rather make it with her than with me?" He called over his shoulder to the woman. "Come here."

"Jesus, Vincent," the woman said in a disgusted tone of voice.

"Come here, bitch!" he said angrily.

Slowly the woman got down from the stool and came over to him. He turned back to JeriLee. "Would you like to go down on her?" he said.

"I told you he was crazy," the woman said.

Vincent stared at the woman wildly and for a moment JeriLee thought he was about to strike her. Then abruptly he dropped JeriLee's arm and walked back to the bar, where he refilled his drink. "Go on, get out of here. Both of you," he said. "You cunts are all alike."

Silently JeriLee opened the door and the woman followed her out into the hall.

"He's got to be higher than the Empire State Building," the woman said as they waited for the elevator. "He's been snortin' coke ever since he got home."

When they came out of the building, the woman signaled for a cab. "Can I give you a lift?" she asked.

"No, thanks. I think I'll walk."

The woman fished in her purse, then held her hand out to JeriLee. "Here's my phone number," she said. "Give me a call sometime."

Automatically JeriLee's hand closed over the folded paper. The cab door closed and the taxi took off. JeriLee looked down at her hand. The folded twenty-dollar bill lay flat in her palm.

"Oh, no!" She took a step after the cab. But it had already turned the corner. She stood there for a moment, blinking back the tears that suddenly came to her eyes.

"Taxi, miss?" the doorman asked.

"No, thank you." The evening breeze was beginning to come in off the river as she boarded a crosstown bus on Fifty-seventh Street.

The driver looked down at her hand as she held the bill toward him. A tone of disgust came into his voice. "For Christ's sake, lady," he said. "Can't you rich East Side broads get it through your heads that there are poor people in this world?"

"I'm sorry," she said, searching in her bag and finding a quarter. She looked out the bus window and blinked her eyes. It really would be funny if it weren't so sad.

The only kindness she had known during the whole depressing day had come from a stranger, a woman whose name she had never thought to ask. But then they were both female in an alien world. Only a woman who had been there herself could sympathize with one who was there now. She was sorry she hadn't taken the cab with her. It would have been good to have someone to talk to.

Suddenly she thought of Licia. There was something about her that was solid and strong. Fred had said that she was into a lot of businesses. Maybe she would be able to help her find a job. She made up her mind to call her when she got back home.

The downstairs buzzer sounded. She took a last quick look around the apartment as she went to press the button that unlocked the outside door. It looked as good as it ever could. She opened the door and waited.

The sound of footsteps came from the landing below. "Up here," she called. "One more flight."

Licia's head appeared as she came up the stairs.

"I forgot to tell you there was no elevator," JeriLee said.

Licia grinned. "That's all right," she said easily. "I never knew there was such a thing as elevators until I was fourteen years old."

JeriLee closed the door behind her. "I didn't mean to interfere with your work."

"You're not," Licia replied. "I usually take Tuesday nights off."

"Would you like a drink?" JeriLee asked.
"Do you have any fruit juice?"
JeriLee shook her head. "Some white wine?"
Licia hesitated. "Okay."
JeriLee quickly filled two glasses and gave her one. Licia sat down on the small couch and put the glass on the cocktail table. JeriLee sat opposite her, suddenly feeling awkward and embarrassed. She took a quick drink of the wine. "I shouldn't have called you," she said. "I'm sorry."
The black girl looked at her steadily. "But you did."
JeriLee's eyes fell. "Yes. The roof was caving in. I felt I had to talk to somebody. The only one I could think of calling was you."
"What happened to the play? Fred told me that Fannon was going to do it."
"It wasn't any good. I didn't know it then but I know it now. I fucked up."
Licia's voice was easy. "Those things happen. I put some money into a few shows. Nothing happened."
"Now I've got to get a job. I can't fool around anymore."
"Fred told me that you wouldn't take any more from him."
JeriLee nodded.
"Why?"
"Fred had his own plans. I had mine. They didn't go together. It wouldn't be right to take his money."
Licia was silent for a moment. "What kind of a job are you looking for?"
"I don't know," JeriLee said. "I'm an out-of-work actress and an unsuccessful writer. The only thing I know is that I want to make enough money so that I can continue writing."
"How much would that take?" Licia asked.
JeriLee laughed, embarrassed. "A lot more than I'm probably worth on the job market. At least a hundred and fifty, two hundred a week."
"That's a lot of bread," Licia said.
"I know," JeriLee said. "But this place costs me over two hundred a month with the utilities."

"What you need is some man to keep you," Licia said.

"Is that how you did it?"

"Yes," Licia said evenly. "I have an eight-year-old son. When he was born his father gave me twenty-five grand to get lost. He didn't want his nice white world to get fucked up."

"I'm sorry," JeriLee said quickly. "I had no right to say something like that."

"It all worked out," Licia said quietly. "My boy lives in the country with my mother. And the friends I made when I was with his father helped me get started in business."

JeriLee emptied her glass and refilled it. "You don't drink?" she asked, noticing that Licia's wine was untouched.

"Never liked it," Licia said.

"What's happening with Fred?" she asked.

"He's working," Licia said. "He's in L.A. right now. He's getting an album together for one of the record companies. When that comes out, they're goin' to send him around the country on a tour. They think he's got a real good chance."

"I'm glad for him," JeriLee said. "He's a good person."

"You haven't changed your mind about him?" Licia asked. "He still wants to marry you."

"No." JeriLee shook her head. "It wouldn't work. We make it in bed and we make it as friends. But that's as far as it goes. If we did get married we'd only wind up tearing each other apart. There's only room for one career in Fred's life."

"You wouldn't consider giving up yours?"

"I would have remained married to my first husband if I felt that way."

Licia was silent for a moment. "Have you had dinner yet?"

"No."

Licia smiled. "What do you say we get something to eat? Somehow problems never seem as heavy on a full stomach."

Chapter 9

THE SAWMILL RIVER PARKWAY was deserted. Disregarding the posted limit, Licia calmly moved the big car up to seventy miles an hour. JeriLee looked at the clock on the dashboard. It was almost nine-thirty. "Are you sure it will be all right with your mother, bringing someone up to dinner at this hour of the night?"

"My mother's used to it. We'll all night people in my family." She began to slow down. "Besides we're almost there. We get off at the next exit."

"You like driving?" JeriLee asked.

Licia nodded. "Especially this car." She laughed. "It used to be a pimp's hog. Man, when he got it he was on top of the world an' he shit down on everybody. Then he got heavy into horse an' completely lost control. His girls georgied on him an' he had to sell it to feed the habit. I got it for practically nothing because he still had some payments on it. But he was one guy I didn't mind shaftin'. He had to be the world's number one prick."

They turned off the main road onto a narrow road that wound its way through the trees to the top of a small hill where a few houses were clustered. "We're here," she announced, pulling into the first driveway on the left.

The front door opened as they got out of the car and a boy came running down the steps and across the lawn. "Mommy! Mommy!"

Licia bent forward and he leaped into her arms. He put his arms around her neck. "You came just at the right time," he said. "There's nothing but commercials on."

Licia laughed and kissed him. "I swear you're goin' to wind up with square eyeballs from watchin' the tube like that. JeriLee, this is my son, Bonny," she said, putting him down. "Bonny, JeriLee."

The boy came to her, his hand outstretched. "Hello," he said. "Do you like television?"

JeriLee laughed. "Yes."

"Good," Bonny said. "We can watch it together. There's a good show just starting."

"You're going to bed, young man." The woman's voice came from the open doorway. "You've got school tomorrow."

Bonny turned back to Licia. "Mommy?"

Licia took his hand and they started toward the house. "You heard Grandma."

"But you just got here," he said. "I won't even be with you."

She laughed. "You wouldn't be with me anyway. You'd be with the TV."

Licia's mother was a tall woman and if it weren't for the fact that her hair was flecked with gray she might have passed for an older sister. Her smile was warm and her hand firm as JeriLee took it. "Nice to meet you," she said.

The house was warmly decorated. Bonny went right to the color television set. "Just ten more minutes," he said.

"Okay," Licia's mother answered. "Then you go right upstairs."

They went to the kitchen. A table had been set up on the screened-in back porch. A charcoal-fired barbecue was glowing in a corner. "I got steaks and salad," Licia's mother said. "I wasn't expecting company."

"That's fine with me," JeriLee said.

"I make great fried chicken, barbecued ribs and greens, but Licia won't eat soul food. She says it's too greasy an' she's always on a diet."

"Mother." Licia laughed.

"Okay," her mother said. "You see if'n you kin get your son to bed. I'll put the steaks on."

"How do you like yours cooked?" she asked JeriLee.

"Rare."

"Like Licia." The older woman sniffed. "I like mine cooked through. I don't hold with eating raw meat."

JeriLee smiled. "Is there anything I can do to help?"

"No. I'm used to managin'. But maybe you like a cold drink? We got all kinds of fruit juices. We don't hold with liquor and no soda pop in this house."

"Anything you have will be fine, Mrs. Wallace."

"Licia likes orange juice, but my favorite is Hawaiian Punch."

"I'll have some of that."

Mrs. Wallace smiled. "I'll put ice cubes in it. Don't taste as sweet that way."

The meat was sizzling when Licia returned. "Those steaks smell good," she said.

"I had the butcher at the A and P cut them special for me," her mother said. "He didn't charge me extra either."

"My mother's got everybody in the A and P under her thumb," Licia told JeriLee.

Licia walked over to the grill. "The meat looks about ready to me."

Mrs. Wallace got out of her chair. "Now you come right back here an' set down," she commanded. "I'm the one who does the cookin' in this house."

"Yes, Mother," Licia said meekly. She looked over at JeriLee and smiled.

JeriLee returned her smile without speaking.

It was after eleven o'clock by the time they finished. During the meal, Licia's mother didn't stop talking. It was apparent that a week's worth of problems and conversation had been stored up inside for this one night. Licia listened patiently—Bonny's school, shopping, the plumber. All the normal trivia came pouring out. And in the telling there was a feeling of pride. She had coped. Licia's approval was obviously very important to her mother. And the woman glowed when Licia gave it to her.

Finally Licia said, "We'll have to be gettin' back to the city."

Her mother was surprised. "You're not stayin'? I got your room all fixed up for you."

"Maybe JeriLee's got some things to do in the morning, Mother," Licia said.

"Do you?" she asked bluntly.

"I don't want to put you out," JeriLee said.

"It's no trouble," Mrs. Wallace said quickly. "There are twin beds in Licia's room."

Licia smiled. "My mother's used to gettin' her own way."

JeriLee nodded, got to her feet and picked up her plate. "Let me help you with the dishes," she said.

"You don't have to do nothin', girl," Mrs. Wallace said. "We got an automatic KitchenAid dishwasher in this house."

There were three bedrooms on the upper floor. Licia had the master bedroom. It was in one corner of the house, separated from the other rooms by a large bathroom. Licia paused in the upper hallway and kissed her mother. "Good night, Mother."

"Good night, Mrs. Wallace. Thank you," JeriLee said.

The older woman nodded and went down the hall to her room. JeriLee followed Licia. A small lamp was glowing between the beds. Licia crossed to the bathroom. "I'll put out a new toothbrush for you. I have extra nightgowns in the closet. I'll get one for you."

"Thanks." JeriLee walked to the open window and breathed deeply of the night air. It smelled fresh and green.

Licia's voice came from behind her. "Not much like the city."

"I'd almost forgoten what fresh air really smells like."

Licia took out a neatly pressed nightgown. She held it up. "This okay?"

"Fine."

"You can use the bathroom first," Licia said, holding the nightgown toward her.

She took the gown and went into the bathroom, closing the door behind her. Quickly she undressed and folded her things neatly over the hanger. She took the toothbrush from its package and brushed her teeth, then washed her face. She had been feeling all right up to now but suddenly she was nervous. She rummaged through her purse. If she remembered correctly, there was a ten-mg Valium in her pill box. When she found it she swallowed it quickly. She felt reassured. Valium always put her to sleep.

Licia smiled as she came through the doorway. "That gown's a little big on you."

JeriLee looked down. The hem was dragging on the floor. "I guess it is," she said.

Licia gestured to the bed nearer the door. "This one's yours."

JeriLee nodded. She went to the bed and sat down. Automatically she reached for a cigarette and lit it.

Licia seemed to sense her nervousness. "Are you okay?"

"I'll be all right. It's just been a bad day, that's all."

"You don't have to worry," Licia said in a low voice. "I didn't bring you up here to hit on you. I never figured we'd be staying."

"It's okay. I'm glad you did. It's the only good thing that's happened to me all day."

"Good," Licia said, going to the closet. Quickly she pulled her blouse off over her head and stepped out of her skirt. She reached behind her to unfasten the brassiere.

JeriLee ground out her cigarette. When she looked up, Licia had slipped into a beige-colored peignoir that was almost the same color as her skin. JeriLee slid down into the sheets.

Licia sat down on the other bed. "What do you think of my little family?" she asked.

"There's a lot of love here."

Licia smiled. "That's why I keep them here. Ain't no way you can get that feeling in the city."

"You're doing the right thing."

"Bonny's growin' fast though," Licia said. "A boy like that needs a father."

JeriLee didn't speak.

"You think he'd put Fred off?" Licia asked.

"Fred loves kids," JeriLee answered.

"What about me?" Licia asked. "He ever say anything about me?"

"Only that he liked you. He respects you."

"But he knows about me. He's seen me with Sam." Licia was silent for a moment. "It ain't that I don't like men, I just went off them. With them everything's a battle. They don't make love, they make war."

"Fred's not like that. He's a very gentle man."

Licia rose to her feet. "I don't know," she said hesitantly. "I got to think some more about it. I don't want to make any mistakes."

"You won't," JeriLee said. "You'll do the right thing."

"You really think so?"

"I think so."

Licia smiled suddenly. "Enough of my problems. You go to sleep." She turned off the light. "Good night."

"Good night." JeriLee watched her go into the bathroom and close the door behind her. Then she looked up into the dark. After a few moments she heard the sound of the water running and closed her eyes. She didn't hear Licia come out of the bathroom. She didn't feel Licia's kiss, light on her cheek, or hear her soft murmur. "Poor little baby." She was fast asleep.

Chapter 10

THE FUCKING California sunshine, she thought as she opened her eyes. Christ. What I wouldn't give for just one rainy day.

Then she was wide awake and thinking about Licia.

For a moment she could almost smell the warm sweetness of her and the smooth sensation of the honey-colored skin against her fingers. Then she heard the voices through the closed bedroom door and the thought was gone.

She sat up in the bed and listened. The voices, a man's and a woman's, were muted. Then the man's voice grew more insistent. A moment later the door opened softly.

Angela peeked into the room. "Are you awake?"

"Yes."

"You were asleep when I looked in just a moment ago. I didn't want to wake you."

"That's okay. Who's out there?"

"George."

"Shit!" JeriLee said. "What does he want?"

"I don't know. He just said it was important that he see you. I'll tell him to go away, that you're not feeling well enough."

"No." JeriLee swung her feet off the bed. George was too self-centered just to pay a courtesy call. It had to be something else. "I'll see him. Just ask him to wait a minute while I go to the bathroom."

"Okay. You let me know when you're ready. I'll send him in."

"No. I'll come out there."

"Don't you think you should stay in bed?" Angela asked disapprovingly.

"What for? I'm not sick. All I had was a lousy little abortion."

The door closed behind Angela, and JeriLee went into the bathroom. She sat down on the john and changed the tampon. She was bleeding more than she had in the morning and she was still sore. She took two aspirin and a Percodan for the pain. Then she washed her face with cold water. She began to feel better. She touched up her lips, used some rouge on her cheeks and brushed her hair quickly.

George got to his feet as she came into the room. "Hey," he said, "you don't look sick at all."

"Makeup." She smiled. She sat in the easy chair opposite him. "What's up?"

"I wanted to talk to you," he said. "I wanted to tell you how sorry I was about what happened."

She looked at him without speaking.

"We shouldn't have rushed it," he continued. "We should have kept the baby."

She couldn't keep the surprise from her voice. 'You've got to be kidding!"

"I'm not," he said earnestly. "I mean it."

"But what about your wife?"

"It would have been okay with her," he said, his blue eyes clear and untroubled. "We talked about it last night. We could have adopted the baby and there would be no problems."

"Oh, Jesus!"

"Margaret would love to have a baby. She loves kids," he said.

"Then why don't you have one?" she asked.

"It's that damn series she's in," he said. "She's got a three-year contract firm. And that's big money, especially with the residuals. She'd blow it all if she got pregnant."

"And how was I supposed to support myself all the time I was walking around with a big belly?" she asked sarcastically.

The sarcasm went over his head. "We talked about that too. You could have lived with us. That way we all would have had a part in it."

"I don't believe it," she said, shaking her head.

"It would have worked," he said. "We were at a party last night at my shrink's. Everybody agreed it was a good idea."

"Everybody?"

He nodded. "Everybody. You know my shrink. He's got the most important patients in town. And once a month we meet at his house for a sort of consciousness-raising session. That's how the whole thing came up."

JeriLee knew his psychiatrist. If you didn't need him when you went to him, you would by the time you finished your first visit. That is, if you were a big enough name and could afford the hundred dollars an hour.

"That really does it," she said in a disgusted voice. "It took me two years to get this town to take me seriously and in one evening you hung the cunt label back on me."

"It wasn't anything like that, JeriLee," he said sincerely. "We're all very honest and open with each other. They all respect you."

"Sure," she said.

"Really. Take Tom Castel, for example. He's producing your picture over at the studio."

"What about him?" she asked, wanting him to confirm what her agent had told her.

"He said that he's talking to your agent about you writing the script based on your book. He says that he's convinced that you're the only one to do it. Especially after Warren's scripts turned out such a disaster."

"Then what is he waiting for?" she asked. "Why doesn't he sign me?"

"He says the studio won't let him go without a star."

"Shit," she said disgustedly. "Nothing ever changes. Which comes first, the chicken or the egg?"

"He said the studio wants me for it. They'll give him the go-ahead if I commit."

She couldn't contain herself. "For Christ's sake, what's stopping you then?"

"That's why I had to see you," he explained patiently. "I read the book. I don't know whether I'm right for the part. It calls for an older leading man."

"Don't worry, you can do it," she said firmly.

"But the age," he protested.

"Remember Jimmy Dean in *Giant?* He played a forty-year-old man when he was still in his early twenties. And you're as good an actor as he ever was. You've got the same quality and excitement."

She could see the actor's ego take over. "Do you really think so?" he asked. "Jimmy Dean?"

She nodded. "What do you think turned me on to you in the first place?"

"I'll be damned," he said in a wondering voice. "I never thought of that."

But she could see that he was pleased. "If you do it I could write the ass off it," she added. "Together we could make sure that everything was perfect."

He nodded thoughtfully. "It's really a hell of a part."

"Once in a lifetime," she said. "An actor's dream. It will put you right up there with McQueen and Redford." She laughed. "George Ballantine. Superstar."

He laughed, then his face grew serious. "But what about the director?" he asked. "Jimmy Dean had Kazan and George Stevens. We'll need a top man. Coppola, Schlesinger, someone like that."

"You name him, we'll get him."

"I'll have to think about it," he said. "I'll talk it over with my agent."

"You tell him what I said. The important thing is that we can work together."

"Sure." But he was already thinking of something else. "Do you think Margaret could play the girl?"

"I thought you said she was firm in the series?"

"She could get out for a feature," he said. "Besides it would look better if we were all together on the project. Especially after what happened."

"Why not?" She nodded. "It would be great box-office chemistry."

"I've got an idea," he said. "Why don't you come over to the house for dinner tomorrow night? I'll have my agent over and we can all talk it out."

That was the last thing in the world she felt like doing. "Why don't you explore it first?" she suggested. "Maybe we can get together on the weekend when I get my strength back."

"Fine," he said, getting to his feet. A rueful expression crossed his face. "Shit," he said, putting his hands in his pockets.

"What's the matter?"

"I don't know what there is about you, JeriLee," he said with an embarrassed laugh, "but every time I'm around you I get a hard-on."

"You do say the nicest things." She laughed. She

got to her feet and kissed him lightly on the cheek. "But you'll also have to save that until I get my strength back."

"He's gone?" Angela asked, coming out of the kitchen.

JeriLee nodded.

"I don't like him," Angela said flatly. "It was his fault you went through all this and he didn't give a damn how you were feeling. He would have gone right into your bedroom if I didn't stop him. The selfish chauvinistic son of a bitch."

JeriLee looked up at her and laughed. "And besides that, he's an actor, which makes it even worse."

"I don't see what's so funny," Angela said. "I wouldn't talk to a man who put me through a thing like that."

JeriLee shook her head. "It wasn't all his fault," she said. "It still takes two, you know. And if I hadn't been in such a hurry I would have stopped to put in my diaphragm."

The doctor straightened up. "You're doin' okay," he said. "You can start getting out tomorrow if you don't overdo it. If you get tired I want you to come home and go to bed."

"Okay, Jim."

"Come into the office after the weekend," he said, "and we'll give you a final check."

"I'm beginning to feel like a used car."

He laughed. 'Don't worry about it. You should have another fifty thousand miles left in you. Besides I have an idea for a new part that should make the motor run without any more problems like the one you just had."

"What's that?"

"I just received the clinical reports of a new I.U.D. they've been testing. It's a small copper coil and I think you'll be able to tolerate it."

"Order one. I'll try anything."

"I already did," he said. "Goodbye."

"Goodbye, Jim," she called after the doctor, then picked up the ringing phone. "Hello."

It was her agent. "Who was that?"

"My doctor," she said wearily. Agents were all alike. They had to know everything.

"What did he say?"

"I'll live. I can start going out tomorrow."

"Good," he said. "We have to have a meeting." His voice lowered to a confidential whisper. "I've got some very big news but I don't want to talk about it on the phone."

That was another quality of agents. Everything had to be top secret. None of them would trust the telephone even if they were reading the headline from the daily newspaper. "Is it about George doing my picture?"

The surprise showed in his voice. "I thought you were in bed. How did you find out about it?"

She laughed. "For Christ's sake. Mike, you know about George and me."

"No, I don't," he said. "What about George and you?"

"That was George's baby that I aborted."

"The son of a bitch!" he erupted. Then there was a moment's silence and his voice lightened. "But that should make things easier for us. He has to listen to you. You can make him take the part."

"I can't make him do anything," JeriLee said. "All I can do is try to talk him into it."

"He owes you something," Mike said.

"Nothing," she said flatly. "That's not the way I live. I'm a big girl. I didn't do anything I didn't want to do."

"Can you come into the office in the morning?" he asked. "I've got to make you understand how important this is."

"Eleven o'clock okay?"

"Fine," he said. "I'm glad you're feeling better."

"So am I," she said. The phone clicked off and she put it down. He was a good agent but he lived in an ancient world.

Angela was on the couch reading the trades. She looked up. "What did the doctor say?"

"I'm better. I can go out tomorrow."

"That's good," Angela said. "Have you thought about dinner?"

JeriLee shook her head.

"Steaks or chicken?" Angela said. "I took both out of the freezer."

"Steak," JeriLee said promptly. "I need the strength."

Angela got to her feet. "I'll get started then," she said. "I'll fix salad and french fries."

"We'll have a bottle of red wine with dinner," JeriLee said. "The good wine. The Chambertin you gave me. I was saving it for a night like this."

Angela smiled. "You didn't forget?"

"I didn't forget," JeriLee said.

"Candles on the table?" Angela asked.

"The works," JeriLee said. "I'll roll a couple of joints. We'll have one before dinner and one before we go to bed."

Angela smiled. There was a happy sound in her voice. "It will be just like old times."

JeriLee watched her go into the kitchen. There was something very touching about her. Like old times.

Only the very young could think like that. Or the very old. There was no such thing as old times. Only good times and bad times. And sometimes the good came with the bad and other times the bad came with the good. It all depended on where you were in your head.

Like the time JeriLee Randall became Jane Randolph. Or the time Jane Randolph went back to being JeriLee Randall. She didn't know which. And that wasn't even old times.

It hadn't been that long ago.

Chapter 11

THE AMBER SPOT set in the ceiling over the tiny platform on which she was dancing blurred everything in front of her and the loud acid rock drowned out all other sounds in the crowded club. Her face and body were covered with a fine patina and the perspiration ran in rivulets between her naked breasts. She gulped for air between smiling parted lips. She was beginning to feel exhausted. Her back and arms were aching, even her breasts were sore from the gyrations of the dance. Suddenly the music stopped in the midst of a wild movement, taking her by surprise. She stood for a moment, then raised both arms over her head in the standard gogo dancer's bow, giving the customers one last free look as the spot died.

As she looked challengingly at the men staring at her from the crowded bar, their eyes fell from her gaze. There was no applause, only the beginning of the swell of conversation. She dropped her arms, came down from the platform and went through the small curtain behind it.

Through the sound system she could hear the voice of the club manager. "Ladeez an' gentlemun, it is with great pride that World à Gogo presents the star of their show, direct from San Francisco, the girl you have all read about, the girl you all want to see, the original, the one and only, the Blond Bomber, Miss Wild Billy Hickok and her twin forty-eights!"

Billy was waiting behind the curtain, her giant breasts thrusting forward against the thin silk kimono. She was holding a small vial in one hand and a short hard straw in the other. "How's the crowd out there tonight, Jane?" she asked.

"Okay, Billy," JeriLee answered, reaching for her terry cloth robe. "But it's you they came to see. All I could do was try and warm them up for you."

"Fuckers, all of them," Billy said without rancor. She put the straw in the vial and held it to her nostril. She snorted once in each nostril. Then she held the vial toward JeriLee. "Want a hit, Jane?"

JeriLee shook her head. "No, thanks. It'll keep me up the rest of the night and I want to get some sleep."

Billy put the vial of coke and the straw in the pocket of her kimono. "The gogo dancer's maiden aunt," she said.

JeriLee nodded. Coke, bennies and ammies. Without them the girls couldn't make it through their nightly four to six half-hour turns, seven nights a week. Billy slipped out of her kimono and turned to her. "I look all right?"

JeriLee nodded. "Fantastic. I still don't believe it."

Billy smiled. Her eyes were beginning to shine as the coke hit. "You better believe it," she said, touching her breasts proudly. "Carol says that hers are bigger than mine but I know better. We went to the same doctor and he told me she stopped at forty-six C and mine are a real forty-eight D."

JeriLee knew she was talking about Carol Doda, San Francisco's first topless dancer. Billy hated her because Carol got all the publicity. "Good luck, Billy," she said. "Go out there and kill them."

Billy laughed. "I know how," she said. "If they don't applaud, I'll just drop these on their fucking heads."

Billy disappeared through the curtain and the music stopped. JeriLee knew that the club had gone black while Billy took up her position. A moment later there was a roaring from the crowd as the amber spot went on. Then the music crashed and the applause and the whistles began.

JeriLee smiled to herself as she started back to the dressing room. Tits were what they had come to see. Now they were happy.

There was no one in the dressing room she shared with two other girls. She closed the door behind her and went directly to the small refrigerator. The pitcher of iced tea was half empty. Quickly she opened a tray of ice cubes and emptied it into the pitcher. Then she poured the tea into a tall glass, spiked it heavily with vodka and took a deep swallow.

She felt the cold liquid running down her throat and gave a light, gentle sigh of relief. Vodka and iced tea helped. It gave her a lift while replacing the fluids she sweated out during her turn.

Slowly she took off the short blond wig she wore and shook her own long brown hair down around her shoulders. Gogo dancers didn't wear their hair long. The customers didn't like it. Sometimes long hair covered the breasts. She opened a jar of Albolene and began to remove the heavy layer of makeup from her face.

The door opened and the manager came in. She looked at him in the mirror. He took out a handkerchief and mopped his face. "It's murder out there," he said. "There isn't enough space to breathe."

"Don't bitch," she said. "Last week you were complaining you could shoot pigeons in there."

"I'm not complaining." He put his hand inside his jacket, took out an envelope and tossed it on the makeup table. "That's for last week," he said. "Better count it."

She opened the pay envelope. "Two hundred forty dollars," she said. "It's all there." She glanced down at the payroll slip. The gross was three hundred and sixty-five dollars but with deductions, commissions and expenses all that was left was two forty.

"You could have doubled that in cash if you'd have listened to me."

"It's not my game, Danny."

"You're a strange one, Jane. What is your game anyway?"

"I told you, Danny. I'm a writer."

"Yeah. I know what you told me," he said without belief. "Where you goin' next?"

"I open in Gary on Tuesday."

"Topless World?"
"Yes."
"Good spot," he said. "I know the place. Lots of action down there. The manager's name is Mel. Give him my best."
"I'll do that, Danny," she said. "Thanks for everything."
There was a sound of applause from the room as he opened the door.
"Wild Billy really turns them on," she said.
He smiled. "She puts on a show. Too bad there aren't more like her. Ten girls like her and I can retire in a year."
She laughed. "Don't be greedy, Dan. You're doin' all right."
"Ever think of having yours done up like that?"
"I'm happy the way I am."
"She pulls a grand a week, for just one turn a night."
"Good luck to her," JeriLee said. She took another sip of her iced tea. "I couldn't walk around with a pair like that. I'd keep falling on my face."
He laughed. "Goodbye, Jane. Good luck."
" 'Bye, Danny."
She turned back to the mirror and finished removing the makeup from her face and throat, then went over to the sink and washed with cold water. After lighting a cigarette she finished her iced tea. She was beginning to feel better. Maybe she could get a little work done when she got back to the motel. Tomorrow was Sunday and she could sleep late. She wasn't making the connecting flight to Chicago until Monday morning.

She saw the car—shining silver and black top—when the taxi dropped her off in front of the motel.
The night clerk looked up from the switchboard in the office. "Your friend came in a couple of hours ago. I gave her the key to your room."
JeriLee nodded.
"Are you leaving tomorrow, Miss Randolph?"
"No. Monday."
"Okay. Just checking."

She went outside and down the walkway to her room. A faint light filtered through the drapes. She tried the door. It wasn't locked.

Licia was sitting on the bed, the pillows propped behind her, reading. She put down the newspaper and smiled as JeriLee came in. "Pittsburgh ain't New York," she said. "The late show goes off at two A.M."

JeriLee smiled and glanced over at the table. The portable electric typewriter Licia had given her was exactly as she had left it, the page still in the roller. "You're right about that," she said. "It's not New York."

She put down the small suitcase she had brought back from the club. "Care for a drink?" she asked, opening the door of the refrigerator.

"Orange juice, if you have it," Licia said.

"We have it." She placed the bottle of Tropicana on the small table. From the shelf above she took down a jar of iced tea mix and a bottle of vodka. "I'll get some ice," she said and went out in the corridor to the machine. When she got back to the room, Licia was rolling a couple of joints. JeriLee fixed the drinks—iced tea and vodka for herself, orange juice on the rocks for Licia. "Cheers," she said, slumping into the easy chair.

Licia passed her a joint. "I figured you can use one of these."

"You were right."

"How's it coming?" Licia asked, nodding toward the typewriter.

"It's not," she said flatly. "I can't seem to get it on."

"What you need is a vacation," Licia said. "You've been on the road for four months. You can't work both ends of the clock."

"That's not it," she said. "It seems that I've suddenly forgotten how to put words together. Like I can't get down on paper what I mean."

"You're tired. You got to stop pushing yourself, honey, or you'll push yourself into a breakdown."

"I'm okay."

Licia looked at the glass in JeriLee's hand. "How many of those do you put away a day?"

"Not that much," JeriLee said, knowing it wasn't true. It seemed that almost every time she went for a drink lately the vodka bottle was empty. "It's cheaper than coke and bennies and it works almost as well."

"Alcohol does things to your gizzards," Licia said. "At least when the other stuff is out of your system it's out."

"I don't know about that," JeriLee answered defensively. "Too many reds can scramble your brains."

"I'm not talkin' about speed," Licia said.

JeriLee fell silent.

"Look, honey," Licia said quickly, "I'm not preachin' at you. I just worry about you."

"I'm okay," JeryLee answered quickly, then changed the subject. "I didn't expect to see you this weekend. Where's Fred?"

"He got held over at the Fairmont in San Francisco," Licia answered. "He comes into the Waldorf next week."

"I thought it was this week," JeriLee said. The grass and the vodka were reaching her head. She giggled. "How does he take to being married?"

"He's not complaining." Then Licia laughed too. "Not that he's had much of a chance. In the four months we've been married, I don't think we've had more than ten days together. He's really getting it together."

"I'm glad," JeriLee said. "He's beginning to get more airplay. I hear him all the time."

"F.M. mostly," Licia said. "They dig middle of the road. We're pushing A.M. radio though. That's the one that pays off."

"You'll get it," JeriLee said confidently. She took another drag of the joint, leaned her head back against the cushion on the chair and closed her eyes.

"Tired, honey?"

JeriLee opened her eyes. Licia had come around behind her chair and was bending over her. She nodded without speaking.

Gently Licia began to stroke her forehead with her

fingers, then moved slowly down to her neck to massage the taut muscles. "How does that feel?" Licia asked.

JeriLee closed her eyes. "Good."

"How would you like me to fix you a nice warm bath?" Licia asked. "I brought some new bath oil with me."

"Sounds lovely," JeriLee said, her eyes still closed. She heard Licia begin to run the water in the tub. A few moments later she felt rather than heard her return. She opened her eyes.

Licia was kneeling at her feet, unfastening her shoes. She massaged her feet. "Poor tired little feet," she murmured. She looked up at JeriLee. "You're beautiful, do you know that?"

"You're beautiful yourself," JeriLee said, looking at her steadily.

Licia ran her tongue across her lips. "I can smell your perfume from here."

"Is it strong?" JeriLee asked quickly. "I didn't have time to shower after the turn."

"It's fantastic." Licia smiled. "It's a real turn-on. I'm wet already."

JeriLee stared into her eyes. "So am I," she said.

Chapter 12

EXCEPT FOR THE faint rays of sunlight coming through the cracks in the drapes, the room was dark when JeriLee opened her eyes. She rolled over on her side and looked at Licia, half buried in the pillow, one arm over her eyes.

In the semi-darkness the black girl's nudeness was like a statue carved out of the night, the full breasts and long jutting nipples like antennas on top of twin peaks falling down into the valley of her flat hard belly, then rising abruptly to the abundantly fur-covered mountain of her pubis. She fought the sudden impulse to touch her, to feel again the hot wetness of her, to taste the mildly salty flavor of her skin. But Licia was fast asleep and she didn't want to waken her. Silently she crept from the bed and went into the bathroom.

Licia was sitting up in bed when she returned. "What time is it?" she asked.

"Almost one o'clock."

Surprise echoed in Licia's voice. "I don't believe it!"

JeriLee laughed. "We didn't get to sleep until seven this morning."

"I never had sex like that," she said. "I never wanted to stop. I just kept on coming and coming and coming."

"The same thing was happening to me," JeriLee said.

"I've never tasted cunt like yours," Licia said. "It's like you're flowing' pure honey. I even lick my fingers after we ball."

"You better stop talkin' like that." JeriLee laughed. "You're turning me on again."

"Keep the good thoughts," Licia said, starting for the bathroom. "I'll be right back."

Just then the telephone began to ring. "You expectin' any calls?" Licia asked.

"No." The telephone kept on ringing. JeriLee picked it up. "Hello."

She held the phone toward Licia. "It's for you. Fred's calling from New York."

"Hello. This is Mrs. Lafayette." She paused, covering the mouthpiece with her hand. "The operator's getting him," she said in a worried voice. "I hope nothing's wrong."

There was a crackling in the phone. "Fred, darling, is everything all right? I thought you were staying on in San Francisco." She listened a moment, then her voice lightened. "That's fantastic! Of course I'll be there. If I leave now I can be in New York by nine o'clock, its turnpike all the way. No, it's perfectly all right. I had some business with the club down here and since I didn't expect you back until next week, I thought I'd stay over and kill some time with JeriLee and see how she was doin'. . . . Yes, she's fine. Going on to Gary tomorrow. . . . Sure I will. 'Bye, honey. Love you."

JeriLee looked at her without speaking.

"It's okay," Licia said quickly. "He's cool."

"You sure?"

Licia nodded. "He's too up to think of anything. Lou Rawls came down with laryngitis and they called Fred to replace him on the Pearl Bailey special that they're taping tonight. It's the break we've been waiting for."

JeriLee was silent.

"I'll grab a shower and get started," Licia said. "I don't want to get caught in the weekend traffic going into the city."

"I'll order some breakfast meanwhile."

"Just orange juice and coffee for me, honey." She saw the expression on JeriLee's face. "Don't be upset," she said quickly. "I tol' you everything was cool."

"I'm okay."

Licia laughed. "There's nothin' to worry about. Fred's just like every other man. They can't imagine anything in the world's better than their cocks."

Through the window JeriLee watched the silver car turn out of the motel driveway onto the approach road leading up to the turnpike ramp. She let the curtain fall and absently began to straighten up the room. The odor of grass and last night's sex hung over the unmade bed. She pressed the vent button on the air conditioner and the whine of the compressor filled the room with a low hum.

Then she went and stared down at the page in the typewriter. Suddenly she was depressed. Angrily she pulled the sheet from the machine, crumpled it, and threw it on the floor. "Fuck it!" she said aloud.

She opened the refrigerator door. There were still some ice cubes left in the bucket. She threw them into a glass and made herself a vodka and tea. Sipping the drink, she crossed the room to the bed and lit one of the joints that Licia had left on top of the night table.

The grass picked up on last night's high and almost immediately she was up there.

She threw off her terry cloth robe and lay back on the bed. She dragged on the joint slowly and with her free hand began to manipulate herself gently. A slow easy lassitude crept over her. She closed her eyes.

Licia's head was between her legs, Licia's tongue was licking at her clitoris, Licia's mouth was sucking the juices from her.

Suddenly she felt herself pop, almost like a balloon deflating. She opened her eyes. The empty room was a prison and the walls were closing in on her.

Quickly she reached for her drink and drained the glass. Then she pulled open the drawer of the night table and took out the vibrator.

This was a modern Green Hornet. It had been made in Japan. Executive size, they called it—no cords, battery-powered with two speeds.

She turned the vibrator on low. Closing her eyes she pressed it gently around her pubis, stroking lightly over her clitoris. She squeezed her eyes closed and inserted the phallus-shaped vibrator.

Now she could see Licia stopping the car and running into the apartment. Fred was sitting at the piano and when he stood up he was naked, his cock hard as a rock. Then Licia was naked too and kneeling in front of him, peeling back the thin black skin exposing the glistening glans. He disappeared into her gobbling mouth but then suddenly he pushed her backward onto the white carpet and her legs were going up in the air to encircle him. Her cunt gaped open and he began to bore into her.

"No!" JeriLee screamed. "That's mine!" Torn from her fantasy, she opened her eyes and stared down at the vibrator tingling in her hands. It was nothing.

Switching it off, she threw it down on the bed and rolled over on her side, fighting back the tears.

JeriLee didn't know why she was so upset. Licia had said she would get jobs for her and she had kept her word. She was supporting herself and writing and should have been happy, but she wasn't.

"I'm not jealous," she said over and over to herself. "I'm not jealous." But every time she blinked her eyes she saw Licia and Fred fucking on the soft white rug.

She looked down at her hands. They were shaking again. She went into the bathroom and popped a Quaalude.

In the mirror she saw the black hollow circles under her eyes. She looked awful. She splashed some cold water on her face.

If she was jealous, was it of Fred because Licia was fucking him? Or of Licia because Fred was fucking her? She just didn't know.

It had been nine months since her affair with Licia had begun, and almost a year since she had been with a man. Until now she had not thought about it.

It was almost midnight when she came into the club. The music was blasting and a girl was writhing in the amber spot on the platform behind the bar. She went through the dark club to the manager's office in the back.

Danny looked up from his desk as she came in. "I didn't expect to see you again," he said with surprise.

"I had nothing to do," she said. "I was bored."

He gave her a shrewd glance. "I thought your friend came down to see you."

He knew, but how? How did they all know everything about everybody? "She had to go home to her husband," she said.

"What are you looking for?" he asked.

"A cock," she said flatly. "The biggest hardest cock in town."

"I don't know," he said after a moment. "Wild Billy has an eye for you."

"I had that last night," she said. "Tonight I want cock."

"There's a half dozen guys out there, any one of them would spring for fifty or a hundred. I get half."

"You can keep all the money," she said.

"Okay. Want to come outside and take your pick?"

She laughed and for the first time he saw the contracted pupils in her eyes and knew that she was coked out of the world. "Don't bother," she said. "Just collect your money. I'll take all of them."

Chapter 13

AT THE BACK of the club there was an old rickety wooden porch that looked out on the ocean. Off to the right JeriLee could see the Santa Monica Pier and overhead the landing lights of the jet planes as they turned over the water and headed for the airport. The night air was turning cool and she pulled the terry cloth robe more tightly around her. She listened abstractedly to the muffled sound of music coming from the club.

Just one more turn and she was finished for the night. The club owners hated it but she was grateful for the California two o'clock law. In some states she worked until four in the morning, in others until daylight. She wondered vaguely if Mike would pick her up. You never knew about him. He lived in a world all his own.

She had met him the day she arrived in California almost a month ago. It was a Sunday and he'd been working in the real estate office she went to when she decided that she wanted to rent an apartment instead of staying at a motel. Besides being cheaper, she had thought it would be easier to write there than in a motel. It would be quieter and she had eight weeks of bookings in the Los Angeles area.

Tall, tan and with his hair bleached almost white from the sun, he didn't look at all like a real estate agent. In jeans and bare feet he looked out of place seated behind the desk.

"What do you do?" he asked, beginning to fill in the information form.

"I'm a writer," she answered.

" A writer?"

"Anything wrong with it?"

"With your body and your legs, I figured you for an actress or a dancer."

"I do that too."

"I got a three-month sublease I think would be perfect for you."

"I only need it for two months."

"I think I could talk the owner into it," he said.

He closed the office and took her out to his car. It was a customized VW with giant balloon tires. The top was completely cut away, with a roll bar running from side to side over the middle of the car. "This is a great place," he said as he moved the car out of the parking lot. "Quiet. Two minutes from the beach. Great bathroom. Even has a bidet."

"A bidet," she repeated. "Sounds expensive."

"You'll love it," he said confidently. "Only three hundred a month. A French lady fixed it up."

"Sound too good to be true. Why did she leave it?"

"Her romance broke up. She went back to France."

The bedroom was small, as was the living room, and the kitchen was little more than a closet. But he was right about the bathroom. By far the biggest room in the apartment, it had a shower stall, sunken tub, two sinks and a bidet.

"What do you think?" he asked.

"It's small," she said.

"Great for a writer. You alone?"

"Yes."

"You don't need anything bigger then."

"But I only want it for two months."

"No problem. Give me a check for two months plus seventy-five dollars cleaning charges and you can move in this afternoon."

"Okay," she said, taking her checkbook from her purse. "Who do I make the check out to?"

"Me," he said. "It's my place." He put his hand in

his pocket and took out a small linen tobacco pouch tied with string. With his other hand he pulled out a pack of Zig Zag cigarette papers. "Do you smoke?" he asked.

She nodded silently, watching him roll the joint expertly with one hand. From his back pocket he took out a wooden match and struck it along the side of his jeans. He lit the joint carefully and held it out to her.

"Two tokes of this and you're away," he said. "Got it straight from Mexico."

She took a deep hit. He was right.

"Sit down," he said. "It'll only take me ten minutes to get my shit together and put it in the car. Then we'll go and pick up your stuff."

"What about the office? Don't you have to go back?"

"I only work there Sundays because the owner likes to go fishing. Besides I did all the business I have to do today."

"Where do you work the rest of the week?"

"I don't. Gave it up when I got out of the army. Ruins your sex life and gives you ulcers."

"What do you live on then?" she asked.

"This apartment. It's enough to keep me."

"Where do you stay when you're not here?"

"I have friends," he said. "Never have trouble crashing someplace. It's amazing how many people are just looking for company and someone to talk to."

She took the cigarette from him while he went into the bedroom to get his things. She took another drag. He was probably right. Dropping out was a way to go. And he didn't look as if he was suffering from it.

He was back in a few minutes with an olive-green duffel bag only half full. "Ready?" he asked.

"Good grass always makes me thirsty," she said.

"I'd offer you a glass of wine, but there isn't any."

She didn't speak.

"There's a liquor store down the block," he added. "I can run down there and get a bottle."

"That's a good idea."

"But I haven't any cash," he said without embarrassment.

She opened her purse and took out two dollars. "That enough?"

He grinned. "This is California. I'll get two bottles."

They smoked, drank and balled through the afternoon, and when night came they went to her motel and got her things so that she could move in. But he didn't move out.

She awakened early the next morning with the sunlight streaming into the room. The bed beside her was empty. She hadn't heard him leave.

In the small kitchen she found a small kettle which she filled with water and put on the stove to heat. She opened the closet door but couldn't find anything but two lonely tea bags. She took one down and placed it in a cup. It would have to do.

She went back into the bedroom and began to unpack. She was setting up the portable typewriter on a table near the window when he returned.

He came into the room, a bag of groceries in his arms. "You're up," he said, surprise in his voice.

"Yes."

"I thought you could use some groceries," he said, crossing the room to the small kitchen and placing the large bag on the table.

"Did you get some coffee?" she asked. "I couldn't find any."

He began to empty the bag. Eggs, butter, bacon, bread, orange juice, milk. Finally he held up a jar. "Instant okay?"

"That's fine."

"I don't drink it myself. Caffeine is bad for you."

"I can't get moving in the morning without it," she said.

"Why don't you finish whatever you're doing?" he suggested. "I'll make breakfast."

She stood there hesitantly.

"I'm a good cook," he said quickly.

She smiled. "Okay."

"Hungry?"

"Starved."

The water in the kettle began to boil. Quickly he

made a cup of coffee and handed it to her. "That should help," he said. "I'll have breakfast in a jiffy."

By the time she had finished setting up her work table with all her papers he called her.

She looked down at the table approvingly. He had set it very attractively with green placemats and white plates.

He gestured to the seat near the window. "You sit over there." He placed three eggs and six slices of bacon on each of their plates. Then he opened the oven door and took out the warm toast. "Okay?" he asked, sitting down.

"Beautiful," she said, picking up her orange juice.

"Coffee now?"

She nodded.

"By the way, how'd you pay for this?" she asked. "I thought you didn't have any money."

"I didn't, but the market always gives me credit when I have a boarder."

She was silent for a moment. "Do you do this often?"

"It all depends on who rents the place," he said. "I don't rent to gays."

"Only girls?"

He grinned. "Preferably. Once or twice I let it to couples. But they usually don't stay too long. It's really too small for them."

She finished her food and drained her cup. Quickly he was on his feet, bringing her more coffee. She looked up at him and smiled. "You do give good service."

He returned her smile. "I try. And when I find a good tenant I try even harder."

"What other services do you provide?"

"Everything—laundry, housekeeping, chauffeuring. You don't have to rent a car with me around. I'm always available."

"What do you do when your tenant's friends come over?"

"I'm very discreet," he said. "I disappear."

"I work at home during the days."

"That's fine with me."

"I work outside nights."

"Are you trying to tell me you're a hooker?"

"No." She laughed.

"I don't understand you then."

"I begin work over at the Rosebud on Airport Boulevard tonight. I have eight weeks of bookings around L.A."

There was an expression of shock in his voice. "But that's a topless joint!"

She laughed again. "I told you I was a dancer."

"But, the typewriter." He sounded confused.

"I told you I was a writer too," she said.

"What else do you do?"

"I used to act," she said. "As a matter of fact, I thought I might check into what's going on while I'm out here."

"Business stinks," he said. "I have friends who are in it. The only work around is in pornos."

"You never can tell," she said. "And since I'm out here, it won't cost anything."

"I have a friend who's an agent," he said. "Maybe he can help you. Would you like to meet him?"

"I can talk to him," she said.

"I'll fix it up."

She sipped at her coffee. "I'll have to rent a car. Do you know a place where I can get one for a decent price?"

"I told you chauffeuring was part of the service," he said. "All you pay for is the gas."

She looked up at him without speaking.

He smiled suddenly. "Okay. I got the message."

"It's nothing personal," she said. "I'm just used to being alone."

"I dig that," he said. "But look at it this way. Why go through the hassle of having to do everything yourself? From what I hear, you're going to be a very busy lady. Working day and night besides all the other shit you want to get into. Why don't you give the service a try for a week? If it don't work out, you can drop it. There'll be no hard feelings."

She thought for a moment. In a peculiar way it made

sense. "Okay," she said finally. "How much extra does it cost?"

A hurt tone came into his voice. "I told you there was no charge. The only thing you pick up is the expenses and the most expensive thing about me is orange juice. I drink three quarts a day."

She laughed. "I guess I can afford that." She got to her feet. "I'll finish straightening up my things and then I'm going back to sleep. I like to be in good shape the first night on a new job."

"What would you like for lunch?"

"No lunch."

"Dinner then?"

"It'll have to be early," she said. "Six o'clock. I have to be on the job at eight."

"Okay. What do you want to eat?"

"Make it steak—thick, tender and rare."

She went into the bedroom and closed the door behind her. She drew the drapes, darkening the room, then popped a Valium 10 and stretched out on the bed.

She felt the tranquilizer taking hold. Maybe it would work. She was always so wound up running around that she almost never had time to really rest. Walter had once said there was nothing like having a houseboy to take care of one. He could very well be right.

She felt herself sinking into sleep. Then another thought ran through her mind. Licia. She had promised to call her as soon as she found a place. She tried to rouse herself but the pill had taken too strong a hold. She gave herself up to the quiet. There would be time to call Licia between turns at the club.

Chapter 14

THE FOG was beginning to obscure the lights of the Santa Monica Pier. In another few minutes they would be completely gone. The door opened behind her.

"Five minutes, Jane," the manager said.

She threw her cigarette over the railing and went into the club. "Mike show up yet?" she asked the manager, who followed her into the dressing room.

"I haven't seen him."

He watched while she checked her makeup. Quickly she brushed a little rouge around her nipples and plucked them to make them more prominent. "A little coke'll really get them up there," he said.

She grinned at him in the mirror. "It's too expensive to waste like that. You don't pay me enough."

He laughed. "I got a little stash. I'd be willing to put it on for you for free."

She laughed with him. "I'll bet." She turned toward him. "How do I look?"

He nodded without speaking.

"Anything wrong?" she asked.

He shook his head.

"What is it then?"

"I just got word from the owners. We're going bottomless next week."

"Total?" she asked.

"No. The girls will still wear pubic panties."

"Shit," she said in a disgusted voice. "When do we start giving them fuck shows?"

"Don't be like that, Jane," he said. "You know our business has gone to hell. Almost all the clubs around have gone bottomless. We held out as long as we could."

"Good luck," she said. "I'm moving on to Zingara's in the Valley next week."

"Same management, same policy," he said.

"I got a firm booking."

He was silent for a moment. "Not if you don't show your ass."

"They can talk to the booking agent about that."

"They already did," he said. "He agreed to an extra forty bucks a week."

She was silent.

"Don't be a fool, Jane," he said. "Forty bucks is forty bucks. The management likes you and so do the customers. What's a little skin more or less between friends? Don't ruin a good thing."

Suddenly she could feel the weariness seeping through her. "I need a pop," she said. She took her handbag from the locked drawer of the dressing table, rummaged through it and came out with a yellow net-covered ampule. Holding it under her nose, she crushed it between her thumb and forefinger.

She sniffed deeply, and felt the rush of heat from the amyl nitrite flood her brain. She took another deep sniff, then dropped the broken ampule into the wastebasket. The first wave of heat had gone, leaving her up and somehow stronger. "I do a hell of an act with an executive-size vibrator," she said.

He smiled. "We can't go that far but I'll be glad to give you a private audition."

She laughed. "I'll bet." Then she turned serious. "I don't suppose I have any choice, do I?"

"Not if you want to work for us."

She thought for a moment. The management that controlled this club also controlled the other clubs she had been booked into. For her that represented eight weeks' work. By the time she found replacement bookings the two months would be gone, along with the money she had managed to put together during the last six months. In addition she wouldn't have the chance to follow up on the contacts she was trying to make while she was on the Coast. The gent Mike had introduced her to thought he might get something for her. Finally she nodded. "Okay."

He smiled. "Smart girl. I'll let the boys know. I wouldn't be surprised if they don't hold you over on the whole circuit."

She watched him leave the dressing room then turned back to the mirror. She still looked good. No way could they take her for twenty-eight, but then there was no way they could take her for twenty-three either. The body was still firm, but the lines were beginning to show in her face. Still, the one place she really felt age was inside her head.

The music pounded at her from the four speakers. She was dancing on the tiny platform behind the bar—the lead spot. There was another girl on a platform in the back of the room but the real action was at the bar.

As she moved she let her eyes wander down the bar. Mike was pushing his way in and there was a man following him. Although she couldn't remember his name, she recognized him as a producer she had met at the agent's office. He made motorcycle pictures—cheap action quickies, as the trade called them. She wondered why he was with Mike.

Mike held up his usual glass of orange juice in a gesture of recognition. She nodded and smiled. The timing mechanism in her head told her that she had about five minutes left of her turn. Time enough to give the producer something to stare at. She let herself get into the music and go.

She was sipping an iced tea and vodka when they came into the dressing room.

"This is Mr. Ansbach," Mike said.

Ansbach held out his hand. "We met at the Gross office."

"I remember," she said, shaking his hand.

"You really can dance."

"Thank you."

"I mean it. Really dance. Not just shake your tits and ass."

"Thank you," she repeated.

"Mr. Ansbach stopped at the apartment," Mike explained. "He said he had to see you right away. I thought you wouldn't mind if I brought him over."

"I don't mind."

"I'm glad now I did come," Ansbach said. "I was interested in one of your story ideas. Gross gave me several of them to read."

"Which one?" she asked.

"The one about the dancer in a sleazy club in Gary who gets ripped off by a gang of bike riders."

She nodded. "Those things happen. And I know the girl it happened to. It was pretty hairy. She wound up in a hospital for six weeks."

"I know they do, but for the movie we have to give it an up-beat ending."

She didn't answer.

"Now that I've seen you dance, I got another idea. Maybe you can do the part. Mike told me you were an actress too. If you can act half as good as you write and dance, we're home free."

"I'm locked in on the circuit for another eight weeks."

"That's okay," Ansback said quickly. "We'll need that much time to get the script ready."

"I'll need more time than that to write it. It was just a story idea."

"You don't have to write it. I have writers who know how I work and can get it together in no time."

"Did you talk to Gross about it?"

He nodded. "He tried to call you but there was no answer, so I got your address from him and decided to give you a try myself."

"How much are we talking about?" she asked.

"Not much. We haven't got big money. Ten-day shooting schedules. Non-union crews. All location, no sets."

"I understand that."

"Two hundred fifty dollars and screen credit for the original story. If we decide you're right for the part, and I don't see why you're not, three seventy-five a week, two-week guarantee."

She was silent.

"It's not much money," he said quickly. "But it's a beginning. You got to start somewhere, Miss Randolph."

"Can I talk to Gross about it?"

"Of course. But try to get back to me tomorrow. I'm committed to start a picture by the end of next month and if it's not yours I'll have to set another."

"I'll get back to you," she said.

He held out his hand. "Very nice meeting you, Miss Randolph. You're a very talented young lady. I hope we can work together."

"Thank you, Mr. Ansbach."

She watched the door close behind him, then turned to Mike. "What do you think?"

"Could be."

"You don't sound up about him."

"He's a weasel. Just get your money up front whatever you do."

"I'll rely on Gross to take care of that." She turned back to the mirror and began to cream her face. "I won't be long," she said.

He looked at her reflection in the mirror. "The word on the beach is that the club is going total next week."

"News travels fast."

"Going along with them?"

"Do I have a choice?"

He was silent for a moment. "You're a strange lady. I really don't understand you. What's so important about making all that bread?"

"Try living without it."

"I don't need that much."

"You're not a woman. You can turn it on any time you want. It's not that easy for me. I've been without and I know what's it's like."

"Still goin' to do it if you get the picture?"

She nodded.

He got to his feet. "I'm goin' to try and talk the bartender into giving me another orange juice."

"Okay." She thought as she removed the rest of the cream from her face that he was acting strange, not at all like himself.

But she didn't know why until he stopped the car in

front of the apartment. When he made no move to get out she turned to look at him. "Aren't you coming in?"

"I'm crashing somewhere else tonight."

"Anything wrong?"

"You have a friend visiting you."

He put the Volks into gear and drove off before she could ask another question. She turned and walked up to the house.

Licia was waiting for her in the living room.

Chapter 15

LICIA'S VOICE was gentle and concerned. "You okay, baby?"

JeriLee closed the door and met Licia's eyes. "I'm okay."

Licia kissed her cheek, her lips soft against JeriLee's face. "I was worried about you. You been out here over two weeks and I didn't hear nothin'."

"I was working." JeriLee went into the kitchen, with Licia following. She took out a container of orange juice. "Want a drink?"

Licia gestured at the four containers of orange juice. " 'Bout time you got smart. That stuff's better than what you been drinking."

JeriLee filled a glass. "It's not mine. It's Mike's. He's a juice freak like you."

JeriLee took out the pitcher of iced tea and made herself a drink. "That stud livin' here with you?" Licia asked.

"Yes," she answered flatly.

"Serious stuff?"

"No."

"Then what's he doin' here?"

"He's the landlord." JeriLee walked back into the living room, kicked off her shoes and sank into the couch. "He makes it easy. He drives, cooks, cleans."

Licia sat in the chair opposite her. "Fucks too?"

JeriLee didn't answer.

Licia reached for a cigarette, then stopped and looked at JeriLee. "Got a joint?"

As JeriLee began to roll the joint, she noticed that her hands were shaking. There was no reason for her to be jumpy. Licia hadn't changed, she hadn't changed, they were still the same people they had been when they were last together. The grass would help. I would take the edge off. She rolled a bomber big enough to put them both way up there. Carefully she licked the paper, sealed the cigarette and went back into the living room.

Licia had her suitcase open on the couch. She held out a red velvet Cartier box to JeriLee. "I brought you a present," she said. "Open it."

Inside, JeriLee found a long rope of oval jade beads.

"Do you like it?" Licia asked anxiously.

"It's beautiful. But you shouldn't have done it."

Licia smiled. "Let me put it on you."

She took the necklace and placed it over JeriLee's head. After a moment she nodded. "Look at yourself in the mirror."

She followed JeriLee into the bedroom. The jade was warm against her skin. JeriLee met Licia's gaze in the mirror. "Why, Licia?"

Licia moved closer, placing her cheek against JeriLee's. Her lips brushed against her hair. "Because I love you and missed you."

JeriLee was silent.

Gently Licia turned her around and kissed her on the mouth. "I missed you so much, baby," she murmured. "You can't know how much I wanted to hold you and kiss you and make love to you."

Suddenly JeriLee felt the tears coming to her eyes and in a moment she was sobbing almost hysterically. Tenderly Licia drew her head down to her breast. "There, baby, there," she said soothingly. "I understand."

She led JeriLee back into the living room and picked

up the joint. She lit it, took a deep toke, then handed it to JeriLee. "Take a good hit," she said. "You'll feel better."

JeriLee took the smoke deep into her lungs. The grass was good. Mike was right. He got nothing but the best. She took another hit and felt the sudden easing of the tensions. She dabbed at her eyes with a Kleenex. "I don't get it," she said in a puzzled voice. "I go up and down like a yoyo."

Licia took the joint from her and sucked on it. Her eyes watched JeriLee thoughtfully. "You've been workin' hard, honey. You can't burn it at both ends without paying for it."

"I have to, Licia, if I don't want to stay in this business until I shake my tits down to my knees."

"You're a long way from that," Licia said.

"It doesn't feel like that at three in the morning after you've done six turns."

"It's not a bad rap, and the money is good," Licia said, passing the joint back to JeriLee. "Who was that little man here with the stud when I came in?"

"He's a producer. He's interested in buying one of my stories for a film. I might even play in it."

"Is he legit?"

"My agent says so."

Licia was surprised. "You have an agent? You have been busy. How did you get to him?"

"Through Mike. He knows everybody."

"What does Mike do?"

"Nothing." She smiled. "He lives off this apartment."

There was a faint note of resentment in Licia's voice. "He's a pimp."

"That's not fair. You don't even know him."

"Maybe, but where I come from, a man don't work, he's a pimp."

JeriLee was silent.

Licia took the joint from JeriLee and put it in an ashtray. "I'm not hitting on you, honey," she said, drawing JeriLee to her. "I'm not holding Mike against you. I know what girls need. Even I can dig a good hard cock once in a while. But I never forget what they really want. There ain't a man in the world who won't put you down if he has the chance."

JeriLee was suddenly weary. She felt the energy drain from her. "Mike isn't like that," she said.

"We won't talk no more about it," Licia said soothingly. "You're wiped out. You go to bed and get a good night's rest. We got the next few days to catch up on our talk."

"How long can you stay?"

"I got a week. Fred's working in Seattle. I said I'd meet him in Frisco."

JeriLee didn't speak.

"I thought it would be nice if you could get some time off. Maybe we could go somewhere and catch up on our rest. I've been going at it pretty hard too."

JeriLee shook her head doubtfully. "I don't know."

"We'll see. Now you go off to bed before you fall on your face."

"What about you?"

"I'll finish unpacking first. I won't be too long."

Licia, watching the door close, was annoyed with herself. She should have known better than to let JeriLee get this far away from her. Especially here where the things JeriLee really wanted were at the tips of her fingers.

She looked around the small apartment. After a moment she had made up her mind. Tomorrow she would look for a more comfortable apartment for JeriLee. Something with enough room for both of them.

The sooner she got JeriLee out of here the better. She could no longer leave JeriLee on her own as much as she had. No matter how much it screwed up her own life, she would have to find a way to bring her back to New York.

Chapter 16

Licia and JeriLee came out of the dust-covered aluminum camper into the bright sunlight. JeriLee's face was covered with carefully applied smeared dirt and blood.

The A.D. peered at JeriLee's face anxiously and called to the makeup man. "I think we can use a little more gore. And rough up the bike suit a bit."

"Where are they shooting now?" JeriLee asked.

"They're on the road. They should be here in about fifteen minutes. They better," he muttered, scanning the sky. "Or we're going to lose the light."

JeriLee followed the makeup man to a small table set under a tree. A wooden crate served as a seat. The makeup man went to work on her face and then with a small razor blade made several cuts and nicks in her bike suit.

Just as he finished with JeriLee they heard the roar of motors. A moment later the big black Harley Davidson screeched up the ramp past the camera. Behind through a cloud of dust came the pursuing souped-up beach buggy. As it sped past the camera they heard the shrill whistle of the A.D. and the director's shouted "Cut!"

The motors stopped and the crew immediately began resetting the cameras. The sun was beginning to slide slowly down the sky toward the ocean and they worked feverishly to gain time against the dying light.

The stunt driver on the bike flipped up his visor. He took a can of beer from the outstretched hand of one of the crew and walked to the edge of the platform that hung out over the ocean.

"Is he really going over it?" Licia asked JeriLee.

JeriLee nodded.

"That's a seventy-foot fall."

"That his business."

"It's not my kind of business," Licia said.

The director came up with the driver of the dune buggy, who was wearing a long blond wig and black vinyl bike suit exactly like JeriLee's.

"You know what you have to do?" the director asked the stunt man.

"Yeah, the minute Tom goes over the cliff I get out of the car and JeriLee gets in."

"It has to be fast," the director said. "We've only got one camera to work with. It will pan out after Tom, then back to the car. The other camera will pick up his fall. You got maybe thirty seconds, no more."

The stunt man nodded. "Okay."

The director turned to JeriLee. "Once you're in the car wait for my signal before getting out. Then you walk to the edge and look down. Take a long beat then turn and walk slowly along the cliff toward the cops who will be approaching you. I'm going to try to catch you in silhouette against the setting sun."

JeriLee nodded.

"We'll be ready in five minutes," the director said. "They're getting the shot of the patrol car coming on the ramp now."

"How are you holding up, honey?" Licia asked.

"Okay."

"You look tired. It's been a long day." She took a pill from her bag. "Better take this. It'll keep you going."

"It'll also keep me up half the night."

"Don't worry about it," Licia said. "We'll get you to sleep. This is the last scene in the movie and I don't want you to look wasted."

JeriLee took the red and swallowed it with a swig of water from the canteen. She felt the instant burst of energy. Her eyes began to shine.

"Feel better, honey?" Licia asked.

"Much better." JeriLee laughed thin and high. "I can go another ten hours."

It was dark when she awoke. There was the faint hum of voices through the closed door to the living room. Her mouth was dry and her tongue felt swollen. She got out of bed and went into the bathroom. Thirstily she drank a glass of water, then brushed her teeth vigorously to get the brackish taste from her mouth. She put on the terry cloth robe hanging on the door and went out into the living room.

The voices were coming from the television set. Licia looked up from her chair.

"What time is it?" JeriLee asked.

"Eleven o'clock."

"I told you to wake me at eight. I was due at the club at nine."

"It's okay. When I saw how deep you were sleepin'. I called the club and told them you were sick."

"It's not okay. They know I was making the picture. They'll figure I didn't want to show up."

"Then screw 'em. You can get plenty of jobs where you can show your ass."

"You know better than that. This is a good club. Most of the places are hustlers' joints."

"Calm down, honey," Licia said soothingly. "Let me make you a cup of tea. You can't keep this up or you're goin' to collapse."

"I got to. I have to keep working."

"Do you? You've been at it steady for about eight months now. You gotta have some money in the bank."

JeriLee's eyes fell. "It costs money to live."

"I know it does, honey, but you only got into this to get enough money to write. You must have enough now to keep you while you get back to work on that play you want to do."

JeriLee was silent.

"Face it, baby," Licia said. "Writin' motorcycle pictures ain't what you started out to do. An' you didn't even write that. They just took your idea and turned it around to suit themselves. You didn't write no sex and sadism story but that's what they made out of it."

JeriLee still didn't answer.

"You don't belong out here," Licia said. "You'll only wind up trapped in all this shit an' never write the kind of thing you really want to do."

"At least I got paid for what I wrote," JeriLee said defensively. "And they talk to me. That's more than I get back East. Maybe this is the beginning of something."

"It's the beginning all right," Licia said. "The beginning of the end. Nobody ever makes it out of these pictures. There's only one way to go after this—down, into straight pornos."

"What makes you such an expert all of a sudden?"

"I didn't just sit here while you were out shootin' this movie. I did a lot of checking on my own. What you made is a double- or triple-bill drive-in movie that nobody watches anyway. The only reason they go to the drive-ins is for hamburgers, hot dogs and fucking."

"Gross says that he can get me a few more pictures after this. He says Ansbach is happy with the film."

"But they'll be the same kind of pictures."

"I don't know."

"You'll see. It'll be like the clubs. Each time you'll have to take off a little more. Next thing, fuck shows."

JeriLee was silent. She knew that a lot of what Licia said made sense.

"I'm not pushin' you, honey," Licia said earnestly, taking her hand. "But someday JeriLee Randall will want to come back and by that time it may be too late. Jane Randolph will have taken over for good."

"I need a drink," JeriLee said.

"Don't drink. Take a Librium."

"I took two before I went to sleep."

"Take another. A drink will only charge you up. What you need is more sleep." She rose from the couch. "I'll get it for you."

JeriLee took the pill with a swallow of water, then Licia pushed her gently back onto the couch. "Now you just sit there and relax while I fix a nice bath for you.

After that you go back to bed and I don't want to hear a sound out of you until morning."

JeriLee took Licia's hand and squeezed it. "I don't know how I'd have gotten through the last few weeks without you," she said gratefully.

"I love you, honey. I want to take care of you."

The tranquilizer wasn't working. Restlessly JeriLee sat up in bed and turned on the light.

The bedroom door opened. "You okay?" Licia asked.

"I can't sleep."

Licia sat down on the edge of the bed. "You need a vacation. A change of scenery."

JeriLee started to laugh.

"What you laughin' at, honey?"

"Look who's talking? When's the last time you ever took a vacation? Even out here, you're always on the telephone running your business."

"There's a difference. I'm doin' what I want to do. You're shootin' off in so many different directions, you don't know what you want anymore."

"I know what I want. I want to write."

"Then do it." Licia paused for a moment. "If it's money that's holdin' you up, forget it. I got enough money to let you do what you want."

"I don't want your money. You've done more than enough already."

"You're being childish."

"I'm not," JeriLee answered stubbornly. "It's important that I take care of myself."

"You wouldn't feel like that if I were a man, would you?"

Licia's sudden coolness took JeriLee by surprise. "What makes you say that?"

"It's the truth, isn't it? It's okay for a man to support you but you can't accept it from another woman."

"That's not true."

"Would you give the same answer to that stud if he offered?" Licia asked. "I'll bet you wouldn't. You'd fall down on your knees and suck his cock in gratitude."

"Don't say that, Licia. You know better. If that was

what I wanted I could have had it a long time ago. It doesn't make any difference whether it's a woman or a man. I still have to make it on my own."

Licia laughed harshly. "You talk a lot about the truth but you don't face it, honey. Why did you call me when you had no place else to go? Because you knew in your secret little heart that I wanted to ball you. And that was okay if we kept it on an airy fairy level but now we're down to the gut and you don't like that. Why don't you come out of the closet, baby, and admit what you are? You're no different than me. You want cunt just as much as I do."

JeriLee's eyes were wide and staring. With trembling hands she reached for a cigarette. Licia took it from her and put it in the ashtray.

"You'll wind up setting fire to the bed," she said. As she removed her robe, her honey-colored skin shone in the glow of the lamp. Gently she drew JeriLee's face to her breasts. Her voice was husky as she spoke. "Here, baby," she said softly. "Mother knows what you want. Mother knows what you need. Let Mother take care of you."

JeriLee closed her eyes and inhaled Licia's warm musky smell. She wanted to sink into the safety of Licia's arms, but she suddenly knew that she could not. What Licia offered was no different from what men had offered. Sex was still the currency of payment. The fact that she was a woman didn't make it a fair trade item. Freedom was the right to be yourself. It was not something that could be bought and paid for. It was earned by being honest with yourself, whether or not you liked what you saw.

She pulled away from Licia and looked into her eyes. "You were right," she said. "I was not being honest. Not with myself and not with you. I'm sorry."

Licia didn't speak.

"I'm grateful for what you've done," JeriLee said. "I want to be your friend. And I want to make love to you and have you make love to me because I enjoy it. Maybe more than any other kind I know. But I'm not in love with you any more than I am with anyone else. Maybe

I'm not capable of love in the same way other people are. All I know is that I don't want to own anybody and I don't want anybody to own me. I have to be free."

Licia's voice was dull with pain. "Even if it means being alone?"

JeriLee looked at her for a long moment, then nodded slowly.

Licia's eyes filled with tears. And this time it was JeriLee who drew the woman's head to her breast and comforted her.

Chapter 17

MARC GROSS ASSOCIATES consisted of one harried secretary and an answering service. Gross himself was a young man who had worked for several of the big agencies before striking out on his own. He drove a Lincoln Continental on which payments were always two months behind and was given to continually dropping names and talking about the big deals that were always pending. Despite it all, he was a likable young man and did the best he could for the clients who happened to drift through his door. The real problem was that the most promising talent was always grabbed up by the more established agencies while he had to make do with the hopefuls.

As JeriLee came into the office he got to his feet, a genuine smile on his face. She was one of his few working clients. "No calls while I'm talking with Miss Randolph," he told his secretary.

"We've got a lot of work to do," he said importantly.

JeriLee nodded without speaking.

"Ansbach tells me that the film on you is sensational. I got him to promise me some clips so that we can have something to show around before the picture comes out. The idea is to lock up a few more jobs and build some continuity for you as a performer." He stopped suddenly and stared at her. "Was that a blond wig you wore in the picture?"

She nodded.

"I saw some stills. You should wear it all the time. Helps build the image."

"It was all right for the part. But it's not me," she said.

"Doesn't matter. That's what the producers want. Gives you a raunchy look."

"A hard look you mean."

"A matter of opinion. I call it the 'I.F.' look."

"What's that?"

"Instant Fuck. Jumps right out of the pictures."

"I'm a little too old to go the sexy blonde route."

"Not true. You're just the right age. These days men are looking for a little more than the dumb blonde. They want a more experienced look, a woman who seems to know what they want and can give it to them. I'm setting up some interviews for you right now and I want you to wear the wig when you go to them."

"Okay."

"When are you going back to work in the club?"

"I start tonight."

"Good. We got to promote that. Okay if I bring some producers over?"

She looked at him doubtfully. "Don't you think that will frighten some of them away? I can't see the studios being crazy about that association."

"Fuck the studios. That's not where the action is. It's the independents who are setting all the trends. The studios do nothing but try to catch up."

"I can't see building a career on motorcycle pictures."

"What's wrong with them? Jack Nicholson didn't do so bad. He made about four of them before *Easy Rider* and look where he is now. One of the biggies."

She was silent.

"I know the money isn't much, but there's a lot of work in that field."

"I don't know."

"Ansbach wants to use you again," he said. "And it's not a bike picture this time."

"What is it?"

"A story of a women's prison camp. There are a couple of good parts in it but you've got the lead if you want it."

"Do you have the script?"

"You know how he works. The script won't be ready until he starts shooting. But here's a copy of the treatment," he said, holding out some pages. "While you're reading, I'll make a couple of calls."

"You want me to read it now?"

"It's the only copy I have, and I need it. He wants me to find some other girls for him. It won't take long. It's only about twelve pages."

She had finished reading before he was through his second telephone call. "What do you think?" he asked.

"I don't think it's for me."

"It's the big part."

"It's out-and-out S. and M."

"It's what the audiences are buying."

"I don't like it. There's not even a pretense of a story line. Just one scene after another of girls going down on girls and girls beating up on girls."

"That's what those prisons are like. Besides it's just a treatment. The script will be better."

"I can't see how a film like that can do me any good. I wind up seeming to be the dike of all time."

"You're an actress. It shouldn't be too difficult for you to get into it."

She detected the subtle change in his voice. "What do you mean?"

"Come on, Jane," he said, putting on the charm. "We're both adults. I know what you're into. I'm not exactly blind, you know."

She didn't answer.

"I've met your friend from back East."

She felt herself flush. "What I do is my business," she said shortly. "I think it's a lousy idea and I don't want any part of it."

"Wait a minute," he said placatingly. "Okay, okay. Ansbach and I thought you might go for it. There will be other things."

"What about the story ideas I gave you?" she asked.

"I'm circulating them. I'll keep you informed."

"Good. You can reach me at the apartment during the day. I'll be at the club at night."

"You'll hear from me soon. I'm setting up appointments for you over at Warner and Paramount." He followed her to the door. "What about that screenplay you told me you were working on?"

"I'll show it to you as soon as I finish."

"Don't forget. I got a hunch we can really break through with that one." He kissed her cheek. "We'll keep in touch."

"I didn't expect you back so soon," Licia said as JeriLee came into the apartment.

JeriLee looked at the closed suitcases standing by the door. "You weren't going to leave without saying goodbye?"

"I don't like goodbyes any more than you do."

JeriLee was silent for a moment. "Where are you heading from here?"

"Chicago?" Licia said. "I spoke to Fred. I told him everything was straightened out here. He was very nice about it. He didn't complain that I was spending too much time with you."

The doorbell rang and JeriLee opened the door.

The man touched his cap. "You called for a taxi, ma'am?"

She gestured toward the suitcases. When the taxi driver left, she and Licia stood looking at each other.

Licia broke the silence. "I guess I better be goin'."

JeriLee felt the pressure of the tears against her eyes. "I don't want you to leave like this. I don't want you to be angry with me."

Licia's voice was even. "I'm not angry, honey. It's just that last night you let me know exactly where I stand. Nowhere."

"But we can still be friends."

Licia let a deep breath escape her lips. "Sure, honey. But the kind of friends I want to be and the kind of friends you want us to be are two different things." She forced a smile. "I better get movin'. Planes don't wait."

They moved toward each other and their lips met gently. " 'Bye, baby," Licia whispered.

They heard a sound behind them and turned to see Mike standing in the doorway. "You leaving?" he asked.

Licia looked and walked past him, then looked back at Mike. "Now you look after my little girl real good. Hear?"

Mike nodded.

"Anything wrong?" Mike asked as the door closed behind Licia.

JeriLee shook her head, tears blurring her eyes. "What brought you over just now?" she asked.

"Licia called me. She said you wanted to see me."

Licia would do something like that. "I can use a drink," she said.

"Vodka and iced tea coming up," he said quickly. He returned a moment later with the drink in his hand. He gave it to her, smiling. "Want the service put back on?" he asked.

She nodded slowly.

"Great! I can get my shit together and be back here within an hour. Should I pick up some steaks for tonight?"

She nodded again.

"Hey, it's goin' to be fantastic. Now that I know where your head's at, it will be even better. I got a couple of cute friends you really will dig."

He was gone before she could answer. She started to roll a joint. Being a little bit stoned would ease the pain of feeling that she just couldn't seem to communicate with anyone.

Chapter 18

JERILEE GLANCED at her watch, then across the elegantly furnished room at Mike. It was after seven and she was due at the club at eight. Mike was standing at the bar talking to their host. She put down her vodka and tonic and went toward them. As she approached they fell silent.

"I'm sorry to interrupt, Mr. Jasmin," she apologized, "but I have to leave for work."

The tall gray-haired man with the deeply suntanned face smiled. "It's quite all right. Now that we've met, you must have Mike bring you here more often."

"Thank you," She smiled and turned to Mike. "If you want to stay I can call a cab."

"No," he said quickly. "I was getting ready to leave myself. I'll drop you at the club."

"I'll have Rick's bags put in your car then," Mr. Jasmin said.

After speaking briefly to one of the barmen, Jasmin returned to them. "I'll walk you to your car," he said.

Jasmin pointed to the pool as they stepped out on the terrace. "We have a Sunday brunch around the pool every week," he said. "Lots of bright fun people. Come by if you feel like it."

"Thank you," JeriLee said, thinking that if they were anything like the people she had just seen they wouldn't be much fun. All the men seemed like reserved business types and the few women who were there had nothing at all to say to one another.

Surrounded by Cadillacs, Mercedeses and Continentals, Mike's VW stood out like a sore thumb. As they got to the car, two men came out of a back door, each carrying a large black valise.

"Put them in the back seat," Mike told them.

"Thanks for the drinks, Mr. Jasmin," Mike said.

"My thanks too, Mr. Jasmin," JeriLee added.

Jasmin smiled at her. "You're welcome. And please try to come Sunday." He was still smiling but there was a hard edge in his voice as he said to Mike, "Rick says to take good care of his things now."

"I will, Mr. Jasmin," Mike said quickly. "You tell him he's got nothing to worry about."

As they pulled out of the driveway, JeriLee looked across at Mike. "That was a strange cocktail party. Nobody seemed to want to talk to anybody else."

"You know businessmen. Heavy types."

"What does Jasmin do?"

"He's a financial man of some kind," Mike answered. "Usually his parties are a little better but today's was a real downer. I'm sorry I dragged you to it."

"It's okay. I'd been at that typewriter long enough. It was good to get away." She glanced at the black valises in the rear seat. "What are you doing with those bags?"

"A friend of mine is going out of town for a while and I promised to keep them until he gets back. He left them at Jasmin's for me to pick up."

"Was he there? I don't remember meeting him."

"He was gone before we arrived."

"Why didn't Jasmin keep the bags? He certainly has more room than you have."

"You don't ask a man like Jasmin to do things like that. Besides, it won't be any problem. I'll just stick them up in my closet until he comes back. They won't be in your way."

They were silent until he pulled the car into the parking lot in front of the club. "Maybe we'll go out there for Sunday brunch like Mr. Jasmin said. I think he likes you. He's not the kind of a man who invites everybody."

"We'll see," she said noncommittally.

"It'll do you good to get out a little more. You've been inside for more than two weeks now."

"I want to get this screenplay finished first." She looked at him. "Picking me up after work?"

"I'll be here." He glanced back over his shoulder as a car pulled into the parking lot driveway behind him. "I better get moving," he said nervously. "I'm blocking traffic."

JeriLee watched him pull out of the driveway. There was something strange about him. She couldn't quite put her finger on it but she sensed a tension in him from the moment they had arrived at the Jasmin house.

The manager came rushing up to her. "You'll have to go on first," he said. "Anne just called in sick."

She smiled. "No sweat, Jack. I'll be ready in ten minutes."

Mike opened the door for her and she went past him into the apartment. "Care for a drink?" he asked.

She shook her head wearily. "I'm really bent. I had to take nine turns tonight. One of the girls didn't show up."

"That's too much."

"I ache all over. I think I'll take a Nembutal and really crash."

"You do that. A good night's sleep is the best thing for you. I think I'll smoke a joint and read the papers before I come to bed."

"Okay," she said. The hot shower eased some of the aching in her muscles. After drying off, she pulled her terry cloth robe around her, popped two sleeping pills and went back into the living room.

Mike was sitting at a chair in front of the window. The faint sweet smell of weed hung in the air.

"I'll have a drag," she said, taking the joint from him. She took a toke, then passed it back. "I thought you were going to read the paper," she said.

"I got bored," he said. "The same old shit all the time."

"Are you sure you're all right?" she asked.

"Me? Sure. Fine. Never better."

She nodded as if accepting his reassurance. Whatever was wrong wasn't her business, especially if he didn't want to talk about it. "Good night," she said.

"Good night."

She went into the bedroom and closed the door. She was asleep almost before she could turn off the light.

The sound of voices reached into the dark and pulled her awake. She moved sluggishly, trying to clear her head. The voices were louder now. Suddenly the bedroom door was flung open.

A man reached in and turned on the lights. His voice was harsh. "Okay, sister, out of bed."

For a moment it seemed like a dream. She was still groggy from the sleeping pills. "What do you want? Who are you?" She reached for the phone. "You better get out of here before I call the police."

"We are the police, lady. We want to talk to you."

She pulled the covers up around her chest. "What about?"

"The two valises your boy friend picked up this afternoon. Where are they?"

Mike suddenly appeared in the doorway behind the policeman. "You don't have to talk to him," he shouted. "Tell him you want to talk to your lawyer!"

A uniformed policeman came up behind Mike and pulled him away from the door. "Keep your fuckin' hands off me!" Mike yelled.

JeriLee stared at the plainclothesman. "What is all this about?"

"Your boy friend's movin' dope. This time we got him. We saw those bags come in here. We didn't see them come out."

"This time?" she asked, bewildered.

"Third time and out. We picked him up twice before but couldn't make it stick. This time we'll tear the place apart if we have to."

"You can't do that without a warrant!" Mike shouted.

The plainclothesman took a paper out of his pocket. "We've got it. We would have been in here sooner but the judge didn't sign it until a half hour ago." He turned back to JeriLee. "Better get something on and get out here." He walked back into the living room, leaving the door open.

JeriLee put on her terry cloth robe and went into the living room. Surrounded by three plainclothesmen and two uniformed policemen, Mike was sitting sulkily on the couch.

The man who had spoken to her in the bedroom gestured to the men behind him. "I'm Detective Collins, county police. Detective Millstein and Special Agent Cochran of the F.B.I. Now about those two valises?"

"You don't have to talk to him," Mike snapped. "You got to inform her of her rights."

"You're a lousy lawyer, Mike," Detective Collins said without a smile. "That's only if you arrest someone. I haven't arrested her. Yet."

JeriLee felt the panic rising. "What are you arresting me for? I haven't done anything."

"I didn't say you had, sister," Collins said.

"Don't listen to him, Jane," Mike said. "He's trying to trick you."

For the first time the F.B.I. agent spoke. "Why don't you make it easy on yourself, Mike, and tell us where the valises are? It would be a shame to mess up this nice apartment."

Mike didn't answer.

"Might as well, Mike. You're nailed this time. We picked Rick up at the airport with two of the suitcases on him. We also picked up Jasmin early this evening and we saw you bring the suitcases here."

Mike stared silently at the floor.

The agent turned to JeriLee. "How about it, miss? Do you know where the suitcases are?"

"No." She stared at Mike, who wouldn't look at her. She was beginning to get angry. How stupid she had been to believe his bullshit about not working, about how living off the apartment was enough for him. Sure it was. If he pushed a little shit on the side. She looked at the agent. "But I think I know where they might be. There's a locked closet in the hall going into the bathroom where he keeps his personal things."

"Do you have a key?"

"No. He has."

The agent held out his hand to Mike. Sullenly Mike took a key from his pocket and gave it to him. The agent gave the key to the other detective. "Let's go."

Detective Collins took JeriLee by the arm and one of the uniformed policemen gestured to Mike. Mike got to his feet and they went through the bedroom to the narrow hallway.

The two suitcases were just inside the closet door. The detectives pulled them out and placed them flat on the bed. Collins tried to open one, then straightened up. "It's a combination lock. Got the number, Mike?"

"No," Mike answered. "Why should I? I'm just minding them for a friend. I don't even know what's inside them."

Collins laughed. "I'll bet." He took a small instrument from his pocket and played with the locks for a moment. He pressed the release buttons and the valises snapped open.

JeriLee stared at the neatly wrapped bricklike squares. There were twenty of them in each valise. Collins took one out, tore a corner of the paper and smelled it. He nodded, holding it out to the federal agent. "The information was right. We can take them in and book them now."

Collins turned to Mike and took a small white printed card from his inside coat pocket. "This is official, Mike. I am required by law to inform you of your rights. Anything you say may be used against you in the court of law. You have the right to remain silent or to consult an attorney before speaking to the police and to have an attorney present during any questioning now or in the future." His voice seemed to drone on interminably and at the end of his speech he turned to JeriLee. "I'm taking you in too, sister."

"What the hell are you arresting her for?" Mike demanded. "You heard her. She don't know anything."

"That's up to the judge," Collins said. "I got my job to do. You're under arrest. I am required by law to inform you of your rights," he said to JeriLee, again reading from the card.

"You're making a mistake," JeriLee said. "I had nothing to do with this. I'm just renting the apartment from him."

"Funny kind of renting," Collins sneered. "You been living here with him almost two months now. I wish I could find a tenant like that."

"But it's true," JeriLee insisted. She felt the tears rising and fought to keep them down.

"You can explain that to the Judge," Collins said. "You got five minutes to get dressed or I take you in like that." He turned to the uniformed policemen. "Take him out to the car, then one of you come back and help Millstein carry out the evidence."

As the patrolmen left the room, he looked at JeriLee. "You're not dressing, sister," he said.

"What do you expect me to do with all of you standing here?"

Collins laughed. "I'll put on a record. You can give us a show at the same time. Or isn't the crowd big enough for you?"

She glared at him without speaking.

"I caught your act a few times." He grinned. "You shake it real good. We wouldn't object to a little private show."

Detective Millstein spoke for the first time. "You can dress in the bathroom, miss," he said. "We'll wait out here."

JeriLee nodded gratefully, still fighting back the tears. She took jeans and a shirt from the closet and some underthings from a drawer and went into the bathroom and closed the door. She splashed cold water on her face but she was still feeling drugged from the Nembutals. She had to wake herself up.

She searched frantically through the medicine cabinet for the Dexamyl. There were two left in the bottle. They would do it.

Quickly she finished dressing and ran a comb through her hair. When she came out of the bathroom Detective Millstein was the only one waiting for her.

"Where are the others?" she asked.

"On the way in," he said. "Ready?"

"I'll get my bag." She took it from the top of the dresser. "Look, you seem like a regular guy. Do I have to go in?"

He nodded.

"What are they going to do with me?"

"They'll probably let you go," he said. "But you'll have to come in anyway. Your boy friend was involved with a pretty big mob. And there was forty keys of grass in those bags."

"Shit, all I did was rent an apartment. And who ever heard of asking a landlord for references?"

He laughed. "I'm sorry, miss."

They went outside. On the way down the steps, he stopped her. "Don't you think you ought to lock your door, miss? You wouldn't want to get back here and find that you've been burglarized."

Chapter 19

DAWN WAS BEGINNING to break as they pulled up the ramp in front of the police station. "Shit!" Millstein cursed when he saw the crowd of reporters and the TV camera truck parked in front of the building. "That asshole Collins couldn't wait to get his picture in the papers."

He kept the car going past the station and down the off ramp. He circled around the block. "How do you feel about publicity?" he asked.

"I don't like this kind."

"I'll try to get you in the back way. Maybe they haven't covered it." He turned the car up the street. "You got dark glasses in that bag?"

"Yes."

"Put them on. At least it will keep them from getting a clear shot of your face."

She opened her bag. She put on the glasses. "How does that look?"

He glanced at her. "Okay. There's a newspaper on the back seat. Take it. You can hold it over your face when we go in."

"You're a good man, Charlie Brown," she said.

"Millstein," he said, unsmiling. He turned the car into the parking lot in the rear of the station. There were not as many reporters as out front but they were all around the car even before he came to a stop. "You don't get out of the car until I come around to your side and let you out," he said.

The flashbulbs began exploding as they tried to shoot pictures through the closed windows. She held the paper up around her face until she heard the door click and the sound of his voice. "Come on now, miss."

He walked her rapidly to the door and she kept her face pressed into the paper. She could hear the reporters shouting.

"Come on, Jane, give us a good picture."

"The publicity will sell out your next show."

"Show 'em you got something else besides tits and ass!"

She heard Millstein's voice. "Watch it. There's a step up here."

She stumbled and almost fell but he held her up and a moment later they were through the door. "You okay?" he asked.

She nodded.

"We'll have to walk up two flights," he said. "The elevator isn't running at this hour."

"Okay, and thanks," she said as they started up the stairs.

He smiled almost shyly. "It's okay." He stopped on the second landing. "You'll have to be booked, you know. There'll be reporters in there but no photographers. You don't have to talk to them. I'll try to get you through as quickly as I can."

They entered the large room through the back door.

They were almost at the sergeant's bench before the reporters saw them. They surged toward her hurling questions. They had been well briefed. They all know her name and where she worked. She kept her head down, not looking at any of them.

Millstein was as good as his word. He whispered across the desk to the sergeant, who nodded and gestured to a side door. Millstein led her through the door into a small room. "The sarge is a friend of mine," he explained. "He'll bring the booking sheet in here away from the mob."

"What did you say to him?" he asked.

He grinned. "I asked him if he really wanted to help Collins make lieutenant."

She began to laugh and suddenly the laughter caught in her throat. The pills she had taken were making her crazy. There was nothing for her to laugh at. Those windows she was looking at had bars on them. This was not a movie or a play. This was for real.

She opened her bag and began searching for her cigarettes. She was sure there had been a pack in there. Finally she looked up at Millstein. Her voice was shaking. "Do you have a cigarette?"

Silently he fished a pack from his pocket and held it toward her. "Ever been through this before?" he asked quietly.

She shook her head. "No," she said, taking a drag of the cigarette. "It's scary. Really scary."

He didn't speak.

"What happens now?"

"After the sergeant finishes the booking report, you turn over your valuables to the property clerk. Then we take your fingerprints and photograph. After that we take you up to the women's holding section, where a matron wil search you and assign you a cell until court opens in the morning."

"I have to stay here until then?"

He nodded.

"In the movies you see people getting out on bail or something."

"Yes, but it takes a judge to order it."

The sergeant came into the small room carrying a large gray-green ledger. "Name, age, address?" he asked quickly, after seating himself at the table.

She hesitated, and looked at Millstein, who nodded. "Jane Randolph, 11119 Montecito Way, Santa Monica, twenty-eight."

"Okay. Collins already filled in the charge sheet," he said to Millstein.

"What did he say?"

The sergeant read from the ledger. "Transportation and possession of eighty kilos of marijuana with intent to sell."

"That's not true," JeriLee protested. "I had nothing to do with it."

Ignoring her outburst, the sergeant rose to his feet. "Do you want to take her over to property or shall I call a matron?"

"I'll take her over," Millstein said. "We go through that door," he said, gesturing to the other side of the room.

JeriLee followed him through the door and into a corridor. They stopped in front of an open counter window in the wall opposite the door. Millstein pressed a small bell to call the clerk.

"It's not fair," she said. "Collins paid no attention to what I said."

A shirt-sleeved policeman appeared behind the counter. "Empty your bag on the counter and take off your rings, watches and any other jewelry," he said in a mechanical voice. "Name and number?" he asked.

"Jane Randolph," she answered. "What number?"

He didn't look up from the paper. "Every prisoner has a booking number."

"I've got it." Millstein gave him a slip of paper. "It's just routine," he said soothingly.

She opened her bag and emptied it on the counter. She slipped her watch from her wrist and put it down. The clerk began listing the items in her bag. She dragged on the cigarette and Millstein noticed the trembling of her fingers. "Take it easy," he said. "I'll stay with you and try to make it as easy as I can."

She nodded but he saw the animal-like glaze of fear in her eyes. As if in a daze, she signed the inventory, went through the fingerprints, mug shots and body search. It wasn't until they followed the matron down the corridor to a holding cell that he saw her stiffen. The matron opened the steel-barred door.

JeriLee turned to Millstein. There was an edge of hysteria in her voice. "Do I have to go in there?"

He looked at her for a moment. There was something about her that touched him, maybe because he was convinced that she had been telling the truth. They had been on the case for two months and this was the first time there was any suggestion that she might be involved. But Collins didn't give a damn. He was bucking for lieutenant and the district attorney was behind him all the way. Both of them were looking for a big score and didn't care whom they hurt. He glanced at his watch. It was almost half past seven. The court would be open in an hour and a half.

"It's okay," he said to the matron. "I'll take her over to the conference room and stay with her."

The matron was a cynical woman who believed that cops were no different from other men, especially when it came to attractive women. "Okay, Officer," she said in a flat voice. "It's your sleep."

JeriLee's knees went weak as they turned away from the cell.

The conference room was small, with a few chairs and tables and a long couch against one wall. The detective led her to the couch, sat down opposite her and held out a cigarette.

"I couldn't have gone in there. I don't know what I would have done," she said, accepting his light.

His voice was not unsympathetic, just matter-of-fact. "You'll have to go there sooner or later."

"Maybe the judge will let me out."

He was silent for a moment. She really didn't know what she was facing. The procedures were designed for delay, not speed. "Do you have a lawyer?" he asked.

She shook her head.

"Do you know one?"

Again she shook her head.

"Then the judge will assign your case to the public defender."

"Is that good?"

"It's better than nothing." He hesitated. "If you have any money, you'd be better off getting your own attorney. The D.A. will make mincemeat out of the public defender in this case. He's after a big score and he won't make any deals. What you need is a lawyer with clout. Someone the D.A. and the court will listen to."

"I don't know anyone like that."

He was silent for a moment. "I do. But he's expensive."

"How expensive?"

"I don't know."

"I have some money. Do you think he will talk to me?"

"He might."

"Would you call him for me?"

"I'm not allowed to do that. But I can give you his telephone number. You can reach him at home now. You're allowed one phone call."

The matron came into the cell with her lunch tray.

JeriLee looked up at her from the cot on which she was sitting. "What time is it?"

"Twelve o'clock," the matron answered, placing the tray on the small table against the wall.

JeriLee looked at the sickly sandwiches. "I'm not hungry," she said.

"Might as well eat. Court won't open again until two o'clock. You won't hear anything before then." She left the cell, closing the steel-barred door behind her.

It had been more than two hours since the lawyer had left her. A tall man quietly dressed in a dark suit with silver-gray hair and a florid complexion, he had listened without comment to her story. When she had finished he asked just one question. "Are you telling me the truth?"

She nodded.

'It's important. I don't want the D.A. springing any surprises on me."

"It's the truth, I swear it."

He looked a her for a moment. "Five thousand dollars," he said.

"What?"

"Five thousand dollars. That's my fee."

"I haven't got that much."

He rose from his chair. "I'm sorry," he said.

"That's a lot of money," she protested, looking up at him.

"You're in a lot of trouble," he said, returning her gaze. "You're right in the middle of the biggest California drug bust of the year. It's not going to be easy to make the D.A. and the judge listen."

She was silent for a moment. "I have about thirty-five hundred in the bank," she said. "I can pay off the rest when I go back to work."

He sat down again. "We have to get you off now. The charges must be dismissed. If they bind you over for trial and you have to go before a jury, you're dead."

"I don't understand. I'll tell them the truth. Exactly what I told you."

"It won't matter. You have to understand the rednecks they have on jury panels out here. The minute they hear the kind of work you do, they'll decide you're guilty. The way they think, only an immoral woman will dance naked in public."

"Shit," she said. "What's the difference between the men who come into the club and watch me and the jury?"

"The same man who came into the club would go against you in the jury box."

"Then what are we going to do?"

"Let me think," he said. "Do you have your checkbook with you?"

"It's down in the police property room."

When he left a few minutes later he had her check for thirty-five hundred dollars as well as a signed note for fifteen hundred dollars. "Try to relax," he said. "You'll be hearing from me soon."

It was the middle of the afternoon by the time he reappeared.

"What happened, Mr. Coldwell?" JeriLee asked after the conference room door had been locked behind them.

"I got it all worked out with the D.A.," he said. "He agreed to separate your case from the others and to dismiss charges if you will agree to act as a material witness for the prosecution."

"What does that mean?"

"It means you're free. All you have to do is appear at the trial and tell your story exactly as you told it to me."

"I can walk out of here right now?"

"In a few minutes. First you have to appear before the judge who will issue the necessary order."

"What are we waiting for then?"

"Okay," he said. "Just remember one thing. Whatever the judge asks you to do, you agree, all right?"

She nodded.

He knocked at the door. "Can Miss Randolph wait here for a moment while I go down to the D.A.'s office and let him know we're ready to appear in court?" he asked the matron.

She looked at JeriLee doubtfully.

"It won't be more than a minute, I promise you," he said quickly. "They're dropping the charges against her and I think she's spent enough time in the cell."

"Okay. But you don't be long. It's against regulations."

"I appreciate it." The attorney glanced at JeriLee. "Be right back."

JeriLee smiled. For the first time in twelve hours she didn't have a feeling of dread hanging over her.

Chapter 20

COLDWELL HAD TAKEN JeriLee out through the back entrance and put her in a cab. "The reporters will have your home address within a day or two," he said. "If you don't want to be bothered by them, my advice is to get out of there as soon as you can."

"I can't stay there anyway," she said. "Mike is my landlord. What's going to happen to him now?"

"The judge set one hundred thousand dollars bail for each of them. My guess is that they'll all be out before nightfall."

"Mike hasn't got that kind of money."

"He's connected with some big people. They take care of their own."

She was silent. It was still hard for her to believe.

"You keep in touch with me," Coldwell said. "When you move let me know where I can reach you."

"Okay," she said.

It was after five when she got to the apartment. As she came up the steps, she noticed that the door was open. That was surprising. She remembered distinctly having locked it when Millstein had reminded her. Slowly she went inside.

The living room was a shambles. Her portable typewriter had been smashed. There were crumpled sheets of paper scattered around the room, and in the fireplace was a pile of ashes.

She picked up a sheet of paper from the floor. It was blank. A wave of fear came over her. She rushed to the fireplace and pulled out some paper that hadn't been entirely consumed by the fire.

She had been right. All the work she had done in the

last few weeks, the screenplay she had almost finished, had been destroyed—burned in the fireplace.

Dully she rose to her feet and went into the bedroom. That room too have been overturned, the contents of the drawers and closets lay around the room in shreds. But that almost didn't matter. What did matter was the words that had been lost. The words that might never be replaced.

The tears were running down her cheeks as she went to the bathroom. All the pills from the medicine cabinet had been strewn in the sink and tub and water run over them so that their effectiveness was destroyed. At that moment the telephone begun to ring.

She picked it up in the bedroom. "Yes," she answered in a cracked voice.

"Jane Randolph?"

"Yes."

"This is a friend calling to give you a little friendly advice. Get out of town. Go as far away as you can. Or the next thing you'll find broken in your apartment is you."

"But—" She was holding a dead phone. Whoever it was had already gone off the line. She replaced the receiver and slowly began trying to straighten up the room.

It was close to eight when she came into the club and she was almost at the dressing room door when the manager caught up to her.

"Wait a minute," he said. "Come down to my office."

She followed him down to the cubbyhole that served as the office. He closed the door carefully behind him and his voice dropped to a whisper. "I didn't expect you tonight. When did you get out?"

"This afternoon."

"I got another girl," he said.

"That's okay. I could use a night's rest. I'll be in tomorrow."

"No."

"What do you mean, Charlie?"

"I got word from outside. I have to let you go."

"You gotta be joking."

"No, they were very specific. You're out."

"They have to be crazy. All that shit in the papers will do nothing but bring in business."

"Don't you think I know it?" he wailed. "But they control the place. If I don't do as they say, zap! I'm finished. No license."

"Okay," she said. "There are other places I can work. They won't pass up the business."

"Janey," he said earnestly, "I'm a lot older than you and I'm going to talk to you like a father, like an uncle. You're a nice girl but you got mixed up with some very bad people. There ain't no place in this town that's going to give you a job. My advice is to go away from here. A long way."

"They got to you too," she said coldly.

"There's nothing I can do. I got my own family to support. But you, you better do as I say. You hang around here and something will happen to you. I know these guys and I know what they already did to some girls who didn't listen to them. It ain't very pretty."

"I was alone at the apartment," she said. "They didn't come near me."

"You're still today's news," he said earnestly. "Believe me, they'll wait. Then one day when the papers have forgotten all about you they'll pay you a visit."

"I don't believe it."

"Believe it," he said sincerely. "If you were my own daughter, I couldn't give you better advice." He opened a small desk drawer and took out an envelope. "I owe you a day's pay," he said. "But you did some extra turns so I'm giving you a hundred even. Okay?"

She took the envelope without speaking.

"You take that money," he said, "and buy yourself a plane ticket to someplace else."

"Sure," she said. This hundred plus the thirty in her bag and the twenty she had in the bank after paying off the lawyer was all she had in the world. She opened the door. "Thanks, Charlie."

"Good luck, Janey." What a business, he thought. If the girls weren't in one kind of trouble, it was another.

"You fucked up, Jane." Marc Gross's voice was harsh and complaining as if what had happened to her was a reflection on him and his business. "I had it all set for interviews at Warner, Twentieth and Paramount, but as soon as they saw the morning papers they canceled."

"Today's papers reported that the charges against me were dropped."

"It doesn't matter. They don't like the publicity."

"What about the story ideas you sent out?"

"They're starting to come back. And not even by mail. They're so anxious to get rid of them they're shooting them back by special messenger."

"What about Ansbach's prison picture. Can I still do that?"

"It's already cast. You didn't think he was going to wait for you forever?"

It had only been a few weeks, but she didn't argue. "Okay," she said, looking directly at him. "Did they get to you too?"

His face flushed. "I don't know what you're talking about."

"I think you do," she said evenly. "Didn't someone call and tell you that it might be a good idea if you had nothing to do with me?"

"I get crank calls all the time. I don't pay any attention to them."

She was silent for a moment watching him. "I'll have my screenplay back from the typist tomorrow," she lied. "I'll send it in to you."

He hesitated, then cleared his throat. "I've been thinking about the screenplay. I'm afraid it's really not the kind of thing I can sell."

"Why don't you just read it first, then decide?"

"I'd only be wasting your time."

She smiled humorlessly. "You're a lousy liar, Marc. But even worse, you're a lying coward." She got to her feet. "I'll let you know where you can send my stories when you get them all back."

JeriLee stood on the sidewalk for a moment undecided about what to do. Then she saw the coffee shop on the corner. It was past the lunch hour rush and she found an empty booth and slipped into it. "Just coffee," she said when the waitress came up to her.

She was engrossed in her thoughts and for a moment didn't notice the man who took the seat opposite her. When she did look up, there was surprise in her voice. "Detective Millstein!"

He smiled shyly. "Coffee," he said to the waitress.

"Are you following me?"

"Not officially," he said.

"What do you mean?"

"I had some time off, so I thought I'd see how you were doing." He didn't tell her that he had picked up word she might be in big trouble.

"I'm not doing so well," she admitted. "My job is gone and just now I found out that my agent doesn't want to represent me anymore. And yesterday when I got home I found my apartment a wreck—my clothes torn and my manuscripts burned. Besides that I got a telephone call telling me to leave town."

"Did you recognize the man's voice?"

"Never heard him before."

"Why didn't you call the police?"

"Would it have done any good?"

He was silent for a moment, then shook his head. "What are you planning to do now?"

"I don't know," she said. "I've got exactly a hundred and thirty-six dollars between me and the poorhouse. I'm trying to make up my mind whether to stick around here and invest it in a month's rent in some cheap place and keep trying to get some work. Or, take eighty-seven dollars and buy a plane ticket back to New York."

"Can you get a job back there?"

She shrugged. "I don't know. But at least nobody

there wants to keep me from working. What do you think I should do?"

"Officially, I have to tell you to stay here. You gave your word to the court that you would appear as a material witness."

"You're not following me officially, so you can tell me what you think unofficially."

"I'll deny it if you ever quote me."

"I won't quote you."

He took a deep breath. "I'd buy that ticket."

"Do you think these men will really do what they say?"

"I don't know. But they're a very rough crowd and they might. I wouldn't like you to take the chance. There's no real way we could protect you short of keeping you in jail."

"If only I could get a few more bucks together, I'd feel better. I hate to go back broke."

'I could lend you a few dollars. Fifty, maybe even a hundred. I wish it could be more but a cop doesn't make that much."

"No, thanks," she replied. "You've done enough already. Shit," she went on after a moment of silence, "just when I thought I was getting it all together."

"I'm sorry."

"It's not your fault. If you're off duty, would it be against the rules for you to help a friend pack and then maybe take her to the airport?"

"No."

"Would you?"

"Yes."

Millstein watched the skycap tag her suitcase and put them on the rack. "Gate twenty-three, ma'am," the skycap said, taking the dollar tip. "They boardin' now."

She held out her hand. "Thanks. You're a nice man, Detective Millstein."

"Good luck. I just hope things work out for you."

"That makes two of us."

"If you come back this way, give me a call."

She didn't answer.

"You know you're still young. Why don't you find a nice young man and get married?"

"And settle down and have some kids?"

"There's nothing wrong with it," he said defensively.

"I guess not. But it's not for me."

"What's better, the way you're living? From hand to mouth, like an animal."

"You're a strange man for a policeman, Detective Millstein."

"I can't help it. I'm a Jewish father. I have a daughter almost your age and I keep thinking the same thing could happen to her."

A sudden smile brightened her face and she kissed his cheek. "Don't worry. It won't happen to her, because she has you for a father."

He put his hand on her arms. "Let me give you some money."

"I can manage. I have friends. It will be okay."

"Sure?"

"Sure." With tears in her eyes she started into the terminal. When she reached the door she turned and waved.

He waved back and waited until she disappeared in the crowds. He sat behind the wheel of his car for a long time before starting the engine. He was sad in a way that he really didn't understand.

What caused girls like this to waste their lives? He wondered what would happen to her now. Chances were that he would never know. She would drop from sight and he would never hear of her again. Another loser in a world full of losers.

But he was wrong. He did hear from her again. It was a year later and he had almost forgotten her name. The letter came from Creedmore State Hospital and was written in pencil in a neat almost schoolgirlish hand.

Dear Detective Millstein,

You may not remember me. I am Jane Randolph, the girl you took to the airport last year. You were very nice and I never forgot it. You told me to give you a call, remember? I never got back to California because I had a nervous breakdown. I have been in the hospital for almost six months now and I am much better and feel perfectly able to take care of myself. The doctors are considering letting me leave here and it would be very helpful if you would be kind enough to write them a letter about me, telling them that you think I am okay and will not be a problem anymore. Even if you don't write a letter, I will understand and still be grateful for your kindness to me the last time we met.

Your friend,
Jane Randolph.

Millstein thought of his wife who had died fifteen years ago, leaving him with a five-year-old daughter, and of his daughter, who was now in her third year at U.S.C. Somehow the girl Jane Randolph had reminded him of her, and perhaps that was why she had touched him so deeply.

He started to write the letter she had requested, then stopped. What was there for him to say? He didn't even know her. He crumpled the sheet and threw it into the wastepaper basket. After a long moment of debate with himself he reached for the telephone.

"Lieutenant Collins," the harsh voice answered.

"Dan, is it okay if I take a week of my vacation now? A friend of mine is sick in a hospital in New York . . ."

Chapter 21

THE RECEPTIONIST'S voice was impersonal. "Patient visiting hours are five to seven P.M. daily."

"I'm sorry," he said. "I just arrived from California last night. I didn't realize."

"Who was it you wanted to see?"

"Jane Randolph."

"Jane Randolph," she repeated. She glanced down at a paper in front of her. "If you'll take a seat over there, I'll get in touch with her doctor and see what we can do."

"Thank you," he said, taking a seat near the window from which he could see the snow-covered trees. He couldn't remember the last time he had seen snow.

He was still amazed that he was really here. He remembered what his daughter had said when he told her why he was going East. She had stared at him for a moment, then flung her arms around his neck, the tears coming to her eyes. "You're beautiful, Daddy. Just beautiful."

"I'm probably just an old fool. The girl must have sent letters like that to everyone she knows."

"It doesn't matter, Daddy," Susan had said. "She's crying for help and you're answering. That's what matters."

"Something in her letter got to me. I remember how frightened she was the day I met her."

"Was she pretty?"

"In a way, I guess. Maybe underneath all that make-up she had on."

"Were you attracted to her, Daddy?"

"What do you mean?"

"You know what I mean, Daddy."

"Why does it always have to be something like that?" he said indignantly. "Stop acting like a romantic child."

She laughed aloud and kissed his cheek again. "I'm not the romantic in the family, Daddy. You are."

He stared at the frosting of snow outside the window. Maybe she was right after all. He was here, wasn't he?

A white-uniformed nurse stopped in front of him. "Are you the visitor for Jane Randolph?"

He nodded, getting to his feet.

"Would you follow me, please. Dr. Sloan would like to see you."

A young redbearded man in a white coat rose from

behind the desk and gripped his hand firmly. "I'm Dr. Sloan, Jane's doctor."

"Al Millstein."

The doctor toyed with an unlit pipe. "Reception mentioned that you came in from California."

Millstein nodded. "I hope I can see her. I'm sorry I didn't know about the visiting hours."

"That's okay. Matter of fact I'm glad you came when you did. I might have missed you otherwise. Are you related to Jane?"

"No. Just a friend."

"Oh. Have you know her a long while?"

"Not really. Just a few days."

"I don't understand. You knew each other only a few days and yet in all the time she's been here you're the only person she has written to or tried to get in touch with."

"You knew about the letter?"

"We encouraged her to write. We thought we could get a line to her family that way."

"You mean that no one's come to visit, no friends, no family?"

"That's right. As far as we know she's completely alone in tht world. Until she wrote you, we had no contact with anyone that she knew."

"Jesus."

"Since you're here I must assume you want to help her. The first thing I have to know is exactly what your relationship with her was."

"I'm afraid I'm going to shock you, Doctor."

"You don't understand, Mr. Millstein. In my profession one learns never to be shocked at anything. I already assumed that you had been lovers."

Millstein laughed aloud. "I'm sorry but you're wrong, Doctor. I only saw her twice and that was never part of it." He saw the puzzled expression on the doctor's face and continued. "I'm a detective with the Santa Monica police and the only contact I've had with her was as her arresting officer."

"If that is all, why did you come?"

"I felt sorry for her. When I met her there was a

very good chance they would send her to jail for something she didn't do. I couldn't stand by and let that happen. When I got her letter, I felt the same way. Something was happening to her that was beyond her control. I had to see what I could do to help."

The doctor was silent as he filled and lit his pipe.

"She said in her letter that you were considering letting her out," Millstein said.

"We have been. She's really done very well since she's been in here. But there were a few things still puzzling us. That's why we've been hesitating."

"What things?"

"Before we get to that, you should know why she is in here."

Millstein nodded silently.

"She was committed here from the East Elmwood General Hospital last September to undergo detoxification. She had a severe problem of chemical drug abuse."

"How bad was it?"

"She was suffering from paranoia and hallucinations resulting from the combined use of various drugs such as L.S.D. and amphetamines in addition to tranquilizers, barbiturates and marijuana. Before being sent here she had a record of three arrests, two for prostitution and soliciting, one for physically attacking a man she claimed had been following and annoying her, which was, of course, not true, but a typical symptom of drug-induced psychosis. In addition she had twice attempted suicide. The first time she tried to throw herself in front of a subway car but was saved by the alertness of a subway patrolman. The second time she took an overdose of barbiturates, which was pumped from her stomach by a fire department rescue squad. It was the last arrest which led to her being here. The man she had attacked dropped the criminal charges against her but she was still hallucinating and she was committed to Creedmore by the examining panel at East Elmwood."

Millstein was silent.

"Were there any signs of this problem when you knew her, Mr. Millstein?" the doctor asked.

"I don't know, but then I'm not a doctor. What I did

notice was that she was highly nervous and at one point very much afraid."

"Do you know if she was on drugs then?"

"Not really. But in California we assume that all the young people are on something. If it's not grass it's pills. If they don't overdo it we try to look the other way. Otherwise we wouldn't have jails big enough to hold them all."

"Well, anyway, I think we have the drug problem cured, at least temporarily. We cannot know what will happen when she gets outside again."

"You're going to release her then?"

"We'll have to. She comes up for re-evaluation by the panel in another two weeks. She'll clear it without any problems I'm sure."

"But you're still not satisfied, are you?"

"Frankly speaking, no. I feel that we haven't gotten to the real problem, whatever it was that pushed her to this. That's why I wanted to get in touch with her friends or family. I'd feel better if I knew she had someplace to go and people who cared about her. I would want her to go into therapy."

"And if she doesn't?"

"She could slide back. The pressures would be the same as before."

Millstein reflected on what a fool he had been to think there was anything he could do. He should have sent the letter and forgotten about it. He wasn't God. He couldn't stop anyone from going to hell in their own way.

"Did she ever mention the name JeriLee to you?" the doctor asked.

"No, who was she?"

"She was Jane's sister. Sort of an idol, I guess. The bright child in the family, the one that got all the attention. Jane loved and hated her at the same time—true sibling rivalry. Part of Jane's problem was that she wanted to be JeriLee and couldn't. By the time she realized that was what she wanted, she had gone too far in another direction and couldn't get back."

"Did you try to locate the sister?"

"The only way we could do that was through Jane and she said JeriLee was dead." He looked at the detective. "We don't have the facilities for personal investigation out here."

"You mean you don't believe her story?"

"I neither believe nor disbelieve it. I just don't know."

"I see." Millstein nodded slowly. "May I see her now?"

"Of course." He pressed a button on the desk. "Thank you for coming in and talking to me."

"Thank you, Doctor. I just hope I have been of some help."

"In my business, everything helps," the doctor said as the nurse came into the room. "Would you please take Mr. Millstein to the visitors' room and bring Jane to see him.

"One more thing, Mr. Millstein. Try not to express surprise when you see Jane. Remember that she's just gone through chemical and electrical shock therapy, which tends to slow down reactions and create some temporary amnesia. The treatments have been halted now but the effects will not wear off for a few more days."

"I'll keep it in mind, Doctor."

The visitors' room was small but comfortable with gaily printed curtains at the windows.

She came into the room hesitantly, half hiding behind the nurse. "Jane, here is that nice Mr. Millstein come to see you," the nurse said in a professionally jovial tone.

"Hello, Jane," he said, forcing a smile. She was thin, much thinner than he had remembered. Her hair was long but brushed neatly and her eyes very large in her pinched face. "It's nice to see you again."

For a moment she looked at him without recognition. Then a light seemed to dawn in her eyes and she smiled hesitantly. "Detective Millstein."

"Yes."

"My friend, Detective Millstein. My friend." She

took a step toward him, the tears coming to her eyes. "My friend, Detective Millstein."

"Yes, Jane. How are you?"

She took his hand and pressed it to her face. "You've come to take me out of this place? The way you did the last time?"

He felt the lump in his throat. "I hope so, Jane. But these things take time, you know."

"I'm better now. You can see that, can't you? I won't do any of those foolish things anymore. I'm all cured."

"I know that, Jane," he said soothingly. "You'll be out soon."

She rested her head against his chest. "I hope so. I don't like it here. They hurt you sometimes."

He stroked her head slowly. "It was for your own good. You've been a very sick girl."

"I know I was sick. But you don't cure sick people by hurting them more."

"It's over now," he said reassuringly. "Dr. Sloan told me the treatments are all finished."

"You got my letter?"

"That's why I'm here."

"You're the only friend I have. There was no one else to write to."

"What about JeriLee?"

A frightened look came into her eyes. "You know about her?" she whispered.

"Yes. Dr. Sloan told me about her. Why didn't you write her?"

"Didn't he tell you that she was dead?"

"Is she?"

She nodded.

"Was she nice?"

She looked up at him, her eyes shining. "She was beautiful. Everybody loved her. Everybody wanted to take care of her. And she was so bright she could do anything she wanted. When she was around, you couldn't see anyone else. At one time we were very close, then we drifted apart and when I went looking for her it was too late. She was gone."

"How did it happen?"

"What?"

"How did she die?"

"She committed suicide," she whispered.

"How?"

There was a tortured look on her face. "She took pills, fell in front of a train or jumped off a bridge," she cried in a pain-filled voice. "What does it matter how she died? It only matters that she's gone and I can't get her back."

He put his arms around her shoulders as she sobbed convulsively against his chest. He could feel the thin sharp bones through the cotton dress.

"I don't want to talk about her anymore."

"All right. We won't talk about her anymore."

"I have to get out of here," she said. "If I don't I will really go crazy. You don't know what it's like in here. They don't let you do anything. It's as if we're less than animals."

"You'll be out soon."

"I want to go back to work. When I get out I know an agent that will get me a job dancing again."

He remembered the typewriter in her apartment and the scripts she told him the agent was returning to her. "How about your writing?" he asked.

"Writing?" she asked, a puzzled look in her eyes. "You must be mixed up. I wasn't the writer. JeriLee was."

Chapter 22

POLICEMEN OFTEN spend their time walking backwards through other people's lives, retracing the steps from the grave to the cradle. It was a habit Millstein had fallen into over the years.

After his talk with Jane he had gone back to Sloan's office. "I didn't expect to see you, Mr. Millstein," the doctor said in surprise.

"You said something about not being able to carry out a complete investigation of your patients, Dr. Sloan, and that you sometimes thought it would be very helpful."

"Yes, I said that."

"You thought that if you knew more about Jane perhaps you could do more to help her?"

"I think so."

"I've got a week off. Would you object to my help?"

"I would be most grateful, Mr. Millstein. Almost anything you can find out will be more than we know. Do you have any ideas?"

"I have some, Doctor. But I'd prefer to wait and get something firm before I go shooting my mouth off."

"Okay. What can I do?"

"You could let me read that commitment paper on her."

"You've got it."

Millstein read it quickly. There wasn't much information. He looked at the doctor. "Where would I get the details behind this?"

"You'd have to go back to the source. In this case East Elmwood General. Back of them are the courts and the police, but you'd have to get that information from East Elmwood's files."

After leaving the hospital, he had gone back to his hotel and stretched out on the bed. The time change had finally caught up to him. When he awoke it was almost dinnertime. He looked at his watch. It would be after four o'clock in California. His daughter should be home from school by now.

Her voice was bright as she answered the phone. "Did you see her, Daddy?" she asked.

"Yes."

"How was she?"

He put it all in one word. "Sad."

There was silence at her end.

"I don't know if I can make myself clear, Susan, but it's as if she split herself in two parts and one part of her is dead."

"Poor thing. Is there anything you can do? Was she glad to see you?"

"I don't know if I can do anything. And, yes, I think she was glad to see me. Do you know what she told me, Susan? She said that I was the only friend she had. Imagine that. And we scarcely knew each other."

"I can't imagine anyone being so alone. I hope you can do something for her, Daddy. You will try, won't you?"

"Yes."

"I'm very proud of you, Daddy," she said.

The hospital was set apart from the rest of the buildings around it. Across the street was a small park, on the corner opposite a large diner was a sign advertising breakfast for sixty-five cents. He paused on the cement steps listening to the voices of the people making their way in and out of the hospital. Most of them were speaking Spanish. Not with the soft accent of the Mexican that he was used to, but still the language of the poor.

A few minutes later he was seated in front of Superintendent Poole's desk in a small office on the ninth floor. To get there he had to pass through the steel-barred gate that separated the women's psychiatric detention center from the rest of the floor.

Mrs. Poole was a good-looking middle-aged black woman, with a warm smile and sympathetic expressive eyes. She looked down at the copy of Jane's commitment report that he had been given by Dr. Sloan. "Jane Randolph?" she said in a puzzled voice. "We have so many girls in here, Officer."

He nodded.

She picked up the telephone. A moment later a young uniformed policewoman brought in a file. "I think this is what you may be looking for," Mrs. Poole said.

The name was typed on the corner of the file. Jane Randolph. It was followed by a number and a date. The date was five months old.

"May I make some notes, Mrs. Poole?"

"Of course. If you don't understand some of the abbreviations I'll be glad to explain them."

He spread the file on the desk and took out his small notebook. Most of it was simple enough. Arrest record, charge, arresting officer, disposition. He copied the important data. It wasn't until he reached the final page that the hieroglyphics baffled him. "Mrs. Poole?" he asked, handing her the page.

"This is our report on her condition and treatment here. Briefly it says that she was admitted in a highly agitated and violent state apparently caused by drug abuse which had induced hallucinations. A bad trip, in plain language. She was kept under chemical and physical restraints for the two days she was here because of the recurrence of the hallucinations and the damage she might do herself and others. At the end of the second day, we were notified that the criminal charges against her had been dropped, and since we no longer had jurisdiction over her our doctors applied to the court for a commitment order. The following morning she was transferred to Creedmore for further treatment."

"I see. Is there anything further you can tell me about her?"

"I'm sorry, Officer. Unfortunately she is only one of many that pass through here and she wasn't with us long enough for us to make any kind of appraisal."

"Thank you for your help, Mrs. Poole."

She held out her hand. "I'm sorry I couldn't give you more information, Detective."

He studied his notes in the taxi on the way back to the city. Maybe he would come up with something more at Midtown Precinct North. The police there should at least remember her. Every one of her arrests had been made in that precinct.

"You come back at eleven tonight and see Sergeant Riordan who's head of our pussy posse," the desk sergeant told him. "He'll fill you in on her. He knows every cunt in the Broadway area."

When he returned a little after eleven that night he found Sergeant Riordan, a tall man in his late thirties, sitting in the corridor in front of the women's holding cells morosely nursing a cardboard container of coffee.

"What brings you here?" he asked after Millstein had told him he was looking for information on Jane Randolph. "She kill somebody out there?"

"What makes you say that? Do you remember her?"

"Fuckin' right I remember her. Every time she came in here she practically started a riot. She was always on something. Spaced out of her mind. It got so I told my boys that if they came across her to look the other way. We got enough troubles in here without cuckoos like that around."

"Did she ever talk about herself or her family?"

"Who could talk to her? I told you she was nuts. Nothing she said made sense. There was always somebody after her. Somebody who wanted to kill her. The last time we had her in here she had beat up on some poor tourist and wrecked his camera. She was yelling that he was a gun from Los Angeles out to knock her off. The poor bastard was from Peoria and was scared out of his fuckin' mind. I think he grabbed the next bus home. He never showed up to file charges."

"What about the other times? Did she say anything then?"

"The first time we picked her up she was brought in by one of my boys dressed like a tourist. She saw him on East Fifty-fourth between Madison and Fifth. She asked him if he'd like a massage up in his hotel room for twenty bucks. He kept on walkin'. There's no law against getting a massage. She followed him. This time she said that for an extra tenner she'd blow his ears off. She told him she really didn't give great massages but she was the best cocksucker in the world. He thought that was funny and wasn't even going to pick her up because she didn't look like no pro to him. Just a kid down on her luck. He kidded her. How about skipping the massage and just going for the blow job for ten bucks, he said and began to walk away. She came after him. Cheap motherfucker, she says, and belts him in the chops. So there's nothing else he can do but bring her in.

"We fill out her sheet and take her over to the tank where we keep all the whores until we can ship them downtown. She takes one look and goes berserk. You ain't going to put me in there like a monkey in a cage, she yells as we shove her through the door. A minute later the whole tank is in an uproar. We finally manage to get her out from underneath a pile of six of the toughest mothers you ever saw, then we get her into restraint and throw her into solitary. We were glad when we could send her downtown in the midnight van."

"What happened to her that time?"

"I don't know. I heard she got bailed out but I don't know. Once they get downtown we lose track of them."

"By downtown, you mean night court?"

"Yes."

"What about the next time you had her in?"

"That was a funny one. We picked her up in a massage parlor called The Way Out with three other girls and seven guys."

"I thought you didn't bust massage parlors."

"We don't, but this was different. They was making a porno movie and it got hot in there from the lights so they left the windows open and one of the neighbors called it in."

"How was she then?"

"On a speed trip. Made no sense at all. Just kept yelling at all the cops to come and fuck her while she kept playing with herself with a big vibrator."

"What happened to her that time?"

"Some smart shyster got them all off on a technicality about an improper search warrant." Riordan shook his head. "I been on this job six years now and it ain't worth a shit. You get no appreciation and the only thing everybody wants to know is how much ass am I getting."

"I was wondering about that. How much are you getting?"

Riordan laughed suddenly. "You small-town cops are all alike. I get enough to keep the skin back. And even with that it's still a lousy job."

"Better than pounding a beat," Millstein said, holding out his hand. "Thanks, Sergeant."

"Any time. Where you going next? Night court?"

Millstein nodded.

Riordan wrote a name on a piece of paper. "My brother-in-law is the court clerk down there. Jimmy Loughran. Tell him you spoke to me. He'll give you anything you want."

Chapter 23

"TO YOUR RIGHT. Apartment seventeen-B," the elevator operator said.

He walked to the end of the green-carpeted hallway and pressed the buzzer. From inside he heard the soft sound of muted chimes.

The door was opened by a slim blond girl.

"Mrs. Lafayette, please. I'm Mr. Millstein."

"She's expecting you. Come in."

He followed the girl into the elegant all-white apartment.

"Can I get you a drink?"

"No, thank you."

"I'll tell Mrs. Lafayette that you're here." He had seen apartments like this only in movies. The wide terrace outside the windows, spotted with plants and dwarf trees, was like a miniature garden in the sky. There were two photographs in silver frames on the white baby grand. One was a head shot of a good-looking young black man, his lips parted in a warm smile. There was something familiar about him and although the detective couldn't place him he knew that he had seen the man before. The other photograph was of a boy, about ten years old, standing with a gray-haired woman in front of a small white wooden house.

He didn't hear the footsteps in the soft white rug. "Mr. Millstein."

He kept the surprise from his face when, turning around, he saw that she was black. She was tall and he immediately sensed the strength in her. Suddenly the name rang a bell. He know now who the young man in the photograph was.

"Mrs. Lafayette." He gestured to the photograph. "Your husband?"

"Yes. That's my son and my mother in the other photo."

"My daughter has some of your husband's albums. Even I like the way he sings. He doesn't drive me up the wall the way some of them do."

"Fred sings pretty but that isn't why you wanted to see me, is it? You said you had some news about Jane Randolph for me."

This was a woman who came right to the point. "You're a friend of Jane's?" she asked.

He nodded, then seeing the expression on her face, he said, "You doubt it?"

"It's hard for me to believe that a policeman would

be her friend. Especially one who comes all the way from California trying to get a line on her."

He took her letter from his pocket and gave it to her without speaking.

She read it quickly, then looked up. "What happened?"

"That's what I'm trying to find out." Briefly he told her what he knew, including how he had gotten her name from the clerk at night court as the person who put up bail the first time she had been arrested.

There was a strange softness in the black woman's eyes. "What happens to her now?"

"I don't know. The doctor told me that she comes up for re-evaluation in two weeks. They are considering letting her out but he's concerned about how she will handle herself after she gets out."

"Shit, poor JeriLee."

"JeriLee?"

"That's her rcal name. Didn't you know that?"

"The only JeriLee she mentioned she said was her sister."

"She never had a sister. Her name is JeriLee Randall. I was the one who gave her the name Jane Randolph when she began dancing. She didn't want people in the business to know what she was doing. She was afraid if the word got out that she was dancing topless they'd never take her seriously as a writer or an actress after that."

"Was she any good?"

"I'm no judge," she said. "But I know she once won a Tony as an actress on Broadway and another time she had a play produced, although it never got to Broadway. So she had to have something. She was always writing. That's why she worked as a dancer. It gave her the days to write."

"Did she ever talk about a family?"

"She has a mother. But they're on the outs. Her mother never believed in the same things she did."

"Do you have her mother's address?"

"Some small town on the Island. My husband knows it. I can get it from him."

"That would help."

"I'll have it for you tonight then. My husband's on his way to Miami for an engagement."

"Did you ever see Jane after that time you put up bail for her?"

"I took her to lunch the same day. I offered to help her but she turned me down. She said when she had the money she would repay the bail I had laid out. I told her I thought she was being a fool doing what she was and that I would give her the money to let her write and there wouldn't be any strings attached. But she turned me down flat out."

"Why do you think she did that?"

"Because we were lovers once. And maybe she didn't believe me when I said 'No strings.' "

"Was she a lesbian?"

"No. I am. She's not. It would have been easier for all of us if she had been. She's bi. It took me a long time to understand that her reaction to our sex was purely physical. It never was like that for me at all. I really loved her."

"Would you still be willing to help her if she wanted it?"

"Yes, but she won't take it."

"What makes you so sure?"

"Because I know her. She has this crazy idea about freedom and independence. She won't take from anyone—man or woman. She left a rich husband for the same reason. She wants to do it all herself, and to be recognized for it."

He was silent.

"Listen, she knew where I was, a phone call would have brought me any time, but look at the trip she took rather than pick up that phone."

"She called you once before. Maybe she will again."

"Twice before," she said, a distant look in her large dark eyes. "There won't be a third time."

For the first time since coming East he felt better. Maybe it was being on the road in a rented car. The Long

Island Expressway might have been a freeway in California except for the white fields of snow stretching out on either side. He turned off at the Port Clare exit sign.

Fifteen minutes after coming off the expressway he pulled up in front of the house.

It was comfortable-looking and the neighborhood was a good one—well-established middle class. The one thing that distinguished the Randall house from others around it was that the shades were drawn and the driveway and front walk were covered with snow. It looked empty.

He got out of the car and made his way through the snow to the front door. He pressed the bell and heard the echoing sound in the house but there was no answer. He turned around at the sound of a car in the street behind him.

A police car had pulled up behind his. A young patrolman stuck his head out the car window. "What are you doing up there, mister?"

"I'm looking for Mrs. Randall."

"She's not home."

Millstein began to pick his way through the snow back to the sidewalk. "I can see that. Do you have any idea of where I could reach her?"

"Nope."

"You were here within two minutes of the time I was. You must have a pretty good system out here."

"This is a small town. One of the neighbors reported you the minute you stopped your car."

"Maybe you can help me." Millstein took his wallet out of his pocket and showed the patrolman his badge.

"Yes, sir," the policeman said respectfully.

"It's very important that I locate Mrs. Randall."

"I'm afraid you're out of luck, sir. She got married again about two months ago and she and her new husband went off on one of them long world cruises. They won't be back until the summer."

"Oh."

"Is there anything else I can do, sir?"
"No, thanks, Officer."

The detective closed his small black notebook and put it back in his pocket. "That's it, Dr. Sloan. You got it all."
"I never bought her story about her sister."
"Neither did I."
"She wasn't trying to kill herself. What she really wanted to do was kill her dreams. Somehow she began to feel that whatever talent she had made it impossible for her to live in the same world as other people. Society tried to force her into its mold and she couldn't make it. The only thing left for her to do was to kill JeriLee. Then she would be all right."
"You've passed me, Doc," Millstein said. "What happens to her now?"
"She'll get out," he said somberly. "We have no real reason to hold her anymore; she's no danger to anyone. She's off drugs, which was why she was sent here. We've done all we can. We're not equipped to give her what she needs now."
"What if she falls back?"
"Then she'll be back here."
"But she could kill herself this time."
"It's possible. But like I said, there's nothing we can do about it. It's too bad that there isn't anyone who cares enough to keep an eye on her. She needs friends more than anything else. But she's cut herself off from everyone." He was silent for a moment looking at the detective. "Except you."
Millstein felt himself flush. "What do you expect me to do about it?" he demanded almost belligerently. "I scarcely know the girl."
"That was last week. This week you probably know more about her than she does herself."
"I still don't know what I can do," the detective said stubbornly.
"You might make the difference between life and death for her."
Millstein was silent.

"It won't take much. Just give her a secure base where she can find herself again."

"That's crazy."

"Not so crazy. There has to be something between the two of you. She wrote you. And you came. You didn't have to. You could have sent a letter or done nothing at all. Right now you're probably the one person in the world she completely trusts."

"Doctor, I'm beginning to think one of us should be committed." He paused for a moment, shaking his head. "Or maybe both."

Chapter 24

MILLSTEIN CAME into the house after his four o'clock tour of duty. He paused in the small hallway listening for the familiar sound of the clicking typewriter. Hearing nothing, he went into the living room, where his daughter was reading a book. "Where's JeriLee?" he asked.

"At the shrink's."

He looked puzzled. "I thought it was Tuesdays and Fridays."

"This is something special."

"Something wrong?"

"No, Daddy. Something good. She heard from the attorney in New York that the shrink suggested she send her novel to. He has a publisher interested in the book and they want to send her the fare to come in and talk to them about it."

"Hmph," her father growled. "I know about those New York shysters. I better run a check on him. What's his name?"

Susan laughed. "Paul Gitlin. And stop being so overprotective, Daddy. She told me he only represents biggies, like Irving Wallace and Gay Talese."

"I'm not being overprotective. It's only six months since she's been out of the hospital."

"And look what she's done in that six months. A month after she was here she got a job nights as an operator at the answering service so that she could write and see her shrink during the day. She's written two original screen stories, one of which Universal bought, and now she's almost completely finished with a novel. You got to give her some credit, Daddy."

"I'm not taking anything away from her. I just don't want her to run herself down."

"She's fine, Daddy. She's not the same woman you brought home. She's beautiful, Daddy. Inside and out."

"You really like her?"

Susan nodded.

"I'm glad. I was worried about how you would feel."

"I have to admit I was jealous at first. But then I saw how much she needed us. Like a child needing approval. Then before my eyes I watched her grow. I watched the woman emerge. It blew my mind. It was like one of those stop motion films where the rose buds and opens all in a few seconds. She's a very special lady, Daddy. And you're a very special man to have seen that in her."

"I could use a drink."

"I'll fix it for you." In a moment she was back with a whiskey on the rocks.

"That helps."

"Rough day?"

"The usual. Just long."

She watched him sink into his favorite chair. "You know she's going to leave soon, don't you, Daddy?" she asked softly.

He nodded without speaking.

"You did what you said you'd do. You gave her back herself. She's strong now. She's learned to walk. Now she wants to fly. You can support a child walking, but flying is something they must do on their own.

You'll have to get used to the idea, Daddy. Someday it will be my turn."

"I know that," he said, his voice husky.

"You love her, don't you, Daddy?"

"I guess so."

"Strange, I felt that the moment you told me you were flying East to see her. You know she loves you too, Daddy. But not the same way."

"I know."

"I'm sorry, Daddy." There were tears in the corners of her eyes. "I don't know if it will help but there's something I think you should understand. JeriLee isn't like the rest of us. She's very special and apart. She'll never be able to love the same way we do. She has her eye on another star. But for her it's something inside herself, while the rest of us may look for it in another person."

She was kneeling on the floor in front of his chair and he pressed his lips to her forehead. "What makes you so smart, Daughter?" he whispered.

"I'm not so smart, Daddy. Maybe it's just because I'm a woman."

Sunlight filtered to a soft glow by bamboo drapes warmed the yellows, oranges and browns of the office. The two women sat in comfortable easy chairs near the window, a triangular table between them. The doctor's chair had a small writing arm not unlike the old schoolroom chairs.

"Excited?" Dr. Martinez asked.

"Yes. Very. But I'm also afraid."

The doctor was silent.

"I didn't do so well the last time I went back East," JeriLee said.

"Circumstances were different then."

"Yes. I suppose so. But what about me? Was I different too?"

"Yes and no. What you have to remember is that you were living under different pressures then. Those pressures are no longer valid. In that respect, you are different."

"But I'm still me."
"You are more you now than you were then. And that's good. As you learn to accept yourself, you grow stronger."
"I called my mother. She wants me to come and stay with her while I'm working on the book. She wants me to see her new husband. I've never met him."
"How do you feel about that?"
"You know how I feel about my mother. She's okay in small doses. But after a while we go at each other like cats and dogs."
"And you think it will be like that this time?"
"I don't know. She's usually okay if I'm not laying any problems on her."
"It could be that you're both more mature now. Maybe she's learned just as you have."
"Then you think I should stay with her?"
"I think you should think about it. It could be a very important part of your coming to terms with yourself."
"I'll think about it."
"How long do you think you'll be there finishing the book?"
"At least three months. Maybe more. That's another thing that's been troubling me. I won't have you to talk to."
"I can refer you to a couple of good doctors there."
"Men?"
"Does it make a difference?"
"I know it shouldn't. But it does. Both doctors I went to before I came to you seemed to treat me as if I were a child to be cajoled into being reasonable and behaving myself. I could be wrong but I think sex had a lot to do with it."
"I'm not clear what you mean."
"If I were a housewife with the kind of problems they're used to hearing they could probably deal with me. But I'm not. When I tell them I don't want to marry or have children, that what I really want is to be able to take care of myself without having to depend on anyone, they just don't understand. I don't want to

settle for a second-place existence. I want to make my own choices."

"There's nothing wrong with that. Theoretically we all have that right."

"Theoretically. But you know better, and so do I. One of the doctors told me jokingly that a good fuck would straighten me out. Only I had the feeling that he wasn't joking. If I'd given him any encouragement I think he would have volunteered his services. The other kept trying to convince me that what he called the old-fashioned virtues were best—marriage, home and family. According to him that is the true purpose of women."

"You'll find many women who go along with that."

"Okay. But that's their bag. They made their choice. I want to make mine. I don't suppose I've said anything you haven't heard before."

"I've heard similar things."

"I even have it in business. I almost sold my second screen original until I met the producer. Somehow things got mixed up in his head and he thought the purchase price included me. When I told him a fuck wasn't included in the sale of a story he said he liked and wanted, he dropped the whole thing. That never would have happened if a man had written it."

"I know of one woman you would like," she said. "It would all depend on how busy she is. She's an active feminist and I think she would like you too."

"I'd like to see her if I can."

"When you have a departure date let me know and I'll try to arrange it."

"Thank you. There's one other thing I want to talk to you about."

"Yes?"

"It's Al. Detective Millstein. I owe him a lot. Much more than money. I don't know how to tell him that I'll be leaving."

"Don't you think he knows?"

"I think he knew I'd be going sometime. I just think he never thought it would be this soon. I don't want to hurt him."

"He's in love with you?"

"Yes, but he's never said anything. Never made a move toward me."

"How do you feel about him?"

"Grateful. Loving. As if he were my father or my brother."

"Does he know how you feel?"

"We never really talked about it."

"Then tell him. I'm sure he'd prefer to hear your true feelings rather than any polite evasions. At least this way he will know that you really do care about him."

Millstein heard the sound of her car in the driveway, then her footsteps stop outside the front door as she searched for her key. He looked up as the door opened.

Her sun-tinted hair fell to her shoulders. She smiled and her face was flushed beneath her tan. "You're home early," she said.

"I had the eight to four today." He could feel the excitement in her. It was difficult for him to believe that she was the same pale frightened girl that he brought from New York. "I heard the good news."

"Isn't it wonderful?"

"I'm very happy for you."

"I can't believe it. It's like a dream come true."

"Believe it. You worked very hard for it. You deserve it."

"You made it possible, Al. Nothing would have happened if it weren't for you."

"It would have happened. It just might have taken a little longer."

"No. I was heading for the sewer and you know it."

"You'll never get me to believe that. If I had ever thought that, I wouldn't have brought you with me. There's something special about you. I saw that the first time we met."

"I'll never understand how you could see anything through all the shit I had pulled over me."

"When do you plan to go?"

"I don't know. They said they would let me know

next week when they want me to come in. I may stay at my mother's."

He didn't speak.

"I spoke to the shrink about it. She thinks it might be good for me if I could handle it."

"And when the book is finished, what do you plan to do then?"

"I don't know."

"Would you come back out here?"

"Probably. I like living in California. Besides this is where it's at for me. Screenplays, television, work."

His voice was suddenly husky. "You always have a home here with us, if you should want it."

She sank to her knees in front of him and put her hands over his. "You've done enough, Al. I can't lay any more on you."

"You're not laying anything on us. We love you."

"And I love you both. You're like family to me. Even more than family. Maybe the only other person I knew that would have done what you did was my father. You have the same gentleness that he did. Mixed up as I was at the time, I knew that. Maybe that was why I wrote you."

He understood what she was telling him. And though there was a feeling of deep disappointment, there was also the great satisfaction of knowing that she cared enough to let him know how she felt. He leaned forward and kissed her cheek. "We'll miss you," he said.

Her arm went around his neck and she held her cheek against his. "I won't give you the chance. We'll always be very close."

He was very still for a moment, then he drew back. He smiled. "Hey! Are you going to give me a chance to read that book they're all making such a fuss about?"

She laughed. "Of course. I thought you'd never ask." A moment later she laid the boxed manuscript on his lap. "Promise you won't read it until you go to bed. I couldn't stand watching you read it."

"Okay," he said. But he didn't really know why she wanted him to wait until after he picked up the manuscript: *"Nice Girls Go to Hell,* a novel by JeriLee Randall."

Beneath that was a short paragraph.

"This book is dedicated to Al Millstein—with gratitude and affection for being the Loveliest Man I Know."

His eyes blurred with tears and it was several minutes before he turned to page one.

I was born with two strikes on me and no balls. I was a girl child. Destined to be delivered direct from my mother's womb into the bondage of my sex. I didn't like it even then. I proceeded to piss all over the doctor who was slapping my ass.

Chapter 25

ANGELA OPENED the bathroom door while she was in the shower. "Your agent's on the phone," she shouted. "He says he has to talk to you right away. It's very important."

"I'll be right out." JeriLee stepped out of the shower and wrapped a large bath sheet around her.

"What is it?" she said into the phone.

"Can you get over to the studio right away? Tom Castel wants to see you."

"What about our appointment? I'm supposed to be at your office in an hour."

"I can wait. I think this is our big chance. I've got him holding on the other line to let him know when you'll be there."

"An hour okay?"

"Make it three quarters of an hour. It looks more sincere."

"Okay." She laughed. An agent was an agent. He even negotiated the time with you.

The doctor had been right. He had said she would feel better by today and she did. Outside of a mildly heavy feeling in her groin there was no pain at all.

Back in the bathroom she finished drying herself, then pulled the shower cap from her head and shook out her hair. It would need only thirty seconds with the blow dryer. She would use very little makeup today, just a touch of mascara and some light lipstick. They all knew what she had gone through.

Angela came into the bedroom while she was dressing. "What did he want?"

"I'm due at Castel's office in twenty minutes."

"Want me to drive you?"

"I think I can manage."

"Are you sure? I'm clear today. I've nothing else to do."

"Okay." She nodded.

"How you feeling, baby?" Tom Castel asked, kissing her cheek.

"Fine."

"Tough shit about what happened. George should never have put you in a spot like that."

"It was my own fault," she said, moving toward the chair in front of his desk.

"No, over there," he said solicitously, taking her by the arm and leading her to the couch against the wall. "You'll be more comfortable. Coffee?"

She nodded and he pressed a button on the side of his chair. A moment later his secretary came in with two cups.

"The old man said to come right over. That it was important."

"How badly do you want your picture made?"

She couldn't resist. "I don't want it made badly. I want it made well."

"Don't get flip with words, JeriLee. I know you're a writer. You want the picture made or don't you?"

"I want the picture made."

"Okay then," he said seriously. "I'll tell you how to get it done. I got the studio to agree to give me a go on the picture if George does it. You get George to do it."

"Why me? You're the producer. Isn't that your job? And besides, isn't he under contract to the studio?"

"That's right. But he's got the right of approval over what pictures he will do, and I can't seem to pin him down. He should listen to you. After all, he did knock you up and you took care of it without making a fuss. I figure he owes you one."

"What if he won't do it?"

"You blow fifty grand and five points."

"What do you lose?"

"Nothing. I got a contract. If I don't do this picture, I do another. But I'd like to get this one made. I think there's a buck in it for all of us. Besides I want to work with you. I think we could come up with a real winner between us. I loved the book."

"Thanks."

"You don't know me. I'm dynamite when I get going. Work day and night. I got a placc out at the beach where nobody can get to us."

She nodded. She had heard about his place at the beach from friends. The only one that believed he went out there to work was his wife. "Okay," she said. "I'll see what I can do."

"Great. I arranged to meet George for lunch at the commissary. I told him you'd be joining us." He smiled. "I know you can sell him, baby. Just give him another whiff of that gorgeous pussy."

"Christ, Tom," she said disgustedly. "It's going to take more than that to get him."

"You don't know your own power, baby. He says that you've got the super cunt of all time and that he can't keep from getting a hard-on whenever he's near you."

"When did he say that?"

"Just this weekend. We had a C.R. session out at the shrink's. It just—"

"Happened to come up," she finished, interrupting him. "I know. I heard all about it."

"I must say he made out a hell of a case for you. Are you really as good as he says you are?"

"Oh, sure," she said, getting to her feet. "I'm a real ball breaker." She walked toward the door. "Where's the john? I think I have to throw up."

"First door on your left," he said quickly. "I'm sorry, I forgot you still weren't feeling well."

"Don't worry about it. That's one of the problems of being a woman. Some things just turn your stomach."

"It's really a very simple deal," she explained to her agent. "Castel gives me the job if I get George to do the picture. On top of that he already told me that we'd be working together out at his place on the beach and he made sure to tell me that he works day and night.

"George says that he loves the whole idea. That he believes in me as a writer and admires Castel as a top producer, but for him the key is the director and he happens to know that Dean Clarke is available because Dean's wife coldcocked the picture he was going to do at Warner's."

"Dean Clarke would be a good director for the project. And I say so even if he's not my own client."

"But you know Dean's problem. If he doesn't get his wife's approval he won't do it. And that's another problem for me. She wants the same things from me that George and Castel want. I've been ducking her ever since we met at a N.O.W. meeting."

"Pictures have been made even with worse problems."

"I've heard of fucking one guy to get a job in this business. But did you ever hear of anyone who had to fuck everybody on the damn picture? Before it's over they'll have me matched up with everyone except the hairdresser and that will only be because he's gay."

"Now don't get excited. Let's talk this out."

"Okay."

"If I could get Castel to go for seventy-five thousand and seven and a half points, would you do it?"

"You're not listening. I wasn't talking about the money. I just don't think I should have to fuck for the deal, that's all."

"I agree with you. But since you're fucking anyway, I don't see what's such a big tsimiss you're making."

"I didn't have to fuck anybody to get them to buy the book, why should I do it to get them to make the picture?"

"They didn't make the picture yet, did they?" the old man asked shrewdly. She started to speak but he held up his hand. "Listen to me, then you can talk. It's almost three years since they bought your book. They did two scripts on it. They were no good and there was no picture. Don't tell me that your book sold forty thousand in hard cover, a hundred thousand in book club and a million in paperback, or that you did fifty radio and TV shows and that *Time* magazine had you on its cover as Women's Lib writer of the year. I know it, you know it and the studio knows it. What the studio also knows is that it all happened three years ago. Since then there have been other books. And, believe me, they would much rather make a fresh start on something new than throw more money into something they have already failed with twice. You talk about what you have to do to get this picture made? Let me tell you what I had to do. For the last year while you were giving away your fucks for free, I was wining, dining and sucking up to every executive at the studio that I thought could push your picture into production.

"Well, I finally got it back on the active list. I got them to turn it over to Castel, one of their top producers, because I know he's a hustler, that he would find a way to get them to make the movie. Well, he found it and now you're complaining.

"I'm an old man. I don't have to work so hard. Soon I will turn the office over to my younger associates. You don't want to make the picture? It's okay by me. It's your book, it's your life, it's your money. I'm a rich man. I don't need it. All I get is a lousy ten per cent anyway." He shook his head sadly. "So go home. We'll still be friends. You'll write other stories, other books. I'll make other deals. But it's really too bad. It might have been a very important movie." He held up his hand. "Now you can talk."

She started laughing hysterically.

"You think what I said was funny?"

"No. It's just that suddenly everything has become so unreal."

"Then let me bring you back to reality." His voice cut like a cold knife. "In this business there is only one truth. It always has been and it always will be—make the movie. Just that. Nothing more, nothing less. Make the movie.

"I don't give a damn what you do, who you fuck. I don't care if you want to remake the world. You can do anything you want but first you will have to deal with the truth. Make the movie. It's the only thing you can do that will validate you. If you don't do it, you're just another cunt who couldn't cut it in this town."

"And you don't care who I have to fuck to get it done."

"I don't give a damn if you have to climb up on the cross and fuck Jesus Christ. You get that movie made."

"I don't really care that much anymore," she said in a tired voice.

"I don't believe that. If you hadn't cared you wouldn't have come out here three years ago. You would have stayed back East and written another novel."

"That's what I should have done. I know that now."

"It's not too late. The planes still fly both ways."

He saw the tears come to her eyes but before he could say anything to her she rose from her chair and walked out of the office. He picked up the telephone and a moment later had Tom Castel on the line.

"I just finished talking to her, Tom," he said in a confidential tone. "Believe me, there's no way you can get her to go for less than a hundred grand. I'll get her to buy the seven and a half points but you'll have to come up with the cash. Right now she's fed up with this town. I have all I can do to keep her from getting on the next plane back East. All she really wants to do is write her next novel."

JeriLee took a Kleenex from the container on the dashboard and dabbed at her eyes. "We can go home now," she said.

Silently Angela put the car into gear and they rolled out of the parking lot. JeriLee lit a cigarette and looked out of the car window. "Shit," she said.

"What's wrong?"

"I just discovered something about myself and I don't like it," she said. "People don't only get fucked by systems, they also get fucked by their dreams."

"You lost me."

"We're all whores," JeriLee said. "Only the currencies are different. By the time we get home the old man will be on the phone telling me he got me a hundred grand to do the picture. And I'll say okay."

"That's a lot of money."

"It's not the money. That's where the old man is smart. He knows it. And uses it. He knows that I want that picture made more than I want life itself. I didn't fool him for a minute."

"I don't see anything so bad about it."

Suddenly JeriLee laughed. "That's what's so beautiful about you. You're the last of the innocents."

"It's been a rough day," Angela said. "Let's get stoned when we get home."

JeriLee leaned across the seat and kissed Angela's cheek. "That's the first sensible idea I've heard all day."

Epilogue—Tinsel Town

ON STAGE the singer was drawing out the last anguished note of the song. In the small crowded control room high in the back of the large auditorium there was a hum of quiet frenzy. This was not just an ordinary television program. This was the live telecast of motion pictures' finest hour, the Academy Awards.

The applause came up as the singer finished. He bowed graciously to the audience, his fixed smile masking his anger. The orchestra had mangled his arrangement and drowned out his best notes.

A voice echoed through the speakers in the control room. "Two minutes. Commercials and station break."

"What song was that?" the director asked.

"Second," someone answered. "No, third."

"It stinks," he said. "What's on next?"

"Best screenplay award. We're picking up the nominees now."

The director looked up at the screens. The five center screens each showed a different person, four men and a woman. The men in their elaborate dinner jackets appeared nervous. The woman seemed almost oblivious to everything going on around her. Her eyes were half closed, her lips slightly parted, and her head nodded gently as if she were listening to some inner music. "The girl is stoned," he said.

"But she's beautiful," a voice answered.

The countdown from the commercial began. The moment it was over a light flashed over the screen that was picking up the master of ceremonies returning to the podium. The director punched in a closeup of the emcee, then cut to a medium shot of two stars, a young man and woman, approaching the podium to the applause of the audience. The applause faded away as they began to read the list of nominees.

As their names were being called out, the men were trying without success to appear nonchalant, the woman still seemed to be in another world.

With the usual pomp, the envelope was called for and ceremoniously opened. "The award for the best screenplay goes to—" The young actor paused for the dramatic moment. He looked at his companion.

She picked up the announcement, her voice suddenly shrill with excitement. "Ms. JeriLee Randall for *Nice Girls Go to Hell!*"

The director punched in on the woman. At first she didn't seem to have heard. Her eyes opened and her lips parted in a smile. She began to rise from her seat. Another camera picked her up as she made her way down the aisle to the stage. It wasn't until she had climbed the few steps and turned to face the audience that they had a clear full shot of her.

"Jesus Christ!" A voice broke the sudden hush in the control room. "She's got nothin' but tits and pussy under that dress."

"Want to go to closeup?" the A.D. asked.

"No way," the director answered. "Give the yokels a treat."

Up on the stage the woman clutched the Oscar to her and moved toward the microphone. She blinked her eyes for a moment as if to hold back her tears but when she opened them they were clear and shining.

"Ladies and gentlemen of the Academy . . ." Her voice was quiet but distinct. "If I were to tell you that I'm not thrilled and happy at this moment I would be very wrong. This is something that happens only in a writer's wildest dreams."

She paused for a moment until the applause died away. "Still, there is within me a lingering doubt and a feeling of sadness. Did I earn this award as writer, or as a woman? I know there would be no doubts in the minds of any of the four gentlemen who were nominated had they won. But then all they had to do was write their screenplays. They didn't have to ball everybody on the picture except the prop man in order to get it made."

A roar came up from the audience and panic hit the control room. "Go to tape," the director ordered. "Delay five seconds." He half rose from behind the control console and peered through the small window down into the theater. "Get me some audience reaction shots," he yelled. "All hell's breaking loose down there!"

The images leaped onto the small screens. There were women rising to their feet applauding, shouting encouragement. "Right on, JeriLee! Tell it like it is, JeriLee!" The camera zoomed in close on a shot of a dinner-jacketed man trying to pull the woman he was with back into her seat. The director cut back to JeriLee as her voice came on again.

"I do not intend to ignore the custom of thanking all the people who made it possible for me to win this award. So my first thanks go to my agent, who told me the only thing that mattered was getting the picture made. He might be relieved to know that I did not have to climb up on the cross. All I had to do was climb on the producer's cock, lick the star's ass, and eat the pussy off the director's wife. My thanks to all of them. Maybe they did make it possible."

"Holy shit!" the director whispered. The noise from the audience was beginning to drown out JeriLee's words. "Cut the audience mikes," he ordered.

Her voice came over the crowd. ". . . Last, but not least, I want to express my appreciation to my fellow members of the Academy for electing me their Token Woman Writer, in honor of which I want to unveil a painting I had done especially for them."

She smiled gently as her hand reached behind her neck. Suddenly her dress fell from her body. She stood motionless on the stage, a huge inverted golden Oscar painted on her nude body. The gold paint covered her breasts and stomach, the flat head of the figure disappeared into the pubic hair.

Pandemonium broke out in the auditorium. The audience came to its feet, staring, cheering and booing as men rushed from the wings to surround JeriLee. Someone threw a coat around her. Contemptuously, she threw it off and marched from the stage in naked dignity.

There was a dazed happy expression on the director's face as the screen went to black for the commercials. "The Academy Awards will never be the same after this."

"Do you think we got on the air?" someone asked.

"I hope so," he answered. "It would be a shame if truth didn't get as much of a chance to be heard as bullshit."

The car moved up the hill and came to a stop in front of the house. JeriLee leaned across the seat and kissed the man's cheek. "My friend, Detective Millstein. Detective Millstein, my friend. You have a talent for turning up when you're most needed."

He smiled. "I wasn't far from the theater. I was watching the show in a bar when you came on."

"I'm glad." She got out of the car. "I'm wiped out. I'll go right to bed."

"Will you be okay?"

"Don't worry, I'm fine. You can go back to work."

"All right."

"Give Susan and the baby a kiss for me."

He nodded and watched her go into the house before he turned the car around and went back down the hill.

The telephone was ringing when she came in the door. It was her mother. "You really did it this time, JeriLee," she said. "I'll never be able to hold my head up in this town again."

"Oh, Mother." The line went dead in her hand. Her mother had hung up. Just as JeriLee put down the phone it rang again.

This time it was her agent. "That was a brilliant publicity stunt," he chortled. "Never in all my years in the business have I ever seen a star made in one night."

"It wasn't a publicity stunt."

"What difference does it make?" the old man asked.

"You come into the office tomorrow. I got at least five firm offers on which you can write your own ticket."

"Oh, shit," she said and hung up the phone. It began to ring again but this time she didn't answer. Instead she lifted it up, pressed down the cradle to disconnect the call and left the receiver off the hook.

She went into the bedroom, found a joint, lit it and went back to the front door. She went outside. The night was warm and clear. She sat down on the porch steps and looked out over the city. Her eyes suddenly began to mist.

She sat at the top of the stairs and cried. And far down the hill, below her, the multicolored lights of Los Angeles shimmered through her tears.